The Last Hundred Days

A Novel

Patrick McGuinness

B L O O M S B U R Y

NEW YORK · BERLIN · LONDON · SYDNEY

for Sarah, who was there

Published by Bloomsbury USA, New York

All papers used by Bloomsbury USA are natural, recyclable products
made from wood grown in well-managed forests. The manufacturing processes
conform to the environmental regulations of the country of origin.

LIBRARY OF CONGRESS CATALOGING-IN-PUBLICATION DATA

McGuinness, Patrick.
The last hundred days : a novel / Patrick McGuinness.
p. cm.
ISBN 978-1-60819-912-9 (pbk. : alk. paper)
I. Title.
PR6113.C483.L37 2012
823'.92—dc23
2011038760

First published in Great Britain by Seren,
the book imprint of Poetry Wales Press Ltd., in 2011
First published in the United States by Bloomsbury USA in 2012

Cover photograph © Andrei Pandele www.ap-arte.ro

1 3 5 7 9 10 8 6 4 2

Inner design and typesetting by books@lloydrobson.com
Printed in the U.S.A. by Quad/Graphics, Fairfield, Pennsylvania

Author's Note

This is a novel and not a work of history or of journalism. It has no pretense to documentary fact. Though the main events happened, many have been altered or imaginatively diverted for fictional purposes.

It is traditional to state that any resemblance to real persons, living or dead, is purely coincidental. However, it would be truer to say that many of these resemblances are deliberate, though the characters created for the novel are composites, if not outright inventions. This includes the narrator.

The city of Bucharest is treated both as location and as, in a sense, a character. It, too, has been imagined and remade for fictional purposes, though always with a view to conveying its reality.

Part One

'And yet, the ways we miss our lives are life'

— Randall Jarrell

One

In 1980s Romania, boredom was a state of extremity. There was nothing neutral about it: it strung you out and stretched you; it tugged away at the bottom of your day like shingle scraping at a boat's hull. In the West we've always thought of boredom as slack time, life's lift music sliding off the ear. Totalitarian boredom is different. It's a state of expectation already heavy with its own disappointment, the event and its anticipation braided together in a continuous loop of tension and anti-climax.

You saw it all day long in the food queues as tins of North Korean pilchards, bottles of rock-bottom Yugoslav Slivovitz, or loaves of potato-dust bread reached the shops. People stood in sub-zero temperatures or unbearable heat, and waited. Eyes blank, bodies numb, they shuffled step-by-step towards the queue's beginning. No one knew how much there was of anything. Often you didn't even know *what* there was. You could queue for four hours only for everything to run out just as you reached the counter. Some forgot what they were waiting for, or couldn't recognise it when they got it. You came for bread and got Yugo rotgut; the alcoholics jittered for their rotgut and got pilchards or shoe polish, and it wasn't by taste that you could tell them apart. Sometimes the object of the queue changed midway through: a meat queue became a queue for Chinese basketball shoes; Israeli oranges segued into disposable cameras from East Germany. It didn't matter – whatever it was, you bought it. Financial exchange was just a preliminary; within hours the networks of barter and black-marketeering would be vibrating with fresh commodities.

It was impossible to predict which staple would suddenly become a scarcity, which humdrum basic would be transformed into a luxury. Even the dead felt the pinch. Since the gargantuan building projects had begun in the early 1980s, marble and stone were requisitioned by the state for facade work and interior design. In the cemeteries the graves were marked out with wooden planks, table legs, chairs, even broomsticks. Ceauşescu's new Palace of the People could be measured not just in square metres but in gravestones. It was surreal, or would have been if it wasn't the only reality available.

I had arrived full of the kind of optimism that, in retrospect, I recognise as a sure sign that things would go wrong, and badly. Not for me, for I was a passer-by; or, more exactly, a passer-through. Things happened around me, over me, even across me, but never *to* me. Even when I was there, in the thick of it, during those last hundred days.

To step onto the half-empty plane at Heathrow that mid-April day was already to step back in time. *Tarom* was the Romanian airline, but its fleet was composed of old Air France Boeings which, like so much else in Romania, had been recycled and brought back into use. It felt more like the 1960s than the 1980s. The air hostesses wore square suits and pillbox hats.

I took my seat in an empty row near the front and read the battered in-flight magazine. Two years out of date, it told of Romanian delicacies and showed blurred models of the 'Boulevard of Socialist Victory', a project described as 'the culmination of modern Romania's vision under Comrade President Nicolae Ceauşescu'. The touched-up picture of

Ceauşescu was on the inside cover – *Tovarăşul Conducător*, Comrade Leader – looking twenty years younger and with the lightly bloated marzipan blush of an embalmed corpse.

Even at Heathrow, with the flights landing and taking off all around us and London proliferating in the distance, our plane had become a capsule of its destination and its epoch. Both felt further away than the three and a half hours it took to fly to Bucharest.

I was still in my suit. I had had no time to change, much less go back to the house before catching my flight. I had attended the funeral with my suitcase and hand luggage, which I left in the crematorium lobby during the service. I hadn't meant to upstage him – there was room for only one departure that day – but that was how it all fell together: my new job, the new country, unalterable plane tickets. 'It's not every day you bury your father,' someone had said to me by way of reproach. *No, but if like me you spent every day wishing you could, the event itself was bound to have its complicated side.* Of course, that's not what I replied. I just nodded and watched them all pretending to pray, straining for that far-away look, something in themselves to help them say, later, how they'd levelled with death this afternoon, and hadn't erred into thinking about dinner or tonight's TV.

After landing we waited for the VIPs to disembark, square-suited men in grey with wives who looked moulded from a mixture of custard and cement. Their luggage was taken out unchecked and placed into anthracite-black limousines. I had seen the cars before too – the Renault 14, the Dacia, made from French prototypes by the Romanian national car plant. The name meant something, as I knew from my limited reading-up. The Dacians, according to Ceauşescu's officially sanctioned history, were survivors of the siege of Troy, poor cousins separated from the Roman tribe, founding their island of Latinity in eastern Europe encircled by Slavs, martyred by the Turks, caught now in the dark orbit of the Soviet Union.

This was April, but we had arrived in a heatwave. Outside the plane everything reverberated in the heat. The tarmac glistened, stuck and puckered underfoot, sweating out its oil. Beyond the perimeter fence stretched flat acres of chalky grass and net fencing over which a horse-drawn plough rumbled. A dead animal lay torn, caught in a tiller's blades and strewn in rags across the ploughlines. From high above, the furrowed fields had suggested musical notation. Up close it was just earth, turned and turned back over, earth that never rested, and those who worked it were hunched and beaten down with drudgery.

The VIP motorcade drove off, the way the wealthy and the powerful do wherever you find them: without looking back, into the next thing.

That smell of airports: the peppery scent of vertigo, exhalations of vacuum cleaners, perfume, smoke, used air. A sublimate of spent jet fuel and burned-off ozone giving the sky its improbable clear blue.

Otopeni airport was a two-storey building with plate-glass walls and red-veined marble floors; overstaffed, but with nothing happening. This atmosphere of menace and fretful apathy engulfed public buildings everywhere in Romania. The next flight, from Moscow, was not for two hours. The previous one, from Belgrade, had been and gone an hour ago. The airport was a place of perpetual lull, perpetual betweenness, as transitional as the plane we had just left behind. But it's the transitional places that hold us all the longer and enclose us all the more.

'Welcome to Romania,' read a tricolour billboard. The Romanian flag, blue, yellow and red with a Party crest in the centre, drooped on its pole and trembled in the faintest of drafts. Militia outnumbered civilians by two to one. Women in knee-high, lace-up sandals pushed dry mops along floors, redistributing butt ends and sweet wrappers over the marble. Great tubular ashtrays overflowed with crushed cigarettes and a miasma of blue smoke wrapped itself around what remained of the air.

The customs officers operated with malign lethargy, deriving so little satisfaction from the misery they inflicted that it seemed hardly worth it. Up ahead, through the glass walls, I saw the black Dacias already clear, coursing down Otopeni Boulevard towards the city that was to be my home.

When my turn came I was made to unpack and account for the little I had. The two customs officers were well balanced. One had a face without a trace of expression, the other a face on which different expressions slugged it out for supremacy, inconclusively. The first spoke ragged English while the second, smoking US cigarettes, spoke fluently in an American accent. If the Romanian police had a fast stream, he was it – expressionless, lean, unreadable.

'What welcomes you to Romania?'

It was a good question, and called out for a witticism, but this was no time to test the national sense of humour. He took my coffee and two chocolate bars and pocketed them with a flourish. His eyes never leaving mine, he added the batteries from my Walkman while his colleague, by some pre-arranged system of equalisation, confiscated my carton of duty-free cigarettes.

'Tax.' Deadpan.

My taxi, a white Dacia with tiger stripes of rust and an ill-fitting blue driver's door, was driven wordlessly by a man whose face I couldn't see and who didn't turn once to look at me.

Coming over Bucharest you noticed the city's contrasts immediately: a rigid geometry of avenues with new housing blocks, high-rise flats and public follies skewering the skyline. Around and between them, a shambles of old churches, winding roads, houses and small parks. As from the air, so from the ground: the old town revealed itself to you in layers; the new town came at you in lines.

Bucharest was not a city that tapered away, suburb by suburb, into countryside; nor did the countryside intensify, street by street, into a central urban hub. There were simply two miles of bad roads and fields; then suddenly apartment blocks reared up, the bumpy track flattened out beneath the tyres, and a city had materialised under and around you.

The flat that awaited me was surprising in its size and elegance: the whole second floor of a large nineteenth-century house on Aleea Alexandru, in Herastrau, a part of old Bucharest which remained for now untouched by Ceauşescu's great 'modernisation' project. It was where Party apparatchiks, diplomats and foreigners lived; where I now lived, for as long as I could take it, or as long as they let me. All over town churches were being torn down, old streets obliterated and concreted over. Here it was possible to imagine otherwise, though the noise of building and demolition was always there.

On the front door the previous occupant's name was still on a card in a small metal frame: 'Belanger, Dr F.' Mine was written on an envelope containing a key and a note inviting me to make free with whatever goods remained. The phone was connected, the fridge and cupboards stocked. The wardrobes were full of clothes that fitted, and there were books and records I might have bought myself, along with a video recorder and TV. My predecessor must have left in a hurry. Or known I was coming. A poster on the wall advertised the 13th Party Congress: Ceauşescu's face rose like the sun behind a gleaming tractor, over which it emitted munificent rays. Beside it was a small, intricate icon of an annunciation scene. It looked old and weathered, the gilt worn, the figures faceless and eroded, yet the golds and the reds inside it smouldered like a fire in the undergrowth. It was dated 1989, this year, and signed 'Petrescu' with a small orthodox cross scratched into the paint with a matchstick.

It was 6 pm. I went to the fridge for one of Belanger's beers, then out onto the balcony. The tiles were hot underfoot and I settled into a frayed wicker armchair to watch the street below.

I must have slumbered because when the doorbell rang it was fully dark and the tiles were cold. In the shadows of the flat, a phone I had not yet seen rang three times, paused, then rang again. I lifted the heavy Bakelite receiver but the caller had gone. There was a tiny click and then the flat tone of a dead line.

The electricity across town had cut out, though here in Herastrau we were spared the worst of the power stoppages. I was conscious, now that traffic had died down, of a constant noise of clattering metal, drilling and thrumming engines. I stumbled through the darkness, unable to find the light switches, only gauging the position of the front door from the repeated buzzing.

At the door stood a short, overweight, lopsidedly upright man with a face full of mischief and an alcohol flush. I knew who he was, though I had never seen him before. I motioned him in with an easeful proprietorial gesture that suggested I had been here longer than a few hours. But I felt at home in Belanger's flat, and even his things, foreign as they were, seemed to confirm me.

'Leo O'Heix. Remember me?' said the new arrival with a mock-military click of the heels, a rolled-up copy of *Scînteia*, the Party newspaper, in his jacket pocket. He jabbed a hand at me but elbowed past before I could shake it. 'From the interview?'

I had not been to any interview. I had applied for a dozen postings, been interviewed for six, and failed to get any. When the Romania job came up I was too disheartened even to turn up to the interview. When, two days later, I received a letter 'pleased to inform' me I had been selected, I thought it was a joke. When the visa followed a week later I realised it wasn't, or that at any rate the punchline was yet to come. 'You were probably the only applicant – everyone else got the good postings and you got what was left,' my father had said. He was unable to piss or shit or even eat unaided by then, but he could still rouse himself for the occasional sally of malice. But in this case, and for the first time in his life, he was giving me too much credit: I had dramatically improved my employ-ability by not even attending.

Nursing my father through the last months was a test of endurance for both of us. I wheeled him through the wards as he fulminated about bad spelling, poor grammar and grocers' apostrophes on the laminated hospital noticeboards. The habits of work remained with him: twenty years in Fleet Street, he had manned the newspapers' hot metal printing presses, setting the pages by hand, learning his trade and learning, as he went, a way with words that a less unhappy man would have put to better use. When they sacked him, along with six thousand other print workers three years before, he stood on picket lines for a few weeks and threw bricks at police cars before one morning going back to work in a reinforced strike-breaker bus, its windows painted over and layered with wire mesh, protected by one of the new private security firms. My father liked his politics intense but changeable.

As he died slowly we kept reconciliation at bay by talking only about trivia. In those last few days of delirium he asked for her, my mother – complained she wasn't there to visit him. Even at the end he was still finding new ways to be angry. The doctor was baffled by the way he fought the illness inch by inch, holding his ground when by rights the cancer should have claimed him months before: 'trench warfare' the doctor called it. I knew what it was that kept my father going: anger.

Leo turned on the lights and made for the drinks cabinet with a manner yet more proprietorial than my own. Pouring a glass of gin, topping it off with a symbolic shake of the tonic bottle, he went to the freezer and tipped in a couple of ice cubes. This done, he sat on the sofa, crossed his legs, and looked up at me. My move.

Leo wore a sweaty flat cap that looked screwed on, leaving circles of red indented grooves on his forehead, and his skin was the texture of multiply resurfaced tarmac. His trousers were the colour of blotchy mushrooms, and though his legs were the same length, theirs were not. His shirt was that special shade of streaky grey that comes from having started out white and having spent years sharing washing machines with blue underpants.

Still dozy, I found it hard to compose myself. But composure was unnecessary: before I could say anything, Leo finished his drink and leapt up.

'We're going for dinner.'

He pushed me out of the flat and into the hallway. The phone rang behind me, but Leo had already shut the door.

'Welcome to the Paris of the East,' he said. Leo is the only person I have known who could be both sincere and sarcastic about the same things, and simultaneously.

The Paris of the East... it was an epithet I'd heard before. Second-string cities are always described as the somewhere of somewhere else. But Bucharest was like nowhere else; that was its sorrow.

Two

Leo was drink-driving, not that it mattered here, thanks to petrol shortages and the seven-year wait for a car from the state car plant. With Leo at the wheel it was like riding dodgems in a ghost town, especially with the CD – *Corps Diplomatique* – badge he'd bought on the black market and affixed to the back of his Skoda. The cranes and diggers that dominated the streets gave Bucharest the look of a deserted funfair. Some of them were still desolately working, half-manned and on half power, hauling the shades of labourers up towards a smoky moon.

The pavements looked empty, but the shadows were crowded with militia in grey uniforms. You only saw them when your eyes had become accustomed to the darkness: they took shape, limb by limb, from the penumbra they lived in. In old Bucharest, rundown Parisian *arrondissements* had been crossed with the suburbs of Istanbul; East and West were in perpetual architectural dance. Plants hung from balconies where people sat in the dark, backlit by the blue of their televisions. Candles flickered in the windows of orthodox churches. Shift workers stood at beer counters, drinking silently, eyes down, their elbows touching.

Leo's car lurched into a vast trafficless square like a small fishing boat propelled into the open sea: Piaţa Republicii, where the palace of Queen Marie faced the Party Headquarters across a vast cobbled intersection. I heard, but much closer now, the same insistent clatter of building works, the hollow peal of scaffolding poles and the chug of cement mixers. I saw the pall of light to the north where they worked, 24/7, on the Palace of the People and the Boulevard of Socialist Victory. A tall building, a skyscraper on this stunted horizon, stood nearby, western cars and black Dacias parked in front of it. Doormen fussed around revolving doors.

Leo had been silent throughout the drive, but the prospect of a fresh glass loosened him up.

'The InterContinental Hotel,' he said, pointing, 'home to the Madonna disco, and prowling ground for the Party's golden youth.' A heavy bass thudding reached us, intensifying and dying down as a basement door opened and closed.

A red Porsche sped across the square and braked hard outside the nightclub, its numberplate – NIC 1 – catching the streetlamp's glare. A man in a white suit and a metallic blue shirt climbed out and was ushered into the hotel lobby, followed by two thin girls in silver miniskirts and shoes with heels so high their every step was a trembling defiance of gravity.

Leo grimaced: 'Nicu. The playboy prince. Ceaușescu's son and heir apparent.'

Capșa, a three-storeyed, French-style building on the corner of Calea Victoriei and Strada Edgar Quinet, was something out of fin-de-siècle Paris. The three sets of doors between the modest entrance and the resplendent dining room were like the decompression chambers of a submarine. They stopped the noise and smells and luxury from seeping out into the street, and kept the street's hungers and deprivations from tainting the Capșa dining experience.

Waiters in white shirts and dark green waistcoats with brass buttons fussed around tables heavy with silverware. Their uniforms were perfect, but their faces didn't fit: sallow and ill-shaven, they were scrappy parodies of the French waiters who had, in the 1890s, brought Paris to a standstill by striking over the right to grow moustaches. Yet Bucharest too had been like this: *An island of Latinity*, so my guidebook said, *of French manners, French style and French food.* I took it out and looked up Capşa. There it was. The guidebook recommended 'Absinthe, Cognac, Bitters or Amers, Curaçao, Grenadine, Orgeat and Sorbet', tempering its advice to sit at the terrace and observe 'Bucharest life in all its phases' with the caveat: 'Chairs placed in unpleasant proximity to the gutter should, of course, be avoided.'

But then my guidebook, the only book about Romania I could find at home, was from 1899 and had cost ten pence from the Isle of Dogs Oxfam. Leo took it from me and stroked its tired cover, the red string of its binding hanging from the spine. 'Dunno about the *Curaçao, Grenadine, Orgeat and Sorbet*,' but the gutter's still there. And as for *Bucharest life in all its phases*, well, I think I can promise you that...'

1899 – ninety years ago. Back then Romanians who returned from France with heads full of the latest books, and bodies hung with the latest fashions were known as *bonjouristes*. Capşa was a relic of that era, and also its reliquary: embossed leather menus, monogrammed tablecloths and heavy silverware. *Chez Capşa* read the cover of the menu: *Bienvenue à la gastronomie Roumaine.* The décor – gold fittings, damask screens and lanky tropical plants with dusty leaves – was matched by a string quartet grinding out some Strauss. The walls were mirrors, smoky from age and minutely fractured. You felt pieces of your reflection catching in the cracks and staying there, like dirt in the grouting between tiles.

Waiters rolled trolleys of food. At the far end of the room, a party of senior politicians was enjoying something flambéed in cognac. The blue flames spat and lit their faces from below.

'There you go,' said Leo, smiling at them sarcastically, 'take a look: the Party has abolished want!' They looked up and grinned, still chewing. '*Bon appétit*, comrades!'

The Maître d'Hôte, splendidly liveried and with a wolfish face, showed us to a table at a frosted window overlooking Cercul Militar. We could see out, but no one could see in. This was the Romanian way, encapsulated in the city's best restaurant: waiters sliced fillets of Chateaubriand with gentle strokes while in the shops beyond, unstacked shelves gleamed under twists of flypaper and the crimeless streets shouldered their burden of emptiness.

Capşa was, Leo told me, the only place where most of what the menu promised was available. 'That's why it's so short.' He placed a packet of Kent cigarettes on the table. These were blocks of currency here, tobacco bullion; to lay them out was to signal your desire for special attention and your ability to pay for it. Leo ordered a bottle of Dealul Mare and it arrived immediately, conjured from behind the waiter's back.

'There's a few things you'll need to know...' Leo begins, sloshing the wine around his mouth and swallowing it back hard. He abandons his sentence and looks me up and down for the first time: 'You look like someone who thought they could travel light but who's already missing his baggage.'

I tell him I'm tired, jetlagged by far more than the two hours time difference between Romania and Britain; that I'm sitting in an improbable restaurant in the half-lit capital of a police state with a jittery drunk; that I'm here because I got a job I never applied for, after an interview I never went to; that my baggage is all I've got to hold on to in these unreal times.

'Enough about me. Tell me something about yourself...' Leo has said nothing about himself. 'You were most impressive at interview. Ticked all the boxes.'

'Very funny – tell me, how much of a disadvantage did not turning up put me at?'

'Well, I pride myself on being able to see beyond first impressions... Professor Ionescu's looking forward to meeting you too. We think we've appointed the right person for the job. Someone who'll, er... grow into it. You'll notice too that we've taken the liberty of adding BA to your name: Bachelor of Arts. A welcome present from me,' Leo pushes a degree certificate across the table, an ornate, multiply stamped and signed piece of parchment with a blot of sealing wax and some ribbon. First Class Honours, *Summa cum Laude*. 'Mind you, if you want a PhD you'll have to pay for it like everyone else.'

Leo shrugs and laughs – he's already onto the next thing, ready to give me *the lowdown*. 'And believe me, it's low.' His joke falls flat (is it a joke?), but he is undeterred. He begins the pep talk he has given many times before. Dozens of people have passed through before me, but none of them stuck it out beyond a few weeks. Only Belanger had looked as if he'd stay the course, but Leo does not talk about Belanger.

Leo explains, Leo contextualises and embroiders. There are things to exaggerate and things to underplay. After a few months here, it will amount to the same thing: life in a police state magnifies the small mercies that it leaves alone until they become disproportionate to their significance; at the same time it banalises the worst travesties into mere routine.

Our waiter, itching with solicitousness, comes to ask 'if all is delicious?' Since we have not yet ordered, this is certainly a good time to enquire. His eye is on the packet of Kent on the table.

Leo replies *Da, multumesc*, yes, all is very delicious.

'These new-fangled ways...' he says, 'asking you if your food's good, telling you to enjoy your meal. I preferred it when they slammed the grub on the table and went off scratching their arses... it's something they've picked up recently from foreign television. When I first arrived in Bucharest, I came here for lunch and one of the cleaning ladies was clipping her toenails on the carpet. That was old Romania. Ah! The old days... now it's all *Hi! My name is Nicolae and I'm your waiter for the evening...*' Leo's American accent is terrible. 'I blame *Dynasty* – they've started showing an episode twice a week. A way of using up a quarter of the three hours of nightly TV. It's supposed to make Romanians disgusted by capitalist excess but all it does is give lifestyle tips to the Party chiefs. Suddenly the Party shops are full of Jacuzzis and ice buckets and cocktail shakers...'

He motions the waiter to take our order: the house speciality, 'Pork Jewish Style,' a dish in which a whole continent's unthinking anti-Semitism is summarised.

Leo eats like a toddler, cutting pieces of food with his knife and skewering them to the end of the fork with his fingers, before changing hands and loading the food into his mouth. 'This is a country where fifty per cent of the population is watching the other fifty per cent. And then they swap over.'

I listen to his bad jokes and already I know they aren't jokes at all, just ways of approaching the truth at a less painful angle, like walking sideways in the teeth of a vicious wind. I eat the food and drink the wine as Leo describes a world of suspicion and intrigue in which he is happy, stimulated, fulfilled. The place suits him, not because it resembles him but because he is so far in excess of it.

But most of all, he loves it: 'It's all here, passion, intimacy, human fellowship. You just need to adapt to the circumstances,' says Leo, 'it's a bit of a grey area to be honest. Actually, I might as well tell you the truth: it's all grey area round here.' He gestures at the world outside Capşa as if it is a correlative of the moral universe we now live in. He motions for a third bottle of Pinot Noir. I wonder if they have aspirin in Romania. Christ, I think, what a start.

But Leo is right. He is not like the other expatriates, who exist in perpetual mistrust of their Romanian colleagues, hush their voices when they come into the room, exclude them from conversations, or socialise with them only at arm's length, nostrils aquiver. He is someone who, for all his excess and swagger, has calibrated his behaviour to those around him, to their extraordinary circumstances and to the violence these circumstances have done to their daily lives.

It's a close call for Leo's special scorn, between the Party apparatchiks who rule their people with such corruption, ineptitude and contempt, and the expats: the diplomats, businessmen and contractors who live in a compound to the west of the city, with their English pub, *The Ship and Castle* ('the Shit and Hassle') and their embassy shop. One of his riffs is to compose designer scents for them: 'Essence of Broadstairs', 'Bromley Man', 'Stevenage: For Her'. Their parties, an endless round of cocktails and booze-ups, are 'sometimes fun, if only for a drink and a chance to read last week's English papers', but the circuit as a whole is, as he puts it 'a *doppelganbang*: where largely identical people fuck each other interchangeably'.

Sitting in Capşa that night I felt two things, two sensations that seemed at odds, but which took me to extremes of myself: a sense of the world closing in, tightening up, an almost physical sensation of claustration; and something else: exhilaration, a feeling for the possible, something expanding around me as I looked out at that empty square. It was as if the agoraphobia the new city was designed to induce, and the political system it existed to make concrete, was translating itself inwards, becoming an intensive inner space. In the way an atom could be split to open out a limitless vista of inverted energy, so now, in the midst of constraint and limitation, my life seemed full of possibility.

The first thing I learned, and I learned it from Leo, was to separate people from what they did. People existed in a realm apart from their actions: this was the only way to maintain friendships in a police state. When Rodica, the faculty secretary, opened our offices for the police to search our things and copy our papers, or the landlady let them into my flat, I said nothing. I knew they knew I knew, and it changed nothing.

For all the grotesqueness and brutality, it was normality that defined our relations: the human capacity to accommodate ourselves to our conditions, not the duplicity and corruption that underpinned them. This was also our greatest drawback – the routinisation of want, sorrow, repression, until they became invisible, until they numbed you even to atrocity.

'Here's the thing, right...' Leo is telling me something – one of the few things – I already know about Bucharest: that it has the largest number of cinemas per head of the population in the world.

Leo judges that I have had enough for the night. Capşa is closing – it's nearly midnight. He wants another drink, but I need to sleep and he is merciful and drives me home, slowly this time, stopping to point places out to me. At the Inter-Continental, the music is still going. Further on, the porch of the Hotel Athénée Palace, a more stately establishment, flickers in the gold of limousine headlamps. Leo drives down an avenue where every other building is a cinema: Buster Keaton, Laurel and Hardy, Harold Lloyd.

'No Chaplin,' says Leo: 'Chaplin's banned – *The Great Dictator*, see? And no Marx Brothers either. Can't work that one out, mind. You'd have thought...'

The Romanian censor has a fondness for those sad-faced Pierrot-types, Keaton and Lloyd, tragic/comic figures at odds with the world of things, Hamlets of the boom-and-bust West. Their comedy featured human beings crammed out of

23

their own lives by objects in a world of surfeit, where material goods shut you out and marginalised you. Here, in Ceauşescu's Romania, all is lack and absence, space unfilled, and the world of material surfeit as alien as the physics of *Star Trek*.

I climbed the stairs, not knowing where the light switches were, following the stairwell with my fingers in the dark. Once in the flat, I found my bed. Not having bothered to lay out sheets and pillows, I lay down on the bristly peasant blanket. My mouth was dry, my head already ached. I looked about me for a pillow, found none, and lay down in the spinning room. I had leapfrogged drunkenness and landed in the middle of a hangover.

In a new bed it is usually the unfamiliar sounds that keep you awake. Tonight it was the unfamiliar silence, a constant rustle just short of movement, tiny shifts in the stillness of Belanger's flat. I woke up several times to piss or to drink rusty water from the bathroom tap. The phone rang, but I could not tell if I had dreamed it or if it was real. Each time I woke it had stopped. Pieces of the day gathered together in my mind: the plane, the glittering silverware of Capşa, the feral eyes of the Maître d'. I was tormented by the recollection of all the postings I might have had, all the cities I might be in: Barcelona, Budapest, Prague. Images of each, none of them visited, coalesced into one, and the place they formed in my mind was the Bucharest I had been in only a few hours: a heat-beaten brutalist maze whose walls and towers melted like sugar, and where the roots of trees erupted through the pavements.

I slept late and woke in sunlight so hot the blood bubbled inside my eyelids. My first morning was given over to paperwork at the Ministry of the Interior. The building dominated a roundabout large enough to outscale even the cranes and diggers that stalked the city's streets like Meccano monsters. A few old buildings stood across the way, precarious for all their seniority. Were their foundations already tingling with intimations of demolition? In a few months they would be gone. From the outside, the ministry was boxy and grey, its only ornament a stucco Party crest. As an interior space, it was barely comprehensible. I remembered those posters by Escher that decorated student walls: physically impossible architecture and abyssal interiors; staircases that tapered into a void, or twisted back into themselves; doors that opened onto doors; balconies that overlooked the inside of another room that gave onto a balcony that overlooked the inside of another room... There were vast desks with nothing on them except for telephones, ashtrays and blank paper; voices loud enough to startle but too faint to understand; unattributable footsteps that got closer but never materialised into presence, then sudden arrivals which made no sound. The rustle of unseen activity was everywhere, like the scratching of insects in darkness. Kafka's *The Castle* came to mind, a book I had not read but that fell into that category of literature that culture reads on your behalf and deposits somewhere inside you. So I imagined Kafka's castle.

After an hour's wait, a man appeared, blinking and smelling of basements. I filled in the forms, leaving only the 'Next of kin' box empty. I had looked forward to the ceremony of leaving it blank, the cleanness of it. 'No kin,' I said, 'no next'; but he insisted I write something. There were no blank forms in this country. I wrote Leo's name.

My photo was affixed to a small card and stamped: my pass to Bucharest's diplomatic shops, special petrol stations and foreigners' clubs.

Outside, clouds of dust billowed from roadworks across the avenue where men worked without helmets, shirtless in tracksuit bottoms and flip-flops. Soldiers sat and smoked on the kerbside, rifles across their knees, beside black vans with barred windows.

Militia were stationed every twenty yards. Last night they had looked sinister and immaterial, restless shades patrolling a missing population. Now they stood and swayed in the heat, badly dressed and bored and serving not as watchers but as reminders of a watchfulness beyond. As I walked, I sensed what was missing. No music came from any houses or shops; no radio, no one whistling or singing; there was nowhere to stop for a coffee or something to eat. No one stood about and talked and those who walked did so alone. The school playgrounds emitted no noise. A newspaper kiosk sold a brown drink called 'Rocola' – Romanian cola – cigarettes, and greygreen stubs of lottery tickets. It was hard to imagine what the prizes were.

Doubling back past my flat, I noticed a commotion. Drawing level with the crowd, I saw a building that gave away so little about itself that I had not seen it despite passing it three times already. Like Capşa, its windows were of frosted glass. This place too served the Party, I realised eventually: it was their discreet, hi-tech clinic, where the bosses and their families went for everything from abortions and gout to heart surgery and chemotherapy. Fronted by forceful iron gates, its marble steps led to a porch with a glass roof, elegant but inconspicuous. Drawn up in front were Party ambulances, white Mercedes estates with red stripes and blue revolving beacons.

Along the building's grey facade, workmen in overalls were slopping white paint over some writing, watched by young men in suits. It was an unequal battle: the bright red letters pushed through their thin emulsion. *EPID – EMIA*, the word's two halves separated by the gates' black bars, along which someone had dragged the brush in a long bloody hyphen. The red gloss had dripped like something from a cheap horror film, a ghastly violent red in a place so grey. Passers-by hurried past, eyes safely down.

I saw that graffiti frequently in the months to come. And when it wasn't there I saw its outline, not sure if I was imagining it or if, from under the layers of feeble paint, the letters kept searching out the light. The word was everywhere around me, but translated into flesh: the emaciated faces of the poor, the sick, the rag-pickers on the scrap heap of Romanian society. Days later, returning from work one Friday afternoon, I saw a young gypsy woman, exhausted and obviously in her last hours. Her clothes were colourful and a necklace of amber beads hung from her neck. A hand was cupped begging, the thumb crossed back over the open palm: that tiny detail sticks in my mind as the very symbol of destitution and hopelessness. I watched from the stalled tram as two soldiers stood over her where she sat on the pavement, piss runnelling down between her legs and over the kerb; snapping on white rubber gloves they slung her into a Dacia pickup. Her ghostly outline remained in sweat against the wall, where her body had wrung itself dry of moisture and winnowed itself to bone and air.

EPIDEMIA: its name was marked out in the eyes of the thin savage young men who stalked the outskirts of the market, where produce was so scarce most of the stalls had packed up and gone by eight in the morning. Items I was used to buying in bags and seeing in heaps were, here, displayed like jewellery, laid one by one and side by side across the concrete tables: green peppers withered like old socks, gnarled carrots, a few lettuces. The only things that seemed in plentiful supply were pickles: pickled vegetables and roots that looked like brains in jars, organs and appendices suspended in formaldehyde, waiting for the jolt of current that would turn them into living limbs, a human body. But what sort of electricity would it take to transform these

27

bowed and broken dollpeople into revolutionaries?

Why didn't I – why did none of us – see it coming? Was it because it really wasn't ever going to come until it came? Maybe. But Leo had seemed to know. 'Hang on tight or get out quick,' he'd say, arching his eyebrows and pointing at something behind or to the side of you: 'Which will it be?'

Three

Someone arriving in a new place registers everything except what is important. The air itself is sprung tight, the slightest detail expansive with meaning: the smell of those corridors, an amalgam of cigarettes, floor polish and sweat brought to pungency by bad ventilation; the walls thickly painted in grey eggshell; the red linoleum floor ripped and scuffed past repairing; the cork boards with staples and drawing pins clinging to shreds of paper; torn corners of posters; out-of-date notices twisting in the draft... all that still seems to me, in its mundanity and disconnection, more real (*more* real?) than what came later: the killings and the mobs, the shooting and the anarchy. That's because in my mind it's these details that bear the weight of all the rest – as if all that was extreme and terrifying was lying dormant, always just a thought away, one wrong turning of the mind.

That first day I arrived at the university and was shown to my office by an old porter. A plastic badge identified him as Micu. He wore grey trousers and a blue tunic decked with medals and tassels. His chest was a wall of decorations in inverse proportion to his status, or at any rate his status now. I couldn't tell if he had been a distinguished soldier, a productive factory hand, or simply someone who had reached an age which in Romania was itself an achievement. If the average life expectancy continued to fall at the rate it had in the last decade, then Micu deserved all his medals. He had to be eighty at least. The government gave out so many medals and certificates – for heroic mothers (those who had five or more children), heroic workers (those who worked three Sundays in four), or heroic tillers of the soil – that it was the people without one who really stood out.

Micu moved fast, despite a limp that gave him the air of dodging invisible but regular obstacles. A soggy, filterless cigarette adhered to his lower lip with a gluey mix of saliva and tar. His eyes were watery and alert. Handing me the key, he pointed at Belanger's nameplate on the door, and made screwdriving gestures to mime out its imminent removal and replacement. This was the nearest it ever came to being removed and replaced.

An old typewriter lay on the table. Tired posters for study trips which none of the students would ever make hung on the wall with dried-out sellotape, along with pictures of the obligatory *Brit-lit* icons, Shakespeare, Dylan Thomas, Virginia Woolf. Stuck to the phone receiver was a yellow Post-it note with some numbers, all local but without corresponding names. I picked it off and stuck it to the window while I tried the line. Dead.

Next door, an electric typewriter hammered fast, backtracking and winding forward in aggressive spurts. Then came a crumpling of paper fast followed by the ping of the balled missile hitting the wastebin's rim and scuttering along the floor. A chain of expletives in English and Romanian came next, then the sound of the roller cranking in another sheet. Leo at work, typing the way he drove.

My first call was to the head of department, Professor Ionescu, a round-faced, affable man who hid his ruthless Party powerbroking under a patina of absent-mindedness. His secretary, Rodica Aurelian, three months into her first pregnancy, looked nervy and underfed, her eyes always fighting back tears. She smiled and welcomed me in, doing what she could to put me at my ease.

An expert purger, it was Ionescu who oversaw the mass sackings two years ago, when the English department was thoroughly 'renewed'. Its former head, a famous Marxist scholar, was now a laboratory assistant in the chemistry faculty. Ex-professors haunted the university buildings, minimum-wage ghosts who dusted their old lecture rooms or polished floorboards on all fours as their ex-colleagues stepped over them. The old joke, that it was in the janitorial strata of Romania's universities that you found the real intellectuals, was, like all good communist bloc jokes, less an exaggeration of reality than a shortcut to it.

Amazingly, no one bore Ionescu any animosity. I once saw him and his predecessor, the latter in the regulation blue overalls, talking amicably and shaking hands in the street. Leo had warned me: people and what they did were two separate things, they and their actions parting like a body and its shadow at dusk. It was a species of reverse existentialism that would have given Sartre and his acolytes something to account for.

The professor welcomed me into his office. Behind his desk large French windows opened onto a balcony that gave onto a skyline broken up with cranes and scaffolding. Down below a vast cavity gaped where a new Metro station was being built. No one worked there now, and a straggle of red ribbons cordoned off the area from traffic and pedestrians. It resembled the site of some space debris that had crashed and burrowed deep into the city's innards. But this was common enough here: buildings were suddenly begun and then just as suddenly abandoned. It was done on a whim, but a whim with hundreds of cranes and diggers and bulldozers, tens of thousands of workers and tonnes of concrete to express itself... the *whim to power* Nietzsche would have called it.

On either side of Ionescu's windows hung portraits of Nicolae and Elena Ceauşescu in academicians' caps and gowns, icons flanking an altar. Ionescu put an arm around my shoulder and gestured at the view, nodding in secular worship of the new Bucharest and of the deities who oversaw its making.

I was invited to sit. Rodica brought tea and Tsuica, the Romanian plum brandy. Ionescu took a sip of tea, sweet and milkless, Turkish-style, then downed the alcohol in one suave tilt of the glass.

It was 9 am, and he was enjoying that morning lift a first drink gives the practised drinker. Later would come the noonday plateau of good humour (the best time to ask him for things), then the mid-afternoon descent when we all stayed out of his way. After a few moments of social autopilot – my flight, my flat, my first impressions – Ionescu, as he put it, *cut to the point*. His English was excellent but full of odd reworkings of set phrases. As he warned me once, wagging his finger and trying to be avuncular, a pretty woman can get what she wants by *fluttering her eyeballs*. Another time, as two colleagues argued over new offices, Ionescu suggested they resolve the issue by means of a *toss off* which he offered to adjudicate.

'I have a job for you – a reference for a very good student, a very good girl,' Ionescu took off his spectacles and pushed a form across his desk – an application for a two-week scholarship at a London college, already filled out and authorised by him. Someone had taken the liberty of filling in my name as the candidate's British sponsor. I only had to sign.

'But Professor, I know nobody here – it's my first day at work. How can I write a reference? I've only met Leo...'

'Exactly, the first day is as fine a time as any to get stuck in. Here, I have had Rodica fill in the reference to save you

32

trouble. You merely... what is the phrase? *append your autograph.'*

I scanned the form. It was made out in the name of a woman, and complete except for my signature. I had never heard of her, and her name, *Cilea Constantin*, was not on my student lists. My reference, neatly typed and in Ionescu's punctilious English, was full of warm praise for this ghost-protégée of mine.

'But she's not one of ours,' I said, wanting to be awkward. It is a sign of how little I understood the protocols of coercion that I thought I was making a stand. To Ionescu's expert eye, I was already relenting. To engage with people like Ionescu is already to have capitulated to them.

'Not as such...'

That versatile, evasive answer. How often did I hear it, from Ionescu, from Leo, from so many others in everyday situations of little legality and no morality? Soon I was using it myself.

I protested a little: it was *unethical, unprofessional*; besides, all he had to do was sign it himself, since it was clear he had dictated it. *No – it was wrong, full stop. This wasn't the sort of thing that happened at home...* I tried out a few such stern rectitudinous phrases. They sounded pretty good, just not mine.

Ionescu changed tack. 'Dr O'Heix tells me you were most impressive at the London interview.' He smiled and inched the form nearer. Had Leo lied to him or were they in it together? Was this Ionescu's way of letting me know that since I had got here on the basis of a non-existent interview, I owed it to him to perpetuate the tradition of phantom appointments?

As I signed he came round the side of the desk and put his arm around my shoulder, as if welcoming me to a club. 'I am very grateful. Come now, do not look so preoccupated, you have already proved yourself invaluable.' Then, like a barman

33

turfing out a customer who has used up his tab, he called Rodica to show me out.

Signing a reference for a complete stranger, obviously a Party apparatchik, should have felt like crossing some sort of border. I should have felt more... *preoccupated*. But no: I thought no more about it.

My life began to take shape: the walk in to work; the long lunch break that drooped over both sides of the short lunch; the walk home and an evening's reading. Leo made loneliness impossible – there was always something to see, someone to meet, expeditions to new parts of the city researching his book on Bucharest. As I returned to the flat each evening I felt there was more and more to come back to: more of myself, more of what could pass for a life and a profession. I worked hard at the Romanian language, liked the students, enjoyed preparing for my classes. My new degree certificate was framed and up on the wall. Apart from that I left Belanger's flat exactly as I had found it. It suited me.

I did not have to wait long before witnessing a phenomenon known as *the motorcade*. By the end I had seen it so often I barely noticed it – so often that when I heard it start up that late December morning eight months later, I ignored it. That was how I heard but failed to *hear* Ceauşescu's 'last motorcade'. Hours later he would be toppled from power, lying like a shot dog across the pavement, and I would be watching it endlessly replayed on television, hundreds of miles away, in Europe's waiting room. It is difficult not to project some aura of finality onto the sirens of the last motorcade, different from all the other sirens as a last breath is different from all that have come before:

First, the roads would freeze up, then diggers and cranes quivered and stopped dead like animals scenting danger. Men in suits appeared from nowhere, by which I mean everywhere, and broke up the food queues. Then you waited. Ten, twenty minutes, half an hour... Then a faraway siren; faint at first, then stronger and stronger until you had to stop up your ears. And the cars. One, two, three, four... six identical black Dacias with black-tinted windows. If foreign dignitaries were being shown Bucharest, police vans unloaded goods and stacked them in shop windows: bread and vegetables, cuts of meat and fruit most people had forgotten existed. The cars slowed down to take it all in. When they had passed the same vans took everything back again to the diplomatic and party shops. If it was just the Ceauşescus, the cars sped down the emptied streets at a hundred kilometres an hour. Nicolae and Elena didn't like to see their people waiting; the place needed to be swept clean of want, of the demeaning spectacle of shortage. At the same time, in two other parts of Bucharest, the same scenes were unfolding: sirens, cars, Ceauşescu's motorcade – the real one and its decoys hurtling through Europe's saddest dictatorship. One of the cars was for the Ceauşescus' dog, and even he had two doggy decoys, a punchline to a joke no one could any longer bear to tell about a world whose brutality was matched only by its absurdity.

Cushioned from the reality of daily life even as I dipped into and out of it, it seemed the easiest thing to separate myself from what was around me. I had had plenty of practice before coming here. Perhaps these were the 'particular skills' Leo mentioned when I confronted him and asked him outright why I had been picked. Even so, looking back I would find it hard to explain the peculiar disengagement between my own life and the life around me, with its shortages and routine repressions or violence. *Hard to explain?* To others certainly. But it was not hard to live. Oppression makes its own normality, levels off amid the everyday. It breaks the surface of our existence, and then our existence closes back over it, changed and not changed by the violence inside. Soon I was shopping in the diplomatic shops, swimming in the diplomatic club, doing the rounds of the western party circuit. I went to the city centre's pseudo-western bars, where cocktails that were parodies of American cocktails were made by waiters who were parodies of American waiters. I was attuned to the place's duality; to its duplicity.

My home attachments fell away – mostly from disuse, but always helped by the Romanian postal service and telecom network. I never broke contact with home – it was nothing so deliberate. It was more like a loosening of the moorings coil by coil until one day, without noticing it, I had drifted out of sight of land. After some desultory letters my relationship with a girl from college dwindled into an exchange of half-hearted recriminations, then into nothing, or at any rate no letters. With my friends, our lives had become so different we barely described the same world to each other when we wrote. Ionescu let me use his fax machine to deal with the solicitor in charge of something called my parents' 'estate', and with Deadman and Sons, 'tailor-made house clearance solutions'. I was due to supervise their tailor-made clearance in July. It was a task I dreaded more than all the militia, Securitate agents and police dogs in Romania, because if, as I hoped, I had begun to float free, that house remained my dragging anchor.

I could never have felt homesick, not after the home I had come from, but I might have felt violently transplanted, especially in those first weeks. Or afraid. But instead it was curiosity that consumed me. Here the lack of options was balanced by the fact that everything you did had consequences. Leo told me one evening: 'You'll like it here. The margin for manoeuvre is very narrow but very deep...' But I had known that from the moment I set foot on the sticky tarmac of Otopeni airport.

When I left home in 1987 to go to college the October after the strike ended at Wapping it was not freedom I found but drift, a sufficiently plausible imposter to have me fooled for the first few months. I even believed that university would let me make good on all the dashed promise of my parents' lives. My father had wanted to be a journalist, my mother a teacher. In a different generation they might have done so: certainly in a different social class.

They came close, at least in terms of physical proximity, the kind of proximity that emphasises only unbridgeable distance: he in the printing works and she as a supply secretary, working from school to school on short-term contracts for the council. Twice she worked at my school for two weeks at a time. I remember one day finding her during the lunch break eating her sandwiches from a Tupperware box, alone and apart from the full-timers who chatted and laughed and smoked together. Her hands were trembling – he had already begun his war on her, his relentless, vengeful campaign of belittlement and diminution – and she looked at me and smiled uncertainly over her sandwich. She looked absurd and pitiable, but school was no place for pity so I looked right through her and passed by.

'Wasn't that your son?' I heard someone ask her behind me. I didn't hear her reply.

She never mentioned what I had done that day. We never spoke about it until a year later when, on my twelfth birthday, he had knocked off from work early to come home and start drinking. She had bought me a present, a model plane, and I had made a start on it. We sat in silence: I with my glue and pieces of plastic, he with his newspaper, cigarettes and glass, she looking into the middle distance as she always did, trying not to move, trying to escape his inevitable attention. Then it began. The insults, the curses, the accusations of being stupid and parasitic; of being sexless and ugly, a *shivering, useless fucking mouse of a woman.*

I leapt up at him and went for his eyes and as his right hand clipped my face I bit into the knuckle, blood filling my mouth as I felt his left rip my hair and pull my head right back. He twisted his hand free from my teeth and punched me in the throat with just the right amount of strength to floor me, gasping for breath like someone drowning. He stood up and rocked on the balls of his feet and laughed at us both, then left the house, crushing my half-built plane underfoot and kicking its pieces across the carpet. My mother held me to her and all I could do was apologise for blanking her that day at school. I kept telling her I was sorry, and she kept pretending she hadn't noticed, or had forgotten, though I knew she hadn't. I knew too that it had hurt her perhaps more than anything he had ever done. I buried my face in her neck, smelled the face cream she wore at night, the washing powder of her clothes, the sweat of her banked-up fear. I kept the tears back, refusing to cry. Who would I have cried for? Not for myself. For her? If I started to cry for her, I thought, I would never stop.

She would have thought of my being at university as a kind of restitution of something she had deserved. He thought of it as usurpation of what was his by right. Perhaps it was the same thing, just seen through two different temperaments.

I had a scholarship and enough money to live on so that for the first time in my life I was financially comfortable. And ashamed of it: I had almost as much as my father had earned in work, and received more than his dole brought him now.

I studied politics, though study isn't the word: I went to lectures on political theory from which I memorised the slogans and disregarded the thought behind them. I threw myself into what at first looked like *the life*. I even sold the *Socialist Worker* outside shopping centres until I became sick of its mix of spite and outrage, the pissing-in-the-wind confrontationalism that masked its complete marginality. I even preferred the abuse I got from passers-by to the cloying liberal guilt of the few who stopped and bought the paper, never read it, and who discreetly binned it a few streets away when they thought no one was looking.

When I decided that we were learning about politics not in order to reimagine the world but the opposite – to continue justifying why it was this way and could be no other – I changed to art history and spent my days touring galleries and reading catalogues. I would like to say it fed something indistinct and unformed in me – a desire for beauty, to appreciate it without needing either to own it or break it, and a way of talking about feelings of extremity without letting on that they were my own. Maybe that was a part of it, but what I really savoured at the time was my father's indignation that I was spending my time and his money – he was always, in his own mind, the living embodiment of that modern Christ-figure, The Taxpayer – in useless, escapist and possibly homosexual occupations. Back from college one weekend, over dinner, I mustered the courage to talk about a painting. I used the word *lovely*. He coughed up his food, wiped his mouth and left the table.

The high point of my first and, as it turned out, only year at university was when I spent a night in a prison cell for decking a commuter who spat into my book as he stepped across me on the Underground at Trafalgar Square. I looked up to find him grinning, a sharp-suited spiv with a briefcase and a humorous tie, part of that eighties craze for accessories that displayed moderate individualism without undermining one's reputation as a 'team player'. I yanked his tie, a pattern of rugby balls and beer bottles on a background of green turf, and his head followed to where I kneed him in the face. He filed for assault, and had the witnesses. I had a police record and a caution. For a few days my father was proud of me. It was the sort of meaningless, self-damaging act that made people like us think for a moment that we were winning, that gave us an extra swagger at the pub or in the dole queue. My first act of violence. *Halfway to your first fuck*, was how he put it, betraying, in that conjunction, something of how he saw the world.

A few months later my father, by then a year out of work, on dole and benefits and coughing blood, collapsed in the newsagent's and called me from hospital. When I got there a neighbour had brought him a dressing gown and slippers and a bag of 2p coins for the phone. The consultant was waiting to see us. Maybe it was the way he explained the cancer – 'competing cells', 'unchecked growth', 'hostile takeover' – but it sounded like he was talking not about a human body but about the stock market. Maybe he thought it was the only language we understood.

Leo hoped I would turn out to be as much of a blank in person as I had been at the interview. I must have internalised the shock of arriving here because he claimed to be impressed by my adaptability. He found me unfazed by it all, though the radical unfamiliarity of Bucharest life was neutralised by my sense of entering an existence that had been tailored with me in mind: the flat, full of clothes that fitted me, books and records I would have wanted myself, pictures I would have chosen for my own walls; a job I was suited for despite never having imagined what it entailed and that had been given to me precisely because I had not sought it. Then there was Leo, who could cram twenty years of friendship into five minutes' conversation. I came away from our first evening together feeling as if he had implanted a rich and textured shared past into my consciousness, that our friendship had preceded our meeting; that it had even preceded *me*.

Leo had his pragmatic reasons for wanting me to feel at home here. He was Bucharest's biggest black-marketeer, with a ramifying network of shady staff and shadier clients, dealing in booze, cigarettes, clothes, food, currency and antiques. He needed human cover, a straight man, and I was happy to comply. In exchange, though Leo would never have called it an *exchange*, he gave me friendship that was unconditional.

Soon Leo was storing contraband in my cupboards. He secreted his supplies in hiding places across town, and my flat, on the cusp of three of Bucharest's slickest suburbs, was a convenient shipping point. Despite his run-ins with the authorities, Leo was at once above and below the law: his clients were usually more important than his persecutors, and he had yet to find a persecutor who could not be turned into a client.

He supplied the embassies with Romanian currency in exchange for luxury goods: wine or *foie gras*, designer clothes, brandy, anything that could be traded or sold on. Sometimes he was paid in cameras or hub caps or hair dryers; but there was nothing he could not sell or barter. It was also Leo who supplied Johnnie Walker whisky to government departments, buying it cheap and selling it on at twice the price to the ministry minions who procured their bosses' luxuries. With a select few, Leo dealt directly: the minister for transport, his source of petrol coupons, the undersecretary for culture, the deputy interior minister – or, as I knew him long before I met him, Manea Constantin. Leo's contacts stretched across Bucharest. They connected it together in occult ways, subterranean branch lines nobody saw but which mapped out a city of their own.

Leo's business partner was known as 'the Lieutenant': a tattooed, multiply earringed gypsy in riding britches and Cossack boots who revved his Yamaha Panther through the slums of Bucharest like an Iron Curtain *Easy Rider*. He wore

41

a blue tunic with gold buttons and officer's chevrons – hence his nickname – and resembled a veteran of some Mongol rape-and-pillage squad. The Lieutenant took care of logistics. He commanded an army of Poles and Romany caravaners who moved about in the night, across fields and mountains and urban wastelands, slid under razor wire and swept over electric fences, insubstantial as the dawn mist. They siphoned off petrol from the state service stations and disappeared equipment from the malfunctioning factories; they subtracted produce from the collectivised farms and re-routed flour and cooking oil from the night convoys. Inventories all over the country adjusted themselves to their passing.

It was the black market that held the country together, kept it afloat by filling its many gaps and rectifying, at a price, its ruinous bureaucracy. It was the system's other self, its shadow aspect. Perhaps the system even owed its survival to it, the way the wall owes its survival to the ivy that sucks it dry before becoming the only thing that holds it up.

But Leo's great project was not the black market. It was Bucharest and the book he was writing about it: *City of Lost Walks*.

'Next of kin?' asked Leo when I told him, a month into my stay, about the form I had filled in at the ministry, 'I'm flattered. Does that make me your guardian? *In loco parentis?* Are there any... duties?'

There was nothing paternal about Leo, any more than there was anything filial left in me, but I could tell the idea grew on him. Such filiality as I had died with my mother. She was so ill for so long that her death was really more of a confirmation than an event. For two years we had made do with her shade, a hologram of the person who had been so tough and substantial that I never doubted she would rise above all my father's calculating savagery. What I learned from her was that when the strong break they break irrecoverably because they never cracked, because they never accommodated themselves to what sought to destroy them.

One day, soon after my thirteenth birthday, I came home from the park chewing my cigarette-camouflaging mints to find her rocking on the sofa, speechless, her face blank but her eyes holding a sorrow beyond what could be expressed. My father was shaking her, telling her to snap out of it and make his dinner: *There's football on in a minute.* He had turned up the television news full blast to make his point: battleships on a churn of grey sea, helicopters and aircraft strafing the sky over the Falklands cutting to a map with an arrow pointing to a patch of land that seemed to me, even in those Union-Jacked times, to be geographically and politically utterly irrelevant. Saying so in school the previous week had earned me a caning from the religious studies teacher and a punch in the eye from one of my schoolmates. My mother had laughed when I explained my black eye. Not for long. My father had blacked hers with a quick, casual flick of his knuckles.

Now I remember the intensity of my sorrow at her dying better than I remember her; and that was a second sorrow, the knowledge that the rest of my life would be her ebbing away: first from the places she had used to be, then from the memory of the child who had loved her. For years I would stop in the middle of what I was doing, drop everything and close my eyes to make sure I still had her image in my mind. Four years later there was only the faintest outline, blanking with overexposure. Now that its object was so faint, it was the mourning itself that I mourned, its lost intensities. They had at least reminded me of what feeling felt like.

I had always been envious when people in books described their parents as *remote*. For me, remoteness would have been a kind of solution.

My father scraped the ceiling of his life, a life he thought he

43

was too big for. But he wasn't too big: it had simply contracted around him from lack of use. My mother was his slave, and as the little she settled for subsided into the even less she got, he paid her in resentment and with violence that was all the more frightening for being rare and premeditated. When she broke down that day she just stopped. It was as if she had died already but left us the body to help us acclimatise to her loss. That was typical of her – the gentleness of her going.

Him I grew to hate, and it energised me. But I couldn't make a life out of it, or not a life that was my own. So I discovered forgiveness, and the secret malice of it: people forgive not out of grandeur of spirit but as a way of freeing themselves. The forgiver always floats free, the forgiven slides a little further down the soft shute to hell. Maybe that's why so many religions use forgiveness as a secret weapon. Thus I forgave him, and made sure he knew it. Throughout his cancer I was there. I dropped out of college for him, left my student bedsit with three carrier bags of books and clothes, and took the train back to Wapping, back to the house, back to the front room where he sat in his favourite armchair, a black sun around whom everything revolved. At the hospice I came in every day; I held his hand and read the newspapers to him while he squinted at the spaces between the letters, measured the print size, scanned the indentations and margins with his failing expert's eye. I showed him how we could have been. *It's not every day you bury your father...* I had been burying mine a little every day.

During the Wapping riots the year after her death, I came home from school and helped my classmates collect the police-horse shit for their grandfathers' docklands allotments. The bags steamed in the cold and the manure juice seeped down our backs as we hobbled under their weight, dodging the bricks and broken glass, the water-cannon puddles and abandoned placards. The harvests of '86 and '87 were miraculous, the allotments bright with vegetables, the old men guarding their patches as the bulldozers moved in to develop the docklands around them, parcelling it up and renaming it in the new language of service-industry English: 'Enterprise Quay', 'Atlantic Projects', 'Sterling Wharf'. And then the jokes: the cucumbers were tough as policemen's batons, the cabbage rows lined up like riot shields, the winter greens sharp as tear gas.

'It all connects up,' my father would say, unboarding the window of his front room as he did every day regardless of the weather. It had been broken so many times he now just nailed a screen of chipboard across the pane. Before his first drink I might catch him philosophising – not wrongly, never that, just helplessly. I might catch sight too, somewhere between the unscrewing of the bottle and the first splash of whisky on glass, of the man who had once told me that thinking about how the world worked gave you the tools to change it. 'It all connects up: from a row of Paddy's allotment carrots up to 10 Downing Street through the crack of a police horse's arse.'

Yes: family life had been a good enough schooling in total-itarianism, eking out small permissions, learning to live under the radar of his vengefulness and failure. There can't have been many people who came to Ceauşescu's Romania for their first taste of freedom.

Leo stared at me as I told him all this. I had not meant to say it. I had never said it to anyone, or not like that, shaking as I spoke, horrified as much by my coldness as by my fragility. For a moment I thought he would tell me his story, the story of how he came to be here. Instead all he said was, 'Christ, we hoped you'd be... I don't know, a little more of a blank slate.'

Four

In his spare hours, between days of teaching and nights of deal-cutting, Leo worked on his book about Bucharest. The longer I knew him, the more frenzied his writing became. He could not keep up with the city's obliteration. The place was coming down faster that it could be described. In the eight years he had been here he had watched nearly a quarter of old Bucharest go down: churches, monasteries, private houses and public buildings. It survived in guide books and memoirs, and in the trove of notes and photographs that lay heaped on Leo's dining table, waiting to be turned into prose. The prose, meanwhile, went from topical to commemorative in a fraction of the time it usually took for such transformations: months, weeks, sometimes days. Leo had begun writing a practical guidebook for a travel company, but had finished up composing an urban elegy, a memorial to a place gone or going at every cobble and cornice.

Against the wall a metre-square map of Bucharest, stuck with lines and clusters of coloured pins, was attached to a cork board. 'Red pins are the walks taken, blue pins are the walks yet to take. Black one are the walks you can't take any more – the lost walks.'

'*The City of Lost Walks...* is that really your title?'

The finished sheets of his book lay piled on his dining table, indexed *quartier* by *quartier*. I read the names aloud:

Dorobanti, Dudesti, Herastrau, Lipscani... while Leo sought out the pages that described where I lived. He handed me a typewritten sheet with lines and arrows in red in the margins:

Beyond Aleea Alexandru, the Ottoman artisans' houses are lined up in a row, their tanneries and stores across the road and further down Strada Rabat. Queen Marie of Romania would visit the tradesmen here in disguise on her frequent incognito trips around the city. A small mosque to the east has Bucharest's oldest minaret and dates from the late sixteenth century. Nearby, a hundred yards to the west, the Church of Saints Cyril and Methodias faces the Lutheran Kirche that serves the German community. The building next door, the nineteenth-century Hotel Particulier that once belonged to the Cazanu family, now houses the Union of Artists.

I knew of no Lutheran church, and though I had not visited every street and square, I recalled no spires mounting the crowded, crane-ridden skyline I saw from my balcony. As for the mosque and the Ottoman workshops, I could not even place where they might once have stood; the nearest I had seen to a minaret was the brick chimney of the clinic incinerator. For people like Leo, however, the city's redesign had not succeeded in obliterating the place's memory of itself; the old town ached in Leo the way a lost limb aches on amputees, pulling on the vacancy it once occupied.

Half of the information in the paragraph had been crossed out in red; then, alongside it, in copyeditor's shorthand, Leo had defiantly marked STET. *Stand* – it was only the words that stood, and only through them that the place now would.

With his racketeering money Leo bought books and paintings and icons. He salvaged from the wrecked buildings, buying job lots of furniture and art from the demolition men, going out with the Lieutenant in a van camouflaged as an ambulance and stripping condemned buildings before the wrecking balls and bulldozers arrived. What he didn't want he sold on or exchanged at a mysterious place I had never seen and which was called, simply, 'Shop 36'. It was better known by its more evocative nickname, *le magasin de l'ancien régime*, where the detritus of old Romania found its way to be sold to tourists, gangsters and Party hacks.

It was as if all that was being destroyed around us was being stored in Leo's flat, where everything belonged to some scattered or abolished set: from unpaired candelabra and antique chairs to erotic photographs, from unframed canvases to paintingless frames. It was all there, a gilded flotsam of salvage, and it occupied every surface, filled every drawer, teetered over every edge. The paleontologist Cuvier could reconstruct extinct species from a femur or a shin bone. Perhaps Leo might rebuild Bucharest from the glittering remnants he had crammed into his flat? The icons, the paintings, the paving stones and shop signs were all tagged and logged and shelved; there were clothes and jewels, old mirrors, street-signs... a small mother-of-pearl box with a forgotten saint's fleshless finger sat on top of the only item in Leo's front room that was not antique: a huge smoked-glass cabinet with a state-of-the-art television, video and hi-fi system.

The walls were papered with photographs Leo had taken of the destruction, not just in Bucharest but beyond, where ancient villages were being razed and old towns all over Romania were being flattened by Ceauşescu's architectural pogroms. Using his network of informers, Leo amassed evidence from across the country for news agencies in Europe and America. The clippings – from *Le Monde*, *The Times*, *Die Zeit* – he kept in a row of scrapbooks on his desk. Shelved nearby was a run of video boxes of action films and horror movies, sequels, prequels and spin-offs: *Rocky*, *Rambo*, *Friday 13th*, *Indiana Jones*. Inside the boxes the spines of the cassettes were marked with a date and a place. These were the films Leo or others had taken of the razing of villages and city streets, the churches and the monasteries.

His flat had become the city's hidden visage, like a backwards portrait of Dorian Gray: as the place itself disappeared around us, so Leo's apartment grew in compressed splendour.

'These places,' Leo said to me one night, pointing at a tiny glass-covered arcade of shops in Lipscani, 'these places are as much under threat as the rain forests or the Galapagos...' A double row of tiny workshops, each with a different trade, twisted to the left, then opened onto a regimented precinct where all the shops had numbers. Six years ago, there had been a stone courtyard with a fountain and a street theatre where the city's musicians, from students of the conservatoire to passing gypsies, met and improvised. Leo claimed he could still hear them. He put his hand on my arm: 'Listen,' he whispered, closing his eyes. At these moments Leo would go into a kind of trance, tuning into something that for him was still going on. His belief in the continued existence of lost places was not just a way of speaking.

The lights were on in a nearby bakery, and the smell of rising dough and warm ovens drew people in, ready to sleep outside for their chance of fresh bread. It was past midnight, and we were using an old map, made in 1920, to navigate the unlit streets. 'This is how you measure what you have against what there was,' Leo said, 'you walk it, what remains of it, you hear the clamour of all that's gone. It's your listening that brings it back.'

We always used old maps or guidebooks, from the 1890s, the 1940s, the 1960s. For Leo, an occultist of place, each gone epoch could be recalled and for a moment brought back. We would cross the dark, cold, kitsch-marbled squares of Ceauşescu's Bucharest using a map that told us we were in a bustling side street full of cafés and cabarets. We walked the length of a wide, new-built avenue following a map that claimed to take us through a web of twisting alleys between two blocks of the brewery quarter. Around us the uniform grid of main roads stretched emptily, but for Leo we were brushing the sweating walls of a *ruelle*, dodging broken glass and with the smell of smoke and hops in our nostrils. He marked out his lost walks on the new maps, overwriting their expanses of blankness and thuggish symmetry with the old streets and buildings, plotting his itineraries. The maps came to resemble geological diagrams, where time was expressed in layers, and where, for all their passing, for all their irrecoverability, all periods existed simultaneously.

On my second nocturnal expedition with Leo to the depths of Dorobanti, we came upon men and women roasting a pig. They drank wine from barrels and sat and talked or danced in lamplight to accordions and fiddles. It was like a dream scene. Nobody spoke, just danced or sang or gestured, offering their food and drink, celebrating something which was never made clear. Passers-by like us happened on it by accident and were amazed. Like me, they thought at first they were dreaming, but Leo was convinced that we had stumbled in on the past, that we had *crossed over*, he said, that the city was full of such ghostly intersections of past and present, seams of layered time ready to be mined. We spent all night there, drifting back into the grey morning in time for work.

I thought I had been drawn into a group hallucination, but Leo assured me it was real. We spent all day arguing about it: we could go back, he said. We *would* go back, that very night. To take a particular walk, walking particular streets in a particular order, was like reciting a magical invocation. The lost walk had its syntax, its word order, like any spell. He was right. We found it again, a midnight fair in the urban clearing, and we visited it twice more before it disappeared. After that,

Leo merely looked for the next thing, like the underground casino we found with a map of the catacombs, where a derelict nineteenth-century machine room beneath the Atheneum had been opened up by a Metro excavation. When we visited, it was full of men and women at gaming tables, with waiters in suits serving drinks and a pianist with an electric keyboard. It was real enough, but Leo was convinced it was part of some subterranean society, that old Bucharest was being rebuilt and repeopled underground. Leo could still find these places. He believed that they were holes in a sort of space-time fabric, time out of time, place out of place.

To balance out the dream of the old city, Leo made me visit the new Bucharest, where whole peasant communities had been forcibly relocated to the cement outskirts. Families were broken up and moved into tiny flats, often without water or electricity or even windows. Many took their animals with them: goats and pigs rummaged around the rusty metal and broken concrete, shat in the corners, rutted in the courtyards. Cockerels, disorientated, crowed beneath builders' floodlights in the dead of night and hens yaffled in the scaffolding. Old men with narrow eyes and calloused hands peeled potatoes and old women sat on deckchairs in peasant dress, watching the cranes stalk the strange horizon, listening to the mixers and diggers, new beasts lowing in the asphalt fields. It was a tragic transplantation. Many wandered off, back to the land, or to where the land had been. They were found, half-mad, walking the motorway hard shoulders; or, if they ever made it out of the city limits, weeping over their flattened shacks, their lost livestock. The few who stayed on the industrialised farms took jobs as machine hands or in abattoirs, or staffing the vast hangars where dioxin-filled pigs were shackled to the ground and fattened on darkness and fear.

Everything was muffled, time-delayed. I listened to the BBC World Service, whose velvety voice of neutrality, patience and *sang-froid* assured us, in the face of the very facts it recounted, that all was as it should be in the world. There was also Radio Free Europe, the US-funded radio station dedicated to making mischief in the Soviet bloc. This was regularly jammed, and though it kept you informed about events in the Soviet Union or Czechoslovakia or East Germany, it hardly mentioned Romania. What you learned was that those places about which you heard the most tales of repression were also, relatively speaking, the least repressed. In Romania we had nothing of the sort. People talked about the Iron Curtain as if there was only one, but Communist East Europe was itself a system of partitions, curtains behind curtains. In the Comecon cosmos, Romania was the dark planet.

From the few bare sentences in the 'News in Brief' sections of the newspapers – a village bulldozed here, a food riot quelled there – you could deduce the clamped-shut world of Romania, and, between the lines, make out the strangled voice of rumour and hearsay, distorted, crackling with white noise, breaking up like a bad phone line. That was the sound of our everyday life.

The silent phone calls continued. Sometimes there were two or three in one day, sometimes nothing for a week. Always the line crackled and fizzed with the static from the listening devices I knew were tapping in, and always there was the caller's indecisive, vacillating breath. Once he – I knew it was a *he* – was on the verge of speaking: there was something there, a name, a word, the edge of a voice.

In the afternoons I walked through Herastrau Park or visited the museums. The Museum of the Communist Party of Romania dominated them all, an empty cavernous place whose lights were on all day despite the power cuts, while the Museums of Romanian History, Natural History and Science stood dwarfed and in darkness nearby. The Party museum advertised an exhibition on the 'Heroism of the Family', alongside its permanent show of 'Omagiu' to the *Conducător* and his wife.

The Natural History Museum offered more stimulating fare: an exhibition entitled 'Evolution and Extinction', illustrated with a poster of a sceptical-looking giant lizard. I had visited the exhibition twice, and bought the poster that now hung on my office wall.

As a power-saving measure, museum visitors were organised into groups and the lights in each room were turned on as you entered and off as you left, the loud click of the switches reverberating in the high-ceilinged halls. It was like a tide of darkness following you, engulfing room after room behind you as you went. Walking past the skeletons of mammoths and brachiosaurs, their bones wired into place and clipped together with metal hinges, their skulls craned upwards and their jaws cranked open into silent screams, you felt the momentum of depletion, the world subtracting from itself faster than it could replenish.

Bucharest's modern parks were flat, planted with dwarfish shrubs and benches arranged to give the sitter maximum exposure and maximum discomfort. You never stayed long anywhere, harried on all sides by an invisible watchfulness. All the fountains were dry. As you walked you passed statues of one of the harmlessly dead: composers, poets, historians, scientists, evacuated from their own stories by these anonymising official monuments. *The safe and useful dead,* as Stalin called them, never shy of adding to their numbers.

The older parks and gardens were more convivial. The nearest one to my flat, Parcul Kiseleff, was overhung with trees and criss-crossed with pebbled paths, canopied with overarching branches and set back from the street. These small groves of privacy were rare in Bucharest, and by now were only to be found in the well-to-do suburbs where foreigners, Party officials or members of the dilapidated bourgeoisie still lived. For most Romanians, leisure was rationed and policed, the regime reaching even into the slow, slack hours of inactivity.

The old enjoyed the benefits of their irrelevance. I would stop and watch them: courteous, dapper little men who tipped their hats to passing ladies or competed with each other to give up their seats for someone older or frailer. The women brought tea in thermoses and pastries in boxes tied with ribbons, shook their heads and tutted at daring propositions, laughing at familiar jokes. Some spoke to each other in that meticulous, creaky, buttoned-up language known as *Capşa French*. Retired technocrats, ex-apparatchiks, *bonjouristes* from the pre-communist era... the police wasted little time watching them.

It was as I passed late one afternoon that an old gentleman signalled with his stick for me to wait for him.

'*Où habitez-vous?*' he asked me. Where did I live? '*Ah, ça tombe bien, je vous accompagne, ce n'est pas loin de chez moi.*' 'That's handy, I'll walk with you, it's not far from my place.'

He introduced himself – Sergiu Trofim – and extended a hand for me to shake. It was small and dry, pocked with liverspots and missing its index and middle fingers. Drawing attention to the neighbouring stumps was a heavy gold ring on his wedding finger, set with a large turquoise stone. His sleeves finished with antique Dior cufflinks.

'*Mon plaisir,*' he said, bowing slightly when I told him my name. Trofim greeted everyone as if he had heard of them before, as if they came to him cresting the wave of a happy reputation.

He wore an old enamel Party lapel badge. The new ones were twice the size, raucous scarlet and made of plastic.

Trofim's was a discrete, weathered crimson; *classy* would have been the word in a different sort of society. It matched the rest of him: clean white shirt, dark grey suit with turn-ups, red braces and polished brogues. He was bald, with white hair on the sides – *degarni*, as the French say, *ungarnished* – with a trilby sporting a pencil stub, like a feather, in the hatband.

As we walked I hung back to keep pace with him, though his slowness came more from wanting to spin out our conversation than from physical infirmity.

Trofim was a considerate conversationalist; he listened to my replies, asked my opinion on matters I knew nothing of, but about which I tried hard to sustain a view. 'Tell me...' That was how all his questions began. His technique was to put you in charge of knowing something, forcing you to live up to his opinion of you, and it was always your better, more knowledgeable, maturer self that Trofim placed within your reach. He spoke to me as if I was a diplomat back from a long foreign mission, his small talk projecting itself across the globe: he talked of statesmen as if they were acquaintances, of world events as if they had happened to him personally. Some of them were and some of them had, as I came to find out from my weekly visits to his flat near the Natural History Museum, which he called simply *Chez les dinosaures*. Afterwards I would accompany him to the park where his friends sat and talked and Trofim played chess with his friend Petrescu, the icon painter, a tall, thin man dressed in black who wore a heavy crucifix around his neck. *The extinct species*, Trofim would say, looking across at the statue of a mammoth on the Museum's piebald lawn, *I think they will be making room...* For a long time, as he said this, I thought he was talking about himself.

That first day we stopped outside a house on Strada Herastrau, a few streets from my flat. In front of the gates was a cream Citroen DS. 'My prized possession. I drove this from Paris to Bucharest in 1968, after the Russians put down the Prague Spring. I haven't driven it for two years. It's waiting for new parts... like me,' Trofim laughed, raising his damaged hand. The car sat under a layer of dust, the bonnet sticky with sap from the tree above. On the dashboard lay a 1929 Baedeker guide to Bucharest. People around here seemed to have guide books for every epoch except the one they lived in.

Trofim saw me noticing it. He opened the passenger door of the DS, took out the Baedeker, and gave it to me.

'A present for you. You won't find the maps much use for getting around any more. Think of it as an urban memoir. It's where your friend Leo lives.'

Later, we sat in Trofim's living room; three walls were floor to ceiling with bookcases and the fourth covered in paintings and photographs: Trofim with Trotsky, Trofim with Victor Serge, Trofim with Diego Rivera, Trofim with a parade of heroes of the tragic left. He worked in their aura, at a small desk by the balcony, while at the dining table his secretary, a grey-faced buzzard with a socialist-realist scowl, typed into an expensive computer. A samovar of tea steamed in the corner.

After my second visit Trofim explained his strange predicament. 'I am writing my memoirs. Every day she takes dictation, and then the papers are taken away for... let's call it *editing*. They return for proofreading completely different from what I dictated. They are taking my story from me. You've heard of the Freudian talking cure, where the mere act of saying something to someone who is listening is sufficient? Well, we always have someone listening here, we are the Freudian state. This is the communist talking cure: they are curing me of my own life. Every day my altered past catches up with me. You know the old joke: with communism the future is certain, it's just the past that keeps changing?'

'I am unable to recover my text,' Trofim lamented, 'and by the time it returns it is no longer mine.' I went across to the computer. There was nothing on the screen other than the menu of options. His secretary copied everything onto a diskette and then put the day's work into the wastebasket to delete it. But she did not know that it needed to be purged each time, and that the files remained on the hard drive. She treated the computer as nothing more than a memorious typewriter. 'Watch,' I said, sliding cursor down to the screen's wastebin and double clicking. There they were: chapter after original chapter. I dragged them out and opened them. I found a disk and transferred them all across. Trofim looked at me as if I had performed a miracle of Lazarine information raising. I felt proud, indispensable – in short, I felt the way Trofim wanted me to feel.

If I had any inkling then that he had stage-managed my miraculous find in order to inveigle me into taking the dangerous job of his secretary, I ignored it. Even now I am not sure he planned it that way, but I know it would have made no difference; just because I was a suspicious person didn't mean I ever acted on my suspicions. If I had I would probably have stayed away from all of them: Leo, Trofim, Cilea and the others. I would not have come here in the first place. But all I have ever learned from past mistakes was to how to commit new ones more knowingly. Self-knowledge for me was always just clarified inertia.

By the end of April I was resurrecting Trofim's deleted files, correcting them with him and taking dictation as he sat and smoked and rolled out his memories. His secretary would take away the text for editing, censoring and rewriting at the State publishing house, while Trofim and I retrieved the files and we worked on the genuine memoirs. Afterwards I took the files and printed them out at the British Embassy library, and later, back at his flat, we edited them together. This is how Trofim's book was born.

'So you've met Comrade Trofim?' Leo said. 'Well, you've shaken the hand that's shaken the hand of Stalin. They say old Trofim's writing his memoirs. That should be interesting. He's swum in some pretty murky waters, has old Sergiu. You'll notice he doesn't have a picture of Stalin on his wall. Odd really, because he knew him as well as any of them, did a few jobs for him too... make sure you ask him about it next time...'

Five

I met Cilea six weeks after my arrival. I was lecturing on essay writing when she came in late and sat at the back of the main hall, a great cavernous place with acoustics that turned speech into drizzle. This was the Romanian way – scale designed to outsize every human manifestation. She kept her sunglasses on, lounged across two seats in the back row and looked up at the dome of dirty glass.

Her body signalled itself. Men and women with their backs to her suddenly turned like dogs at an inaudible whistle. It was not just that she was beautiful – there was enough beauty to go round, and Cilea had none of the consensus-beauty of the catwalk model or the men's magazine. Her face was dark, her eyes at once stormy and aloof. Her skin was tanned, her mouth lipsticked bright red and her hair black and shiny as a Politburo limousine. *Arresting* was the word, though we tried to use it sparingly in a police state: her mix of carnality and untouchability, along with the way she wore the best and latest western clothes, not the way people wore them around here – with preening amateurism, labels pointing outwards – but casually, from an inexhaustible stock. She looked like someone from another epoch as well as another country: 1960s Italy or France seen through the prism of late 80s US buying power. Everyone noticed her; everyone seemed to know her too. I lost my wording when she came in, stumbled through the rest of the lecture, squinting across the rows of empty seats to where she sat.

Afterwards she came to thank me for my reference. I felt clumsy. I wished she had come when I was giving a poetry lecture, when at least I might have looked less like a glorified grammar teacher, or during a class on the modern novel. Instead, behind me on the board were written those expository phrases found in that fatigued genre, the 'topical essay': *in the final analysis, on the one hand/on the other, it might be objected that...* No one wrote like that, except in international English, that committee-language sieved to a fine inexpressiveness through the strainer of compromise and neutrality.

We went for coffee in the dismal canteen. This was her country, yet she made me feel that I had to justify the place to her, even though – and I must have known it even then – she was part of the system which made it what it was.

The queue stretched from the entrance to the till. No matter that there was nothing worth queuing for. If there was a queue you queued. The only coffee on offer was known as *ersatz*, a thin flavourless substitute that tasted different each time because its ingredients always changed. Students with whom I was friendly avoided us and looked away.

We waited. Our small talk got smaller. When we finally got our *ersatzes*, Cilea grimaced at her first sip and pushed hers away.

'It's Ionescu you should be thanking,' I said, 'he's the one who told me to write the reference. All I did was sign it. '

'I know, but he wouldn't have done it without your permission.'

'I wouldn't have given my permission if he hadn't made me. I don't know you. You're not even one of our students.'

'True, but then again one of your students wouldn't have got the visa and you'd have wasted your reference. Ionescu was being practical: fill in the forms, do it right and waste the place on someone who can't use it, or bend the rules and use the place, and someone gets something out of it? I went, and I got something out of it.' Cilea lit an English cigarette, something else she had got from her trip to London.

Cilea looked at her watch: *she had somewhere to be getting back to.* She spoke an English that marked her out immediately: the English of the frequent visitor, contemporary, fresh, and not the embalmed patter we studied in the university's Cold War grammar books. Most of my students would never leave Romania, but Cilea was different. She had words for material goods most contemporaries did not know existed; she had been to Italy, France, Spain, and even spent a term at Boston university on some scholarship designed to enhance the prospects of disadvantaged East European students. She could talk – about American films, French food, West End theatre – but never about where she got her money from, or what she had to do to live as she did, wealthy and untouched by her country's miseries. But she never hid it either, and even when I found out, it was impossible to say to how far she was implicated in the system and how far she was merely living in its interstices, better and more happily than most, but nonetheless uninvolved in its brutality. Never once did I hear her say anything positive about the regime or the Party that protected her and kept her in luxury, but neither did she express any regret for those who made do with Romania's poverty-line basics, or whom the regime persecuted or ostracised.

Not long after we started Leo had said: 'Ah, Cilea – a girl of many layers'; then he elaborated: 'layer upon layer of surface...' I still cannot be sure I knew Cilea, not until it was too late for both of us, but I know now that Leo was wrong.

I might not have come across her again if I hadn't tried for that second meeting. It was a last-ditch attempt as she rose to leave. I stuttered out an invitation, the kind that comes swallowed up in its own embarrassed retraction. She turned it around, saying she would fetch me next day for lunch. I had a class but I didn't tell her. I'd cancel.

The rest of that day I spent in an itch of erotic expectation. I did two more hours of teaching and knocked off at four. The last thing I saw as I closed the door behind me was the top sheet of unmarked essays on my desk trembling from the electric fan as it chased the same air around the room. I called on Leo in his office. He was on the phone, speaking in quick, agitated bursts of Romanian. I understood a little, that the conversation was about Rodica and that she was in hospital. There had been some sort of complication with her pregnancy.

Leo snatched a jacket from his chair and a fresh carton of Kent cigarettes from the filing cabinet, then pulled me out into the corridor.

'I'll tell you all about it in the car.'

But he didn't. Leo drove nerve-wrackingly slowly, desperate not to be stopped: out of the university car park, past the library and down Academicians Avenue, out through the city centre and towards the north-east suburbs. Further beyond I caught sight of the *Boulevard of Socialist Victory*, a vast avenue that didn't so much vanish into the distance as use it up, drawing everything around into itself. At one end, in a sort of urban phantasm, the steel frames of a vast palace reared up: the 'Palace of the People'. It was going to be the biggest building in the world. What old buildings remained nearby had no choice but to submit to the gargantuan scale of its pettiness. With the sun behind it, it looked translucent, traced in the dust it threw up around it.

All around were apartment blocks in different gradations of grey. Ten minutes from Bucharest's picturesque and ragged centre, the streets straightened, stopped having names, and sank into numerical anonymity: 'Strada 4', 'Calea 9', 'Piaţa 32'. We passed two schools, also numbered, and turned at a large roundabout in the middle of which people were selling machine parts. The pieces were strewn across white sheets on the ground, amid puddles of oil and piles of tools. It looked like the scene of a robot's autopsy. A few shabby queues poked out of shops, but the pavements bore little by way of pedestrian life.

There was even less traffic, just battered trams and buses gasping dirty fumes. The car followed the concrete rim of a waterless canal that bisected the city, then turned over a bridge and waited at a junction for the lights to change. No cars crossed. To my left the rubble of an old church was being boxed up and placed, stone by stone, into waiting lorries. The stones were tagged and numbered, the whole strange ritual supervised by men in suits. A few black-clothed people looked on, some with crucifixes, others crossing themselves and muttering.

'The church is being dismantled,' said Leo, 'then it'll either stay in storage or get put into some open-air museum.'

'A working church?'

'Still consecrated, yes, but it depends what you mean by "working"... they locked it up a week ago, and pulled it down yesterday. It's one of the lucky ones. Most just get flattened and the stones get used as ballast for the new apartment blocks. Dig up any of these building projects and you'll find the pieces of some old church or monastery underneath.'

'Those men...'

'The men from the ministry they deal with the Moonies, the Seventh-Day-Adventists and even the odd Christian, it's all the same to the men from the Ministry of Cults... that's right: *The Ministry of Cults.*' He laughed grimly. 'In the old days peasants on the border would build their churches on wheels, so they could shift them every time they were invaded by the Turks. They should have thought of that here.'

When the car moved again Leo explained where we were going.

'There should be a hospital somewhere round here, but it's got no name, and since it's brand new I can't find it on the map. Rodica's had a miscarriage... her husband's on work detail in Cluj and can't make it for a while. But that's not all. Some fuckers from the Securitate took her into the police station for losing the baby. Losing babies is a tragedy in most places; here it's a crime.'

'A crime?'

'As the Man himself, President Comrade Beacon of Progress Nicolae Ceaușescu, Danube of Thought, said – and he meant, oh yes he fucking did, he meant it literally too – *the foetus is the property of the people*... basically, no one wants to have kids in this godforsaken place, but old Nick has decreed that each family shall have at least three children. The population needs to rise! No matter that we can't feed them or find them jobs, or that their lives are shit... oh no, fuck that, contraception is a crime, abortion is a crime, the pill, that's a crime. Now losing your baby – that's a fucking crime!'

After a month here I could believe anything, even that women could be criminalised for losing babies. It was another ten minutes before we reached an anonymous avenue where Leo realised we were lost.

'Fuck it,' he shouted and thumped his hands on the steering wheel, 'where the fuck are we?'

I didn't need to look at the rectilinear void around us to know this was a rhetorical question. If it was possible to build suburbs that were so bland, so empty of landmarks that they became unnavigable, it had been done here. The place was traceless. The eye sought out something to fix on, but kept rolling off the surfaces. Even the inhabitants must get lost; most, judging by the places they would be coming home to, would probably find that a mercy.

Leo reached for a map but it was no use. 'Half the fucking places on this map don't exist any more – I only bought it last year! I thought this was where we were, I just couldn't recognise anything around me. Christ, this used to be the red-light quarter, the place full of cafés and by-the-hour hotels.' He shook his head angrily. 'The only red lights you see these days are the bloody brakelights on demolition trucks!'

There was no one to ask for directions, no car to flag down. Leo got out and found a phone box. These were plentiful in Bucharest, in an inversely proportionate relationship to what you were allowed to say once you got inside. I watched him kick it a few times, find another, and shout into the receiver.

Things moved fast after that. Within ten minutes we were at the gates of a dirty-fronted hospital, half an hour and two world economic zones from the plush clinic where I had seen the EPIDEMIA graffiti. Rusty Dacia ambulances stood around, their drivers lolling beside them smoking or swigging Tsuica. Leo parked right up by the front door, and we walked unchallenged up the stairs and into the lobby. The reception desk was empty. There were no signs or notices or arrows pointing where to go; only the drag-marks of blood along floors and walls provided orientation. An open bin was full of crusted bandages on which flies feasted noisily. I swayed at the giddying smell.

'I know you've had your share of Thatcher's NHS, but you'd better be prepared for this,' said Leo grimly. 'Don't even bother to press for the lift...' He launched himself up a filthy staircase three steps at a time. My foot made contact with something which turned out to be a tooth lying on a bed of its own coiled rootage, like a jellyfish heaped on its tentacles. It was not the hospital's dirt or mess that frightened me but its apparent emptiness: everywhere signs of illness, damage and trauma, but no one around.

When we reached the ward, Rodica was the first person we saw, our eyes drawn to her bed by the mess of blood on the sheets. She was pale and clammy, in deep but precarious sleep. Leo took her hand. I think he was checking she was still alive. That would have been my first reaction too, had I not been so stunned by what I was seeing. The sheet rose and fell gently as she breathed. Her arm was punctured by a transparent plastic drip and some piping led from her nose to a square box with dials on the bedside table. The box was switched on but its pilot light was out.

All around lay women in various states of pregnancy: some with their babies alive and well beside them, others, like Rodica, in bloody sheeting, the incubators empty, others still waiting to deliver. The mothers-to-be watched the mothers who had lost their babies, and vice versa; the successful births were ranged alongside the stillbirths and miscarriages. The room, above the penetrating odour of sweat, of human and clinical waste, smelled of fear and crushing sadness. A male nurse smoked and played solitaire at the end of the room, a bottle of Tsuica at his elbow. Leo walked up to him. Voices were raised: Leo waving his arms, the orderly turning away and lighting one cigarette off the other, making to resume his card game. Leo grabbed him by the lapels of his white coat and the man pushed him away. There was a pause, and then Leo reached for a packet of Kent cigarettes. Things changed after that.

Some bottled water and a wet flannel were brought to Rodica's bed for me to administer. The water was cold, straight from the fridge. I pressed the bottle's flank across her burning forehead, then soaked the flannel and ran it over her face. The nurse got up and shouted down the corridor, and within minutes a young woman doctor came in. She nodded to Leo and came over to Rodica, checked the temperature, and asked me something in Romanian. I expressed my inability to understand, and she asked me in English: 'Are you a relative?'

'No, I'm a friend. A colleague. At work.'

She headed towards Leo, then turned back to me: 'If she wakes up come and tell me. Keep doing what you're doing. It isn't useless.'

That double negative expressed the horizon of the doctor's expectation, where the best that could be hoped for was that the worst might omit to happen. She couldn't have been much older than me.

What had happened to Rodica, we slowly found out, was terrible. Last night, alone in her flat, she had begun to lose blood. She lived on the eighth floor; the lift was broken and there was no phone, but she managed somehow to get down the stairs and wake a neighbour who helped her to a friend's car. She had arrived here at 3 am, unconscious and losing blood. Rodica had lost the baby, but by 6 am her own condition had stabilised. She had come round long enough to drink a little and eat some chocolate she had brought with her. A message was put through to her husband, an engineer in Cluj, but he was refused leave to come home. In any case, he had no idea of what had happened afterwards.

Rodica and her husband were part of Romania's 'technocracy', the educated, Party-affiliated middle class who helped run what was left of the country after the regime had finished with it. If this was how someone like her was treated, it was difficult to imagine what those lower down the scale went through.

At 10 am this morning, two Securitate men paid her a visit. All miscarriages in Romania were investigated. The statistics on illegal or self-administered abortions here were frighteningly high and frighteningly grisly, Leo explained later, and many of them produced the dramatically disabled children discovered, not long after the regime's collapse, filling the country's orphanages. Party members went to clinics for safe and secret terminations. Ceauşescu planned to increase the population from twenty-three million to thirty million by 2000. A 'celibacy tax' was imposed on women who could have children but did not, while officials were sent to interrogate women about their sexual habits. 'Anyone who avoids having children is a deserter,' proclaimed Ceauşescu, announcing the 'Mama Eroica' scheme to reward mothers with five or more children. But there was no milk, no food; it was impossible to find sterilised feeding equipment; electricity was now as random and inscrutable as Acts of God had been for ancient civilisations.

Rodica, traumatised and in pain, was taken from the hospital for questioning. Two hours later, she was left in the street outside the police station and somehow found her way back to the hospital. By the time she returned she was bleeding heavily. Her body had gone into toxic shock. Her interrogators had refused to confirm whether or not she would be 'charged'. Leo looked up the offence in the penal code: 'Crime against the integrity of the Romanian family'.

The young doctor was not ashamed. She was not resigned or fatalistic or sorry. She didn't avoid our eyes. She was angry, defiant, daring us to implicate her in all this. It was the second time today, though for different reasons, that I had felt challenged to account for something I had nothing to do with: once by Cilea, who circumvented all the miseries of her country, and again here, by Dr Ottilia Moranu, who lived and worked in their midst.

'She'll be OK; there's not much you can do here unless you think seeing a friendly face will help. It might.'

Leo pressed a carton of Kent on Dr Moranu, but she refused it. How long would she keep that up? All the best people here put up token resistance to being bribed. I trusted them more than those who gave in straight away, but the few who never gave in were genuinely suspicious. 'The dirty bastard's clean!' Leo exclaimed on the rare occasions he encountered someone he could not bribe or blackmail. Now he said nothing, just scratched his head and looked pleadingly at Dr Moranu. She was young. Perhaps she hadn't yet worked out that taking bribes didn't make you worse, or that refusing them didn't make you better.

I took the cigarettes from Leo and threw them onto Rodica's bed. 'For Christ's sake take them!' I said, suddenly sickened by all I had seen here, 'keep them for yourself or give them to him...' I jerked my head at the male nurse who eyed us from his card table, 'it doesn't matter – just make sure you take them for her.'

The doctor stared at me, at first surprised I had spoken at all, and then furious that I had presumed on her corruptability. Leo stood back. I could feel him watching me, waiting to see how this would turn out. Dr Moranu looked across at the nurse and then back at me. *I am not like him*, her expression said. She went to Rodica's bed and picked up the cigarettes, holding the carton away from her like contaminated goods.

'Is this how the private health care we've heard so much about works in your country?' she asked sarcastically, her eyes full of anger.

'Quite the diplomat, aren't we,' Leo whispered as we left, 'I knew you were the right man for the job.' As we took the stairs back down to the lobby, we passed the nurse from Rodica's ward carrying up boxes of medicine and a fresh saline drip. He grinned at us through his cigarette smoke. For the short time we had bought him, he would be completely at our service. You knew where you stood with people who were corrupt, I thought, giving him a brisk, decisive nod.

We had no trouble finding the way home. It was nine o'clock. The sun was sinking fast, the sky speckled with powdery light. Back at his flat, Leo opened a bottle of red wine and poured out two full tumblers. We sat in silence and ate bread and cheese and corned beef as the sun wavered and dimmed out across the western suburbs.

An hour later I walked home through a city with no electric light. Standing on my balcony I looked out and thought of home without longing or regret. Back towards the city centre the frenetic, floodlit building site of the People's Palace inflamed the undersides of the few passing clouds. Beneath me the blackness was punctured by a flash of sulphur as someone on the pavement lit a cigarette and cupped its glow back into the shadows. Like a ripple down the street, others followed.

I slept well that night. *The sleep of the uninvolved*, joked Leo, not really joking.

Six

I woke early next day and drank my coffee on the balcony. It had not rained since I arrived, and the smells of Bucharest were becoming increasingly emphatic: petrol fumes, the juice of rubbish bins, the sharp, empty scent of hot dust.

On the ground below me was a cluster of cigarette ends, where the man who had trailed me home from Leo's had waited and watched. There was no one there now, only people walking slowly to work or killing time between trams. The *Scînteia* vendor was in his kiosk, drinking from a tin mug. He gave me a small wave good morning, looked up and down the street and then at the circle of butt ends on the ground. Below me the *concierge* was back from market. She looked up then quickly looked away, fumbling for keys to a door that was never locked. Nothing had changed, yet everything had that slight emphasis that comes from an awareness of being watched, as if the whole street were now suddenly in italics.

In films, being tailed is represented in an atmosphere of threat, a ratcheting of tension that must always lead somewhere, culminate in something. In reality, the relationship between follower and followed is an aimless affair, a pedestrian shaggy dog story with no beginning, middle or end. There's nothing dramatic about it, and once the clandestine savour has passed, it becomes another of life's minor reassurances, like a regular bus service or dependable weather forecasts.

At first it unnerved me. Last night's struck match had not been mere clumsiness on the part of the man outside. He had been showing me that the darkness was full, but there was no need to watch me all the time. After this, I would be watching myself. That was how it worked: you ended up doing the job for them. Making a second cup of coffee, I became conscious of every movement; starting to sing in the kitchen, I stopped; in the shower I closed the bathroom door, even reaching to bolt it shut. This is what surveillance does: we stop being ourselves, and begin living alongside ourselves. Human nature cannot be changed, but it can be brought to a degree of self-consciousness that denatures it. So it was that the feeling of guilt and furtiveness that had suddenly grown inside me I now projected over the whole indifferent street.

I called Leo but there was no reply. He had probably come back late and was sleeping it off, or was at Ioana's, splayed across the sofa fully clothed.

The phone rang.

'Leo? Is he over there with you? Can you put him on? He's meant to pick me up and take me to the station. I'm going to miss my train.' It was Ioana, Leo's fiancée.

'Ioana? I thought he was with you. I've tried him at home and there's no answer.'

'Well he's not. What were you up to last night?'

I told her, avoiding most of the details.

'Poor Rodica. I will have to go and see her when I am back. Typical that Leo didn't call me. Anyway, where is he now, that is the question?'

'Ioana, I don't know – I left his flat around ten and came straight back here. I assumed he went back to the hospital and returned home later.'

'Doesn't look like it. Which hospital?'

I had no idea. The place had not seemed to have a name,

72

and there was no way I could retrace our steps. I tried to describe the building to her.

'Mmm... that narrows it down. Thank you very much.'

'He's teaching at ten, so he's bound to come in for that.'

'He is not *bound to* do anything. This is Leo we are talking about. And what about my train?' I heard her shuffling papers. Her voice had a strained receiver-in-the-crook-of-the-shoulder tone. 'I will ask the neighbour to take me over. Tell him to ring me at my parents' this afternoon. He knows the number.'

At the department I knocked on Leo's door. No answer. As I turned Ionescu intercepted me: 'Ah! The very chap!' he said brightly. The morning Tsuica was discreet but unmistakeable behind his cologne that smelled of fly spray. 'Our friend Leo has got himself into something of a scrape. Shall you and I go and fetch him from his current lodgings?'

'And where are they?'

'Central Bucharest police headquarters, apparently.'

Ionescu called for a car, which arrived after twenty minutes during which he sat at his desk and ignored me, typing and munching through a plate of strudels. He picked up the phone and held a brief staccato conversation in which I could only make out Leo's name and that of some gravely titled personage Ionescu addressed as *Domnul* – Sir – a form of address to a superior officially abolished for *Tovarăşul*, Comrade. It was still in one's interests to have it to hand when, as often around here, life turned you into a supplicant.

'So – are you going to tell me...' I began when we were sitting in the car.

Ionescu cut me off. He raised a finger to his lips, and then to his ear, and looked out of the window with an exaggerated interest in some lorries, just then unloading sacks of cement.

'It's good to see so much building going on. That's what Bucharest needs: a proper Metro.'

Though there was only me and the driver, Ionescu spoke as if he were addressing a group of strangers, which, given the likelihood that the car was bugged or the driver an informer, was a sensible wager. Everyone was adept in this public-private voice, used for statements that meant nothing, or that slid inconsequentially past whoever one was with. This second degree dialogue was transcendent in its banality, pure and meaningless as a sheet of water. We all spoke it. Flaubert had dreamed of writing a book about nothing, but found it was impossible, that language cramponned onto things, that there was nothing he could do to break the shackles that bound it to the world. Here in Romania, they had made a real start on the Flaubertian mission.

In front of the station, a statue of The Comrade in white marble dominated the little that there was, Ozymandian against a background of broken stone and half-erected pillars. A gypsy on a stepladder was buffing the leader's clear brow. Ceauşescu sculptures were always one-and-a-half times life-size, so that when you stood beside them you were outscaled, but realistically – diminished yet in a discomfitingly human way. Saddam Hussein or Kim Il Sung had seventy-foot sculptures of themselves; not Ceauşescu. He made sure he looked as if he was simply made differently, a superior version of the human, as befitted the leader of an atheist state that believed in the superhuman and not the supernatural. With Ceauşescu statues, it was their very moderation that made them so excessive, so troubling to be near.

We reached the police compound; Ionescu tensed up at the checkpoint, his hands gripping the armrest of the Dacia. He needed a drink, but smoked one Carpati off another instead. In front of the building, he told the driver to wait, took me by the elbow and walked through the double doors.

Ionescu flapped open his identity card in front of a succession of checkpoint staff. I assumed he had phoned to arrange Leo's release, but I caught nothing of the whispered transactions that were going on now. All I saw was that we made our way easily past guard after guard. Each time Ionescu's ID card opened there was a flash of dollar bills: a butterfly with wings of cash. We descended further and further into the building, finally in a lift so small we could only use it one at a time. As I stood in it the fear crossed me that it was a trick, that I'd never leave here, but the lift went back up, bringing Ionescu to join me. He walked, I thought, like someone who knew his way around places like this. But from which side of the bars?

Finally, we reached the end point: a long corridor with smaller barred corridors going off it, like the set of a Soviet-bloc *Alice in Wonderland*.

The tunnels narrowed as we went. They were made of brick, painted in beige lacquer, with curved roofs and square electric lanterns that swayed on their chains in the draft. It smelled clean and antiseptic; the chilling hygiene of the frequently cleaned. It was a place where violence was not wreaked or loosed or unleashed, or any of those emotive, dynamic, driving verbs; violence here was administered. Distant bars clanged and echoed, but there was no human sound. We waited at a plastic table. Ionescu, arms crossed and looking at his shoes, breathed deeply and looked down. I focussed on an efflorescence of rot that had climbed the curved wall beside my knee. As I stared it seemed to be moving, growing in front of my eyes. I leaned across to touch it, and it came away as powder on my fingers.

We heard Leo before we saw him.

'Oh yes, I wish to speak with your gynaecological security unit immediately!'

He was interrupted by the sound of a dry slap, which echoed along the corridors but only stopped him for a moment.

'I want the fuck police. I called the emergency number, but no answer. Maybe they're still in the sack, doing their patriotic duty?'

The men who delivered Leo and who, I assumed, were responsible for the black eye and the bleeding lip, looked exasperated rather than evil. They were functionaries of violence, and though they were the ones giving it out, they looked oddly passive beside their victim. One even patted Leo's shoulder. The knuckles of his left hand were raw. His colleague puffed out his cheeks and exhaled, relieved to be getting back to more straightforward power relations. Leo saluted them as they left, shaking their heads. It was they who looked hard done by, two teachers handing over an unruly child to his parents.

Leo was bullish. If anyone could come out from a night in a Romanian cell in better shape than they'd gone in, Leo could. He smelled bad – sweat and alcohol and a topspin of piss – and looked worse, his split lip caked in a black crust that didn't look like a healing scab. His left eye had closed up. A deep gash sliced through his eyebrow which was sticky with blood and shreds of tobacco where he had applied a cigarette paper to stanch the flow. He needed stitches. Nonetheless Leo vibrated with energy, high on drink and pain and sleeplessness.

He threw open his arms: 'Comrades! You shouldn't have. I was just leaving anyway...' He wiped his mouth, leaving a smear of blood across his hand.

The journey back into daylight seemed to take hours. This time, with no bribes to give out, each checkpoint and each security desk took longer to pass. People to whom Ionescu had only minutes before given dollar bills appeared to have no recollection of him. They just furrowed their brows and strained to spin every transaction out to its limit. 'Even the corruption doesn't work properly around here,' – Leo's loud stage whisper. Papers were checked, taken away and examined. I found a packet of Kent and two ten dollar bills in my jacket pocket, and gave them to Ionescu, who slipped them to one of the officials. As we finally stepped outside, the three of us flinched and shielded our eyes from the sun.

'Where's your car, Leo?' asked Ionescu.

'I left it in the Athénée Palace car park. If you'd be so kind as to drop me there, I'll drive home and do a bit of grooming. I might just catch my eleven o'clock class.'

'You're off today, Leo. I don't want to see you. Your classes are covered.' Ionescu continued sternly in Romanian. Leo listened and answered brightly, trying to turn whatever was being said into a joke. He turned and tried to wink at me with his good eye.

At the Athénée Palace, Ionescu dismissed the driver, telling him we would walk the rest of the way. Out of electronic earshot, he gave Leo a sharp smack on the shoulder. 'Do you have any idea how dangerous this is?'

'Well, Professor, take a look at me – I'd say I've developed a rather clear idea of how dangerous it is...'

'You make light of everything! This is not a game. Being a foreigner won't always get you off the hook. Being *you* won't always get you off...'

'Sorry, boss.' Leo put on a look of exaggerated contrition and rolled his eyes at me.

'Look, things aren't straightforward for me at the moment. My position isn't safe enough for me to take risks like this, and anyway, I don't have the time to bail you out each time you get into trouble... I've barely got the time to wipe my own arse these days...'

'Professor, I hope that's one area where you aren't cutting

corners. For your colleagues' sake if not your own...'

Ionescu looked at Leo and shook his head, then put his arms around him. Leo sagged forward and closed his eyes. They were both exhausted with sorrow and relief and for a moment Leo looked small and defeated. I looked aside. Eventually, Ionescu pulled away and adjusted his spectacles.

'And by the way, Dr O'Heix. That's fifty dollars you owe me, and a packet of Kent and twenty bills for our new colleague here!' He began to walk away, leaving us in the car park.

'Cheque's in the post!'

'Ha!' Ionescu's hand rose and swept the air with a grand carelessness.

Leo patted his pockets and found he had lost his keys and wallet. 'Gone. Car keys, house keys, office keys. Money. ID card. The lot. Shit. Must have been my cellmate, the fake drunk with the real Tsuica. Phone Ioana, she can let me back in the flat at least.'

'Ioana's gone to Iaşi. She called this morning. Wondered where you were.'

'Well, looks like you'll be giving your old chum Leo somewhere to kip for a few nights.' He walked over to his car. It was parked diagonally across two spaces, and had been clamped. Leo scratched his forehead, raised his foot to kick the car, held himself back.

'I'm up for a drink,' he decided, settling beneath a parasol in the hotel's beer garden, 'You'd better get them in – I'm barred and out of cash.'

The Athénée Palace bar was a drinkers' Capşa: elegant and retro and discreetly underlit. Its only concession to the twentieth century was a long strip of lighting underneath the lip of the bar, which brought out the carpet's wavy design. After a few drinks you got seasick looking at the floor.

It was empty but for some Cuban businessmen cutting a

deal over whisky and club sandwiches. It made me hungry to watch them, and I ordered some for us. I was hungry all the time in Bucharest, I realised, though I myself never had difficulty getting hold of food. I was absorbing the place's hunger without ever experiencing it.

A lethargic prostitute looked up at me from behind the ashtray where she was rolling the ash of her cigarettes into a sharp point between puffs. Her eyes were hollow and bloodshot and her thin, wasting body was at once garishly on display and in sunken, hollow retreat. Girls in her state were not usually allowed into tourist hotels. When their bodies and faces became overwritten with illness, they were moved on. I gave her a few weeks before she would be servicing drunks on building sites outside the city limits. And then another few weeks. Two others, hard-faced but with a worn and savvy beauty, were reading a German lifestyle magazine at the bar. They raised their heads as I came in, horses jerking from grazing, then looked back down.

'Yes. Now are you going to tell me what happened?' I asked.

After returning to see Rodica, Leo had stopped off here, at the Athénée Palace bar, had several drinks and started a fight with some German businessmen. 'To be honest, I've forgotten what the bone of contention was. Something I said probably... or was it something they said? ...anyway, this big Kraut grabs my throat and starts banging my head into the table. But they're guests and I'm not, and they've got a couple of hookers and a bar tab the size of my arm, and I get thrown out by a couple of heavies.'

'So of course you did the sensible thing and went home?'

No. Leo had found himself outside the hotel, where he spotted a black Mercedes Benz with German plates. His next step had been to carve *arsehole*, or rather – because he had the German and wanted to use it – *ARSCHLOCH* across the bonnet. That might have been it, but Leo had decided to go back in and explain the joke. When the German businessmen laughed, Leo was puzzled. When two Romanian policemen came in, dragged him outside and clubbed him on the arms and legs with their truncheons, he saw that the joke was on him. The car belonged to the Romanian Ambassador to Germany, who was entertaining ministers in the Athénée Palace. Leo had been lucky with a night in a cell and a moderate beating. He had shared a bottle of Tsuica with his cellmate, a good-natured drunk who was probably a Securitate plant, dozed a few hours, and was now back at the scene of the crime.

'Yep...' he concluded, mulling it over, 'it could have been a lot worse.'

The club sandwiches arrived, toppling towers of toasted bread and meat. Why had Ionescu been so keen to get Leo out? What, for that matter, could an old university professor do?

'Yes, Ionescu's a good man. Takes care of these things. You have any trouble, real trouble I mean, get onto him.' What Leo said next shocked me: 'You'll find it helps to have a Securitate colonel as head of department.'

He refused to elaborate. I pressed him for details; I asked for more background, some stories. But all he said was: 'I've told you all I know,' which translated, in this place and at this time, as: 'That's all I'm going to say.'

I gave Leo my keys and watched him jump into a Herastrau-bound tram. He had left his belt at the police station, and as he leapt into the tram I saw he was holding the front of his trousers up with one hand while with the other he grabbed hold of the moving handrail. You can know people for years. Everything about them can change, but somehow there is one image that defines them for you. For me, thinking about Leo, that was it.

Back at the department I passed Ionescu's office and hovered at the open door, as if by looking once more at his books and furniture I might learn something about his clandestine life. He sat in his usual place, the windows open behind him and the net curtains flapping like ghosts at his back. His glasses were balanced on the tip of his nose as he read. His eyes swivelled up at me, head perfectly still. 'Yes?' he said, in a tone of such neutrality I wondered if I hadn't simply daydreamed the whole morning.

I called Leo to see if he had settled in. When he answered, there was loud music in the background and a bath running. 'Great, yes, thanks. Just freshening up!' He promised to have dinner ready for me. I visualised a meal of semi-defrosted bread, baked beans and anchovies – the only things Leo kept in his own kitchen. That was bad enough, but his speciality was *Chicken Chassewer*. I had never tried it, but Ionescu had: 'If you think that unfortunate title is just Leo mispronouncing his French, then think again: one mouthful of *Chicken Chassewer* and you know the dish could be called nothing else.'

An hour later than arranged, Cilea walked into my office without knocking. A car was waiting, engine running, with a driver in pale blue jacket and cap. He drove us to the botanical gardens, and parked outside, right across the words 'NO PARKING' marked in bellowing yellow letters.

Cilea took my hand. She must have felt how much I wanted her from the way my body jolted as she touched me, because she took off her sunglasses, smiled the distant, modest smile of someone used to letting men down gently, and let me go again.

She had brought a bottle of Greek wine, which she opened and set on a tartan blanket on the lawn. Then she lay back and pushed her sunglasses into her hair, letting the sun into her eyes. Her shirt rode up, revealing the skin of her midriff and the top of her black pants above the line of her jeans. I had not seen much of her body, but I wanted all of it and most of all I wanted the taste of her skin, close and perspiring and smelling of Chanel and sweat; skin so smooth and so deep that it seemed to be tanning in the sun as I watched.

The earth had just been watered and the hexagonal domes of the greenhouses were quiet but for the faint sucking of soil hydrating. In the tropical palmhouse, the plants were livid, leaves like upturned hands supplicating something beyond the glass that held them in. Many had leaves edged with brown: sudden drops of temperature, too much or too little water. They were dying slowly, from the outside in. This was more like a sanatorium than a greenhouse, full of gasping, stricken patients. Coal fires were gone to ash and electric two-bar heaters stood disconnected in corners. In between the resident exotic flora, dandelions grew to terrific proportions, fat and bloated dockleaves had crept in and begun replicating across the mounds of humus while bindweed curled and twisted around every stalk and trunk.

'So, what made you come to Romania?' Cilea rubbed a leaf between her fingers, smelling the plant's scent: exotic, mentholated, clean. She asked it as if it were a trick question. Perhaps the only trick was in the answer: my simply having no idea I was falling in with the machinations of Leo, Ionescu and who knew how many other people I didn't know and might never meet? I told her instead that I had wanted to visit a country whose language I could learn, and that I was politically in sympathy with the ideals of communism if not, or certainly no longer, their execution.

'I think you knew nothing,' she said, matter-of-factly.

'That's true, or else I wouldn't have come. I'm glad I'm here though.' That second statement was not strictly true, or not then. I tried it out and it sounded plausible. By the end, which was not so far away after all, I meant it.

'No one knows about Romania, about us, our culture, our problems. We're the forgotten country. We're not sexy like the Czechs or plucky like the Poles. We don't have our Havels and our Walesas...'

'You don't look like you've got that many problems.' I looked at Cilea, then thought of Rodica in her hospital: 'You've got Greek wine, Italian sunglasses, you dress like a westerner – better than most westerners... you drive your own car, no sorry, *you get driven around in your own car...* you – you personally I mean – you don't look like you need any Havels or Walesas. Not sure about the majority of your compatriots though...'

'I'm not part of all this...' she said, gesturing at all that lay nearby, outside, beyond, 'if that's what you mean...'

'*Part of this?* Part of *what* exactly? It's not your fault or you just don't have to go through what the rest of your people go through?'

I thought I'd ended our relationship before it had begun.

'You don't know – you've got no idea, and I'm not going to explain to you, some gap-year deprivation tourist...'

Nice phrase. I wondered if she'd prepared it. Cilea flushed, and when she was angry I seemed to smell her more: the closed spicy scent of her perfume and body heat.

'Are you sure you didn't come here so you could be part of something you'd never need to live with?' she asked, as if she were sorry for me, as if I were a stranger to my own motivations. I didn't answer. The sun hid for a moment behind the clouds and the temperature dropped.

'Come, I want you to see this...' Cilea pulled me up by the hand and took me to a small, immaculate glass dome set apart from the rest of the gardens and guarded by a man in green overalls with a walkie-talkie and a holstered revolver. Even the garden attendants had a paramilitary air. The *nomenklatura* had their own shops and clubs and travel agency, their own schools and spas and restaurants. Apparently they even had their own greenhouses in the Botanical Gardens.

Inside was a plant that flowered every decade. We were catching it just at the end of its span, turning inwards, readying itself for another cycle of sleep. There were insects that lived half a day, whose existences were frenzied miniatures of life, and there were plants, like this one, that existed a hundred years, but lived only for a week every ten. This one crammed all its life into a few tight petals around a delicate stamen. To me it didn't look like much – one part flower and three parts reputation – but it was sufficiently rare for the greenhouse to be empty of any other form of botanical life. For the remaining nine years and fifty-one weeks of the decade, viewers had to make do with a colour photograph stapled to a wooden frame. A notice alongside announced proudly that other examples of the plant were in the *Tuileries* and the Oxford University Botanical Gardens. In a glass case to the right, a faded newspaper image from 1979 showed Nicolae and Elena Ceaușescu bending over it, and a sepia photograph of Queen Marie of Romania holding the infant plant, or one of its ancestors, in a terracotta pot. We stood there in the glass room, perspiration beading on our bodies, as an attendant ladled water over a tray of burning coals. My skin prickled in the swaddling heat. The place smelled musky, like a bed after sex, the air twice breathed.

Later, I tried to kiss her mouth. She turned away. 'Please don't try to kiss me.' Not hurt or offended; fending off clumsy advances was just par for the course.

It was early evening when Cilea took me home, her driver's eyes, half-shielded by a cap, looking me over in the rear-view mirror. At Calea Victoriei we became stuck in human traffic:

84

a long queue of people walking slowly down the avenue, hemmed in on all sides by soldiers blowing whistles at them. They marched to an unseen, unheard band, in step to some collective hallucination, half there and hollowed out with boredom. Some had poles in the air, others raised and lowered their fists in unison. A woman with a loudhailer and a stopwatch was growling orders at them to stop and start and wave their arms at precisely timed intervals. She was dressed in a tracksuit, looked like a cross between an Olympic shot-putter and an army major, and was probably both. 'They're rehearsing,' said Cilea, 'for May Day.' The bull-jawed woman stomped over to the car and looked in. The driver flashed some paper at her and she nodded, backtracked and yelled something at the soldiers, who parted the crowd to let us through. As we passed she saluted. I looked back to see her watching us, full of admiration and disgust.

Cilea dropped me off outside my house with a kiss on the cheek and a wave. That was it. The whole afternoon, so promising, had sunk into anticlimax. The wine had given me a headache and my mouth clicked with dryness. I took a long deep breath before going into the flat.

Leo lay on the sofa wearing my dressing gown. His eye was still oily and closed over, but his mouth was cleaned up. He let out a long rolling fart, muffled by the towelling of my dressing gown, and lolloped sideways off the sofa. Through a slit in the gown I saw his swollen balls the colour of boiled ham and a boot-shaped bruise on his inner thigh. Two cigarettes lay in the ashtray, and a cold *cafetière* half-full of sodden coffee grits stood beside a British Embassy mug.

'There's a hell of a show on Calea Victoriei...' Leo said, putting on the kettle, 'some big woman, a Brezhnev in drag, making all these poor sods march in step. Looks like a wake.'

'It's May Day. They're rehearsing for the parade.'

'No shit? Thanks for that. Been here a few weeks and

already telling old Leo the low-down?' He poured himself a scotch. 'Should get yourself a job on the Foreign Office Romania desk with that kind of insider knowledge. May Day, eh...?'

'Bugger off, Leo. Put some clothes on and give me back my dressing gown.' I looked at him, then at it, and thought of Leo's flatulent puppy-fat broiling away in something I myself would wear. 'Actually, you can keep it now. I'm going for a wash.' I remembered I hadn't eaten. The thought of what Leo was capable of in a kitchen was chilling. I suggested we go out to a restaurant.

'Already taken care of, Comrade. Your job is to open the *apéritif*. We'll be eating in an hour or so.'

I thought of the dinner I was having with Cilea in some luckier parallel universe: a meal somewhere expensive, candles and wine, finishing with a smooth Dacia ride back to her flat and a bed suddenly made whole by my presence.

I went for a shower. The bathroom floor was soaking, and my only towel had been used as a bathmat. The soap was inlaid with pubic hair and a soggy, discoloured toe-plaster was curled up on the floor tiles. Back in the living room, Leo had put on the World Service so loudly I heard the frame of the radio vibrating around it.

In a move interpreted as further evidence of Perestroika, Russian premier Mikhail Gorbachev has called for limited liberalisation of trade and freedom of expression in the Soviet Union, and indicated a readiness to remove Russian troops from eastern bloc countries. Meanwhile wildcat strikes in Poland have led to a state of emergency in several cities. Solidarity leader Lech Walesa...

'It's happening. It's happening,' Leo called out. 'Can you hear me? Hang on tight. They say it'll never happen here but it will. You watch... hey! ... you listening?'

'Yep, every word, Leo, every word...' I closed the door on him.

I lay on the bed, dozed and dried in the air. I woke with a start as the doorbell rang. Leo was showing the new arrival to the kitchen: the Maître d'Hôte from Capşa, tucking some hard currency into a back pocket and carrying two suitcases. Leo was dressed and had shaved in his usual pyrrhic manner, clumps of bloody toilet paper stuck to his cheeks and chin.

'We're having dinner cooked at home,' he explained, 'Capşa style. I've hired Dumitru – just one of his mid-price menus mind: consommé, beef stuffed with olives and crêpes Suzette. Now stop looking so grumpy and wanked-out and knuckle down to some proper pleasure.' He threw me a corkscrew and pointed at a row of bottles.

In the kitchen, the Maître d' slid two slabs of beef from their wrapping, a double page of *Scînteia* on which it was possible to make out the Ceauşescus in traditional costume receiving some mountainside homage from a group of peasants. The Maître d's fingers worked at the beef, slippery with blood, seasoning it then slitting it open like an envelope and stuffing it with olives and rice and chopped onions, then tying it with string. The black market in meat had led to a black market in animal slaughtering, and makeshift abattoirs had sprung up in the most unlikely places: the back rooms of restaurants, basements, even the city's two morgues – *after all, the equipment's there*, Leo explained. In the shops, it was impossible to tell, aside from by the smell, how long the meat had been in transit. This way, though the hygiene was questionable, you knew it was fresh.

The food was delicious, for all that watching its preparation had made me nauseous, and served with a surreal degree of expertise. The man from Capşa had changed into black tie and now served clear soup from a silver tureen, then wine with the bottle wrapped in a napkin and a brisk twist of the neck at end of each pour. Leo and I sat at either end of the long dining table like a baronial couple reduced to candlelight and their last manservant.

Later, after our chef, waiter and retainer had brought the flambéing pancakes, Leo tipped him in Kent cigarettes and shook his hand. The man left, taking with him his silverware and crockery in the two suitcases which clattered as he went down the stairs, home or to another assignment.

'Well, what d'you think? Capşa dining in your own home,' Leo enquired.

'Very nice, Leo, thanks. You could have asked. That's one sinister bloke, and I'm not sure I wanted him sniffing around my flat.'

'I don't think you get a choice here of who sniffs around your flat. The best thing you can hope for is to stay on good terms with whoever's doing it.'

'With you, you mean?'

'Low blow, low blow, and I'll put it down to your feeling tired and emotional after your trip down the old central police HQ.'

Leo poured the dregs of a bottle of Tokaj and lit a Cuban cigar from a box on my mantelpiece. Another of Belanger's limitless stock. The phone rang again, the receiver going down and the click of the line-tap outlasting it by a few seconds. Again no one.

Seven

With Leo around, daily life was felt less as Stalinist terror than as shady ineptocracy – brutish and clumsy, sometimes comical, usually absurd. Our sense of the system's viciousness was offset by our belief that it was not sufficiently organised to implement that viciousness. We were wrong, but when one knew a man capable of getting out of as many scrapes as Leo, one developed a risky sense of untouchability. It never occurred to me that irrelevance might feel much the same.

What was Leo escaping from? He too had been translated from another life – maybe that was what he saw in me when he picked me for the job – but it was hard to make out the original that lay behind. Most of us carry the mark of what we've run away from, a sort of bas-relief of damage, error or regret. Leo's ran deeper than most: estranged children, a crashed marriage, a successful academic career scuppered on drink, affairs with students, and all-round unreliability. He had written a book on travel literature, still in print after fifteen years: a small classic in its field from which he received royalties that, though symbolic, were a useful hard-currency bonus in Romania. I found a copy in the university library. It showed Leo on the back flap, fifteen years younger, a full head of hair, clean-cut and sharply dressed. Not the Leo whose features now blended and blurred into each other, jowly and decadent-looking, half connoisseur and foodie, half gutterjuice-swigging reprobate: the Leo whose life was all subplot and no plot.

After one of his guided walks through the disappearing city, I asked him how he had finished up here. The verb *to finish up* seemed appropriate when it came to explaining one's presence in the English department at Bucharest university in 1989, but never more so than when Leo used it: 'One day I just woke up in my bed in East Molesey, and thought: "Apart from a wife, two kids, mortgage, home and job, there's nothing holding me here..." and now look: here I am, Comrade, here I am!'

A few years ago, Leo had begun to run out of storage room for his salvage. He now used basements in the Museum of Natural History and the National Gallery. With these came semi-professional help, packing crates and even manpower. The museum directors too had an interest in Leo's game. It enabled them to collect for themselves objects from pre-communist times, but with the museum as alibi. This or that object was catalogued and stored or put on show, while the reverse of its label designated its true owner by an elaborate code Leo had devised: a minister here, a general there, retired politburo members, artists and theatre directors and writers. Only Leo knew who owned what.

Highly placed officials used Leo to store their own *ancien régime* furniture, icons or modern art, and would come and admire them every few weeks. The obese minister for work, a man with the fleshiest and least toil-tested hands I had ever seen, would visit Leo's flat with his latest mistress to admire the jewellery he stashed there. Rotund, jolly, ruthlessly corrupt, he came each month with a different adolescent girl. Leo was not fastidious in his business dealings, but there was a class of person – mostly ministers and pimps – after whom he always washed his hands.

Leo hosted auction parties in his flat, where people came to buy or watch others spend their way to ownership of fragments of the old world. He laid out the pieces, each priced and with a short paragraph of explanation, date and provenance, and waited for the bids, which were always made to him privately in the course of the party. Nobody knew who bought what: 'untraceability all part of the service'. Bids were camouflaged as conversation, and gradually the small red 'Sold' stickers filled the price list. Those objects that could not be transported were photographed and the photographs laid out on the table to be fingered and passed around like pornographic snaps. The first time I attended one of Leo's auctions, early in May, he was selling a fifteenth-century carved screen from a demolished church. It was bought by the minister for cults, who had ordered the demolition and wanted the screen for his bedroom.

Leo knew a cross-section of Romanian life: Costanu, the chief of museums, a melancholy, cultivated man who took refuge in his poky office in the National Gallery and read poetry, cosseted in the 1930s' heyday of his imagination; the tennis ace Nicolescu, for whom Leo procured Mercedes parts, Burberry clothes and champagne; the brutish pimp, Ilie, whose network of girls and Securitate-sanctioned honey-trap bars supplied sex and bad drugs to foreigners, and hired out the photographers who snapped them, *in flagrante*, for the secret police to blackmail. Leo called on favours from a gallery of Romanian ambassadors and envoys for whom he arranged the import of western goods using his network of gypsies or Poles in Polski Fiats. For these people, the country's intensively patrolled borders were no obstacle. Stereos and magimixes made their way from Germany or Austria, fridge-freezers and washing machines slipped through the barbed wire. I imagined Leo's 'turbo-Poles' driving iceberg-sized frigidaires strapped to their tiny cars: ants dragging carcases ten times their size into their underground feasting chambers. Leo once oversaw the migration of a thirty-foot Jacuzzi from a German luxury bathroom shop to a villa in Snagov, on the outskirts of Bucharest. As Leo told the story, he understood it was for Nicu Ceauşescu's weekend bachelor pad, though he never discovered for sure. Just in case, he and his crew had relieved themselves into it as they filled it up and switched it on. 'The Whirlpool of History,' Leo baptised it as he unleashed a bladderful of beery piss.

Then there was the most poignant of all the people I encountered through Leo: 'La Princesse', an aristocrat who had lived in Paris for thirty years and reputedly been Paul Valéry's last mistress. She had made the mistake of returning to Bucharest in the late 1960s and found she could never leave again. She had no money, and lived in two rooms of her family's former *Hotel particulier*, the rest of which was given over to workers' accommodation. Every Wednesday she went to the French Embassy for the coffee morning, to eat croissants and stretch the diplomats' diplomacy with stories of 1930s Paris and Romanian émigré culture. Then she would visit the consulate and ask if her visa had arrived. The visa, stuck somewhere in the bowels of a frozen ministry, had been in process – the official term was 'active' – for nearly twenty years. Each time she walked home via the patisserie on Calea Victoriei, where the manager took pity on her and gave her an elaborately ribboned box of yesterday's pastries.

She was always invited to the embassy functions, where she stood in her haggard finery – outrageous feather boas in the summer, 1940s Chanel two-pieces and moulting furs the rest of the year. Her once-luscious minks now hung off her like peelings from stray dogs. French ambassadors and cultural attachés still called on her, though less and less – she clung to them, her dry fingers clasping their hands too long, crowding them with desperate courtesies. With everybody else, she was an imperious, unreconstructed middle-European aristocrat. Then there was her crew: a feudal retinue of ultra-orthodox religious types and monarchist dreamers. All were unpaid and basked in her disdain. She held annual parties for the King's birthday which the authorities monitored and treated as a piece of folklore: hand-kissing, curtseying and crossing. The telegram from the exiled King Michael, sent to her care of the *Ambassade de France*, was solemnly read out and followed by prayers. Her flat was a place of icons and stewing tea, incense and old books. Even Capşa French was too rough-hewn a medium for her. Hers was elaborate, baroque, ceremonial, a Louis-Philippe chair among languages: fragile, substanceless, overstuffed.

In Paris she had been *La Princesse Antoinette Marthe Cantesco*. Here she was citizen Antoaneta Cantescu, the only person we knew who had a servant, or rather, who had someone officially designated as such, since there were plenty of examples of servitude. Hers, an old lady almost her own age whose own family had been employed by the Cantescos for generations, lived in a single room in the building's basement. The maidservant never looked happier than when her mistress criticised her stoop, castigated her for her ugliness or found fault with her cooking. The look of beatitude on her face when *la Princesse* called her idle was the only expression of complete spiritual transport I have ever witnessed.

We went to see the Princess as one goes to visit ruins; and like all ruins there seemed something permanent about her, the indestructibility of the already felled. She lived, broken and poor and anachronistic, without once letting on that she knew it, or that her every waking minute was a triumph of wilful fantasy over reality. She shared her madness with her minions, who looked to her to sustain both them and it.

It was Leo who had finally, in May this year, secured her visa. He bribed and cajoled and called in favours until it appeared, stamped and dated and ready for customs. And it was Leo who paid for her one-way flight, *Air France*, to Paris.

Leo and I took her to the airport. In the car I watched her face as it failed to comprehend the avenues of new apartments and office blocks, the fantasias of scaffolding and cement. Perhaps she never saw them; perhaps all she saw was the long-demolished Bucharest of her youth, the ghosts of its buildings. The airport baffled her, *habituée* of the Orient Express, whose family once booked whole Pullman carriages for their trans-European journeys. It was an evening flight, and from the departure lounge we could hear the cicadas, tiny engines thrumming in the trees. At the passport control she handed over her documents and kept her gloved hand out a few seconds for kissing. The young guard looked at her and laughed. On the other side of the plate-glass wall, she turned back and waved us away. Servants dismissed.

Or so we thought. She came back a month later, broken and beyond reach now, where before she had just been far away in time and place. 'Properly crackers this time around,' said Leo as he caught sight of her, swaying in the arrivals queue, dishevelled and staring out across some vast inner distance. No one knew, and she never said, what had happened in Paris.

We drove her back from the airport. She was dramatically thin and hollow-eyed, dressed in the same clothes she had left in and smelling of urine.

Leo and I helped her up the stairs back to her flat. Her maid curtsied and struggled to straighten back up: she too had aged a decade, symbiotically with her mistress. She had kept the flat exactly as it was left; had gone on polishing the silver, buffing the icons, dusting the books and furniture. The Princess looked around her as if seeing it all for the first time:

the grimy stairwell whose walls had once displayed her family's portraits; the banisters where she and her brothers – one dead in the First World War, the other disappeared when the Russians invaded – had played and slid down the handrails; the hallway where she had modelled ballgowns as a debutante now partitioned with chipboard, walls stuck with public notices and racked with jimmied-open letter-boxes. The old chandelier remained hanging, fragile and denuded, its crystal long gone. Three forty-watt bulbs strained to keep the vast space lit. Mosaic tiles that had once covered the floor were missing or chipped, clumsily refilled with cement, and behind the elaborate coving the faulty circuitry buzzed and crackled.

Paris, now that she had returned to it, was further away than ever. It no longer even existed in her imagination. When she lost that, she lost, too, the madness that had kept her sane. As Leo put it: 'Madness is not living in a fantasy world – she has lived in her fantasy world quite happily for years, perhaps we all have. Madness is the space between the fantasy world and the real one, where you find yourself cut off from both. There's no way back from that.'

Eight

May Day was a national holiday across the eastern bloc. In Romania it was an excuse for a minutely planned display of spontaneous celebration. The rehearsals had taken up three evenings of the previous week, the workers of Bucharest honing their spontaneity under the malignant watch of the police. When the day itself came, there was, exceptionally, no building work going on anywhere in the city. The morning was taken up with the hanging of placards and tricolour bunting; kiosks were stocked with Rocola, beer and sausages; news-stands sold celebration issues of *Scînteia*. 'A true Bacchanalia,' Leo gasped in ironic awe as he watched the preparations. Banners proclaimed joy in work, fulfilment at home and respect abroad. Everywhere you looked or listened you encountered the rhetorical rule of three: *People, Party, Ceauşescu! Peace, Prosperity, Plenty!* and, Leo's favourite, *Epoch of Light, Dignity and Joy!*

Leo, Ioana and I were drinking and smoking dope on the balcony. The TV was on with the sound muted while we listened to the parade outside: patriotic music, a bloated slurry of pomp that sounded the same whatever country you were in. Leo had found some liqueur chocolates which he had stacked in a cascade on a salver and displayed with an ambassadorial flourish. He was already drunk, singing communist party songs, a joint between his thumb and forefinger. Open on the table before him was the literary magazine, *Luceafurul*, named after the hero of Eminescu's national epic, the fallen angel who became the evening star: Lucifer. The front page printed a new 'Ode in Homage to the Couple of Light' by some Union of Writers' poet Leo knew and which Leo now translated.

'I've known Palinescu for years – he's got to be taking the piss! Listen: *The Light that illuminates our epoch has a source! Two Suns that burn as one!* Jesus, I hope they paid him well for that...'

'Palinescu's a wimp. He'd sell his grandmother for petrol tokens,' Ioana cut in.

'*Twin lighthouses by which the ship of state, trusting* – surely that should be *rusting? – navigates the perilous waters...*' Leo went on, 'Ioana darling, it's your country, but I shouldn't have to tell you that the world's not divided into wimps and heroes. It's not like that. There aren't enough of either to really make a difference...'

'It's exactly like that. Palinescu's a human oil slick – his kind spreads and spreads until nothing else can breathe.'

'Ioana, it's just some harmless crap poetry – and everyone knows it's crap: he does, his bosses do, the magazine does, only Nic and Elena believe that stuff. They'll check he's mentioned the right number of tractors and stuck in some Romans and they'll forget about it. We all will. Most people just want to get along and reach the day's end unscathed, not weigh up the moral rightness of everything they do and say. Nothing wrong with that, and...'

'It's the lies,' Ioana said, more despondent than angry, 'all the lies. They eat away at you until you believe nothing; you feel nothing. That's what I'm saying – if everyone believed it they'd be idiots, but they'd actually be believing. The part of themselves that believed would be there still, still getting used, not dying away like this, dying into irony and cynicism.' She gestured at us, at *Scînteia*, at the television indoors, then at herself. 'Instead we just listen to nothing, take nothing in, we think we're resisting by laughing it off. The lies are wearing everything away... wearing us away.'

'No, that's not true.' Leo was serious now, something he did not enjoy. 'It's *because* they're lies and we know they are that they can't reach us. If we're going to be lied to on this scale, let's know it.'

Ioana waved the conversation to an end and looked down at the floor. In Leo's eyes the worst social crime you could commit was to lead one of his conversations into seriousness. He saw it as a kind of ambush. Leo could be angry, righteous and passionate, but he found seriousness hard. He preferred to exaggerate or play things down; seeing them in their proper scale disturbed him.

Ioana was a disapproving girl, with a lot to disapprove of: from the local details of her life (Leo, principally) to the state of her country. It was hard to know which was the more easily remedied. Leo sat puffing into the sky and tapping his feet out of time to the music, the alcohol flush adding a scorched quality to his face. They were an unlikely couple, Ioana tall and slim and with features as sharp as her manners, Leo short and baby-faced, manic and idle. By starting a relationship with her, Leo was demonstrating his commitment to remaining in Romania; she, by starting one with him, thought she was staking her commitment to getting out.

The doorbell rang. I was expecting no one, but when I answered I found Cilea, a Burberry bag over her shoulder. She kissed me on the mouth and walked straight in.

I introduced her to Leo and Ioana but there was no need. These people knew each other, though for my benefit they went through the motions of meeting for the first time. Suddenly, Ioana's roaming disapproval had fastened on an object. Cilea seemed unbothered by the change she had brought to our small party. Did she even notice? She took a seat and opened the bag from which she produced a bottle of chilled French wine and some Italian olives.

Ioana was the first to go, making up some engagement at the other end of town, not until now mentioned. Leo wavered and exchanged a few stilted pleasantries with Cilea before following. If any of this offended Cilea, it didn't show. Without asking the way, she went to the kitchen for a bowl and glasses; Belanger's flat clearly had a history of hospitality. The wine was so cold the glass beaded with condensation.

Cilea handed me the corkscrew and opened the olives with her teeth. I noticed a small line of newly applied lipstick along her front teeth and remembered its waxy red taste as I had tried to kiss her on our last meeting. I opened, she poured. My mouth was parched. Leo's dope was rough, but rougher still was the Turkish tobacco it came with. Cilea's wine tasted as perfect as it looked. A top-end Chablis, it was nearly impossible to lay hold of here, even in the diplomatic shops and western hotels, whether you paid in sterling, dollars or Deutschmarks.

She was in a different mood from our previous meetings. This time I knew she had made a decision about me, though I couldn't yet tell which way that decision had gone. Her body language was more open. She was less careful, less guarded. For the first time too she was interested in me. I was half-stoned and half-drunk, but these two halves seemed to amount to a plausible whole. I found myself quicker off the mark, readier to engage her and better able to stand her scrutiny.

It was nearly five o'clock. The parade had been going for four hours now, four hours of music, marching and cloud-scraping military flyovers. Occasionally, the television would revel in a close-up of some dignitary. Colonel Gaddafi was one I recognised from the rogue's gallery of western bogey-men; Mugabe fronting a row of elaborately uniformed Africans. Yasser Arafat, always a reliable guest at Ceauşescu's celebrations, sat beside the *Conducător*. Months later, he would be guest of honour at Ceauşescu's final Party congress. Behind them I recognised people from the diplomatic circuit. All looked blankly ahead. The British Ambassador wore his customary expression of very faint strain, a tightening of the eyes and mouth that could denote anything from a stifled fart to moral outrage. The close-ups of Ceauşescu's face were more interesting. He was man on perpetual watch. His small black eyes missed nothing of what was going on around him, alert and twitching with paranoia.

The next bottle, from Belanger's stock, was warm and sweet and difficult to enjoy. It proved the law of diminishing returns that governs daytime drinking: the more and more becoming less and less. Cilea seemed happy enough, though I feared the afternoon would fizzle out into nausea and headaches before seven, and bed by ten. Alone. Cilea tasted the wine and scrunched up her face.

'Come on,' she said, 'let's join the parade – we'll find you a placard. Actually, we'll be the only spontaneous marchers there.'

As we left the flat, Cilea put her arm through mine. She walked jauntily, pulling me along. At the corner of Aleea Alexandru we found ourselves in the midst of the parade. I say 'parade', but it was more like a chain gang with invisible shackles. They marched as if their ankles and elbows were threaded together, heads bowed or facing straight ahead at the backs of other heads. Many held brightly coloured banners, yellow and red and black, and party crests modelled on Roman military insignia. They moved forwards in one drab, articulated shuffle.

The placards were mostly of Ceauşescu and his wife. A

few posters bore the likenesses of other men, presumably ministers, but these were strictly rationed, and one or two had portraits of Marx and Lenin. Far up ahead the music continued, while the parade progressed joylessly: a sudden stop rippled its way to the back of the three-kilometre-long file of people, and what on TV looked like a tidy mechanical progression was really a sullen, fettered grind.

Cilea tapped one man on the shoulder and asked for his placard. Suspicious at first, he was only too glad to hand it over and rest his arm. The picture was a magnified passport mugshot of Manea Constantin, treated in communist baroque style: sensible grey jacket, buttoned shirt, penetrating gaze, and framed with hammer and sickle motifs. There were only one or two of these in the waves of Nicolaes and Elenas; after all, no individual must look better, or appear more frequently, than the country's leading couple.

She handed it to me to carry. It is a sign of how inured I had already become to the grotesquery of things that when I recognised the man's face, and knew it was her father, I merely noted it down as an odd piece of serendipity and continued walking.

We processed onwards, hand in hand, for about ten minutes down Calea Victoriei. Cilea, tipsy and laughing and well dressed, drew scowls from the rest of them. For myself, I had never been a great dresser, but I was dismayed to see how well I blended in here.

The mood was aggressive and despondent. People stepped on each other's heels, elbowed each other in the kidneys, spat on the floor, strutted and squared up to each other only to retreat in a fade-out of grumbling. The smell of sweat and dirt was everywhere, punctured by Cilea's perfume as she zigzagged ahead of me. At one point the line stopped suddenly and I was pushed into her from behind. She arched her back and pressed her head into my shoulder, her neck against my mouth. Her hair was warm and heavy.

'When they get to the stadium, they'll have to stop and stand around for three hours of speeches and ceremonies,' shouted Cilea above the noise. She didn't seem especially sorry. The sun beat down. For most of these people this 'day of joy' consumed the whole of their public holiday. Many of them would then trek home through building sites and urban dustbowls to their flats in the outskirts. They moved along, penned in by soldiers and militia. Every now and then an individual would try to make a break for it, try to disappear down a side street, only to be slapped and dragged back into line. It was human cattle herding. Only Cilea and I dodged through the crowd, snaked our way through the lines. Once or twice someone in a suit came to push us back in, but Cilea showed them her identity card and they saluted. Months later, these young men would be the people shooting at their compatriots during those unreal days in the strangulated city. I had no idea where she was taking me. Two kilometres down the road, the Romanesque gates of the Stadium of the People lay open.

Without warning, Cilea pulled me into a side street and up into a gated avenue, where a guard clicked his heels and let her through. I had never seen such a place: overhung with cherry trees, their scattered petals on the pavement; a shop with frosted windows was guarded by a uniformed militiaman; the roads had been hosed down to cool them and the air smelled of wet pavements. Black Dacias and Mercedes were parked along clean kerbs. A gardener was bent over some perfect tulips, as if taking their pulse. Everything was fresh and opulent. Cilea led me into a shady courtyard where a fountain rippled quietly and balconies were crammed with fat-leaved plants. I followed her into a cool stairwell that curled upwards in a spiral. The clean smell of newly brewed tea hung in the corridor. Her flat was on the first floor.

I had known, without being conscious of knowing it, that Cilea was the daughter of a top party member. So much was clear from the aura of untouchability she carried, which seemed, for all that we were in a *classless communist state*, the aura of lightness that rich and privileged people have everywhere you find them. It was as if the material world, the air itself, parted for them as they moved. You knew them from the way they passed through life untouched by life. Cilea was one of them: part of that international, borderless community of ease. What I had not known until this afternoon was that her father was more than just a member of the *nomenklatura*. The flat Cilea lived in alone would have housed two families. The living room looked furnished from a Nordic minimalist catalogue and full of US films and magazines, British books, Japanese electronics. The kitchen was stocked with olives, amaretti, French wine and English biscuits. There was Romanian art on the walls and shelves of photographs: Cilea and her father in front of Big Ben, the Pitti Palace, Harvard boathouse. In one photo a small girl, recognisably Cilea but perhaps five or six years old, played with other children on a green lawn. At a table nearby sat a group of adults enjoying a spread of food in the open air. At its head, and with Elena to his right, sits Nicolae Ceaușescu, elbows on the table. Behind him stand two minders. The servants, arranged just on the edges of the photograph, had the feudal air of self-erasing ubiquity you saw in the margins of photographs of nineteenth century royalty. They might have been attending on any Czar, Emperor or Sultan.

At the centre of all these pictures was a photograph of a beautiful young woman with the same dark brown eyes and thick black hair as Cilea, the same golden-tanned skin and red mouth. From her hair and clothes I judged it had been taken in the mid-seventies, against a background of blue sea, sun and shiny white passenger ferries. The only way you could tell it was taken in Constanța and not Cannes was by looking at the grey-faced, ill-dressed communist apparatchiks around her, from whom she stood out as vibrantly then as her daughter did today. She wore the same necklace Cilea now had on, a crescent moon of beaten silver on a chain so fine it ran like water through your fingers. Cilea and I had that in common: she had lost her mother young and still mourned her in that imprecise, blurred way I understood because it infused everything I felt and did. 'My mother died when I was eight. If I want to remember her, I look at that photograph. If my father wants to remember her, he looks at me.' Cilea laid her head on my lap. I leaned back and stroked her hair, then lifted her face and kissed her eyes which were hot with tears that never fell.

That afternoon we went to bed. I never knew and I never asked what had changed her mind about me, why she'd come to my flat, or how she even knew where to find me. If I had I might have been better prepared for what would happen, or at least known my place in it all. But already I had learned not to ask, not to wonder, not to dig too deep.

Cilea's lovemaking was frank, demanding, without prudishness. I had preconceptions about eastern bloc fucking from watching Czech films on the arts channel that started at midnight: the smell of hairspray slugging it out with body odour and plum brandy; grey sheets, armpit thatch and a backing scent of garlic. This was more like pampered women's magazine sex, and I was having it in all places in Romania, a country where even the Bulgarians imported their own food.

Cilea's passport was on the bedside table, beside some French contraceptive pills: two of Romania's most controlled subjects, travel and fertility, side-by-side. Having these was an imprisonable offence, but Cilea had nothing to fear. I thought of Rodica in the hospital surrounded by sorrow and death, and of Dr Moranu, the challenge of her anger. It looked like I was in a different world from them, here in Cilea's flat, but in some strange way they felt connected. I pushed away the thought. *I'm not part of all this...* Cilea had said. It was enough for me at the time because I wanted it to be enough.

The regime dealt in counterfeit: counterfeit goods, counterfeit money, counterfeit feelings. It gave you solitude instead of privacy, crowds instead of community, reproduction instead of sex. Sex was the one act in which all of daily life's privations could be exorcised, the one sphere into which the state couldn't reach. But Rodica knew differently. In other communist countries your body at least was your property, perhaps the only property that was not theft. Fucking was escape. 'Poor man's aspirin,' they called it here. But really only the privileged fucked recklessly; for the rest, it was another furtive, precaution-racked release.

In other eastern bloc states abortion and birth control were statutory rights. Here they were a dangerous, illegal business. The black market in condoms was ferocious, and they were so hard to find that people used them again and again, washing and drying and rolling them back up. AIDS was still a secret, and didn't officially exist, but you knew it was out there, taking hold, making its way in along the channels of denial and official secrecy. I had seen it: EPIDEMIA, the letters burning like a fever; I heard its tills ringing in the night, in the shuffle of banknotes in the hotels and clubs where the whores worked.

On Cilea's Swedish stereo Joni Mitchell sang, 'Oh I could drink a case of you, darling/ And I would still be on my feet,' to the steam of an espresso machine. She brought two scalding coffees and some Swiss chocolate which she broke into blocks and spread across its foil on the bed. She lived in a world without friction: nothing scraped or dragged as she went through life; there were no obstacles. When I was with her I shared that frictionless world, lived on a cushion of air where the only intensities came from the pleasures we shared: the nights when, as she slept, I would hold her from behind and press my face into her shoulders until she wriggled sleepily out of my arms and kicked off the sheets. That first afternoon the breeze dried the sweat off our bodies and Cilea's arm lay weightlessly over my chest, while mine held her tightly to me.

We dozed to the *finale* of the day's celebrations: a choir of hundreds singing a song – with helpful subtitles: totalitarian *karaoke* – about Ceauşescu's exploits in the anti-fascist resistance. Ceauşescu's speciality was third-world leaders who could always be relied on to take up and reciprocate invitations to 'state visits' or, as *Scînteia* put it, 'fraternal exchanges between helmsmen'. The speed at which these regimes collapsed or were overthrown ensured a steady supply of international helmsmen at Cotroceni Palace.

By now Ceauşescu's public engagements, which had once involved the likes of Nixon, Khrushchev and the Queen of England, had dwindled into a rotation of pigmy-plenipotentiaries and micro-dignitaries. He had been in power nearly twenty-five years; they eddied around him like a shallow stream around a rock. Marx talked about history as the great force propelled by logic and necessity, which could be prepared for and ridden but not hurried along; Mao had replied, asked if the French revolution had worked, that it was 'too early to tell'. Just as religion had once promised rectification and reward in the next world, so Marxism offered us life as perpetual prelude. It was customary to take the long view – looking around us, what other view was there? – but History was not playing the long game with this lot. This was not History flattening out its dialectical kinks over generations, perfecting the conditions of its own unfolding. This was History as stopwatch: you could hear it at their backs, timing them out.

Nine

'I fancy a *Kojak*...' Leo announced.

Ceauşescu's love of *Kojak* was legendary, and tempered the fear his name instilled with just enough ridicule to allow for a glimmer of humour. Most evenings on a good day the *Conducător* would watch a *Kojak* in his private movie theatre to prolong the warmth of his greatness. On a bad day, to take the edge off his quotidian tribulations, it was to the golden-domed Hellenic-American lawman that he also turned. Either way, Ceauşescu was reputed to fancy a *Kojak* much of the time.

I fancy a Kojak: the phrase was Leo's opening line whenever he was proposing an evening out. When, later, we met in a restaurant or hotel bar, he would open his arms wide and drawl, 'Who loves ya baby?' And before you could reply, Leo did it for you, arms extended and hands open in mock homage: 'Ya People and ya Party!'

Leo was inviting me to the highlight of the contraband calendar. Twice a year he hosted 'museum parties' where guests could visit the official exhibits at one or other of the museums before viewing, in secret, the unofficial collection that Leo kept in the underground storerooms. His favourites were the Sutu Palace on Bratianu and the Natural History Museum on Kiseleff, whose directors were both customers and shareholders in Leo's business. This one was to be held at the Sutu Palace.

Coded invitations were sent out on museum stationery for a certain day at a certain time. You added six days to the day, and six hours to the time, so an invitation to the Monday 3 pm reception was for the following Sunday at nine. The museum windows were blacked out, and the place would then be lit up inside with gas lamps and candles. Waiters from across the city materialised the way people did in Bucharest, appearing at your shoulder dry though it had been raining, warm-handed despite the frost, fresh and unhurried despite heatwaves, stalled trams and cancelled buses. Marshalling them from the shadows was the Maître d' from Capşa: a man whose ubiquity was matched only by the sheer difficulty of getting from place to place in the city. I think of him not as someone who arrived or left, who came and went, but as a being who, like a light, switched himself on and off, into and out of place.

Then the guests: they came in cars with dimmed headlamps and silently filled the museum lobby. Everyone whispered, not because there was any need to, but because it fitted the occasion: muffled, excited, faintly dangerous. Coats were lifted off shoulders and hung up as trays of wine glided through the crowd. The Maître d' discreetly took the entrance fee, a steep ten dollars for the apparatchiks and racketeers, a few hundred *lei* for the artists and writers, or for Leo's friends, flush with Romanian currency but with nothing to buy. A string quartet played quietly, canapés did their rounds, people mingled and admired the collections, the objects enveloped in gaslight.

These gatherings divided into two groups. First there was the old bourgeoisie; discreet, educated and delicately mannered, they had lost everything in the transition to communism, seeing their homes requisitioned, their savings nationalised and their social networks shattered. Most were denied Party membership and endured a purgatory of *déclassement*, eking out livings as concierges, museum attendants or theatre ushers, jobs designed to confront them daily with what they had lost: their homes, their pasts, their culture. A few managed to climb the Party rungs in spite of their family's past, occasionally, like Manea Constantin, becoming powerful members of the *nomenhlatura*, ministers and diplomats in much the same positions as they would have been under the *ancien régime*. Then there was the new breed, people who owed everything to the Party, and more specifically to Ceauşescu, who preferred people like himself: semi-educated, crude but full of low cunning; unquestioningly loyal and wholly corruptible.

At the back of the room, in front of an expressionist painting of a yellow-skinned nude, Trofim had been cornered by the British Embassy's ecomonic *attaché*, Giles Wintersmith. Wintersmith talked and munched peanuts at the same time, so that the contents of his mouth resembled the churn of the weekly rubbish as the jaws of the bin lorry closed on it. After years of cocktail parties, his fingers had set into a kind of tapered simian scoop with which he shovelled up bowls of snacks. Beside him was Franklin Shrapnel, his opposite number at the US embassy, an overweight civilian with an army fetish and a penchant for military attire with zips and multiple belts and holsters. Shrapnel strove to give himself the air of a presidential bodyguard on a dangerous state visit: he tweaked his ear in pretence of listening to a hi-tech earpiece and his eyes darted around the room unmasking extremists. Their friendship was a parody of Anglo-American cold war relations: Shrapnel admired Wintersmith's phlegmatic limey wit and Wintersmith looked up to Shrapnel as a man of action.

Wintersmith's big obsession was identifying 'contacts' to press for information or to interpret rumours. He was asking Trofim if he knew of any dissident movement likely to capitalise on the unrest elsewhere in communist Europe. I had not been here long, but I knew enough to see this was the wrong approach. In a world where there were no direct answers, only fools asked direct questions.

'What a gross approach,' I heard Trofim say, in perfectly enunciated English, 'and unworthy of a diplomat, even one of Thatcher's, sir.' *Sir...* the way Trofim hissed it out, drenched in contempt, was withering. Wintersmith shrank back. Shrapnel puffed out his chest and muttered some item of superpower machismo.

'Does the man think he is James Bond?' Trofim asked when they had disappeared.

'The name's Wintersmith,' I laughed, 'Giles Wintersmith.'

A tap on the shoulder. 'Your consort,' Leo pointed across the room, 'she's not on the list, or not on mine anyway...'

Cilea stood at the door, handing her coat to the Maître d' and slipping him a banknote.

'I didn't invite her...'

Leo raised his eyebrows. 'Of course not. Still, better make her welcome.' He took her a glass of *Sovietskoi* sparkling wine and she smiled innocently.

'How did you know about this?' I asked her.

'Dr O'Heix's *soirées*? Highlights of the Party calendar. You don't think the cloak and dagger stuff is for real do you? You couldn't get away with this kind of thing without the say-so of someone up there...' She pointed up at the ceiling. 'I'll bet you a new Dacia that for every five guests here one of them is an informer. But one in five of those informers is watching the other four. They're the ones to worry about. That's the beauty of the system.'

The beauty of the system... what was beautiful about this *mise-en-abîme* of paranoia, this endless recession of spies being spied upon?

'Anyway, I'm here to check up on some of the family collection.'

'You've got some stuff here?' I asked, paying new attention to the exhibits.

'My father's family were diplomats in the old days. The *ancien régime* they call it now. His grandfather and father were ambassadors. *Haute-bourgeoisie*,' she stage-whispered, her breath candied with lipstick, haunted by wine and duty-free cigarettes, 'most of their belongings are stuck in museums. Every now and then he buys a bit back, or splashes out on a new piece...'

'How d'you *buy a bit back* from a national museum?'

'How d'you buy anything?' she answered, unfazed, reaching for a bowl of green olives skewered on toothpicks. If indifference was like armour, then nonchalance was a finely spun, weightless chain mail. Cilea was *nonchalant* – my life had never given me much use for that word until now.

'Show me.' I took her arm and she led me through the crowd. We toured her father's belongings: a Renaissance peasant chest, a pair of ornamental swords, Afghan rugs, paintings by Romanian artists in the manner of famous western masters now considered 'decadent'. Cilea showed me a Romanian cubist picture of a lady climbing from an Orient Express carriage, her movement plotted as in Duchamp's more famous picture: in the electric wake of her passing, a flurry of hats and furs, noses and eyes, legs and arms, bracelets and jewels, laid their mark on the air and delineated her descent.

'*Tainted with the sickness of individualism and bourgeois materialism*,' Cilea recited with mock-sincerity, 'that's what we were taught at school – all this stuff: *decadent and aesthetic and foreign to the concerns of socialism...*' She laughed. 'But she's so beautiful – look at that dress, that necklace...'

'She could be the Princess in the old days,' I said, looking at the Chanel two-piece and the fur boa, the pale oval face and the dark eyes topped with a straight black fringe. Cilea laughed. 'Christ – it *is* the Princess!' I cried out, astonished. There it was, written in gold on a small lacquered plaque at the bottom of the frame: 'Portretului Contessa Antoaneta Cantesco'.

At that moment there was a disturbance across the room. The Princess herself. As always, she had spotted something that had once belonged to her family and was demanding it back. Leo always mollified her, even, sometimes, buying whatever it was back and presenting it to her.

'There's always an outburst by some ex-aristocrat over reassigned property,' Cilea said wearily, taking me by the hand and leading me upstairs to the lobby. After the hot crowded basement, it was a relief to reach the cold marble of the atrium, to feel the sweeping draught of the staircase as we climbed, the sweat on my back drying in the cold. I followed Cilea into a side room in the gallery, the curator's office. We kissed at the door as she expertly unlocked it behind her, then she pulled me backwards, a hand on my belt buckle, until she bumped against a table. She swept it clear without turning around and lifted herself onto it, wrapping her ankles around the back of my calves. She was already wet, and I lifted her skirt and fucked her quickly. She kept her face away from me, watching the door, and with my mouth against her neck I tasted the bitterness of her perfume that had smelled so good and musky moments before. When I put my tongue in her mouth it was burning. Cilea bit my lip as she came and held me inside her. My lip bled but she kept her mouth there, running her tongue along the cut so that it stung.

Someone called her name. She held me to her hard, sighed and kissed my face, then rearranged herself. She rubbed a trace of blood off her upper lip. 'Give me a few minutes to leave first,' she said as she left, 'I'll call you tomorrow.' In the lobby stood Titanu, her father's bodyguard, a hulking, bullet-headed Moldovan ex-wrestler. He had suddenly appeared on the scene when Cilea and I began seeing each other – 'my father likes to keep an eye on things,' she said, whether as warning or reassurance I still couldn't tell and was unlikely to ask. When she reached the bottom of the stairs, she looked up and blew me a kiss. That was what Cilea was like. I had no idea she would come tonight, and now I had no idea where she was going. Yet again I had that sense of her – the sense by which I remember her – as someone who could give you everything and then leave you alone with it.

'There you are!' called Leo from the shadows when I went outside for air, 'I've been looking for you.' He stood beside his Skoda. 'Get in.'

Minutes later we were on the outer perimeter of the Boulevard of Socialist Victory, parked on a street with a few kiosks and a one-storey glass-fronted supermarket. The shelves were stacked with pyramids of tinned carp. There was nothing else. The darkness was diluted here and there by streetlamps so weak they succeeded in illuminating only the miasma of moths and midges that pulsed around them.

'This way,' said Leo, guiding me down the street. 'You need to come to it from the front to get the full effect.'

We turned down a wide, new avenue, full of unfitted shops and offices. Bent saplings were planted at intervals along the pavement and held upright by splints of wood. Wires and piping stuck out of the ground. Incongruously new and polished shop signs had already been put up – butchers, bakeries, clothes shops and supermarkets – but the places they designated had yet to materialise. There was even – black humour – a travel agent, already decorated with posters of Hungarian lakes and Black Sea resorts.

The avenue was more than uniform, it was relentless: eight storeys of flats and offices with identical doors and windows, and facades clad in identical blocks of white funereal marble. Leo stopped at a huge roundabout and waited. As I walked to join him, I saw narrower unfinished streets that stopped abruptly a few hundred yards further down in a mass of rubble and slabs. One of these came up against an old monastery that blocked its path and stood there, contemplating its next move. A painted wooden gate with carved posts and a small roof stood between it and a ramshackle cemetery where gravestones were scattered haphazardly like grazing sheep. Beyond them, lights burned in the monastery windows. Diggers and dumpers stood outside, their articulated claws hanging slack, open jaws silhouetted against the clear sky. I thought of the dinosaur skeletons in the museum: it was as if they lived once more and had the run of the streets. I reached Leo, in the middle of the roundabout, where a white plinth stood with nothing on it. Four vast avenues, all also incomplete, met here, intersecting on this vacuum of a monument.

And on the pedestal these words appear:
"My name is Ozymandias, King of Kings:
Look on my works, ye mighty, and despair!"
Nothing beside remains. Round the decay
Of that colossal wreck, boundless and bare,
The lone and level sands stretch far away.

Leo declaimed, puffing out his chest, 'Shelley's "Ozymandescu"... required reading around here...'

'Very funny, Leo. What are we doing in this Stalinist Legoland?'

His answer was to take me by the shoulders and ceremonially turn me 180 degrees.

'I give you... The Boulevard of Socialist Victory. The Palace of the People.'

Seen from a distance, the place hulked over the city, the butt of so many jokes that we no longer thought of what it cost in money and human suffering. It merely absorbed them and gave them back as idiot magnitude, laughable bad taste on a mammoth scale. Face to face there was nothing harmless about it: standing there on the main avenue it felt like an attack, a gaudy, brutal, humanity-denying mass of stone. Instinctively I raised my hands to shield my head – the sight of it came down in blows.

The Boulevard of Socialist Victory, wider than the Danube and twelve storeys high, was assembled with that mix of careless sloth and paranoid haste that characterised eastern bloc public projects. In different parts of the vast building site, men and machines worked in deafening noise and blasted white light. But here, almost a kilometre away, it was darkness. Open holes around us disgorged bilious water that smelled of rust, metallic effluvia and industrial decay. As we approached, an open gutter higher up the slope seethed with waves of slurry that rustled and sucked as it descended an uncompleted marble staircase. Up close, with Leo's pocket lamp, we saw what it was: a moving carpet of rats, and their sound the high-pitch static of rodent panic as they tumbled in a collective rush. It had not rained for weeks, but here the air was lacquered with a kind of fetid, effluent damp.

We moved into a shell of a building. The walls sweated, and already greyish-green stalactites hung from the ceilings. This room had mosaic tiles for a floor, three large chandeliers and marble walls. It had never been used, but already it looked like the mouldy inside of an old fridge. Leo guided me towards a ball of light, a campfire in the far distance.

'Ah! Leo – *Salut!*'

Leo: '*Salut! Vintul, ce mai faceti?*'

In the shadows, lit by a petrol-soaked rag torch, was a

group of young men and women smoking some rank-smelling dope. They sat cross-legged, leaning forward into an acrid open fire so their faces were lit from below. They were the counterparts, the distorted reflections, of the group of party hacks I had seen in Capşa on my first night, their faces illuminated by brandy-flamed crêpes. More and more I had the sense here that everything had its counterpart, its other self, that everything, even the opposites, corresponded and connected up – perhaps especially the opposites.

I hung back while my eyes learned the darkness. Four men and three women sat around the fire. Two fat joints circulated and a ghetto blaster played the Grateful Dead. Everyone looked young and all were dressed in clothes you rarely saw here. One girl had a bandana and piercings that made my eyes water, they emerged through her eyebrows and cheeks and in the taut skin of her throat above her voicebox. All of these would have been self-administered: sterile needle through skin numbed with ice or deodorant spray. All had long hair and wore flowery shirts and flares. Aggressive-looking peaceniks, they eyed me suspiciously. Leo had broken protocol by bringing me here. The pierced girl said something to me in Romanian and they all relaxed a little when they saw I was foreign. She held the joint out to me.

'Mel – Melina...' she smiled, watching me wince at the first hit of dope. She had big eyes and freckles around her nose, which was pierced by a faceted glass stud that caught the fire-light. I passed the joint on, feeling its smoke spreading along my lungs, hitting the downstream of my blood. It tasted wrong, dipped or cut with some chemical. In a country where they put sawdust into flour to make the bread go further, there was no telling what they used to spin out the drugs. My heart felt as if it were being suddenly drained of blood then pumped full again. A conversation began that I couldn't understand. 'Friend of the Devil' was playing. I thought I detected the first signs of a flattening battery, the distending lyrics, the spiralling guitar chords... or maybe it was just the nauseous high taking hold. *The Grateful Dead... such a ferocious name*, I thought as I slid down the damp wall and hung my head between my knees, *such graceful, spiralling music*.

The young man who had first addressed Leo was the most alert of the group.

He prodded me: 'Leo's friend, eh?' Sardonic, detached, effortlessly in charge.

'Is that a question?'

Leo explained: 'You said you'd like to make yourself useful. I took you at your word. How much more useful than meeting Vintul – *Le Vent... The Wind* – and hearing what he's got to say?'

The young man was bearded, long-haired and wiry. Even crouched on the ground he looked powerful, ready to spring. Everyone around him was druggy and slack, but he exuded tension and resolve. He looked at me and held me with his eyes. I tried to square up to him, sit up and shake off the dope-torpor. My saliva was sticky and tasted of burning.

'OK,' I said, 'anyone fancy telling me what's going on?'

'We help people leave. Leo has been helping us for four years now, and Belanger did,' said Vintul. Leo looked uncomfortable at the mention of Belanger, and dragged hard on his joint. 'We're a group that helps people cross the borders into Hungary or Yugoslavia. But we need people like you and Leo to get them papers or letters of invitation from foreigners... to find someone to take care of them when they get out.'

'And stump up the funds when there's people to pay off,' chipped in Leo.

Vintul looked at him with distaste. 'As Leo says, there is a financial dimension, but we do not make money from this.' *There is a financial dimension...* Vintul's English was exceptional: formal, precise, elegant, and wholly out of keeping with his appearance.

Leo was leaning over Mel's chest, getting a furtive eyeful of her cleavage as she bent forward to roll another joint. Her skin was clear and milky, and her piercings crude and out of place, all that metal diving into her flesh. 'They're all at it,' said Leo, taking the joint from Mel and drawing in deeply, 'Petrescu – he doesn't just paint icons, he doctors passports, makes rubber stamps and visas; Ionescu does a line in headed notepaper from US universities... nicks the stuff from conferences and brings it back here. Costanu at the natural history museum – he's been known to lend us a couple of packing crates... a few holes for air, some straw, and Bob's your uncle: a tidy little first class compartment for a courting couple in search of a better life.'

Vintul was not enjoying Leo's levity, nor his readiness with people's names. I looked at Leo and the handful of bleary-eyed youngsters around the fire. What an amateur operation: some hippies and a motley band of painters and professors up against one of the world's most ruthless security apparatus.

'You had much success?' I tried sound offhand, to recover my footing in the conversation.

'More than you think,' answered Vintul.

'What happens to the failures?' I asked.

'That's not your concern. We are living in terminal times...' a brisk nod towards Leo, 'did you know it was Leo who brought us capitalism? What do you call it? Supply and demand, everything with its price and its price always changing – depending on how much Leo thinks you want it. That's the new world we all want to get to now...'

'You're the one who's been ringing me?'

'We have been trying to get in touch but your phone – Belanger's phone – is bugged. All phones are bugged. Now we will make an arrangement for our meeting, if you wish to help us.'

'How?'

'You can write references, check things, carry stuff around for us. We can use your passes and currency. You can help in all sorts of small ways, not all of them dangerous. What do you want in return?'

'I don't want anything in return. I came here to see what I could do...'

'We all want something in return. Money, influence, a good conscience... what is the difference?'

'If I'm doing this at all it's because I think there *is* a difference – don't you?'

'If you say so.' What he meant was: *I've had this conversation with better people than you.*

Leo put an arm around my shoulder. It was a protective gesture and it jarred – Leo rescuing me from a better opponent. Vintul told me I would be called some time in the next few weeks and all would be clear when the call came.

When he had finished Vintul took a swig of red wine and rolled up a fat joint which he kept to himself. Someone had changed the tape: we now heard something aggressively ethnic in which violent bursts of folk music were crossed with electric dance rhythms. Vintul jerked his head in time to it and drank from the bottle. I noticed his muscular arms and neck, his lean, strong face. Everyone around here was flabby or emaciated, unfocussed and vague, but not Vintul. Two of the girls had fallen asleep and the three boys were doing a drunken peasant dance around a stepladder they had set fire to. On top of it they had arranged empty bottles, re-corked, which now exploded loudly one by one.

Suddenly we saw the criss-crossing of powerful torch-beams outside, followed by shouting and the barking of dogs.

'Out! Now!' called Leo, pushing me hard towards the corridor.

'No,' said Vintul. 'They'll be expecting you to go out. You've got to go further in. Come.'

Vintul jumped up, surprisingly agile for a man who had been smoking dope and drinking all night. The drugs had little effect on him, but the others looked dazed. He shook them awake, split us into three groups and pointed us in different directions. I felt sick, Leo even greener-gilled than usual. The music pounded from the tiny ghetto blaster on the floor.

We heard a snarl in the darkness: a pair of yellow-flecked eyes catching the torchbeam. Then another. Two German Shepherds.

'Go right, always right, no matter what you see,' said Vintul. Then to me: 'We'll be in touch!'

Leo turned out the flashlight and we moved off into the depths of the building.

For what seemed like hours, we bore right, though corridors and halls, always with the sound of dogs and voices at our backs. Time was distended: drugs, fear, adrenalin. It cannot have been more than twenty or thirty minutes, Leo and me retching in the darkness and two of the girls with us, but it felt like a stumbling odyssey. Somewhere along the way we lost the girls. We walked into paintpots and concrete buckets, tripped over cables and leads. Every now and then Leo would stop and lean against a wall and puff. Once there was no wall, just a screen of plywood, which came clattering down as Leo sank his weight onto it. Leo had lost the torch, so we saw nothing but flashes of moonlight or streetlamp outside. Finally we came to the shell of a ballroom and found a damp corner where Leo sat and fell asleep. I listened out for noise, but there was only the hollowness of the building echoing to itself.

Hours or minutes later, I woke. A grey morning light

gathered and the marble cladding all around looked pale and bony. Leo was snoring. I had vomit over my shoes – mine or another's, I could not tell or remember. We were in the same room in which we had begun. Vintul had sent us in a circle, calculating that by the time we returned, the place would be safe again. It seemed to have worked. The fire was still warm, a dust of white ash and half-consumed sticks. Where had the girls gone? The chandelier's cut glass was starting to catch the light that came in through what I now saw were vast French windows overlooking a balcony the size of a squash court. Leo came to, grunting primordially, a large caked cut on his forehead. He touched it, feeling the scab. 'Oh Christ... I'm too old for this,' he said, then closed his eyes again and adjusted his position against the wall. Then he was snoring again.

A scatter of rats was busy in the corner. I tried to see what it was they were occupied with, but could not make it out: a coat draped across the floor? My eyes adjusted. It was an empty cement sack. I could hear the rats' jaws clicking wetly. I pulled myself up on the ledge of an unfinished windowsill, stepped over Leo and crossed the room.

The bodies of two German Shepherds lay side by side. Someone had slung the cement bags over them, but blood had seeped through the dirt nearby. I prodded them with my boot – they were already stiff – and nudged the bag off. Their eyes were open, fixed on death's middle distance. Their throats had been torn, and beneath the mess of tumbled viscera the blood had run and mixed with a small pile of cement dust. A small hard mound had formed. I kicked it, but it had already set: rust-coloured, veined with red.

'Jesus,' – I hadn't heard Leo behind me. He swallowed back a retch and looked away. 'Two militia hounds with their throats cut. Who the fuck does that?'

'They're not cut, Leo, look. They've been torn or bitten, straight through the windpipe.'

'Let's get out of here. These buildings are full of people living rough, gypsies, alcoholics, druggies, homeless... It's like a shanty town, a fucking dangerous one.'

It was 4 am by the luminous hands of Leo's watch. Outside, cranes started up and vans emptied workers along the pavements. The men were undernourished and thin, some were ill or lame, others looked like gangsters. Armed guards herded them into work details and led them off. We hung back behind a cement lorry until they had cleared.

'Prisoners,' Leo said. 'Prison vans. Army numberplates, probably from the Jilava prison... Look: yellow trousers and shirts, numbers on the back and chest. Forced labour. These buildings are all forced labour now.'

'I'm not sure I see,' I said to Leo once we were back in the car, 'the point of that unpleasant interlude.'

'You will,' Leo checked his mirrors and started up the car, 'you will.'

Ten

There was nothing formal about my relationship with Cilea: I rarely knew where she was, who she saw, whether she even studied except in the nominal sense of being listed as a university music student.

As for my jealousy, which ranged over the blankness of the time she spent away from me and invented ever more painfully sluttish and disloyal ways for her to fill it, I kept it to myself. Admitting I had once followed her home and watched her flat, and that because I had found nothing suspicious I had followed her again the next time and the time after, would have been to give in both to her and to my jealousy. Besides, the jealous one always at some level wants to be proved right. Investing in suspicion is like investing in anything: after a while you want to see a return.

Cilea and I met by appointment only, and when I was not with her I heard nothing of her and never encountered her in any of our usual haunts. Sometimes I would arrive somewhere and the sense that she had only just left would overpower me – I would run out into the street in the hope of seeing her, or catching sight of her car, or (it would have been enough) just smelling her smell.

Then one day she told me her father wished to meet me. *Wished*: so much more elegant, and at the same time so much more authoritative, than a mere *wanted*. I was delighted. I thought it made our relationship official, made us a couple. We attended events together, I accompanied her to the theatre or to concerts, and when she sang in the Atheneum choir's summer concert she booked me a seat in the front row reserved for family members. I still never saw her outside the times she arranged with me; there was never any question of *dropping in* on Cilea unannounced, and when I was not with her I might as well have been living in a different city since I never bumped into her or met mutual friends (we had none anyway). But I had become comfortable with how little I knew about any of them: Cilea, Trofim, Ionescu, even Leo. Partial knowledge was a condition of every friendship here.

'You going to ask him for her hand over brandy and cigars?' Leo mocked when I announced I would be meeting her father, 'tell him what a fine prospect you are? Orphan, drop-out, what was it she called you? *Gap-year deprivation tourist?* Don't delude yourself: he knows exactly who you are, he's probably got your file, just wants you to know he's got his eye on you.'

When the phone rang one mid-June morning at 4 am, I answered as if it was a perfectly normal occurrence. Crossing the hallway I stepped over a suitcase that stood by the front door. I was due for my first trip back to the UK next month, my first 'home visit'. I had packed my small luggage ten days early and left it here, hoping it might accommodate me to the dread I felt at having to return. The voice on the phone was hesitant, heavily Romanian-accented but with an American intonation. Everyone around here picked up their English from 1970s US cop shows, and my students could call each other 'punk' and 'dork' and feelingly throw out phrases like 'This was a decent neighbourhood once,' long before they had absorbed the niceties of everyday conversation.

'Hi... Dr Belanger?'

'No, I'm afraid not.'

'Then can I ask who is speaking?'

'Can I?'

There was no answer. For a moment the line went quiet, as if the phone was being held to the chest or the speaker had his hand over the receiver and was consulting with someone at his side. It was an amateurish moment, my interlocutor not sure what to do next, though he had spent nearly three months working up the courage to speak. I knew it was the same caller – our silences being as unique as our singular pitch or our trademark turns of phrase. By now I was attuned to the way he hovered on the edge of speech, the sound of his breath drawing in, the lungs' faint wheeze.

The line went dead. It was not what I was expecting now that we had finally made contact, but I shrugged and turned back to the bedroom: it was progress. I looked at Cilea asleep. She had her back to me, but I could see her in the full-length mirror propped against the wall. The room was silver with moonlight, and the rucked-up sheets she had kicked off had the grey shine of oystershell. I climbed in, kissed her on the small of her back, inhaling last night's sex. I touched the inside of her thigh and she wriggled sleepily back onto me.

Suddenly I knew what was happening. I jumped out of bed, went to the balcony, and looked out across the street. A few yards down, I saw the phonebox. In some situations, paranoia is no more than an ability to read life's hidden signals, no longer an unhappy fantasy but a sixth sense. I knew immediately that the call had come from there, and that I was meant to know it.

I pulled on some clothes and crossed the road. At the kiosk, the phonebook chained to the counter lay open at the name of a large supermarket in town. A few pages further on a bookmark made out of the side of a cigarette packet was inserted at a page where the first digit of an address, the 5, had been circled. If that was code, it was easy enough to break.

Thus it was that at 5 pm that afternoon, without telling Cilea or Leo, I stood in the lobby of the fittingly named Monocom supermarket, a shop where all there was came in one variety. Among the greyly lingering customers, a young man stood out: shoulder-length red hair, faded scarlet shirt and light-brown, fitted leather jacket. He was examining a Russian camera, pointing it at me and laughing. He turned the lens, focusing in and out, pretending to take pictures. The camera covered his eyes and nose, but the broad smile beneath it was unnerving: genuine, unfeigned, without ulterior meaning. That alone was suspicious. I stood and watched, waiting for him – if it was him I had come to see – to make his move.

Slender and bearded, he looked too thin to be among the system's winners, yet there was no obvious sense in which he was one of its losers either. In a world of conformity, he seemed to know just how different he could be without paying the price. He had a kind of measured swagger; stood out, but not in a way that invited suspicion. He was well groomed, wore John Lennon glasses and was smoking a roll-up. Over his shirt, open at the neck, his 1960's leather jacket was scuffed but elegant. His jeans were flared and his tall Cossack-style boots looked at once military and bohemian. He put the camera back on the counter and darted out of the shop.

His thin, quick body provided all the colour in the street: following him was like tracking a fox in the snow, the russet streak zigzagging in and out of doorways, always pushing on to the next turn, the next set of traffic lights. It was rush hour, and though there were few cars, the pavements were thick with people and the trams and buses were nose to tail on Calea Victoriei. Somewhere, a few blocks away, the sirens sounded for The Motorcade but he pressed on, past the ministries and embassies, towards Lipscani.

Lipscani reminded me of old photographs of pre-Haussmann Paris: leaning houses of different builds and different heights, a teetering slum-jostle of styles and materials. A hundred years ago it had been a perfect setting for rumour, disease and crime; now it was a place of escapism, surprise, *flânerie*. The cobbles were uneven and some roads were without pavements. Private cars were scarce, and the trams wound their way through the backstreets, sparks flying from their wheels.

The place was rough, chaotic, apparently unpoliced though always watched; thick with informers gone native, natives turned informer, or those – most of the people I knew – who oscillated between the two. It was also the gypsy area of town. Its spectacular old buildings had been left to decay and filled with Romany who helped the government along by running their homes down in preparation for Lipscani's eventual demolition, scheduled for 1990: campfires in living rooms, horses stabled in the hallways, walls knocked down and the roof-lead sold off.

Gypsies stood or sat soaking up the afternoon sun, eyes closed, their arms extended and palms open as if receiving a transfusion of empty hours from Time itself. The outdoor life was hardwired into them. As they went in through the tall arched doorways of their buildings they ducked instinctively even though they had several clear feet of space between the doorframe and their heads – all indoors, however spacious, was a confinement, a shrinking, an unnatural inward turn. They left their homes at 5 am and returned after midnight. The day was their living room, their place of work, their habitat; and the homes they had been given merely places to store the body in the dark hours.

The boy was slowing down; people stopped him and

127

exchanged greetings, or waved at him from across the street. This was his territory. At a small art gallery there was a launch or opening of some kind. Judging from the nervous look of the guests, it was unsanctioned by the Union of Artists – such gatherings could be broken up at any time. If you were lucky, the local informer would wait until he or she had eaten and drunk enough before calling the Securitate and the party would at least have time to catch light. There was Leo with a plastic cup of red wine, talking with Ioana and Petrescu the icon-painter. Petrescu caught my eye over Leo's shoulder, but if he saw me he showed no sign of it. I recognised Campanu the pathologist, smoking and wearing a cream jacket over his blue morgue shirt. In the window hung a large painting of workers sharing bread and milk against a background of gleaming cogs and pulleys.

I had lost sight of the boy in the scarlet shirt. A few yards away, a cast-iron tavern sign of a Carpathian Boar hung from the lintel of a doorway. I had to stoop to go in, and the door was stiff and ungiving. I found myself in a noisy crowded bar so low that if I stood on tiptoe I could scrape my head on the liver-coloured ceiling. Just below it, covering the faces of the drinkers like mountain mist, hung a layer of smoke. This was no mist, but the fug of Carpati, the cigarette that shredded your lungs with every gasp: you didn't inhale Carpati smoke, you chewed it. Everyone, young or old, looked bohemian here: students sat with pensioners, workers with hippies. There were even – a rare sight – gypsies at tables with non-gypsies.

'You have failed Securitate surveillance training – please report to your commanding officer!'

I turned. The boy was there, holding two frothing beers, enjoying his cloak-and-dagger moment. We shook hands and looked each other up and down. I liked him straight away, that mix of mischief and serenity. He offered me a roll-up from a dented pewter case: Turkish tobacco and a leavening of good, sweet dope. It was what Leo called an 'office hours' measure, just enough to give the bottom of the day a gentle lift without spinning it all into orbit. His smile was open, full of warmth and amusement. We looked at each other grinning stupidly, stranger to stranger.

His fingernails were long and clean. He noticed me noticing, and ran his fingers over the strings of an air guitar. In his top pocket was a Walkman, rare in Romania and new even in the West. He pulled a cassette tape from an inside pocket: 'John Cale – *Paris 1919*,' he said. 'You like?'

I liked. 'I am sorry,' he said after we had both taken long slugs from our beers. 'I am Petre and I am happy to meet you.'

The lights dimmed and a small jazz band started up in one corner of the room. 'You like jazz?' His English, like my own beginners' Romanian, began with basic likes and dislikes. I knew the form: speakers laid claim to extreme opinions about subjects they cared little about just to keep the conversation turning over. I followed protocol and expressed a deep, life-long love of jazz. Petre nodded, satisfied, and waved to a punky girl at the bar wearing a Mrs Thatcher T-shirt. It was a startling thing to see, but unlike at home it could not immediately be construed as ironic.

Petre was a music student at the university and a classical guitarist. He told me about his next concert in the Atheneum – Bach, Villa-Lobos and Federico Mompou. Did I want to come? He handed me a pair of tickets from a book of stubs. But I soon learned that Petre was also lead guitarist in *Fakir*, a semi-underground rock band whose concerts were tolerated by the authorities but closely monitored. Leo had played me a bootleg tape of theirs. All their recordings were bootleg: since they were not members of the Musicians' Union they had no access to studios or concert venues. I looked him over: his skin was smooth, his hands soft and delicate; his hair shone, his well-worn clothes were clean. A heavy celtic cross hung over his shirt.

'Petre!' called out the double-bassist, a stylish young man in a 1950s three-piece suit and Teddy Boy haircut, the retro's retro.

'You will stay here. I see you after. We can talk.' Petre rose and joined the band.

I sat drinking beer and listening to a medley of silky jazz impromptus. After a forty-minute jamming session Petre returned to our table, his hair matted with sweat, his shirt sticking to his back.

By the time we left the tavern it was ten o'clock. Lipscani was the only part of Bucharest where there was an organic life after 9 pm. The hotels and bars in the town centre were either tourist traps or snazzy playpens for party apparatchiks. Here there was street life: drunks tightrope-walking kerbs, beer gardens spilling onto the pavements. People were buying and selling things that you couldn't see and that maybe didn't exist – it was the transactions that counted, not the goods. Transactions symbolised life, subversion, rebellion: flurries of haggling around absent commodities. Gypsy music came from the courtyards or open windows. The BBC World Service was loud but impossible to locate in the jumble of sidestreets: the pips dwindling into Lillibulero, and then the soothing voice of Bush House. I thought of the building, there on the Strand, of what London must be like now: the Tubes full and pubs heaving, the neon letters trademarking the air, the disposable income evaporating in the London night.

This was the time I liked best in Bucharest: people out for their last walks, the few cafés still open crossing into the indoor twilight of late drinking. Moths with frayed wings pounded against mosquito nets and as the night cooled, the day's smells thickened and separated out – pollen, burned fuel, late baking, cigarettes, all distinct now in the prickly air. There was something about the way Petre breathed it all in, eyes closed, like a connoisseur savouring the fumes of a good bottle, that reminded me of Leo.

I asked where he lived, but there was no answer. We walked on, though I was now comprehensively lost. We came to a small square where Petre sat down and crafted himself another cigarette. I asked again, and he mentioned a new estate beyond the city circle. The buses and trams had stopped, and taxis were unlikely to go that far out now. Where would he sleep? He gave an empty-handed gesture of unconcern. 'It is warm.'

I was meant to meet Cilea in my flat. I toyed with asking Petre back, but knew this was exactly the wrong thing to do. Besides, he had still not said what he wanted from me. Then I thought: they were both music students at the university... perhaps they knew each other?

'You are asking yourself why I have made contact with you?'

'I suppose I am, yes. I assume it's something to do with my meeting Vintul the other day.'

'Something to do, yes.'

'You want to get out?'

He laughed. 'This is my country. Why should I leave? I would not be me if I left and never returned, and that is why I stay in spite of everything... how hard it is to live, to make a good life. But I want to travel. I want to go to Spain, to Britain, to Canada, to the US.... It is difficult to go, but right now it would be impossible to come back. I want to come back. So I will not leave. Maybe that means I will never leave. But my friends, many of them, they want to go. Many have already left. I help them, and you can help us.'

'What about you? Is it freedom you want too?'

The crudity of my question disappointed him. 'I know

131

freedom. Don't make the mistake of thinking that we do not know what it is. I have had freedom, but I have not *lived in* freedom. But I can wait because I know I will never be free unless I am free in my own country. What freedom have you known?'

'I'm not sure.' I wasn't. I had a sense of freedom in the abstract, but there were few concrete examples of my having really *used* my allotted portion. Was that perhaps itself evidence of freedom – that I had never had to measure and quantify it, that I had never had to answer for what I had done with it? I decided to stick to specifics: 'This is about you not me. I am free, I can vote and say what I want and travel where I like...'

'Perhaps you have lived in freedom but not been free?'

'Perhaps. Perhaps if I knew what you meant...' I was tired of the relentless obliqueness of these discussions: long sessions of quickfire goalpost-shifting between westerners who acknowledged only money and buying power as markers of civilisation and Romanians who insisted on their dignity by pretending that their régime, however appalling, promised a better future even if it no longer intended it. Petre reminded me of Trofim in this respect: he was still holding out for communism to deliver on its ideals.

I watched him take a long draw on his cigarette and lay his back against the bench, sliding his body forward so his backside hung over the edge of the wooden slats. I felt a speech coming on and looked at my watch. I needed to leave, to find my way home. But what Petre said stayed with me; not because it was penetrating or intelligent or even true, but because of its extraordinary purity, its ingenuity, and ultimately its complete and heroic wrongness.

'I have known freedom in my life. I live in a place that is not free, but I have made freedoms that have gone deep. Short freedoms, only moments here and there, but freedom. I am not a stranger to it. The mistake you make in the West is to think we are just victims, bowed heads... to think that we do not keep safe a part of our lives in which to be normal and happy and become who we want to be. Many things are the same for us as they are for you: loving, dying, friendship, pleasure, the taste of good food and drink – when we can get them,' he laughed, 'and they have the same value, the same meaning...'

'I try not to make that mistake about people...'

'Maybe you, and maybe a few others. But I know how you look at us because we are not free the way you are. But what are you free for? To buy things? To choose twenty different models of camera? To give your children six different brands of cereals for breakfast. Is that autonomy? Is that why my friends are leaving the country, risking their lives to cross borders to live in places where they can make a big choice about eating Cheerios or Coco Pops in the mornings?'

'Petre, save that stuff for the right person. I'm not arguing with you; I don't pretend that the West is perfect. But you can't say there's any equivalence between what you suffer here and what we have in the West, even if we waste so much of our freedom on crappy things. These are small choices, but they stand for bigger choices, about who rules us, and what we are allowed to choose to say and do and believe. Perhaps a choice of cereals is a sign of a country where there's a choice of governments.'

'That's not freedom,' Petre said, 'that's being a customer. You are all customers. You live in a customer country. What is it Mrs Thatcher said? *There is no such thing as society...*' He gave a dismissive laugh.

'That may well be true when she's finished with us, but it's not true yet...'

'I am free because I stay here, not because I leave. I choose to stay, that makes me free – even though I cannot say what I want, even though they are always watching me, destroying my city, even though they will stop me from playing my music and I always have to have my concert programmes approved in advance... I am free because I *choose* not to run away.'

I had no answer. Petre believed in the intensity of freedom as it was lived, not in its quantity thinly spread across a range of minor choices: what to wear, which brand of detergent to buy, the 'freedom' to choose who treats your piles or your bad teeth. But here, now, in the circumstances he found himself, Petre had no choice but to believe what he did. I had never heard anything so persuasive and yet so manifestly untenable, so ill-fitted for any of the kinds of life that were on offer to him. It was a philosophy of extremity that depended on extremity in order to exist. But it only *seemed* idealistic – really it was pragmatic: after all, when you cannot spread out freely, you dig down, and that was what he had done: he had created a logic where intensity replaced quantity. Petre had adapted, because he had adapted a theory of freedom to make sense of all the constraint.

Petre was twenty-three, two years older than me; he seemed to know nothing but to believe already in too much. There must have been plenty in his short life to knock all this belief out of him, to make him cynical and hard, but there was a calmness to him I had seen in no one else. He was more out of place here than I was, yet at the same time he was entirely adjusted to it. There was something about him: as if he was from a better but recognisable version of this place and time, in which higher versions of ourselves circulated uncontaminated by the gross realities we had created and which had in turn made us. That was my first impression and, as I came to know him, that impression deepened.

He had a half-sister, a doctor, with whom he shared a flat. His parents, now dead, were born into the Transylvanian

134

peasantry and became engineers in Timişoara. His grandparents had been farmhands on an aristocrat's estate and then
worked in the first collective farms. Petre was proud of that:
from illiterate peasants to engineers in one generation.

'I am the grandson of peasants, the son of engineers, and
now I play guitar. In three generations of one family we have
gone from pointless toil to efficient technocracy and now to
useless art. That is progress. You show me that in your
country!' He laughed, crushing his cigarette butt with his heel
and putting a hand on my shoulder. 'It's time for me to go. We
would like you to help us. You have spoken to Vintul, and very
soon we will ask something of you. We have a project and we
would like you to join us in it.'

Petre embraced me then disappeared, leaving a faint smell
of leather, patchouli oil and tobacco. It was already eleven – I
was late and I was lost. Cilea would have let herself in and
found something in the fridge to graze on. I was the only
person in the small square, and I could hear water rushing
somewhere ahead, in roughly the direction of home. Choosing a likely looking sidestreet, I walked on. It was by now so
dark I could orientate myself only by the occasional glimmer
of a candle or paraffin lamp in the windows. I heard the
scrape of a zippo flint. A flame swelled up and a face took
shape, eyes looking directly at me, then fell back into darkness. I smelled drink and heard him breathing, saw the
cupped glow of a cigarette end as he inhaled, and the shiny
black rim of a policeman's cap.

I heard voices, saw light lapping at the cobbles at the next
turning. Some music funnelled its way down the alley.

I emerged into a gaudy little red-light zone. Beneath a sort
of bridge of sighs that connected up two decrepit buildings,
young girls wearing rubber shoes and short skirts sat in lamplight, reading crumpled German magazines. Drunk soldiers
stood around and argued; builders drank from bottles or old

pickle jars. Men in ragged suits and frayed ties counted money, exchanging wads of banknotes and cigarette packets. A brand new stereo system played western disco tracks. One of the girls struggled dopily upright, pulled herself up by a crumbling windowledge, and put out her small dry hand to take mine. There was no strength in it; her fingers grasped my wrist, her cracked, painted nails scratched my arm no more deeply than a bird's claws, then fell away as I passed. Her eyes were ringed with shadow, sunken back into their sockets, circles of rouge painted onto her hollow cheeks. She looked like a broken doll. Behind her, the girls sitting on the ground with their backs against the wall had the air of marionettes propped up in the wings of a puppet theatre. Had I seen her in the InterContinental that day with Leo? Yes, I was sure now: there was a little less of her now; and the eyes... more than before afire with fever.

Some builders in dusty work clothes sat playing cards, an upturned crate serving as a table. Two prostitutes stood behind them, resting their heads on their shoulders like escort girls at a high-class casino. No one paid any attention to me – I was walking through someone else's dream. People looked past me as I wandered through this underworld, an inner-city limbo of prostitution and racketeering; the smell of boredom, sickness, victimhood. Then the stench of human excrement and vomit and the grunting of paid sex. My shoes nudged through soft shit and broken glass. A figure stepped out in front of me. The policeman had followed me, but had somehow finished up ahead. He took my papers, wrote something down in a little booklet then mock-saluted me past, leering, as if we had just shared some secret, binding experience.

I left my shit-caked shoes outside the door and went imme-diately to shower. Cilea was curled up on the sofa in front of the TV. She smiled up at me, a box of expensive chocolates on the armrest, and made room. She had painted her nails, and the smell of varnish hung in the air. The video was the latest James Bond, and I had arrived in time for the set-piece casino scene, in which 007 coolly fleeces the playboy-psychopath of money and *amour propre* before a gasping public.

Cilea teasingly nestled a foot into my groin. When I failed to respond, she paused the video and went to the kitchen to fetch some wine.

'Do you know all the other music students?' I called out.

'I think so – but I don't go to all the lectures...'

'Petre Something – you come across him?'

'There's a few Petres... it's a common name... Red or white? I went to the Diplomatic Shop this morning...'

'Nothing thanks, I've had too much already. I was out with Leo.' I realised I had let on that I knew Petre, and that I might have to explain myself to Cilea. 'Don't know the surname – long hair, plays the guitar, looks slightly spaced-out... you know...?'

Cilea stood in the doorway now, her black dress half-ridden up her thighs where she had slid forward on the sofa. She frowned – trying to remember or trying not to?

'Ah, you mean *the* guitarist? *The Fakir* himself...' Cilea laughed quickly, 'that's what they call him apparently. The girls go for him, but they say he's not much interested in them... I've seen them in concert though, last year. Why?'

'Oh... I just passed by the Atheneum and saw his name on some concert programme. I thought I might go. I bought some tickets actually... well, just one... I assumed you wouldn't want to go.'

'Probably not,' Cilea was back on the sofa and Bond was back on the job, climbing a vertical cliff face in a dinner suit. I needn't have worried. She had no interest in my life outside the time I spent with her, and this in itself was enough to make me uneasy: while I worried about what she was doing and who she was with, her interest in my activities never went beyond polite enquiry. For the jealous, jealousy becomes the marker of passion, of authenticity of feeling; unrequited jealousy was just as bad as unrequited love.

I ran my hand along her thigh to see if the intimacy on offer earlier was still available. She opened her legs slightly and pulled my mouth to hers, keeping her eyes on the screen over my shoulder as I carried her out of the room.

Eleven

'Sure about this?' Leo asked, pulling up to the kerb and slinging my meagre luggage into the boot of his Skoda.

I was not. "Course I am – why shouldn't I be?"

'Leaving your chums behind, the lovely Cilea, the holiday resort weather... who knows? There might be a revolution while you're away... you might come back and find it all gone. Someone might knock your building down. Or your girlfriend off...'

Leo roared down Otopeni Boulevard, the speedometer of the Skoda touching 120 kmh. Motorcade speed. It was hot, and the tyres were sticky on the road. My suitcase thumped against the metal shell of the boot as we jammed to a halt at a checkpoint on the city limits. 'No worries,' Leo said. 'Because you're so anal we're two hours early as it is.'

I was on my way back for my first home leave. I was due two weeks, and I intended to finish clearing out my parents' house, sell up and settle my father's debts. I had said goodbye to Cilea the night before. We had walked home from the Athénée Palace at 2 am, Titanu tailing us discreetly in the Dacia. She kissed me on the steps of my house and climbed into the car, claiming it was unlucky to sleep with someone the night before they went away. The darkness had been thick and humid, but today the storm it had preluded had failed to come.

At the terminal building Leo parked in a diplomatic slot and put a crested permit card on his dashboard. It read, in English, French and Romanian, 'Ambassadorial Business' and referred any queries to the Consular section of Her Britannic Majesty's Embassy, Strada Jules Michelet. 'I won't stay long,' Leo explained, 'I'm not really a goodbyes man.'

My flight was not for another two hours. I checked in my case and joined Leo at his table in the 'Progress Bar and Lounge'. The airport's glass and concrete shell was almost empty of travellers, the usual battalion of officials with no precise duty sat or stood in postures of resentful vacancy. A flight from Belgrade was due, and a line of ministry limos waited on the tarmac, their drivers' doors open. Trolleys of food and wine were wheeled into the VIP lounge full and rattled back out empty. Glasses clinked and corks popped – and the visiting dignitaries had not even arrived.

'I thought you weren't going to hang around,' I said to Leo, though really I preferred him to stay, 'you don't do goodbyes, remember?'

'Greetings are more my thing, as you know. Actually, I'm interested in who's arriving. There's some kind of welcoming committee here, and it pays to keep your ear to the ground... looks like a Yugo delegation.'

Leo ordered a whole bottle of wine and poured us both a glass: What did I plan to do with my leave? Beyond seeing through the arrangements for selling up and clearing out the house, I had no plans. I barely wanted to go at all, but these were arrangements I had held on to, something to steady myself amid the buffetings of my new life.

I had only just met Petre, but much of the short time we had known each other we had spent together. I was drawn to him. Unlike Leo, whose life consisted of imagining a different world and making it happen in flashes by means of imagination, nostalgia and dirty money, Petre lived in the here and now. He managed to exist in it without either escaping or giving in to its crudity and greyness. He too had his plan for the city, his plan to link it all up into a single network. But not by lost walks. Petre was no more interested in Leo's old guidebooks than he was in the brutalist blueprints of Ceauşescu's architects. He had something else in mind. *The Project* he called it: *The Co-operative.*

With Petre I visited the new Bucharest with its factories and housing blocks, its identical new model suburbs. It was the counterpart to the old city of guidebooks and Baedekers, the city Leo was salvaging from a mass of broken stones and memory. But it had its beauty, its unlooked-for heroism and dignity: people trying to live normally, sending their children to school but supplementing the days of state indoctrination with unofficial classes on science or literature or history; men and women exhausted from banal and overmonitored jobs coming home on irregular buses to empty shelves and power cuts; old people eking out their pensions, younger ones struggling to fill their lunchboxes or put a square meal on the table. Everyone lived with the tug of hunger, the drag of boredom, a world and an epoch away from the Party bosses, the diplomats, the foreign businessmen. Leo's louche, beautiful Bucharest was of no concern to these people, if they knew it existed at all.

They had their citizens' groups which took care of the sick or the bereaved, distributing essential goods like medicines and baby milk, and Petre's dream to was to co-ordinate these groups into a single, well-planned counter-economy – one that would make good the failings of the system without contributing to the corruption of the black market. He was building what he called a 'skills bank' where teachers, plumbers, engineers, medics and other essential workers would pool their time and talents. The teacher would teach for two hours and buy two hours of an electrician's or a plumber's time. He could use them or exchange them or keep them until needed. There would be no interest rates, no economics based on cash or investment – just on time and work, from which the central administration would take a percentage to build up a welfare system for the sick, the workless or the old. The Social Fund Petre called it. What Petre dreamed of was a society within a society, a huge, Bucharest-wide network that would eventually spread across the country. Versions of it existed already in apartment blocks or villages. What it needed was countrywide co-ordination. Petre showed me his plans, his maps, not of streets and buildings but of people. 'Sounds an awful lot like communism to me,' I said when he had finished explaining it last week in the beer garden of the Carpathian Boar. He nodded but didn't answer, just dragged on his cigarette and blew the smoke into the air. 'Like a world before money,' I added. This time he turned and corrected me: 'After money. *After.*'

Then there were the concerts Petre's band gave in darkened warehouses to hundreds of students, close-packed and sweating, smoking bad dope and drinking flat beer; the *samizdat* songbooks and bootleg tapes they passed around, copying and recopying so often that the music became blur and the words became shadows on the page. This was the Bucharest that was left over when Leo had finished idealising it and the state had finished bulldozing it. 'This is what we must start with, Leo: *this,*' Petre had told him one night after a concert, pointing at the mêlée of thin, sweat-drenched students squeezed onto the temporary dance floor they had cleared in the abattoir that was *Fakir*'s venue for a night. The place smelled of detergent and blood. 'You must work with what you have, with what's there. Otherwise who will inherit the old Bucharest you love so much?'

That had been three weeks ago. Since then Leo's habits had changed. In his black market deals he always took a cut for

Petre and Petre's friends, bought up school books and unglamorous, unprofitable essentials like flour and sugar and tinned food. His associates complained – *it was heavy stuff, cheap; there was no profit margin. Why didn't he stick to whisky and watches, to the easy-to-carry, fast-selling luxuries the rich Party bosses paid so well for?* And whenever there were medicines involved, Leo always short-changed the buyer or over-ordered from the supplier to keep some back for Petre. Petre had changed the way Leo did business, had given him a focus for his sprawling, chaotic kindness that so often missed its mark or became lost in a tangle of double-dealing. It was through me that they communicated, and my role as go-between gave me my first real sense of being involved in Bucharest life. I arranged pick-ups and drop-offs, relayed messages, supervised payments and part-exchanges. Petre's Social Fund was taking shape. For now he needed Leo's racketeering, defectors' escape fees, and all the tawdry trappings of a corrupt police state. But not for long. These were the start-up costs, he said, necessary to buy time and lay the foundations of the social fund, and it was Vintul who oversaw it all: Vintul the banker.

I was spending more time with Petre than with Leo. Leo had started to notice, but if it hurt him he hid it well. Leo's world of Capşa and cocktails, his fin-de-siècle Bucharest of battered luxury and threadbare high-life, had become too rarefied for me. Besides, between Trofim, Leo, Petre and Cilea I felt I was living in four different Bucharests, across four different epochs. None of them met except through me, and yet, because I kept them apart from each other, my own life didn't even meet itself.

I lived in crowded isolation, moving from one to the other, keeping them separate but running them in parallel: Trofim's book, Cilea's bed, Leo's black market, Petre's concerts...

whatever was left over by the time I had subtracted them all from my life must, I supposed, have been myself.

'There's something... not quite real about Petre, isn't there?' said Leo one day, adding, 'you know, something temporary...' Maybe, I wondered now as I sat at Otopeni airport thinking of all I was leaving behind. Maybe. Though Petre was real enough, I knew what Leo meant. It was that unpindownable feeling that however much you knew him, however much he trusted you, there was something being kept back – not because he was hiding it but simply because there was more to him than you could take in.

Then there was Cilea. My hold on her was slim enough as it was; how would two weeks away affect us?

I was afraid to go home, afraid of those days stretching ahead in the empty house: that smell of fermented stasis, compacted carpet pile, the old cigarette smoke that was all that remained of my parents' breath... And their things: the sunken cushions where their now cremated bodies had sat; the heartbreaking worn slippers beneath the table that held the phone and the mostly empty address book, each page a window onto the blankness of their lives. That Larkin poem – what was it? – 'Home': 'It stays as it was left, shaped to the comfort of the last to go...' The great, enveloping sadness of it all... I could smell it from here; or rather, it was in me already, the foretaste of its pastness.

'Second thoughts, eh?' Leo read me, and I realised I had not spoken for several minutes. 'Still, home's home,' he said, hewing at my resolve.

As the Belgrade plane came in, a group emerged from the VIP lounge, headed by a large, jowly man in a black suit, muscle run to fat, flanked by aides and followed by some lean-faced, watchful young bodyguards. They had the familiar Securitate suits with the gun-bulge in the left breast pocket. These people wore flares not from retro fashion sense but for easier access to the second gun that was strapped to their calf. The man in front, sweat filling the folds of his skin, exuded physical strength and ferocious malice, and looked as if he got plenty of practice exercising both. His eyes were close together; in anyone else it would have made them look dim, but in his case it gave him an air of mean, low cunning; the eyes of a man who sought in those around him the lowest motivations and always found it. A crew-cut emphasised the bulkiness of his scalp, which joined the collar of his shirt not via the intermediary of a neck but through five thick rolls of flesh that resembled a stack of pink bicycle tyres: a Slavic Mussolini.

'Stoicu, Ion Stoicu... Interior Minister, Cilea's dad's boss for one thing. He's a real piece of shit: a fat boorish peasant, but sadly no fool. He's one of these people who's so terrifying that he doesn't need to kill people to get things done. He just kills them as a sort of free extra. He's reduced his ministry to a small hate-filled village ... it's now self-purging, you know, like those self-basting chickens? He's Ceaușescu's most trusted lieutenant. Stoicu owes everything to Ceaușescu, and has absolute loyalty to him.' Leo had his eyes half closed, and spoke slowly, as if reading from files stored in some inner archive. 'Just a petty criminal in the forties, a fascist Jew-baiter who burned down a synagogue in Iași, then did time in the same prison as Ceaușescu, apparently for rape. The official story is that he was a close comrade of the young Nicolae and helped him activate the successful revolution. Actually he was in clink, wanking and thinking of ways to kill Jews when the communists took power. They say history makes the people who make history... *cometh the time, cometh the man* and all that bollocks. It's not like that. History just crawls along on its belly picking up parasites... Stoicu, Ceaușescu... the lot of them... crabs on the pubis of history.'

The plane had landed. A red carpet was being rolled out by crouching henchmen who stumbled backwards as they went. It was a civilian plane decked out in military colours, green and khaki patches through which you could still see the name of the Yugoslav national airline, JAT, not quite painted over.

Stoicu stood flanked by his deputies, ready to greet the delegation.

Leo drained his glass. 'Ceauşescu picked him out and gave him a job running the Iaşi Party. Made him mayor. He purged the party, shut down the synagogues and started the process of selling Jews to Israel. Then Ceauşescu brought him here and put him in charge of the Interior Ministry. A real piece of shit – one of the people responsible for shafting your chum Trofim, who's a shifty customer himself... Stoicu was in charge of the first "Romanianisation of the executive" programme in the early seventies. His job was to purge Jews, ethnic Hungarians and Germans, Moldovans and anyone else not one hundred per cent ethnic Romanian from government posts. In 1972 Stoicu walked into the Snagov villa of one of the anti-Ceauşescu Politburo bosses and shot him twice in the head. He was screwing the man's wife anyway, but told the Big Chief he'd done it for him, that the poor sod was plotting against him. He got promoted, got the woman, and kicked his own wife out into the sticks. Business with pleasure... then he dumped her and married a niece of the previous president, Gheorgiu-Dej.'

There was no way Stoicu's fat fingers could fit through the trigger guard of a handgun, I thought, but around here they probably made revolvers for the larger customer.

First off the plane were paramilitary bodyguards in combat gear and mirror shades; then a dozen officials in standard-issue, elephant-grey communist suits, tieless and with their top shirt buttons fastened, followed by young men in jeans

146

and leather jackets sporting mullet haircuts, western watches and biker boots. One, his jacket over his shoulder, had an eagle tattoo on his upper arm. At the back of the group, indisputably in charge of them all, was a short man with steel-coloured spiky hair and a round, fleshy face. Everyone stopped and waited for him, watched him for cues as to when to walk, stand still or shake hands. Stoicu stepped out onto the red carpet and embraced him first.

The Yugoslav flag hung out in welcome was different from the usual one: in place of the red star at the centre, it had a crest on it, two white eagles face to face, like the tattoo on the young man's arm.

'Serbs...' Leo said, more to himself than to me, 'the Serb flag. You see it everywhere since Tito died... I don't think this is an official visit, look – there's no Yugoslav Embassy staff to welcome this lot.'

The group was waved through an unstaffed customs booth into the VIP lounge. On cue, two trolleys of elaborate canapés and cakes emerged from the airport restaurant and disappeared inside.

'OK, I'm off to do some homework on this lot. Check a few things out. Have a good trip!' Leo was suddenly business-like, in a hurry to leave.

I was flagging now, playing for time. I suggested another drink – my flight was over an hour away and the airport a desolate place to be alone in, full of other people's business, the continuities of all their lives arching like flight routes across the globe.

Leo pressed his advantage: 'You don't want to go, do you? Just like me on my first trip out – I got here, checked in, sat around for an hour and turned back.'

'OK Leo, you win, take me home.'

'Home! *Home?* Well, you said it!' Leo clapped his hands in delight.

I tried to get my case back from check-in, but the attendant refused to understand my request. No matter: my half-empty suitcase would tumble out in a jostle of bags and cases and finish up orbiting the luggage belt, unmatched, in the Heathrow light. After a few hours someone would pick it up and convey it to lost property where it would sit out its time with others of its abandoned kind. I tried to follow it with my mind. Where did the story end for lost things? Would it be used again, dumped, thrown away? As a child I had been haunted by the way nothing disappears... until I saw that yes, there is one thing that disappears, it's people. Their clothes, shoes, false teeth, suitcases and bags all rumble on in some form or other, landfilled, incinerated, compacted, shredded or scrapped. But people? They just go.

That was what I had been going back to, and perhaps that was what Bucharest could help me with, not by overcoming it but by interposing its own dramas and sorrows between me and my own life. It had done so for Leo. Why not for me?

There were tears filling my eyes but I blinked them back. Leo said nothing, just walked me gently to the car. We passed the roadblock, the road clogged up now with angry gesticulating foreigners who had yet to learn the first and only law of communist queuing: like quicksand, the more you fought it, the deeper it sucked you in.

I wondered if in not taking that plane I had failed to confront something. Leo pulled up outside the university and turned to me: 'No. That's just psychobabble – all this "confronting the past" shit, all this bollocks about "closure" and all that. There's no rule that says you have to keep going back, nothing to say you *need* to confront things. Your past doesn't own you. That's just a way of keeping you shackled to it, it's the shrinks and the gurus and the TV chat-show shitemongers who say that. No. You can get up and leave whenever you want. Take it from me: if you can, keep on running, and if you ever *have* to stop, just start running on the spot.' Leo O'Heix: lifestyle guru.

Ionescu let me use his fax machine, the only one in the building with an outside line, to cancel my arrangements. I left a message with the solicitor and Deadman house clearance to sell what could be sold and throw out the rest.

Back in my office I shuffled my papers and switched on the fan. Waves of stirred air cooled my face. I looked around. Stuck to the wall were the Post-it notes I had removed from the phone on my first day. For the first time I noticed that the number I saw written there, in Belanger's tight hand, was Cilea's. Of course I always knew without really knowing – it was how we knew most things here, the informational equivalent of peripheral vision – that they had been together. It had never bothered me before. Now I felt I was involved in a replay, a sequel, not in life itself, and maybe not even mine.

I looked at Cilea's number and decided not to call her. She would know soon enough I was still here. My non-return sat more easily on me now. Maybe Leo was right. The plane would have landed, my suitcase abandoned to its fate, trapped in lost-prop limbo. And that house, radiating sorrow like a damaged reactor... I was out of sight at least, if never quite out of range.

'You're best off out of it.' Leo knocked, walked in, sat down and put his feet on my desk, as was his wont, in a single flowing movement.

'Out of what?' I asked, looking up and rubbing my eyes. Belanger's Post-it note was stuck to my fingers.

'Out of... wherever it was you were just then.'

'Who was Belanger? I mean, really? What did he do? Apart from work in my office, live in my flat and fuck my girlfriend?'

'I rather think, if we're doing this logically, chronologically, that he'd be the one to ask you those questions, not the other way round...' We walked to the canteen and ordered a couple of *ersatzes*.

'I've done some detective work,' said Leo proudly. 'What we saw earlier wasn't a Yugo official visit, it was a Serb delegation. It's the new Serb president, Milosevic, and he's got some meeting on later with Ceauşescu, fraternal greetings and all that. But I'll bet you a Capşa steak there's more to it. The shit's about to hit the fan in Yugoslavia, it's going to break up piece by bloody piece. I expect the new man's doing the rounds of the friendly socialist countries, seeing whom he can rely on to keep their noses out. There's an old Serb saying: "There's only two people on the side of the Serbs – God and the Greeks." Maybe you'd add Romania. Anyway, we won't be seeing much of them.'

We saw them sooner that we expected.

Later that evening Leo and I went to the InterContinental. It was not a place we went to often. Leo saw it as enemy territory, expensive and sleazy, and the headquarters of a rival black-marketeering outfit, the darkest and most powerful of Bucharest's undergrounds – Party-protected, maybe even Party-run. It was from here that Ilie the pimp ran his girls and pushed his drugs.

On my way here I had stopped by the music faculty, remembering that Petre would have been rehearsing, and invited him to join us. The only way his band got time to practise was when they booked the concert hall as a classical chamber group. Every member of *Fakir* doubled as a classical musician, and after an hour of formal rehearsal, once Micu the porter had safely locked up and taken out his hearing aid, out came the guitars and synthesisers, the drum kit and the saxophone.

Now, in the half-deserted basement nightclub, I saw that inviting Petre had been a mistake.

Cilea was there, with some of her friends: Elena Ralian, the daughter of the Bucharest party chief, an imitation of Cilea – same clothes, same hair style, down to the perfume, a lost girl whose identity had been pieced together from duplicated facets of other people's; Ion Stoicu's son, damaged, ferret-eyed and with an air of someone preparing a chilled dish of revenge without having decided who to serve it up to; the dim-witted Nestor Postelnicu, son of the foreign minister, who went by an idiomatic nickname the nearest English equivalent of which was 'Two Planks'. There were a few others wearing western clothes and perfumes but unable to shake off the aura of a closed society. Only Cilea got away with it. Even Leo, with his Monocom trousers, yellow nylon shirt and Bulgarian moccasins, looked more like westerner than they did. His clothes were the visual equivalent of a perpetually tuning-up orchestra, but he carried it off

The *nomenklatura* youth were out in force tonight to entertain the savage children of the Serb chiefs. They were all drinking hard and chatting up the girls. At the bar, the callgirls were waiting for the drink to wear down their customers' inhibitions. Ilie the pimp had put on his best shop window. His girls looked disposable, carnal, professional. They waited to be asked. They didn't hustle.

When Cilea saw me she looked at me first in astonishment, then in anger. She shook her head, warning me not to get involved.

Leo had already seen her. 'Bad move,' he said, trying to bring me back out of the room, 'let's try the Athénée Palace... a bit more class.' But I pushed on and headed for the bar, indicating the table we would be sitting at.

Stoicu, Constantin and the Serbs were dining upstairs while the golden youth entertained themselves down here. A row of ice-buckets stood on the table. When a bottle was finished, they upended it and shouted for another. Cilea sat among them but apart from it all, smoking, laughing politely, looking at her watch. Beside her, one of the Serbs was too close, peering down her front for a glimpse – more than a glimpse, a luxurious tracking shot – of her cleavage. When he lit her cigarette he looked her in the eye, touching her hand as she tried to steady the lighter.

One of the Serb boys crossed the dance floor and went to the little stage on which the resident singer, 'Doina the Diva', was performing. She had put on a brave show so far, against the drawn-out insult of their boorishness. Leo knew her slightly – a matronly woman who each night squeezed herself into leather trousers and tight, breast-enhancing shirt. She sang anthemic pop songs like 'Total Eclipse of the Heart' and 'I need a Hero' with a backing band that looked like starving undertakers. In her thick make-up and overblown wig she looked like a transvestite, but she was in fact an attractive woman beneath it all. Did that make her, Leo wondered, a 'trans-transvestite'? 'Voice like a bag of broken glass,' he joked, but Doina was a Bucharest institution. Sometimes, after closing time, the curtains would be drawn and a new clientele of musicians, students and other nostalgists arrived to hear her sing the old peasant songs she had learned as a child in Banloc.

The Serb climbed onto the stage and barged her off. She retreated with dignity, her high heels teetering, the flesh so tight-packed and the leather so ungiving that she walked like a robot, moving only at the joints. I scanned the clientele: foreign businessmen, German truckers, lost tourists and the odd local slipped through the net, looking in at how the other half lived.

It was the time of night when men start to edge towards the prostitutes; one of the truckers, a regular on the Frankfurt-Bucharest route, had already made a start. Norbert he was called, 'Norbert the Talker', because he liked to pretend that he was charming and chatting up the girls, that the money he gave them was a gift they could take or leave, and not a payment. He bought them dinner and a night in a luxury hotel.

The DJ stood aside as two of the Serb boys took over his decks and unleashed a round of techno-ethnic funk. The Serbs made for the dance floor and danced something violent and atavistic, a cross between heavy metal headbanging and frenetic folk dancing. They finished with a salute; two of them drew a finger across their throats.

'Music to kill Jews to,' whispered Leo in disgust, 'or is it Muslims these days?'

Across the room, standing in the doorway, stood Petre, open-mouthed. How long had he been here? I felt embarrassed and guilty. Then I felt angry: this was his country not mine, why should I feel responsible? But I could tell the scene horrified him; he seemed to be looking through it, into some future that chilled him. I should have left then, or taken him somewhere else. But I was staying to watch Cilea. I motioned Petre to sit down, and he walked cagily towards us along the periphery of the room to avoid crossing the centre.

'Jesus, why d'you bring him here?' Leo asked.

'Why d'you bring *me* here, Leo?' I was drunk, my anger balling up inside me without my knowing who it was aimed at.

The music and lights pulsed like the inside of a migraine; the drink had an evil underpull. Cilea had been cornered by one of the Serbs. I saw her push his hand away from under the table then look at me, signalling me to keep my distance.

At the edge of the group, alone at his own table, Titanu watched over her. He drank orange juice through a straw, and the segment of orange perched on the rim of him glass gave him an absurdly camp look.

I went to the toilet, hoping Cilea would get the cue and come out to speak to me. I was swaying slightly by now, and pushed aggressively past one of the Serbs, who looked at me with delinquent eyes, then forgot the slight and stumbled on. In the toilets there was the sound of fucking from one of the cubicles. The door opened and one of the Serbs leered at me mockingly, 'Good yes?', and washed his hands. One of the prostitutes flushed the toilet and followed him, smoothing her dress, blood at the corner of her mouth.

In the lobby Cilea was waiting. She kissed me and looked nervously around.

'I was going to come by tomorrow,' she said into my ear.

'I wasn't meant to be here...' Something crossed my thoughts, something like a bird's shadow on the ground as it flies, but I couldn't catch hold of it.

'No, of course. I'd forgotten. Anyway, you stayed. I'm glad...' she said. 'I have to go. I don't want them coming to find you here. I'd prefer you to leave actually.'

'What, so I don't cramp your style with that bunch of yobs?'

'No – so I can get through the night without being spied on. Anyway, I'm OK, Titanu's watching.'

'This is horrible – a fucking horrible night,' I told her.

'You haven't seen anything yet,' she said, sighing, 'at least it'll be over soon. Please go.'

Petre was behind me tiptoeing out, trying to get away from us. I called him back. 'Petre,' I said, 'this is Cilea Constantin. Cilea, Petre Romanu, a friend of mine. You must know each other? Surely you've met?' I was drunk and truculent. They looked at each other and shook hands, but I knew immediately that I should not have done it. Petre went pale and looked down, avoiding her eye. Cilea was angry and flustered. She tried to hold his hand a moment too long but he pulled it back and disappeared. Now she made to leave, avoiding my eye.

'What's up with him?' I asked viciously, 'one of your exes? He certainly seems to know you...'

Cilea shook her head sadly: 'I'm not getting into this. You

seem to think everything is there to be known, asked about, brought out into the open. It's not. When you apologise to me, make sure you apologise to him too.'

The pogrom rock was getting louder. Cilea, back at her table, held her nerve even when the Serb who had stuck to her all evening pulled her onto the dance floor. I watched his hand slip down to the small of her back, only for her to lift it out again. He nuzzled into her bare shoulder, inhaling her underskin scent. She held him at arm's length but was no match for him; he pulled her closer until their faces touched. When the song ended, he kept hold of her. Titanu sat in complete stillness, his elaborate cocktail untouched, watching.

I had had enough. I pulled myself up and tried to get to her. Leo stopped me. 'Stay here. You don't dick around with these people. You stay put or I get you out of here. She can look after herself,' he added, 'she knows how to handle this – she's been doing it all her life.'

Leo was right. The boy held on to her a moment too long and then, with a practised, emphatic little push, she unhooked him and moved back to her table. He spat on the floor then danced solo for a few minutes to keep face, cupping his balls.

Stoicu and Manea Constantin came down with Milosevic and the rest of the Serbs. The dislike between Stoicu and Cilea's father was obvious. Manea behaved as if he was slumming it with yobs and gangsters. Even the most ruthlessly equalising system failed to get rid of his upper-middle-class demeanour, but alongside his squat, pug-faced boss Stoicu he looked like an aristocrat. He winced as he entered: the dreadful music, the hot, damp air, the flashing lights and glitter. He scanned room and stopped when he saw our table: Leo and me, with Petre between us. Petre flinched and looked away, moving his whole body sideways. I was sobering up enough now to realise I had made a big mistake bringing him into this cavern of slime.

Stoicu was in his element – dollar-flashing, flurries of waiters and racks of Johnnie Walker. He eyed up the girls at the bar, banking their images, making mental notes for later. He was probably staying at the hotel, as most of the Party bosses did when they were on a night out, or kept a city-centre flat for adultery and hangovers. 'Politburo Shagover Pads,' Leo called them. Stoicu held his champagne flute in his fist and bolted his drinks. Constantin sipped from his, holding it between thumb and middle finger. He spoke a few words to Cilea. She ignored him. He put his hand on hers; she violently brushed it aside. He rose, kissed her on the top of the head and left. At the centre of it all, Milosevic the Serb chief sat and watched, his champagne untouched.

'Why did you make me come here?' Petre was asking me. 'This place is hell. It makes me ill.' It was true that Petre looked profoundly sick, but he looked afraid too. Even Leo, a veteran of Bucharest sleaze, was finding it hard to extract much humour from the evening. 'Bet you wish you'd taken that plane now?' he whispered. Over at the VIP table, it was that time of the night when, by some animal law of entropy, the group starts to turn on itself. 'Two Planks' was being ribbed with increasing nastiness. Someone poured champagne over his head, another flicked fag ash over his hair and shoulders; he laughed a feeble, stoical laugh – years of knowing that the nearest he would come to joining in group humour was becoming the butt of its jokes.

His humiliations were put on hold by a new arrival, an unsteady, leering figure. The DJ pulled the plugs on his decks and the sound died.

Nicu Ceauşescu swayed in the doorway like a man on the prow of a storm-tossed boat. His legs were parted to steady him, his face flabby with sated appetites, but eyes alive with appetites renewed. Two minders stood a little behind him, a parody of the western playboy: open-necked shirt, gold chain, Pierre Cardin shirt, Adidas trainers. Three nervous adolescent girls waited behind him.

'Shit – I've been here eight years and I've never had to be in the same room as that bastard. Now, thanks to you, here we are...' Leo knocked back a drink and refilled his glass.

'Thanks to me...?' I trailed off and looked at Petre. He was aghast.

Nicu's companion, a famous gymnast and all-too-recent child prodigy, had won a silver at the Los Angeles Olympics five years back, and was tipped for a gold next time. She was thirteen back then. Nicu had his arm around her, but continued to scan the room for flesh. His relationship with an opera singer his own age, his official consort, was common knowledge, but everyone knew he preferred them young. The gymnast, Paulina Iliescu, had big wide eyes; her slim, toned body was wrong for here, a place of protrusion and ornament. Stilettos and a miniskirt made her long legs unsteady, and she had the air of a foal taking its first steps. Her lack of cleavage was accentuated by a low-cut top, around which she kept putting a defensive, muscular arm.

'Christ knows what lives those poor girls live – steroids, drugs, kept prisoners in these athletes' camps, then taken up by him. They lie back and think of Romania and hope he finishes quick, which fair play he apparently does. At least athletes are allowed to go on the pill...' Leo stared at them, talking to me out of the corner of his mouth.

Nicu sniffed and wiped his nose with his thumb and forefinger, then wiped them on his trousers. Stoicu showed him to the bar and ordered drinks: champagne and Johnnie Walker. Nicu looked around at the prostitutes. Stoicu introduced him to the Serbs, who greeted him without enthusiasm. Milosevic especially looked unimpressed – where others saw power and status, he saw a slob, a police-state playboy with the shakes, a parasite on a rotting system. He shook Nicu's hand and sat back down, ignoring him.

It did not take Nicu long to turn his attention to Cilea. They knew each other, that was clear enough, despite the twenty-year age difference. He ordered a big round of drinks, put his arms out in welcome to the guests, and proposed a toast. He whispered something to a minder, who went to the DJ, quivering like a tracked beast behind his podium and changed the music to some 80s slow dances. 'Ah,' said Leo authoritatively, 'groper's classics. I've had occasion to request them myself.'

Nicu tried out dancing partners, a feudal *droit de seigneur* played out to eighties disco music. This was what he did in his own fiefdom, Iaşi, where he was Party chief and where no one went to nightclubs or restaurants for fear of bumping into him. Nicu's first dance request was with Elena Ralian. She rose hesitantly, slotted her good body against him, biting her lip and closing her eyes. His hands went all over her, down her back, across her buttocks, where he squeezed a little; she flinched but he just gripped her harder, liking the tension, needing something to exert himself against. All the time he was looking at Cilea, for whom Elena was the warm-up act. His gymnast companion, fiddling with the straw of a coca-cola, looked relieved – she might yet get the night off. After three songs, Elena Ralian was released and returned to her seat, where the effects of whatever 'Two Planks' had had his drink spiked with were beginning to take hold. He lay with his head on the table, sleeping, a mound of cigarette ash on his wet hair.

Nicu made his move on Cilea. As he jimmied himself in beside her she got up and changed tables. Undeterred, he followed her, calling her back. She ignored him. Everyone was watching. Even the music seemed to drop in volume, slow down in tempo. Nicu put a hand on Cilea's leg but she pulled it off and threw it back at him so violently it looked as if it had separated from his body. He lunged at her, took her by the throat, and pushed his mouth onto hers.

Titanu moved so fast that we saw nothing happen. Only after it was over did we piece it together: he had Nicu in a bear hug, arms pinned to his sides and hands flapping helplessly at his waist. Nicu was screaming obscenities while Stoicu tried to unlock Titanu's arms. Nicu's face was red and bloated; he coughed between screams, launching his head back against Titanu's chest. Titanu stood and waited until Nicu had exhausted himself, then walked to the lobby and dropped him hard onto the marble floor. Nicu's gang of girls looked terrified. They would be the ones to reap the consequences of tonight's humiliation. His minders hovered on the edge of the drama, more concerned with calming him down than taking on Titanu, who now stood beside Cilea like a block of granite. Cilea was rubbing her neck, breathing hard, holding back tears. Her friends had moved away, all except 'Two Planks' who was still out cold. I started to get up to join Cilea, but Leo held me back. The way she looked at me told me all I needed to know about staying out of it.

Stoicu was yelling at an impassive Titanu – 'You're fucked! You and your boss! Finished!' At Cilea: 'You little snob slut, you bourgeois cunts never change their ways, you still think you're better than the rest of us.' There were flecks of foam around his lips, the saliva spraying in the disco lights, behind him the muffled sound, half blood-curse and half infantile weeping, of Nicu Ceauşescu.

Cilea gathered her things and left a few minutes later, Titanu escorting her through the hotel's back door. Neither gave a signal of recognition as they walked past me.

'Jesus, that won't be in the papers tomorrow...' Leo was

shaking his head. The prostitutes were clipping shut their cigarette and condom-filled purses and paying their bar tabs. No one would be needing them now. Doina the Diva gave a quick thumbs up to Leo and treated herself to a large Courvoisier from the untended bar. In the lobby the barman stood with a silver salver and a bottle of Johnnie Walker from which a hyperventilating Nicu slugged.

Though Nicu was a slob, a rapist and a bully, this would not have happened ten years ago, or even five. His treatment tonight was a barometer of the closed internal politics of Romania, more significant than a food riot or demonstration. These things were just flashes of desperation from a powerless people; what we had now seen was a testing of the structures of power. I could tell that was how the steel-eyed Serb chief had seen it, and how Stoicu himself now saw it as he sipped Tsuica, all pretence at sophistication gone: the peasant at his plum brandy, projecting his village machinations country-wide.

Milosevic slipped away, tapping his room key against his leg as he walked. He ordered a pot of coffee from reception and left, cold sober despite all the drink, looking like a man just getting down to work. 'Two Planks' was standing up, groggy and with a line across his forehead where he had slept against the table's edge. He had missed it all, but he would be the only one left when the Securitate got here, stuttering dim-wittedly that he had seen nothing, heard nothing.

'Time we went.' Leo took me by the arm and we left through the staff exit. In one of the offices, someone was excitedly telling her colleagues what had happened. The rumour mill was turning. By morning it would be all around Bucharest, filling the offices and factories, reaching the foreign embassies and newspapers.

I remembered Petre. I looked around for him but he had gone. I was glad – it saved me apologising to him, but I would need to do it soon enough, and to Cilea as well. This was his country, but tonight had been my doing.

Twelve

My involvement with Petre and Vintul's border-crossing operation came sooner than I expected. It had been brought forward and now, a week after the incident with Nicu Ceauşescu, Leo and I were heading to the Yugoslav border. Petre, Vintul, and five others would reach the same place by a different route. We had stopped at a roadside for a dashboard meal of bread, white cheese and Rocola. Leo was doing penance for the evening at the Madonna Disco, and had foresworn fine food and drink. I had not seen Petre or Cilea since. He had gone to ground, no one knew where, and now he was behind us in a stolen car. I would see him soon, at least. I would explain. I would apologise. As for Cilea, she had not returned my calls, and I had failed to get past the guard at the gates of her building. The messages I left on her answerphone alternated between abject contrition and unrepentant accusation. Only once did she pick up. She heard my voice and put the phone down.

It was early evening, and after the city limits of Bucharest the farmland stretched for hours of flat road. On the horizon's cloudless rim a red sun boiled. There were no animals; nothing moved or grazed. To the north-east of us, the petrochemical towers of Craiova disgorged their smoke. It looked like it disappeared, but really it impregnated the air, attached itself to it molecule by molecule, and the sky's metallic blue was in fact a screen of pollution. That summer's intricate sunsets were all pollution too: petrol-fume, carbon-dazzle... there was no rain and the only rainbows we saw were in the oil-slick puddles beneath the construction lorries.

There was a weak point on the border with Yugoslavia, a narrow stretch of the Danube that was barbed-wired and patrolled but not guarded. Romania shared frontiers with five countries, but an increasingly disunited Yugoslavia was a favourite crossing-point. It was a step westwards. Leo had been on three of these trips so far, but only a few of the escapees gave a sign from their new lives: coded postcards or messages that passed like Chinese whispers along the channels of the underground.

We arrived at our destination, a small town called Hinova a few miles from the border, at around nine o'clock. Leo had booked us into a hotel where we were the only customers. Leo ordered some wine and asked for the menu, which was orally transmitted and five syllables long. After watery stew and *ersatz*, we walked outside. The shadows were closing in on the small central square. The town was untouched by Romania's modernisation project. It exuded irrelevance: parched lawn, dry fountain, some busts of forgotten men crumbling in limestone. In the shadows of their plinths a pack of dogs lazed and snarled at the nothing that was happening. Old men sat on benches, and folk music came from a shuttered café. The town's only modern building was the Party headquarters, a small breeze-blocked square iced in grey concrete, with faded flags and rusty slogan boards.

We met the others in a car park on the edge of town. Vintul, Petre, three other boys and two girls, only one of whom I recognised: Mel from that night on the Boulevard of Socialist Victory. Tonight her name was Ana. Each had a rucksack wrapped in bin liners strapped to their back and was full of nervous courage and big talk. Only Petre and

Vintul were calm, Vintul because he was in charge and focussed, Petre because he seemed to float above it all. He shook my hand and smiled. 'I'm sorry about the other night...' I began. 'Not now,' he said, 'and anyway, it's all finished, I have already forgotten.' Our friendship remained, I was sure of that, but he had withdrawn a little, whether to protect me or to protect himself I could not tell. My acquaintance with Cilea troubled him enough to ask if I knew her father, but he relaxed when I told him I did not. In any case, I was unlikely to meet him now.

We separated into three groups, me and Leo heading off first and Petre and Vintul each taking some of the others in different directions. We walked for about an hour across terrain that looked as anonymous as motorway hard shoulder, before reaching a range of bare, tinder-dry hills that took us to the edge of thick woods.

We walked carefully, stopping every twenty yards and waiting, listening out. The wood looked made of shadow. As we entered, the temperature dropped suddenly and our steps were padded with springy undergrowth.

'Fox traps,' whispered Leo, 'they're not for the foxes.'

At last, about two hundred yards into the wood, Leo brought out a torch. There was a path of flattened nettles and brambles, and great coils of bindweed thick as a child's wrist. There were plants here that existed in permanent shade, like those fish that live miles below sea level, fleshy and filled with darkness. 'Wolf shit.' Leo aimed the torch's beam at a pile of whitened, chalky turds. The torchlight made the ground sway beneath us. I tripped and as I fell forward I caught sight of a fox trap, gaping and rusty, the fanged zero of a shark's mouth. People had been caught in there and bled to death or, if managing to free themselves, hobbled home, bones crushed and flesh gouged. A hand steadied me from behind and covered my mouth before I could call out. Vintul had come up suddenly from behind us, poked his stick into the trap and snapped it shut. He had been behind us all the time.

Eventually we reached the end of the forest, and before us in the gloom rolled the Danube, thick and dark and oily. Against the moonlight, standing a few hundred yards upstream, was a single watchtower with its lights out. Between it and the water stood a twelve-foot screen of barbed electric wire. We could hear it buzz, a thin insect hum.

Vintul now made an owl call. Silence. We waited. Then a reply came from across the water. I saw the flash of a torch on what I assumed was the opposite bank. It was hundreds of yards of water away. Vintul made one more call then there was nothing.

'Have a breather. We're waiting for the next power cut. Stay by the trees.' Leo was puffing, bent over and with his hands on his knees. The others sat and waited on the edge of the wood. No one spoke, nothing moved. There was only the sound of the wire, the deadly voltage coursing through it.

Finally the current stopped and the wire shuddered. A little beyond it, thin razor wire, its edges catching the light, flashed then disappeared back into darkness. This was a well-chosen spot, as close as it came to being safely unobserved. There were holes in the wires, carefully made and easy to reset when the operation was finished. Vintul went first. With strong pliers, he began to untie the electric wire – 'have to keep the wire connected between operations, or the circuit breaks and they'd know it's been penetrated. Then we couldn't use it again,' Leo explained. 'Every break in the circuit sets off an alarm.' Slowly Vintul loosened the wires and opened a few feet of electric fence and parted it. He climbed through, and did the same with the razor wire. With the moon on the river and its light being reflected he was dangerously silhouetted, but he worked fast. A few minutes later he had made a series of holes in the wire large enough to pass through. He crawled to the riverbank, stopped, then turned around. The route was clear.

The current was strong. We could see the water twisting fast, catching the light in flashes, the river's muscle flexing. I watched them go, two of the boys first, then the girls, and then the last boy. The water closed over their bodies. The two high-fiving boys, all bravado gone, looked terrified. We watched them all slide in, holding back cries as the cold water filled their clothes and shoes, weighed them down. One of them seemed to float rather than swim, silently letting herself go downriver. Then they were gone.

Vintul was back on the rocky bank and mending the electric wire. They had lost a few minutes somewhere along the line, and it was a race now to rejoin the broken ends of fencing. He was just in time: a few seconds after pulling back his hands, the current started again, its electric dirge drowning out the slop of water against the banks.

Petre smiled and embraced me. 'Your first mission! We will toast it soon.' Then they were gone, back into the forest. He and Vintul would follow the river as it pulled back inwards, then head deeper into Romania, towards Vânju Mare. 'There is a small village where we know people. We will make our own way home,' said Vintul, and turned to go.

Leo and I headed back to Hinova, the light gathering faster than we could walk. When we reached the hotel it was nearly 5 am. We passed the unmanned reception and went to our rooms.

'Why did you want me here, Leo? What good did I do? I just stood around and watched...'

'You did a great job,' replied Leo, '...you *stood around,* yes, *but you stood around getting implicated,* and that's much more useful to them, to us, than anything you could actually *do...*

besides, you'll be up to your neck in it soon enough, so you may as well take a back seat while you can.'

After breakfast we drove through the villages of Craiova county and the vineyards of Segarcea. After the grey privations of Bucharest, it was a shock to see such fertility Everything grew. On all sides there were tomatoes, corn, cabbages; orchards heavy with fruit and bright fields of vegetables. The earth threw it all forth, and the sun ripened it generously. In the vineyards the fat white grapes hung on their boughs, the vines rising in perfectly aligned terraces. Melons the size of footballs lay on the earth, umbilicals ranging off across the dark soil; greenhouses and polytunnels stretched off into the distance. 'All for export,' Leo saw me scanning the fields, 'most of the poor sods in the factories have never even seen a melon, except in *Dynasty*. This is naturally a land of plenty; it's the bloody destitution that's artificial.'

A week passed and Petre failed to make our appointment at the Carpathian Boar. Vintul made no contact with Leo either, though he had promised to ring the next day. I looked for Petre at the music lectures but there was no sign of him. He missed the first *Fakir* rehearsal, then the second. The concert scheduled for the beginning of July was cancelled.

Cilea still refused to see me. Something had happened that night, something other than Nicu Ceauşescu's humiliation, but I could not make it out. Coincidence had placed them all together in that terrible disco – the Serbs, Nicu, Stoicu, Manea and Cilea – and the fluke of my last-minute decision not to leave Bucharest had brought me there too, and with me Leo and Petre. Had that chance grouping set something in motion whose consequences were being played out without our knowing what they were? Cilea was avoiding me, Petre had gone, Leo brooded and hid away in his flat.

Leo heard the first rumour three weeks later: a German

trucker, Norbert the Talker's colleague, boasting that he had been with the same prostitute in Hamburg, a Romanian girl, three nights in a row. This girl, Ana, was new to the game and he reckoned he had 'broken her in'. Leo asked for a description and got what he feared: the girl had a nose stud and piercings, and was under the constant guard of her Yugoslav pimp.

'Of course it's not her!' I said, 'there's probably hundreds of those poor girls in every port. In any case, Hans couldn't tell the difference between a Romanian and a Russian.' There was something in my voice, shrill and desperate-sounding...

Leo and I decided to find out where Petre lived. He had told me the name of the estate, but Leo found the address on the university database. It was just as well, since the twelve identikit blocks that made up 'Housing Estate 14' were impossible to tell apart. A seasoned observer, judging from the mould and crumbliness of the facades, might perhaps be able to tell which of the blocks had gone up first, the way an expert might assess the maturity of different blue cheeses, but to the layperson such distinctions were impossible.

Leo parked at the base of Block Seven and unpacked a soya salami. 'You'll see it in glow in the dark – the bean fields are right in the Chernobyl wind.' He waved a speckled, flesh-coloured baton from the car window, and sent me up.

In the lobby, the lift squatted at the bottom of its cage. I pressed the button, but nothing happened. I had eight flights to climb. The concrete was rough and crumbly, and the stair-well was a vortex for disconnected, discontinuous sounds: human voices, the squealing of babies, the seepage of a single TV programme ramifying identically across each floor. The walls were damp and all around me I heard echoing droplets of water. One landed on my upper lip. It tasted of vinegar and chalk.

I came to the eighth floor, and stopped to get my breath

back. The smell of thrice-boiled cabbage filled the corridor, but it was better than the smell of dogshit and decaying scraps on the way up. I found the door. On a sellotaped square of card was typed:

Romanu, P.
Moranu, O.

There was no answer when I knocked so I waited, crouching at the bottom of the door. In the darkness I heard some keys rattle and steps heading up to this level. Emerging from the stairwell, pale and exhausted, in a dirty, once-white clinical coat and flat-heeled shoes, was Ottilia Moranu, the doctor from the hospital. She had a torch, and as she saw me struggling to stand up, she shone it full in my face.

'Who are you?' She made for the door and kept the torch in my eyes.

'We met. In the hospital.' I spoke in English.

'Get away from me,' she edged back into the doorway.

'My friend, my colleague, Rodica... you were the doctor on duty. That terrible night.'

Ottilia quickly recovered: '*That terrible night?* You mean that normal, regular, standard night in a Romanian hospital you happened to visit once?'

The flat was tiny, a single sitting room/kitchen/dining room, with a bathroom and a bedroom to the side. Ottilia put on a gas lamp. In its unsteady flames, the ceiling lowered itself onto us, the walls contracted. She flicked on the light switches just in case, but there was no current.

'Tea,' she offered. 'Or water?' She lit a hob connected to a portable butane bottle. A tin of North Korean pilchards stood beside a half-loaf of bread covered with a damp cloth. We sat down, she at the bar stool in front of her food, I on the sofa bed. I made space, moving the blankets and pillow that were folded across it. A guitar case and an amplifier leaned against the wall.

'He's not been back for those?'

Ottilia had her back to me, her elbow on the table and the fork hovering between tin and mouth. The fish was a rust-coloured marine sludge and its smell filled the room.

'No. No word. No one has heard anything. We expected to hear straight afterwards, and he would not have escaped, certainly not without saying something.'

'I was there. We saw no sign that he was thinking of leaving. In fact, he headed back into Romania.'

Ottilia looked at me, surprised. 'What were you doing with them? You're just a tourist here. Sorry...' she refined '...a *visitor*.'

I explained. Then I asked her what she had to do with Petre.

'He's my half-brother. Different fathers. Petre was born when I was four. We grew up together.' She looked me in the eye. 'He said nothing about you.'

'Maybe not, but we're friends. I hope we are friends.' Something stopped me from phrasing that in the past tense. Ottilia sensed it anyway, that implied pastness, because she stopped eating and put her face in her hands.

'I'm worried. I've heard nothing. No letter, no calls, nothing. There's no one from the group left to talk to. Petre hasn't been to classes or rehearsals since, and he's never missed one. His friend Vintul's gone too.'

'What do you think's happened?'

'I think they've been captured. But if they had there would be something, some message, some word. And most importantly reprisals against friends and family. Me, for example. There's been nothing. In any case, Petre is as unlikely to leave the country as I am.'

She sat for a minute and said nothing. 'He always left

messages at the hospital...' The sentence petered out. There was nowhere for it to go except into the darkness that talking keeps at bay. Ottilia put down her fork, flipped open the pedal bin, and dumped the tin into the clanging cylinder. She looked defeated.

'I was afraid this would happen. I told him: "Please – stop this, or at least get out yourself once and for all." But he told me not to worry, that he'd never leave, that he was protected. He liked to say that there were two kinds of people – people who lost themselves in exile and people who found themselves. He knew he'd lose himself, and I know he'd never leave.'

'What did he mean, *protected*?'

'I asked but he never answered. Who would protect him?'

I put my arm around her, and felt her thin shoulders through the blouse, the tight strap of her bra biting into her. Her feet were swollen and her hands scrubbed and raw. I ran my finger along her bitten nails, the skin red and flaking where she had attacked the cuticles. Her face was thin and drawn. I tried to imagine what she would look like happy, well slept and properly fed. There was something Greek about her, with her dark brown eyes and high cheekbones, her thick crinkled hair pulled back with a Monocom clip but which kept tumbling over her eyes: a ruthlessly suppressed beauty.

I offered her images of hope – Petre hiding out underground, Petre out of the country waiting to make contact, Petre shopping for guitars in Carnaby Street... She did me the kindness of nodding once or twice, tightening her fingers around mine as I spoke.

I made some tea, the British reflex. As the water rolled to a boil, I watched her on the sofa. Her head hung down; her knees were clamped together, her hands clenched. Then, as I poured the tea, Ottilia was up and rearranging herself. She went to the bathroom and I heard the tap splutter. A few minutes later she returned, barefoot and wearing a home-made dress of colourful peasant cloth, her hair free to fall where it wished, her cheeks scrubbed and full of colour. She smiled – pure fortitude – and got out a bottle of Tsuica, slugged back a bracing nip then wiped her mouth with the back of her hand.

'I must work now – I have things to prepare for tomorrow, case notes which no one will read, and then sleep. Thank you for coming. I will tell you as soon as I hear something.'

'Well?' asked Leo. Then, seeing me wince as I climbed into the car, 'sorry – I've farted up a bit of a storm in here. The old soya salami I'm afraid. It'll clear up once we start moving.'

As the breeze cut in through the open windows, Leo listened to my account of meeting Ottilia and said nothing. I kept saying the same things in different words, as if by doing so I might surprise some new meaning in them.

'OK, OK,' said Leo, 'I get the message. Just let me think for a moment.'

But after ten minutes he had still said nothing. 'Leo, what is it?' I asked. 'I know you're thinking something. Just tell me!'

'You're not going to like this, but fuck it, I'm probably wrong anyway, and if I'm right it's not really your fault, it's the fault of the bastard system. But here goes: you introduced Petre to Cilea, didn't you?'

'Yes, just the once,' I replied, unable to see the point of the question. I was tired and my tiredness was making me obtuse.

'Once is enough around here. So: they meet, but obviously don't want to speak to each other, in the InterContinental hotel, with Nicu Ceauşescu, Manea Constantin, Ion Stoicu and fuck knows how many other trolls, hacks, spies and stooges all around them. She's the daughter of a top Party boss, he's... what? Some student up to his neck in trouble. Then a few days later, Petre and Vintul go off on a mission they've done ten times before, and suddenly they disappear.'

It was more than a possibility now, it was likelihood, and it had been there, inside me, feeding my unease, my vague guilt for weeks. Now it was there fully formed, a sick wrenching feeling: something had happened and more likely than not it could be traced to me.

'You don't know. No one knows anything for sure.' Leo was backtracking now, a sure sign that he thought he had hit on something, 'there's all sorts of reasons they might have got caught, all kinds of ways someone might have found out.'

He was driving so slowly that a policeman flagged us to the side of the street and demanded our IDs. There was no backchat or bonhomie from Leo, just sullen co-operation. The policeman checked our papers and waved us on, puzzled. He knew Leo's reputation and expected something more lively, an extravagant bribe or a *risqué* joke.

'I'm dropping you at your flat. I want you to forget about this for now. Just leave it. And whatever you do, don't go and have it out with Cilea. Let me see what I can find out.'

Thirteen

It was the fourteenth of July, Bastille Day, when the expat community looked forward to the French Embassy's big *soirée*. The only person who refused the invitation was the Princess, who each year sent back the same letter. It began 'I thank his Excellency the Ambassador for his kind invitation, but he must know that I do not consider the fourteenth of July to be a day of celebration...' and went on to elaborate a long history of Republican atrocity and failure. Someone walking along Bucharest's Piaţa Republicii on July Fourteenth 1989 would have agreed with her. Even with the daily queues and shortages, the ubiquitous police and Securitate, the place felt even more purged and prostrate than usual.

I had nearly reached the university by the time I realised why. The streets were full of people carrying typewriters. This was no easy feat: most of the machines were the old iron models, with Bakelite keys on long articulated fingers, beautifully kept antiques in perfect order. From the TAROM offices two men were carrying out an electric typewriter the size of a baby elephant. Office girls with manicured nails and immaculate hair stood outside looking sad as the beast was hauled into a waiting van.

This scheme, known as 'typewriter day', was an annual event, designed to keep records of any instrument that might be used for dissident or *samizdat* publications. If so it was a laborious way of keeping track – sending dozens of officers around town to test typewriters must involve massive administrative time and cost. But then this was not reactive repression but preventative. Leo had told me about the 'National Handwriting Archive', brainchild of Elena Ceaușescu. This was the machine version, logging the imprint, tug and slant of every key of every typewriter in the land. The old joke was that Professor Doctor Mrs Ceaușescu had invested in research into telepathy to set up an archive that recorded the accent and timbre of one's thoughts.

I went to the staff room to make coffee, a reflex action that occasionally surfaced from a previous existence, since there was never any coffee and the hob had long ago broken. The perpetually out-of-order photocopier, a hulking East German contraption, had chosen today to begin working again. A small crowd, for whom the machine's operational state was just a sort of urban myth, watched excitedly. It ground out a limp sheet of paper, sputtered, then stopped.

There was a note on my office door from Professor Ionescu asking me to pay him a visit. He was twitchy. A gleaming, typewriter-shaped square of desk in front of him was framed in a border of dust.

'Please go to the university car park, where someone is waiting for you,' he said.

'Who?' I asked. Ionescu's sobriety was an ill omen. 'You have a visitor. Deputy Minister Manca Constantin has asked to see you. I do not know what it is about, and it may be that I will not be here much longer to find out. I may be joining the janitorial staff. Now please go.'

Outside I found a black Mercedes with Party plates. Two smiling young men, well-groomed, smartly suited and smelling of French aftershave, climbed out. They were polite too – another worrying sign.

'*Domnul*, we would like you to come with us. You are invited to meet somebody,' said the first, firm but unthreatening in the manner of those who do not need to threaten. I wondered whether they knew the clichéd nature of what we were playing out. Given the black market in American action films and Mafia sagas, it seemed probable that they did: two minders in a black limo making me an offer I couldn't refuse.

'That would be terrific, but I'm afraid I'm working. I have a lecture to give.'

'Everything is fine. It has been taken care of with your professor. Now please,' said the other, gesturing into the tan-upholstered interior of the car, 'we will bring you back after lunch.' The Mercedes' windows were of smoked glass and the conditioned air inside was icy. Morgue temperature, I thought as my teeth chattered.

There were no checks for us as we slid into the courtyard of the Interior Ministry, parked and walked into the building's lobby.

I was taken upstairs and shown into a vast room with blank walls and high ceilings with hammer and sickle mouldings. There was one desk, a vast reinforced-glass slab on two marble trestles, and behind it French windows flanked, as usual, by portraits of the Ceauşescus. The figure behind the desk stood with his hand out in greeting: Manea Constantin, the deputy Interior Minister, in a charcoal suit and Savile Row shirt that was the rich dark blue of a winter afternoon sky. A few papers had been pushed to one extremity of the desk, and an espresso machine sat squarely in the centre, foreign magazines in a haphazard pile alongside it. An atomiser of *Signor Ricci*, retailing at thirty-odd quid a bottle in duty-free, served both as eau de cologne and all-round room freshener.

In an annexe, two secretaries typed. One was square and matronly, the other slim and beautiful and so much like Cilea that I had to look again to make sure it wasn't. She turned and smiled; she exuded mistresshood, the unattainable sexual availability of the powerful man's consort.

'Call me Manea,' he said charmingly. As *if*, I thought, my sweaty hand in his, two not-so-secretly holstered flunkeys on either side of me. 'I thought we might spend a morning together... getting to know each other. I like to know who my daughter's friends are.'

'*Were*,' I corrected, 'I haven't spoken to her for a month and she hasn't returned my calls.'

'But first a shave,' he said, ignoring me. It was not how I expected the morning to go.

The car took us, through halted traffic and disregarded traffic lights, to the InterContinental Hotel. I was starting to feel that the place was cursed, and I cursed always to return to it. The manager dropped some tourists' luggage with a crash and showed us to the hotel's 'Aesthetic Centre', where two barbers were waiting on our arrival.

We sat side by side as the hot towels and razors came out. Manea Constantin spoke to me in the mirror. I kept turning to face him, but the barber had my head jammed. Just as well – the razor was so sharp it would probably not even hurt when it cut, not until I saw the blood. The blade was hot, the steel smooth in its thin, lethal slide on wet skin. My eyes watered as he hitched up a nostril and the blade scraped right up into the cavity. I fought back a sneeze.

'Vlad the Impaler used to slit open the nostrils of his enemies so they flapped like rags in the wind,' said Manea, by way of putting me at my ease.

The barber sprinkled some mentholated astringent over our heads and necks and began a Turkish cranial massage. It felt as if my skin was being peeled off, stretched out and tanned across my skull. I felt a high of physical health.

Constantin was practised at mirror talk, and enjoyed the

symbolism of it: everything inverted, him talking to me via my reflection and I talking to him via his. He was an intelligent and graceful conversationalist, and I found myself forgetting that he was probably as corrupt as the rest of them, and as ruthless. He was certainly his daughter's father: he had that same detachment from all he was implicated in, that same nonchalance in the midst of responsibility. The difference was that where Cilea could merely distance herself from it all, Manea implemented it. I asked him about what I had just seen in the university, about what might happen to Ionescu.

'That charade this afternoon, the typewriters...?' He laughed, 'it is now a tradition, like folk dancing and basket weaving, but nothing to do with me. Orders from the highest place. As for the demotion of your professor, that is the responsibility of Comrade Stoicu. I do not interfere in his affairs. How do they say it in England? I do not cross onto his patch.'

'The National Handwriting Archive?' I began. He cut me off with a laugh. 'Yes, I too have heard of that. Again, Comrade Stoicu's department. A very expensive and very stupid initiative. Next you will be asking me about the research into telepathy...'

Manea settled back and relaxed. We said nothing more until the barbers were brushing the hairs from our collars.

'Now you will be my guest at the Politburo restaurant in Snagov.'

Forty minutes later we were there. The journey out of town had taken us across some rubble-strewn roads. In Leo's Skoda it would have been a boneshaking nervejangler of a journey. In Manea's ministerial limo it was like a car journey on a fifties film set, the landscape rewinding in the tinted glass.

The Snagov 'Socialist Village' was a twenty-acre gated compound of villas and facilities for highly placed Party officials: health clubs, gyms, saunas, skin care and anti-ageing treatment centres. There were shops with blacked-out windows selling white goods, luxury food, designer clothes. Politburo wives shopped and dined while their children rode western motorbikes to cinemas showing US action films. Unlike Bucharest itself, the place was orderly and shiny; a cross between Switzerland and the retirement belt of Florida – an Iron Curtain *Costa Geriatrica*.

What brought the average age down was a two-abreast file of uniformed boys and girls. 'Young Pioneers', the Party's children's corps, were goose-stepping with knapsacks on their backs, compasses and water bottles around their necks. They walked in step and sung heroic songs, a phalanx of communist Tintins marching to the beat of an automated childhood. 'Two Planks' sped past on a red Vespa, wearing Ray-Bans and a Lacoste polo shirt.

'This is the Central Committee compound,' explained Constantin, 'though some of us prefer to live in town. I'll be hosting a Foreign Office delegation from your country here in December. I shall send you an invitation.'

Thanks, thanks very much, I thought. Come Christmas, that would be all I needed: standing in a suit while Romanian Party bosses mingled with diplomats, sleazy defence contractors and some damp-lipped Tory undersecretary for closet arms sales. 'I'll pencil it in,' I replied in Romanian, trying for sarcasm, a difficult nuance in a foreign tongue. The worst was that I knew I would probably go.

We were shown our table in the modern dining room. Unlike Capşa the room was boxy and ascetic; also unlike Capşa, it had an extensive menu with a prodigious wine list. Everything was available, from the oysters to the wild boar, the Cheval Blanc to the Chateau Talbot. The waiters looked seconded from some defence academy. They probably doubled as paratroopers, ready to protect the Party's higher echelons in the event of an uprising. Or, it struck me later, to watch and incarcerate them in the event of a *coup*.

In the corner was a group of senior army officers. The conversation was loud, the drinks being poured and downed so fast the bottles barely had time to touch the tablecloths. Constantin ordered a gin and tonic, which came in a tall Party-crested tumbler. I had a Coca-Cola. The ambient music that came from the loudspeakers sounded like a crematorium organ played at one-and-a-half times normal speed.

'The Comrade has his Palace here,' said Constantin, pointing beyond the ponderous stone terrace. Below it, small pedalos and leisure boats bobbed along a clear blue lake. Over and beyond the grounds, I could just make out the turret of a tower around which the helicopter circled. 'Looks like he's home,' I said brightly, pointing. Ceauşescu had forty-one villas and twenty-one palaces, each with a retinue of staff on alert. Each probably had a helicopter circling around it too. 'I hear Nicu lives nearby too,' I added.

At the mention of Nicu, Constantin put down his glass and wiped his mouth with a hammer and sickle-crested napkin. One of the waiters twitched but managed not to turn around.

'The Comrade's favourite son, yes. Our minister for sport and youth affairs is a troubled young man, but we have learned to deal with his personal problems. Something he has yet to do...'

People went out of their way to greet Manea as they passed. I recognised some faces from the *nomenklatura* shops and restaurants, the nightclub-and-foreign-embassy circuit. With some he conferred in a low voice, or wrote times and dates for meetings into his Party diary. He seemed popular, and it struck me that he probably didn't just rely on power to get things done but on something approaching loyalty and fellow-feeling. Not least significant, I thought, was the number of junior people who spoke to him, and the staff he treated with courtesy, though never once hazarding his air of power both copious and withheld.

The army table was joined by Stoicu, who gave a dry contemptuous little nod towards Manea, looked me over and sat down. He showed no sign of recognising me from the night with the Serbs, but it was impossible to read those tiny frisky eyes pinned into the rolls of flesh that enfolded any expression before it took hold on his face. He proposed a toast: 'To the Comrade!' It meant everyone else had to get up, as to be seen not to do so would be cause for comment. Manea, in the middle of his *coq au vin*, had to join in. More toasts followed: to Elena, to the Young Pioneers, to the anti-fascist struggle, so that by the end most of the dining room was up and down every two minutes. People began to hurry their meals and leave.

We took our coffee onto the terrace, Manea lighting up a Sobranie and I sticking to my Carpati. 'Going native, I see,' he commented. Inside, Stoicu's clan had started singing. Manea jerked his head back towards them: 'You can abolish class differences, but somehow they always come out during meals, don't you think?'

'I thought you were starting to deal with that by abolishing meals altogether,' I replied, 'for the populace at large, I mean...'

'*Touché!* Yes indeed, a quick riposte. But I must say your appetite has remained unaffected by the hardship. The way that veal went down, that *crème brûlée*...'

'True enough – I've learned to compartmentalise.' I took a long draw of my Carpati.

'Oh, I think you knew how to compartmentalise long before you came to Romania... Cilea tells me you helped her get that trip to London. I'm very grateful. If there is anything I can do for you, you will let me know. You will also, I hope, treat her well.'

'She can look after herself, and as far as I can tell that's all she ever does...' I said.

Manea put down his glass and laughed. 'Yes, a lot of people think that of her. I wish I thought it was true, though...' He became serious: 'She says you're blaming her for something that happened to your friends. I don't want to know the details. But I can tell you it's nothing to do with her.'

'You seem very sure of this... this thing that you don't know about.'

He finished his cigarette and looked out over the terrace, an arm over my shoulder, and spoke up close. 'Let me tell you how you perceive it, or how you are being encouraged to perceive it: Cilea finds out what is going on through you; she then tells me; I then give orders. Your friends are gone. But why should I care about what a bunch of hippies does? Suppose I already knew, have known for a long time, and never did anything? Why would I act now?'

'*Did* you know?'

'That is not the point – if so, I did nothing about it.'

'Perhaps you passed on the information to someone who did...' With napkins tied around their necks, hunched over their food, each one with crew-cut hair, small ears, and a flaccid pink face, Stoicu and his minions looked like the pigs in a cartoon of Orwell's *Animal Farm*. I turned back to Manea who was, in more respects than not, one of them. 'Anyway, people don't just disappear!'

Manea raised his eyebrows and laughed. 'Oh no? Are you quite sure about that?'

He stirred his coffee for a few moments, then spoke confidentially: 'I am telling you this – and it is dangerous for me, even I have to report on our conversation now – I am telling you this because of Cilea, and I too am sorry that she is no longer with you. I will explain why another time, but for now let me say this: you can think what you like of me, but she has nothing to do with any of it. None of us is safe at the moment. It's department against department, minister against minister. Every organisation, every group of friends is infiltrated. Everything is known, it's just a question of who acts on that knowledge and when, and why they decide to do so. You find out *why* your friends have been pulled in – *if* they have been – and you'll know who did it.'

I nodded. I saw the sense in that; more exactly, I understood the contortions of state paranoia that caused it to make sense. Someone somewhere always knew what you were doing; several people at a time did. But what did they do with the knowledge? Use it? Trade or barter it? Perhaps several people knowing at a time, each with different or conflicting agendas, cancelled out the knowledge, gave you a cover second only to anonymity, which was in any case impossible? That was how Leo worked, relying on the informational bottleneck to pursue his shady career and to pursue, too, his acts of restitution and commemoration.

Behind us was a group of ministers brandishing building plans and two architects in black-framed spectacles and roll-neck sweaters. Manea took my elbow and whispered: 'Everything's tightening up. It happens from time to time, because some part of the system's unstable, or just because the Comrade is afraid. It may loosen again in a few months. Perhaps things will be clearer then. For now, you keep your head down.'

Others joined us on the terrace. Manea stopped talking and we listened instead to the architects and their ministers. One of the ministers was explaining that the artificial canal currently being dug in the city centre was to be re-routed. The map, opened out across his knees, bore a crude red line straight through several districts. One of the architects quietly but steadfastly pointed out that this involved not only the refilling of the vast and now useless ditch they had spent the last three months digging, but the demolition of two old suburbs. The young and eager-looking woman minister replied with a well-known slogan: 'These are uncharted waters, but we are well-captained.' The architect argued his case, never raising his voice, running his finger along the fat red line that tore through the map of Bucharest. There was a silence, as always follows one who has gone too far. The minister changed tack, asked him outright if he was ready for the consequences of abandoning the project. He said he was. He made to get up and leave, thanking her for lunch. His colleague shuffled in his seat. One of the deputies, until now silently watching, put down his coffee, laid his hand on the architect's shoulder, and spoke slowly, calmly, in a menacing stage whisper designed to be overheard.

'Listen, you bourgeois pig. This is how it goes: you leave here and we do the work anyway, except it'll be you and your whole clan of Yids digging the new canal seven days a week. It's goodbye nine to five and the flat in Herastrau, and hello nightshift and worker's hostel. Your kids... what are they? Four and six? Might get rehomed in one of our State orphanages – you know about them? – maybe down in Iaşi. If you like your black pullovers and your Johnnie Walker, and your wife likes her western tampons, you just nod your head and we'll all forget about your lapse in socialist taste.'

The architect was alone. His colleague turned away. The minister looked down at her shoes. The others at the table pretended not to hear, but like us they would remember every word. Manea put down his coffee and shook his head, though he must have said and doubtless done worse things himself.

Then a remarkable thing happened. The architect dislodged the man's hand from his shoulder and walked off, throwing his napkin onto the table. His colleague buried his head in his hands. The minister was speechless; there was no slogan to hand for this eventuality. The enforcer smiled a thin, vicious smile of humiliated sadism.

I must have been watching and listening too obviously, as Manea took me by the arm and guided me across the terrace and into the gardens.

'Jesus, that was brave. What'll happen to him now?'

'He'll get a cooling-off period, and if he doesn't play, some of what that bastard threatened will happen. Most of it probably. Don't worry – to get this far he must have done some pretty unsavoury things himself. We've got no heroes here. Or if we have this isn't where you'll find them.'

I imagined a day of reckoning in which scores were settled and judgments meted out. Here in Romania, I envisaged a set of trials in which the judges would find the accused guilty, then swap places with them. In the end I was not far wrong – except about the verdicts.

Manea received a message on his pager. Seconds later, the black Mercedes lounged down an avenue of linden trees. In their threadbare shade, the Young Pioneers were eating a picnic of soya salami and Rocola. There must have been forty or fifty children sitting in a circle and eating in silence, facing straight ahead, heads still and jaws munching, like clockwork infants.

Manea spoke again: 'Your friend Trofim must be enjoying writing his memoirs. I hear they are the memoirs of a good communist, but dull. He may wish to keep them that way. But if he doesn't he may be needing friends. And in this case I do not mean friends abroad.'

'Is that a threat?' I asked.

'You persist in misreading me. It is not a threat. On the contrary. *He* will know what it is. Tell him.' Manea was exasperated, the slick Party man hurt at not being trusted. As we drove back, I wondered if I had offended him with my smart-arse comments and my readiness to interpret all he said in the worst way possible.

Stepping out of the car I turned back and apologised. 'I'm sorry. I didn't mean to be cynical, it's just habit. I don't need to tell you how hard it is know who to trust...' Manea brushed away the slight, and as his arm moved I caught a whiff of his aftershave, still fresh and clean and lemony despite the heat. I was sweating, uncomfortable inside my skin, conscious of my own smell.

'Of course you shouldn't trust me, but maybe you should believe me...' he smiled, 'you still don't know the difference?'

I was no closer to finding out what had happened to Petre and Vintul, but I had seen the way things worked, and I believed Manea when he told me that Cilea had had nothing to do with it. Whatever *it* was. Would Leo?

On my way back to my office I stopped on the landing of the second floor and looked out across the Bucharest skyline. Somewhere out there, the architect was waiting to learn his fate. Somewhere perhaps, Vintul and Petre and the others were being kept or, I hoped, were in hiding. The cranes jutted out everywhere; there was not a single piece of the horizon that wasn't crane-crammed and prickling with scaffolding. That Snagov dining room was the symbol of the new Bucharest: behind communism's inert symmetries, the great dead surfaces of marble or granite, there were the convoluted, winding schemes that took root and flourished and devoured both themselves and those who engineered them. Manea, Stoicu, Trofim, Ionescu, the purged and the purging... all were part of that tail-chasing paranoia, that frenzy of self-policing that boiled away inside the expressionless monolith of the Party.

What I noticed first were the boxes outside Ionescu's office.

Framed diplomas were being wrapped in old copies of *Scînteia* by a snuffling Rodica and placed into boxes by Micu, who, in his elaborate uniform, looked like an old soldier burying his fallen comrades on a battlefield. Inside, Leo and Ionescu sat looking mournful with a bottle of Tsuica.

'How am I going to break it to her indoors? I suppose I shall just have to lay it upon her straight.' Ionescu's gift for peculiarly off-key English was still with him, though he might not be putting it to use in his new job.

'It's not a purge, not really. Think of it as a shuffle. You'll be back in no time,' Leo was spinning for the positive: 'Look on the bright side – at least you don't have to oversee the computerisation of the faculty!' Ionescu's expression confirmed his refusal to cave in to optimism. 'When's the new man coming in?' Leo continued, 'And more to the point: who is it?'

'I have not been told. Nobody will tell me,' Ionescu emitted a tragic exhalation.

We loaded his things into Leo's car. So far down the pecking order had the rumours percolated that even the drivers in the staff car pound knew of Ionescu's demotion. Colleagues looked away or crossed the corridor to avoid him. Some might visit him when things calmed down, but for now it was the arm's-length principle. He was starting to become invisible, disappearing at the edges. His nameplate would be off the door by 5 pm, his books off the library shelves by Monday. As we said goodbye, a man in blue overalls, his own purged predecessor, came to shake his hand.

The next stage would be even harder for Ionescu: explaining to his wife why she had to move out of her Herastrau duplex and into some already-decrepit brand new two-roomer on the outskirts. That's if they were lucky enough to be staying in town.

Ionescu would be back next Monday to hear about his

new job. It could be anything from provincial parking attendant to kitchen porter in the canteen's ghost-ship of a catering wing.

'Library assistant!' Leo called jubilantly down the receiver, 'he's been made library assistant! Here!'

It was the Saturday morning. I was alone with the radio on, listening to a World Service programme about the Polish Solidarity Movement. I had spent the night in a turmoil of nightmare, and had woken at 4 am screaming into my sweat-drenched sheets and vomiting into the sink from a shock so violent it had gripped my body as well as my mind. My recurring nightmare, that I thought I had left behind in London, was back: my parents, calm and happy together as they never were in life, beckoning me from across an enormous room. Now that I was in Romania, that room became the mouldy marbled cavern on the Boulevard of Socialist Victory, the hellish disco or the Snagov dining room I had been to with Manea. As I came closer to them, I realised that they were warning me to stay away, begging me stay away from them. They writhed and held themselves, doubled over in pain, then finally burned away at the edges like leaves, their faces turning to bone and ash as they screamed in silence.

The dream had been with me for years, even when my father was alive. Here in Bucharest I thought I had escaped it. Now it was clear it had merely been internalising the new décor. It came back more ferocious than ever, and though I had been up for hours its aura still had not cleared. I could still smell burning.

After months of seemingly effortless adjustment, everything I had left behind was crowding back into me, using sleep as its means of entry. Cilea had left me; I was guilty of something, I didn't know what, to do with Petre and Vintul; I was caught up amid icebergs of corruption I barely saw the tips of, and at every moment of every day I was in danger from one or other of the activities I was involved in without ever being *part of.* Worst of all, I had nowhere and nothing to go back to. *Well, wasn't that what you wanted?* I heard myself ask.

'And that's the good news?' I asked, unable to rise to Leo's enthusiasm.

'Think about it – it could have been a hell of a lot worse: he could have been cleaning toilets in Turda...' I recalled a place of that name, somewhere to the north-east, and possessed of a small seat of learning, 'he gets to read, doesn't have to leave town, we get to see him. Trust me, it's better than it could have been.'

'What's the bad news?'

'The new boss, Popea. Slimeball. Informer. Yes-man. Brontë specialist.' These faults – was Leo listing them in ascending or descending order of perfidy? Ion Popea, a paranoid apparatchik so focussed on finding hidden meanings in everything you said that even your remarks about the weather were scrutinised for political content. Leo joked that Popea submitted everything he said to the Party's 'Workplace Conversation Unit' a week in advance. 'But it's OK, I've got something on him,' added Leo mysteriously.

I told Trofim what had happened when we met in the park that afternoon. I had still not shaken off my nightmare, and felt weak and exhausted.

'The first law of a good purge is that it must be random; the second, that it must culminate in a promotion that sets the other pretenders to the job against each other and not the system; the third is that people must spend more energy trying to work out what it means than complaining about its unjustness. Sounds like a classic example of the genre. Very nice.' Trofim was evaluating it aesthetically, a dealer approving of a fine *objet d'art.*

'Why would they sack Ionescu? He's done nothing wrong, he's a respected academic, he's obviously a good Party man...'

'In his way, yes he is. It's possibly nothing to do with the university, but an internal Securitate purge. Ah, the old days... after the purge, the interpretation of the purge,' Trofim settled himself on the bench and lit his pipe. 'I do miss it, the intrigue, the back room deals, the whole chess game of Party politics... my guess is Ionescu was unreliable, erratic, or using his Securitate position to further his academic career. That's the wrong way round. He's been getting better-known and better-liked, his work has been getting published abroad. He's been letting things slide! People aren't afraid of him, he's respected, he runs a happy department, insofar as that's possible here. These things get noticed you know...'

'Everyone knows he's as ruthless as the rest of them. I've seen him in action. He just hides it well. He's just not a complete bastard.'

'I remember Ionescu when he started out. A junior lecturer. Long before Ceauşescu – late fifties. Young and keen and razor-sharp, but always the gentle persuader, that was Ionescu. He had a boss and mentor, a kind, cultivated old gentleman, and a good Party man. Serafim he was called, a Jew who had survived all the purges of the forties and fifties. He helped Ionescu onto the ladder, put him on committees... launched him. He got Ionescu this coveted job in his department, promoted him, sponsored his rise up the ranks. One day, during one of the 'Romanianisation' purges, the old man arrived at work and found his things had been moved out and left in the corridor – this was before they did you the courtesy of providing boxes. The old prof's first reaction was to visit Ionescu. He found Ionescu outside *his* office, with all *his* things in the corridor. "My poor friend," said the old man to his *protégé*, "I am sorry to have implicated you in this. It is too late for me, but I will do my best to have you exonerated."

Ionescu, so the story goes, said nothing; he simply took Serafim's office key out of his hand, walked straight into his newly vacant office and shut the door. What about that? The poor man thought Ionescu was getting purged too! When all the time it was Ionescu who had fingered him to get his job!'

'I can't believe that,' I said, 'Ionescu would at least have explained...'

'Explained what? I am just telling you the story as it happened. That's how Ionescu got his first senior post. No one underestimated him after that... But do not get worked up. Life is full of such stories, ours at any rate. We all take our turn.'

Trofim took my arm: 'You mustn't think that I have no regrets. I do, it's just that there were – there still are – contexts for all we did wrong. I know that to you I am one of the many people who made this place what it is.' He looked at me but I said nothing. It was himself he was talking to – I was just the context for him to speak it aloud. 'There was a price to pay and at the time it was the right price, but it was never meant to remain like this. One generation of repression, perhaps two. And yes, some killing. But it was not an end in itself. We thought we had time, you see: we played the long game. But it was never a game.' He shook his head: 'And there was never long enough.'

'Will you write that in your book, I mean in those words?' I asked.

'Yes, if you can remember them when we get home,' he laughed sadly and took my arm.

Trofim's secretary was just leaving as we arrived. Her hair, like some industrial-modernist sculpture, looked coiffed in fully set cement, and the room smelled of the spray she used to hold it in place.

He disappeared into the *bijou* kitchen. Trofim had that habit, peculiar to those with little domestic know-how, of holding utensils and staring at them, waiting for clues to their use to be transmitted through his palm to his cognitive faculties. There was a new coffee machine on the windowsill, gleaming in designer black and silver, and definitely not from Monocom. Trofim peered round the back of the machine, looking for somewhere to put in the water, or the coffee, or both. Ten minutes later he came out onto the balcony with his usual long-handled Arabic coffee pot, a present from a UN PLO delegation, steaming with sweet cardamon-scented coffee.

'What we have on the computer today is the morning's dictation. Up to and including the last Olympics. I think there will be one more chapter, say, two weeks' more work, and then we can think about the next step.'

I suddenly remembered Manea Constantin's message and passed it on to Trofim. 'I'm not sure how to interpret it, but there it is anyway,' I added in a throwaway tone that I hoped disguised my curiosity.

'Very simple. The minister knows, or thinks he knows, I am up to something. This is his way of saying that other people do too, people who may not be as – what? – tolerant as him. He is offering me something, in exchange for which I must offer him something.'

'What?'

'He does not know yet; nor do I. But yes, thank you for the message – it is good news, I suppose.'

We spent the afternoon on his files. Our routine: first I fished the day's file from the computer's virtual trash can. Then I scrolled down paragraph by paragraph, while Trofim, sitting to my right, dictated his additions. It usually took us two or three hours. I then copied everything onto a diskette and replaced it in the trash, before taking the files to be printed in the British Council library, a tatty prefab building inside the embassy grounds.

Today, as I left the building with the printed sheets, Giles Wintersmith loomed up behind me. 'The draught,' Leo called him, a reference not just to his ability to chill a room, but to the ripple of shivers by which one sensed his imminence. I had that now, and turned to face him: grey watery eyes, pale oily skin polished to translucence, a sharp thin beard and hair that grew a sheen of grease even as you watched. Since the ambassador, like some public school headmaster, had declared summertime 'shirtsleeve order', Wintersmith wore a white short-sleeved shirt with brown semicircles of sweat under the arms. The inside of his open collar looked like the ring of dirt in a bath. His arms were white and pimpled, crossed over his chest and bent upwards like deep-frozen chicken wings.

We were now on page 180 of Trofim's memoirs. I held the day's papers to me, fifteen pages, the only copies of the latest instalment. Beside them, the diskette with the first two thirds of the book. Wintersmith noticed me clutching the satchel.

'Drink?' He tried for a smile: a thin, vampiric leer of yellow teeth.

I sat in the Shit and Hassle while Wintersmith ordered at the bar. The place smelled of sweat and smoke and old lager. Beer towels hung sweating but never drying over bar pumps: Worthington's, Skol, Guinness. The tabletops were streaked with bullet-shaped burn marks where forgotten cigarettes had consumed themselves on the veneer. The windows were open but the air had no intention of clearing. There was a darts board with one drooping arrow stuck in the bullseye, and an Aunt Sally range that doubled as a children's play area. A calendar of *Page 3 Lovelies* was pinned behind the bar. We might have been in any pub in middle England, but this was like a film set; you half-expected the scenery to clatter to the ground. To counterbalance the diplomats, there was a different crowd of Brits: Embassy security guards, ex-police or ex-army; construction workers or decorators sent from home to do up this or that wing of the compound; a few businessmen on foreign sales trips thirsty for a familiar brand. A few tables away a Geordie handyman, beyond tipsy, was loudly going through a roster of people in line for one of his Glasgow kisses. At the back of the room an embassy wife, pale and graceful and etherealised with boredom, watched her children squabbling over last month's *Beano*. A Friday afternoon in the Home Counties.

Wintersmith sat down. 'You've rather thrown yourself into things out there, haven't you?' he asked, waving his long fingers at the world beyond the embassy gates. 'We don't see you much at embassy dos either. We do our best, you know, trying to put together a sort of scene...' It was phrased as an apology but the tone implied I was arrogant and thought myself better than my own people, whoever they were.

'Cheers,' I took a deep drink from my pint. The room was cool but the sweat stung my eyes. I wiped my brow. Wintersmith hesitated over his half-pint and watched me. A piece of advice from my father came to me, the only advice he'd ever given me: *never trust a man who drinks halves.*

'Are you all right?' Wintersmith asked, interested but not concerned.

I nodded and asked him bluntly what he wanted. I wouldn't get a straight answer, or even a short one, but it would do no harm to get him started. Most diplomats conversed like telegrams: short objectless phrases delivered in staccato rhythms. Not Wintersmith. His sentences came out in coils. 'I suppose that with all that time you spend with Leo O'Heix you've been getting to see quite a lot of what goes on? And word has it you're close to – if that's the right term these days...' he smirked, 'the daughter of a highly placed official...'

'Not especially – I do my job, see Leo, have a few friends.' I drank fast. Only two good gulps then I could leave.

'Bad news about Ionescu though – any thoughts on how that came about?'

I shook my head, tried to pull myself up from the table but felt woozy and sat back down. No lunch, all that coffee at Trofim's, the heat... all the same, it was only a pint of beer. Wintersmith watched me over the rim of his glass. 'It would be very helpful if you could keep your eyes open, if we could trust you to keep us informed...'

'Of what?' I was being obtuse. I knew what he was getting at. He knew I had access to all sorts of information and rumours, but really I *knew* nothing. There was no inside track, or there were so many inside tracks it didn't matter. Ionescu had been purged. So what? Did it mean anything more than if he hadn't? I had seen a booze-up get out of hand with some Serbs. I had seen Nicu Ceauşescu get kicked out of a night-club. What else? Gossip – unreadable, uninterpretable gossip. What bothered me was the whereabouts of Petre and Vintul. Would dealing with Wintersmith help with that?

He couldn't be trusted. I was used to that. But was he untrustworthy in ways I could rely on?

'You might find all sorts of information that means nothing to you. But it may mean something to us if we connected it up. If you just passed things on, no matter what... your predecessor Belanger was very helpful. He kept the Romania desk busy with titbits for two years.'

Belanger again, I thought. 'Any of it much good?' I asked.

'Sometimes just knowing is enough,' he replied. 'To help with the narrative, flesh out the context.'

'Anything in this for me, or is it a one-way deal?'

'What do you want?' Wintersmith sighed loftily as he said it: a pro dealing with an amateur.

'Find something out for me?'

I took the leap – more a leap of calculated mistrust than a leap of faith, but it would mean I owed him, and that was itself hard to swallow. I told him about Petre and Vintul. I told him the where and the when of the operation, leaving out my own and Leo's involvement.

'Who wants to know?' he asked. 'I mean, is it really you or is it someone else you're putting out feelers for?'

I wanted to leave Ottilia out of it. And Cilea. I invented some distant colleague who was related to one of the group and left it there. Wintersmith squinted at me, trying to decide if I was lying. My deceit had improved remarkably since my arrival in Bucharest, but I was not yet sure I could outwit the professionals.

Fortunately Wintersmith's need to give me a realpolitik lecture got the better of his scrutiny: 'What's happening is that all over Europe these regimes are falling. Not here. We've got a trade mission coming with the Foreign Secretary in a couple of months, and they're hoping to sell a lot of planes and helicopters. It'll be one of the biggest deals outside the Middle East. We're going to be stuck with Ceauşescu for a long time, believe me, so we're going to have to work with him. Look at it out there: the city's coming down around our ears, the Securitate's more powerful than ever. There are no dissidents. No one looks like they'll make anything happen. The Romanians won't – it's not in their nature. No one helps those who can't help themselves. The place is a basket case, but a basket case with money.'

I wasn't interested. Rising to leave I asked him: 'Will you see what you can find out about those two boys?'

'Will you keep me up to date? What's going on in the university, student groups, any flashpoints of discontent you hear about? Knowledge – it's a market, a commodity. Anything you can find out...' Wintersmith had been eyeing my satchel throughout our conversation. I kept it on my lap, one arm crossed over it. 'Writing a novel?' he asked. 'Only I saw you printing off a ream of paper back there. Must let me read it sometime.'

I tried to look dismissive. 'It's nothing. Just some translations I'm working on, a bit of poetry...' As I stood at the pub door, I felt nausea closing in, first in tiny ripples, then in stronger, rolling waves. 'You OK? You're looking... unsteady.' Wintersmith held out a hand towards me. The white, bony fingers were inset with a few strands of thick black hair. The hands looked suddenly disembodied, the hairs quivering like tentacles. I headed for the toilets to throw up.

When I returned Wintersmith was inspecting his right hand with a puzzled look. 'You'd better stay here for a while, you're in no shape to go home. As luck would have it, the embassy doctor's down for a few days this month. He's here now. I can get you seen first thing tomorrow.'

I stumbled out of the embassy and headed in the rough direction of home. After five minutes at a half-run, I steadied myself on the corner of the street. Somewhere, Motorcade sirens started up. I sat in the doorway of a closed bakery and rested my head on my knees.

I must have looked like an ordinary passer-by, exhausted with drink or apathy, or a day-shift worker dozing between connections. But my head span, my stomach lurched. I was producing sweat so fast my clothes were saturated.

A fierce kick to my thigh broke into my nausea: thick-heeled ankle boots, flared trousers. Securitate standard-issue. A young suited man stood over me, blocking the sun and jerking a thumb in the air, a signal doubtless picked up from US crime shows in which petty thieves in the Bronx are rousted by square-jawed cops. Perhaps he too watched *Kojak*. At least he had the right clothes. I tried to haul myself up, but my legs were shaky and the kick had deadened the muscle. He took my ID.

'Open.' He said it in English, pointing at my satchel.

'University papers,' I replied in Romanian. I was groggy, and the swirling sirens unbalanced me.

'Open.'

I opened the satchel, careful to let the sheets of Trofim's manuscript fall sideways blank side up. He put his hand in and felt around and was lifting the papers out when a burst of shouting broke from his walkie-talkie. He dropped the papers and answered a one-syllable affirmative. I strapped the satchel closed and made to leave. His hand took my shoulder and pulled me back. He raised his right hand and put his middle and index finger to his eyes, then pointed them back at me – *we're watching you*. He was thin and sharp-featured, not much older than me and six inches shorter. The Securitate's footsoldiers: taken in late adolescence from state orphanages and trained in combat and surveillance, they owed all they had to the state. I had no trouble remembering he was a trained killer: it was his blankness, the vacancy in the eyes, barely masked by the darting, paranoid agitation that passed for life.

I walked fast in the opposite direction, my spinning head now exacerbated by a thumping heart. Had it really been only ten minutes since the sirens? Time was distended; I was walking through syrup, every step slow and sticky and unreal. At the intersection, nothing but more Securitate and the road's tyre-beaten cobbles giving back the sunlight. The stale afternoon light was breaking up, and through a sickly prism the colours began to separate out. I felt top-heavy, swaying along the kerb. I stumbled off into a shop entrance to vomit again. Several painful dry heaves, and I was empty, wrung out. I could feel my body dehydrating, my skin tightening over the bones.

I pressed on through the backstreets, the long way round but clear of roadblocks at least. The sirens had faded but still no cars passed. They must have cordoned off the whole quarter, not just the roads the Comrade or his decoys were using. I heard a rush of engines behind me, their sticky tyres ripping down the one-way street. The Motorcade. Four black Dacias at seventy or eighty kilometres an hour down the small street, horns blaring. I jumped sideways and fell, my satchel strap catching at my throat as I went. The first car passed, and then the second. As I rose I drew level with the passenger window of the third. Behind the smoky glass I saw a pair of small startled eyes, the pinched face and pursed lips of the Comrade. He waved uncertainly, half shielding his face. The real Ceauşescu or his double?

Fourteen

It was Leo who found me on my living-room floor, 'splayed out like a dried-up starfish', and Leo who brought Ottilia, who now leaned over me with a thermometer and a bag of pale liquid, a saline drip that shone opal in the declining sun. I brought my hand to my eyes but felt a tugging. I was plugged into a variety of tubes, and my bedroom was laid out like a field hospital.

'Welcome back. Leo!' she called out. Leo lumbered in, a pile of Sunday supplements under his arm.

'Don't worry – the good doctor stood aside while your old chum Leo took your trousers off and squeezed them dry. No job for a lady.' He dropped the magazines onto the foot of the bed and patted my leg. 'Don't put that thermometer in your mouth, by the way.' He winked at Ottilia, who smiled and left us to it.

'What's wrong with me?' My voice was hoarse, my throat ached from all the empty vomiting. A basin of liquid shit was on the floor beside the bed, swampwater-thin and brackish, with flecks of grey foam on the surface.

'Ready for the good news?'

Leo bent over me, spectacles on the end of his nose, pretending to read from a clipboard in the manner of the fat consultant from *Doctor in the House*. One or more late after-noon drinks haunted his breath. 'You've been here two days.

Touch of amoebic dysentery, we all get it to start with. Lucky I found you though. The lovely Ottilia's been getting all the medication you need to spare you going into hospital. Know what they say about hospitals here in the socialist paradise: "There's always a bed, the problem is, you never come out..." All fine now. That's the good news.' I propped myself up. Leo continued. 'Bit of a bummer this, but you're not allowed to move for another week – doctor's orders.'

'Has Cilea been?'

'Yes, she popped by yesterday, but you had a thermometer up your jacksie and were raving about Wintersmith. She left some good wishes and a bunch of flowers. Didn't get the sense that sickbeds were her thing really... She's been away, Belgrade, just got back.' His expression clouded as if he had just remembered something. I motioned for the phone, but Leo shook his head. 'Not now. Wait a bit. Let yourself settle.'

Thanks to Leo's manoeuvrings Ottilia had all she needed to treat me, she said, and didn't want to know where it came from. The drips had Greek writing on them, and the plastic nappy I wore came from a Red Crescent box with Arabic and Turkish packing. The boxes of pills and flagons of medicine were in enough different tongues to constitute a United Nations to themselves. I felt resigned, comfortable, helpless. Everything had a strange convalescent distortion: the lights glittered, the doors and windows were blurred at the edges, and the bowl of rare if not exotic fruit – oranges, apples, apricots – made a vibrant still-life on my bedside table.

The red light of the answerphone flashed. I played the message: it was Trofim, his voice a snarl that made me recoil from the phone. I closed my eyes again and blacked over into sleep. I was aware, some time later, of Leo's voice as he found me, unfastened from my drips and turning weakly in my burning sheets. Sometime in the middle of that night, I heard the World Service; later I was roused by terrible noise, like an oar scraping a rubbly riverbed. I reached out for the bedside lamp and fumbled the switch to find Leo snoring, fully-dressed, in the armchair. I called out, shouted, lobbed a biro at his head but failed to wake him.

On the fourth day I was released from my drips, strong enough to get up and go to the bathroom unaided. I had lost half a stone. My cheeks were sunken and my eyes bottomed out into dark semicircles. My skin was yellow, and my arms puncture-bruised. I walked to the living room where Leo had set up camp. He was there now, reading *Luceafarul* and listening to an English-language broadcast on Radio Moscow. The answerphone still flashed its red light. I played the message again:

My friend, I hope you are well. You never arrived on Sunday. Or Monday. I became worried about you, and of course about what had become of our work. Let me know. I shall be studying chess moves in the park, in my usual place, as usual. Otherwise, you know where to find me. With best wishes, your friend Sergiu Trofim...

Trofim's answerphone messages were like letters: he always began with a greeting, always spoke in perfect sentences, and always signed off with good wishes and his name. This was the message which, in my fever, I had imagined as some sort of vicious encryption.

'I need to speak to Trofim,' I told Leo. 'Urgently... He hasn't heard from me for nearly a week and I've got something of his.' I noticed my satchel flapping open on the doorhandle. I looked inside, but the papers and diskette were gone.

'Dealt with,' said Leo lazily. 'Where d'you think he'll have the launch? Capşa? Banqueting rooms of his old ministry? A two-bunk, eight-man cell in Jilava Prison? After all, he's a graduate of that establishment...' I was taken aback. Trofim had not exactly hidden anything from Leo, but he had kept even close friends underinformed about what he was writing, its state of completeness and his plans for publication. Even I did not know the last of these, though I knew he was in touch with a French publisher through someone at the Belgian embassy. Trofim kept the different parts of the picture separate, jigsaw pieces secreted across town, across languages and across social spheres.

I saw that Trofim had left me an old book of poems by Tudor Arghezi, Trofim's favourite poet and also, I knew, Ionescu's. It was signed by Arghezi, and there was a small United Nations compliment slip inside bearing Trofim's name. As Leo fussed in the kitchen and made some lunch, I leafed through it. It was not the words that caught me – I was too tired and unfocussed to read those – it was the yellowness of the pages, the way they had begun to crumble and break rather than tear. They were the texture of rice paper and serrated at the edges like the wings of moths that had been battered by endless strivings against lamps and windows. As I turned them they emitted a pervasive, smoky dust that caught my throat and made my eyes itch.

Tudor Arghezi... collaborator in the war of 1914-18, antifascist in the war of '39-45, dissident in the Stalin years and National Poet in the Gheorghiu-Dej era. After the second war, the poet had been denounced by the Stalinists. In an article in *Scînteia* entitled 'The Poetry of Decay and the Decay of Poetry', they vilified him as the bard of the bourgeoisie, the poet of sickness and decadence; 'pathological', 'perverted', 'a putrefied consciousness...' I knew all this from Trofim's memoirs. Trofim had known Arghezi a little, first as his persecutor and then his rehabilitator, but always as his admirer and most avid reader. Trofim knew Arghezi's work by heart, despite being the Politburo member with special responsibility for Arghezi's 'critical reappraisal', a reappraisal which resulted in the poet's expulsion from the Union of Writers and the banning of his poems.

There was a chapter in Trofim's memoirs – the genuine ones and not the fake ones he was writing for the official publishing house – about how, after the war when he was out of favour, the old poet had made his living selling cherries from the orchard in his Bucharest garden on Strada Martisor. Trofim had bought some one day, finding Arghezi sitting on a wooden stepladder at the roadside. The old poet had no reason to know one of his tormentors was in front of him, since already evil could be done, as Trofim put it, 'by remote control'. *I felt contemptible,* Trofim had written, *I do not know what he sensed in me – perhaps nothing, how could he? – but he drew all my guilt and self-hatred to the surface with his sly, knowing eyes. He drove a hard bargain too: I paid twice the going rate. He knew I was guilty. It did not matter of what. He just knew.*

Trofim had planted one of the cherry stones in his Herastrau garden. The tree had blossomed; indeed it never failed, over forty years, to welcome the spring with a promising flourish of flowers. But it had never yielded a single cherry.

'Remote control', Trofim had called it: of course, he had not sullied his own hands with the day-to-day business of defaming Arghezi. He had picked an ambitious young academic for the job. The dirty work of smearing Arghezi in the press and coercing his friends and readers to desert him was done by the Party's attack dogs, led by the young literature professor. When Trofim had supervised Arghezi's rehabilitation ten years later he had chosen the same professor, no longer so young, to make the case for the old man's status as 'National Poet and Treasure of our Literary Life'. Trofim had not named the literary apparatchik in his book, and always refused to tell me when I asked. I had assumed he was dead or had fallen into irrelevance.

Now, as I went to the last page of Arghezi's poems, there

was an envelope stuffed with yellowed press cuttings. They were arranged in order of escalating vitriol. The first, dated March 1965, was headed 'The Poetry of Bourgeois retreat'. The next, a few weeks later, was called 'Emotional Pornography'. After a couple more, 'Putrefaction and Decay: Arghezi's insult to Life' argued for the expulsion of Arghezi from the Union of Writers and his removal from the curriculum. All were signed Andrei Ionescu.

Ionescu! It had been Ionescu doing Trofim's bidding! Further on in the pile of cuttings, a decade later, the process began again, but in reverse: an article claiming that socialist taste was now sufficiently embedded to admit of experimentation with what it termed 'the vagaries of subjectivity as a counterpoint to the self-evident truths of scientific materialism'. By the end 'a giant of World Literature was emerging from the neglect in which, by his own modesty and gentleness of temperament, he had too long suffered.' It was eye-wateringly hypocritical stuff, comical now, though there was no mistaking the brutality and fear that underwrote it all. Leo noticed me scanning the articles. He had already read them.

'Terrific isn't it? Old Ionescu destroys the poor old sod's reputation, then a few years later proclaims him the greatest poet of the century! You couldn't make it up! Wait till I tell Ioana – it makes what goes on today look principled.'

I closed the book and replaced it on the shelf. I felt sad and disappointed. In what exactly? In whom? After all, I knew all this – not the details, but I knew. About Trofim, Ionescu, Cilea, Leo and all the others... I was complicit in it too and I even knew that. But now I felt both crowded out and alone, implicated and out on a limb, in a world whose terms were perpetually shifting, yet whose rules would never change.

'I don't care what he's done.' Leo cut into some argument with himself, since I had said nothing, 'he's all right is Ionescu, poor bugger. There are no winners here. Even old Trofim hasn't won. He's got his nice flat, he's had the power, the mistresses, the money, the foreign visits. But for what? For a system that's on its knees in a city that's coming down around his ears. That's not evil out there, that dark cloud, the Securitate, the motorcade, the decoy dogs... it's not evil. It's failure, that's all, failure. Colossal, ongoing failure: taste it! It tastes like a bottle of expensive Pomerol and a chateaubriand from Capşa, and it tastes like a crust of yesterday's potato bread and some tinned pilchards from Korea. Whether it's Cilea's Chanel No. 5 you're inhaling or the station baglady's armpit juice, it's still the same smell. Failure.'

I didn't answer him. Sometime later, half-asleep, I smelled Ottilia beside me. She was still in her working clothes but smelled of soap and scrubbed skin. As she leaned over me to tuck in the other side of the bed, her hair brushed my face. I caught a very faint floral scent, though not of any flower I knew. I half-opened my eyes, a movement she seemed to hear as if my eyelids had made a tiny noise. She leaned down and put her fingers gently on them, closing them to restore the darkness. Then I was conscious of some whispering next door and the quiet latch coming down on the front door as Leo took her back home.

That night I dreamed a sequence from Trofim's book as if I were seeing it with my own eyes. I remembered it word for word. I had typed it, and in doing so I must have archived it, perfect in every detail and in all its cold sad beauty. It had been Trofim's *epiphany of pragmatism*, as he put it, when he decided to fall in with Stalinism. He reneged on his allegiances and friendships, de-judaified himself, joined the purges and was quickly promoted.

On the flight to Moscow to meet Stalin in 1951, it all came clear: *I looked out of the porthole of the plane: the dying sun behind its wall of ice, those fields of cloud and burning cold, the pressure of empty air, that press of void that held the plane up and kept it safe while at the same time threatening its destruction... 'That's all there is,' I said to myself, 'that's all there ever was, a regulated vacuum.' Over the next decades, whenever I was in a plane, whether it was a TAROM local flight or Kissinger's private jet, that vision was always there, reminding me... 'That's all there is.' I still believe that, but much of what I did in view of that belief I would undo or do differently if I had my time again.*

Leo arrived the next morning at nine. 'Sorry I didn't come back last night. I got held up. We'd got word that the old church of Saint Paraschiva in Lipscani was being demolished. Ottilia came too – wanted to see what it was like. The wrecking balls had done their job by the time we got there, but I snatched a few shots.'

Leo slotted a video into the machine: in the slow, misty dusk, men were tearing the copper strips from a dome. It stood in the rubble like a giant tortoise as they attacked it with hammers and pliers. The picture was blurred and wobbly, taken from some nearby window whose wooden pane kept intruding on the image, framing it up and letting it go again. Lorries came and went in silence as the ghost of a sun rose behind the ruins. A few minutes in, a hand came from the left and covered the lens. That was it. Leo ejected the video and replaced it in its box: Chuck Norris, *Missing in Action*.

Cilea visited for the first time a week later. I still spent most of the day in bed and Leo had used my illness to take up residence in my flat. Ottilia called in most days, usually in the mid-morning before her shifts at the hospital. Trofim visited twice. The interruption to his work was frustrating him; they had replaced his cement-haired secretary with a computer-literate Party loyalist, Hadrian ('The Wall') Vintile, who erased each new file and took away the only copy at the end of every day. For the first time there was an urgency to the project, a sense of time running out.

Cilea brought chocolates, flowers, a fat pineapple with leaves like a cartoon explosion and an atomiser of her father's cologne to fragrance my convalescence. I asked her why it had taken her the best part of ten days to come and see me.

'You were being taken care of. I would just have been interrupting. I saw you were in good hands, then left it until you were well enough.' She sat at the end of the bed, her smell mingling with the room's nameless chemical odour. She had had her nails varnished, I noticed as she lit another Pall Mall, puffing the smoke out of the window, her concession to the medical context. She looked more tanned too, in her crisp white shirt and jeans, sunglasses pushed up into her hair, wearing the same clothes as when we had first met. The Inter-Continental's 'Aesthetic Centre' had been busy. Either that or Belgrade had been blisteringly sunny.

I struggled out of bed and manoeuvred us to the living room, away from all the signs of illness and dependency. Wrapping an embarrassing tartan dressing gown around myself, I sat on the sofa and let her make tea. When she returned, I touched her arm. She stiffened up.

I knew then, from the coldness of her skin, the contraction of her body at my touch, that it was finished. She was all solicitude and dead libido. And it was decisive, the way only a body decides. The mind's slant can be changed, the rational mechanisms can always review and go back on themselves, but the body's knowledge is irreversible. I knew that was why she had avoided me these last weeks, why she had not spoken to me or contacted me since that night with Nicu and the Serbs. Something had changed.

'I came to see how you were,' she said redundantly.

'And?'

'And what? You showed me that night what you really

thought of me, I saw it all: the way you watched me, like you owned me, the way part of you was excited seeing those bastards touching me, and the other part of you wanted to kill them... I thought we might be together, but it's obvious that will never happen. You don't trust me, I'm not even sure you're interested in me. I know you think you are, but when all the fucking and the high life is over you hold me in contempt. You followed me. Checked up on me. You thought that was love but of course you knew no better. I'm sorry for you. My God, you even suspected me of having something to do with what happened to those boys...' She looked away.

'And what *did* happen to those boys?' I asked quickly.

'I don't know. Why should I? But you thought I was responsible.'

'That's not true. I was besotted with you. I still am. You know that.'

'I thought I did. Now I know that you thought I just wanted to be a westerner, and that I was not as noble or pure as those who suffer, as your new companion Ottilia for example...'

'There's nothing going on with Ottilia...'

'No, maybe not – because she can see through you. I didn't, that was my mistake. Your friends hated me from the first day. Leo, hiding behind his buffoonery; your "pure" friends who were better than me, Ioana with her perfect credentials, Ottilia with her work in the hospital...' Cilea swallowed, tried to continue, dragged on her cigarette and puffed the smoke out towards me. Her fingers shook. She closed her eyes. There was something else. 'And anyway, I know now that I'm not free, I probably never was.'

'"Free?" Don't you start. I've had enough of all these bloody speeches about freedom...'

'Shut up – I mean free to be with you. I shouldn't have started this.'

'So you *have* been with someone else? I bloody thought so!'

'No. I *was*, before we met – never while we were together. You know who it was. Here, in this flat, you know that of course. So do they – ' She meant Leo and Ioana. 'Belanger...' She paused. 'It's complicated...'

'I never finished college but I think can grasp the basics of a story where my girlfriend goes back to her ex while I'm supposed to be clearing out my dead parents' house! How inconvenient of me to stay behind! How inconvenient of me to come to the InterContinental that night!'

'It's not like that. He called me, asked me to come back to him. I promised nothing. Just to see him. My father hates him, made him leave the country, so I went to meet him in Belgrade. I'm sorry. I shouldn't have led you on.'

'It took you six weeks to prepare that?' I asked with as much derision as I could muster. I had already lost. 'Or was it just between dances with Nicu, manicures and visits to Capşa that you put your mind to it? I've spent the last month begging you to forgive me, humiliating myself on your answerphone, and all that time you've been holed up in Belgrade screwing your ex?'

Cilea turned to go, eyes burning. 'I'd expected better from you. But really you thought so little of me that deep down you think nothing of yourself for having been with me. Well, you saw what you wanted to see, and got what you wanted to get. I am sorry. I'm leaving now.'

I was suddenly exhausted. I tried to rise and stop her going, but sagged back into the chair. I heard the front door close behind her.

Leo returned with Ottilia later that afternoon. I had fallen asleep on the sofa and woke in an icy sweat. The first days had been full of convulsions, as my body pounded the sickness out of me. Now it was slower, a glacial detoxification that felt too much like illness itself to persuade me I was getting better. They were both laden with shopping bags and bottles, and in a blistering good humour I could not match. Leo had persuaded Ottilia into one of the *nomeklatura* shops. He was breaking down her resistance.

That evening Ioana joined us for dinner while Leo, helped by Ottilia, cooked a messy and desynchronised meal in which everything that should have shared a plate arrived as a separate course. The food thus took us far into the night, with whoops of delight and laughter coming from the kitchen, clattering pots and pans and at least once a shriek of what sounded like terror, then modulated to relief, and then finished up as laughter. I asked Ottilia what she had made of the Party shop. The place had horrified her, though it enabled her to put an image to the rumours: there was nothing there she did not already know about, and seeing it had liberated her. It was not so long ago that I myself, a westerner used to groaning supermarkets shelves and all-night convenience stores, had been dumbfounded at the luxuries on offer to the privileged here. How much more shocking must it have been to someone like Ottilia.

Ioana was in a better mood than I had ever seen, though Ottilia's and Leo's closeness had at first made her suspicious, something for which she blamed me. During her one visit she mentioned something about Leo's 'sudden interest in medicine', implying that I was a convenient alibi for their budding relationship. She was wrong, but Ioana was not one to acknowledge mistakes. She just moved on from them, mere obstacles on her march towards the truth. And it always was *the* truth with Ioana: singular and indivisible and clear, not the multiple, blurred or partial truths Leo dealt in.

I watched Ottilia eating: a few experimental mouthfuls, a sip of French Embassy claret, and then she got into her stride. She caught me looking at her, smiled, and spiked a piece of Leo's stuffed pork loin onto her fork.

'I think I can count on the fingers of one hand the number of times I have eaten meat like this.' She pushed the morsel around her plate, mopping up sauce. 'I exaggerate, but... well... it is not far short of the truth.'

Ioana looked at her. 'You spend time with these two and you'll be the biggest carnivore in Bucharest. As for Cilea Constantin, our friend's paramour here, she's a walking reminder of why the rest of us have to eat boiled cabbage and soya salami.' That was Ioana's idea of a lighter moment, and she gave me a quick flinty smile.

'Ex,' I said, in a tone I hoped conveyed manly insouciance. I had not eaten properly for days, and the food lay heavy on me. 'Ex-paramour.'

'Ex?' Leo chipped in. I told them about our meeting of earlier, and explained what I now firmly believed: that Cilea had had nothing to do with what had happened – *if* anything had happened – to Petre and Vintul. Yet the thought crossed my mind: she knew *something* had happened to them, didn't she? *Those boys...* she had said.

'You know as well as we do that she's behind it. It may not be her fault, she may not have intended it, but she came into our circle, a Party chief's daughter...' Ioana interrupted. I regretted bringing it up.

'What you're trying to say is that I'm the one who brought her in, isn't that right?' I said.

Ioana did not deny it. 'You did what you thought was best. You behaved the way it is normal to behave for you. It is not, strictly speaking, your fault.' *Strictly speaking...* there was no clearer indication that Ioana thought it was my fault.

I was not letting go. 'I don't think it was. I think you've made a mistake, we all have. It doesn't make sense. There's something else. I don't know what, but the answer is elsewhere. Why should Cilea care what Petre and Vintul do? It doesn't affect her – she was never interested. Not once did

212

she ask. Isn't that strange?' But I was uneasy. I still believed Cilea had nothing to do with it, but there was something about the way she had said it, as if she knew there was something specific... If I hadn't been so consumed by my need to attack her, or to trample what was left of our relationship, I would have pressed her.

"There's something to that,' said Leo, 'what's in it for her, getting involved in something like this? Ioana – I thought the reason you disliked Cilea was that she was unconcerned by anything other than living the good life? Why should she get involved now? In any case, she's always been on the scene one way or another...'

'Cilea's no fool. She's watching and reporting like the rest of them. She hangs out with dictators' children, goes to the US, shops in the hotels... and what about her and Belanger, have you forgotten that? No, Leo, you think she won't dirty her hands to protect all that? There are no coincidences. Coincidences were abolished by the communists.'

I started to ask about Belanger but Ioana cut me off with a sweep of her hand. They all mentioned his name, but no one ever said *who* he was.

'Please stop,' said Ottilia, 'No one knows anything for sure. It doesn't help me to hear only speculations and recriminations. It won't bring him back or help me find him again.'

The film Leo had taken of the aftermath of the demolition of St Paraschiva's was aired on German news the next day. Then it did the rounds: Italy, Spain, France, the US, Britain. The Shit and Hassle had a new wide-screen digital TV for news and on a big screen the demolition seemed even more sinister. You could make out the actions better too: the predators tearing at the grounded dome, the Securitate watching and filming the demonstrators. Scattered about the wasted site, which Leo had caught in a wide-angle tracking shot, the

213

bulldozers and wrecking balls were still, their work done.

All this had been going on for years, but for the media any story only begins the moment it is noticed. Perhaps because of the upheavals in Prague, East Germany, Poland, there was now real momentum behind the reporting of Romania. By August it was a big story. On the World Service a lisping young fogey from the Prince's Trust for Architecture condemned the vandalism of Ceauşescu's regime. There were a few aerial shots of the Palace of the People, cut with comments on the crudity and kitsch of the buildings. The human tragedy of Romania was irrelevant. Ceauşescu had been imprisoning, starving, brutalising and lying to his people for the best part of two decades, mostly with the connivance of the West. But his real crime apparently was bad taste.

There was excitement at the embassy. The country was in the news; we were on the map of dissent. No longer the forgotten kingdom, somewhere between Albania and Bulgaria on the ladder of irrelevance. The Romania desk at the BBC had been moved, as Leo had it, from the broom cupboard to the landing. 'Any minute now they'll be staffing it.'

Wintersmith was riding high. His bureau chief, the inappropriately named Jim Bossy, was being sent home on medical leave of absence. A gentle and nervous man, Bossy had spent all his life running from the authoritarian implications of his name. He deferred to everyone, even his chauffeur, and his body was prone to so many tics and jerks that he walked like a robot made of jelly. He had been having a long, discreet breakdown for years. Wintersmith was now Acting First Secretary.

Leo spent more time on his expeditions around the country, recording and photographing the destruction. With his contacts abroad, he set up a scheme in which villages and towns in the West 'adopted' counterparts in Romania that were earmarked for 'modernisation'. 'SOS Romanian Villages' caught on. By the beginning of September forty villages had been 'adopted'; western mayors, local politicians, school-children and local history societies wrote to newspapers calling attention to what was happening to their town's Romanian 'twin'.

The black-marketeering had now been delegated to the Lieutenant and a junior Polish diplomat Leo christened 'the apprentice'. It was hard to keep track of Leo. I had to replace the 'Back in 15 minutes' on his door twice because students had defaced it. Finally, I laminated it and just wiped off the graffiti every few days. He missed his lectures, stopped attending meetings, failed to hand in reports. Under Popea, the atmosphere at work became morgue-like. Even the draught had stopped blowing. When I went for my first meeting with Popea in Ionescu's old room, the place was bare and the desk had been moved into a corner from which both door and window could be seen. The deskchair was backed up into the tightest angle where the walls met: the Feng Shui of paranoia.

Each time I called Cilea she was either out or not answering. I waited at the gates of her avenue, unable to get past the guard, while the black cars drove in and out and I peered through their tinted windows. As I loitered on Cilea's street one night after another fruitless stakeout, Titanu blocked my way. He looked at me, looked up at her window, then shook his head. I realised I had never heard him speak, even when he kept guard for us as we fucked in theatre stalls, hotel rooms or the Dacia he drove her around in. It was a warning, and a friendly one by his standards. I nodded and turned back. As he let me past he patted my shoulder, a gesture so unexpected, of such repressed gentleness, that when he had gone I found somewhere dark and quiet and cried into my hands.

Ottilia now had her own room in my flat. Her own was no longer safe since she had been assigned two new flatmates. One was an informer, the other a devious lecher who made a pass at her as soon as he arrived. She had called us and when we picked her up she had a crumpled, sagging sports bag with some clothes and two framed photographs. 'We'll get the rest in the morning,' I said. 'There is no rest,' she answered.

At weekends Ottilia and I walked through the parks before my visit to Trofim. Sometimes she came with me. At first she was suspicious of the ex-Party chief in his expensive flat, surrounded by capitalist luxuries accumulated over years of enforcing communist privations. To her he was one of the architects of the world we lived in. Yet they became friends. Both had a gift for the sort of friendship that grew unspokenly, that communicated itself in imperceptible exchanges of thought and feeling. She gave him her arm as they walked or visited museums without me; he saved her copies of medical magazines and took out a subscription to *The Lancet*.

By mid-September, the book was ready for the printers. We stood on Trofim's balcony watching the sun sink and feeling the start of autumn's slow closedown. We toasted its completion with the Belgian Embassy's vintage champagne, raising our glasses to the three hundred sheets of type. Trofim and Ottilia had already chosen the photographs: Trofim in childhood with his Rabbi father and his two sisters; his young wife; Trofim at party meetings, completely de-judaiefied in a suit and tie. The young Trofim in prison, and, a few yards behind him, Ceauşescu. Jailed under the fascists, then under the communists ('same prison, same food, change of warders, that is all...'). Trofim with Stalin, with Khrushchev, with Kennedy.... The last photograph in the book was of him with his son Ion, now Iacub, the Tel Aviv rabbi, and his grand-daughers Sara and Rachel.

The decoy book was ready too, text and images back from 'retouching'. This one was celebrated with a glass of warm *Sovietskoi* fizz, the only sparkling wine available in Monocom. The cover was apartment-block grey with a rust-coloured lettering, and felt as if it was already biodegrading in your hands. Hadrian was with us, sharing the glory. 'Comrade, I have taken the liberty of writing the dedicatory foreword to President and Doctor Ceauşescu. I have followed the template, but you may add a few personal touches of your own.' Trofim thanked him and asked him with gentle sarcasm to put in some personal touches on his behalf.

Trofim was enjoying himself. He had arranged for both books to be launched on the same day: the seventh of October.

'What will you do now?' I asked him later, clearing the glasses after Hadrian and the Party cronies had left.

'I had better practise my chess.'

On the twentieth of September Wintersmith called. 'Found out about a shooting near the border. One casualty.' Was that what I had wanted? *Wanted* was not the word, I told him, but certainly the dates fitted, if the number didn't. 'Just one?'

'That we know of,' he said, 'but it's pretty reliable. Border guards on the Yugoslav side heard one shot across the water. Later, during a cross-border security meeting, the Romanians produced the official story: one attempted crossing, one armed man acting alone, who shot first before he was taken out. "Organised criminal elements", says the report. The Yugos don't buy it, but they've got other things to think about. It's taken a while to get back to us from the Belgrade office, but it's *bona fide* info. Our man there, Phillimore, he's gone native but he's got the contacts.'

'But just one shot?' I asked, 'that doesn't add up. How could he have shot first if there was only one shot?'

Wintersmith sounded satisfied with himself. 'I never said

the story added up. I said the source was *bona fide*. As is the next bit of info...'

'What's that?' I asked.

Wintersmith had watched too many films: he was spacing out his revelations for maximum dramatic effect. 'They found two bodies next day.'

Part Two

'In history as in nature, decay is the laboratory of life'
                                                    – Karl Marx

One

When Ottilia returned from work at midnight exhausted, I said nothing and let her sleep. When she woke, I brought her breakfast and gave her Wintersmith's news as she lay in bed. That way there was nowhere for her to fall.

Leo had called in so many favours, indebted himself to so many people to get information about the bodies, that even his network of contacts dried up. He spent hours on the phone, paid out hundreds of dollars for leads, but it came to nothing except a few expensive dead ends.

It was Leo who suggested I contact Manea Constantin. After what had passed between me and Cilea, it was unlikely he would want to see me again.

'You sure you want to get involved with him again?' asked Leo, starting to backpedal.

'It's probably the only chance,' I said, 'and besides, if he has anything to do with it, and it's my fault in the first place, then it's the least I can do.'

'Are you sure you can face finding out?'

'I'm not sure I can.' We both turned. Ottilia stood at the door, her face sallow and tear-stained, fingers bleeding where the cuticles were bitten down. 'I am not sure I want to know, not this way.'

Not knowing had its advantages, and for me it always had: not knowing about Cilea, not knowing about Belanger, not knowing even half of what Leo got up to on the black market. But it had been two months now with no word from Petre and Vintul.

'Someone will call for you and the girl tomorrow morning.' Manea's voice was brisk and ministerial on the line. He had been quick – I had left a message on Cilea's answerphone and she must have relayed it to him. It gave me some comfort – at least she was still listening to them. 'Be ready by eight,' he said.

No one slept that night. Leo lay on the sofa, claiming to be too drunk to drive home, the first time he had shown such compunction. Videos played in silence and the TV cast its blue monster-shadows against the wall. Ottilia went to bed early but her light stayed on. I dozed, read, paced about, stood on the balcony and listened for the sound of building and unbuilding that accompanied our nights. Light the colour of blood and egg yolk broke across the sky: the raising up and coming down of buildings was ever-present, like the breath or heartbeats or pulse that kept a body alive and drew it ever closer to death. Even on the slowest days, the most languid weekend afternoons, it was always there. I even heard it in my sleep, and on the rare occasions when it stopped I heard it inside my head, a sound that had become a part of me.

I was up at five. Leo was sleeping deeply in front of the TVRom testcard. Ottilia was flat out, fully dressed and spread across the bed in deep, forgetful sleep. She snored lightly, one eyelid trembled, the eye half-open, a short circuit somewhere in her body fizzing on after the rest had shut down. I leaned across and closed it, staying a moment to touch her hair. Her sports bag lay on the floor, unzipped, her few poor possessions laid out: a photograph of her parents and an old house I knew immediately had been demolished. Pastness clung to it. A photo of Petre in his leather jacket and jeans, smoking and smiling his life-devouring smile. A skirt hung on a coat hook, and some jeans were folded on the floor beside a pair of working shoes. An alarm clock on the windowsill marked time with a scratching sound, grinding the minutes into dust.

Downstairs the news stall was opening to the empty clatter of regulation lunchboxes against belts. *Scînteia*'s new slogan, 'One Nation, One Paper', beamed from the awning. The sardonic newspaper vendor pointed up at it as I bought my copy.

'They forgot to add "One Reader",' he said, thoughtfully sipping the coffee I had brought him, concentrating on the taste. He was a man of few words and only one joke, which fell into the category of jokes that became funnier with repetition: waving a string of lottery tickets at me as I left each morning, he would call out, 'Feeling lucky, *Tovarăşul*?'

I heard the shower splattering the walls, the floor, probably the light switches in the bathroom, then Leo's long expectorating growl as he cleared his throat into my toilet.

'What happens when Constantin's boys come to get you? Any idea at all where he'll take you?' he asked.

'You heard what I said. He asked me to be ready with her and I said yes. I'm about as clued up on this as you are.'

'Well, you're the man with friends in high places...'

'One friend. And he's hardly a friend. Besides, that's rich coming from you.'

'Ah no, you see what I have is many, many friends, and they're mostly in low places. I find it works better that way.'

Leo turned the dial of the long-wave radio, his ear pressed to the box like a safe-cracker. It was difficult to avoid the touch-tag of velvet revolutions across eastern Europe: Poland, Czechoslovakia, Hungary... Gorbachev's *Perestroika* and *Glasnost* might now be part of the English language, but they still felt a world away from Romania.

Ottilia was disorientated from sleeping deeply but not enough. We tried to tempt her with breakfast, but she barely acknowledged us. The radio droned on: small African wars,

Britain's European opt-out, Thatcher and Reagan's nuclear courtship... Ottilia disappeared into the bathroom.

'You're going to have to look out for her,' Leo said. We watched for Manea's car. 'I don't know what this will do to her. Part of me wants it to be him so we can close things up. The other part of me dreads it will be.'

'What d'you think it's doing to me?' I asked. 'If it turns out to be him lying there, where does that leave us?'

'This isn't about whose fault it is. It's not about you. It's about her, and what's going to happen to her, knowing or not knowing...'

Ottilia emerged from her room washed and dressed and in a different frame of mind. She had put on some make-up Cilea had left in the bathroom. Her mouth was lipsticked, her eyes shadowed and outlined by mascara. She wore her one pair of jeans and sandals, one of my shirts tied up at the bottom over her belt. She looked changed, as if by entering a new personality she might spare her real self the brunt of what was coming.

'I'm ready,' she announced, braced and standing tall in the face of whatever lay ahead. She went to Leo and kissed him, took my hand and led me downstairs, closing it tight in her own. At his kiosk, Mr *Scînteia* gave us a big double thumbs up.

'Good morning, Sir.' To Ottilia, '*Buna ziua Tovarăşa.* Please.' It was the same young man as the first time, just as polite and well groomed and at his ease. He must have known something of Ottilia's situation, since he was gentle and considerate, which put her on edge more than the predictable thuggishness would have done. When he touched her to help her into the car, she flinched. His apology was genuine. Manea might be in charge of a large section of the repressive apparatus, but he employed people who looked intelligent and humane and capable of fellow feeling. In the car, there was no conversation. Ottilia had still not let go of my hand. I put my free arm across her shoulder, and she moved her body further into mine.

As we walked through the ministry's atrium Ottilia looked about her, comparing the reality with all the versions she had heard over the years. In a few weeks she had visited the fabled shops and sampled the pleasures of the society within a society that constituted the Party's inner circle. Now she was going to meet a minister to find out if her brother was dead.

With Manea there was none of the customary waiting that people in the upper echelons put you through as part of the protocol of intimidation and obstruction. He shook my hand and introduced himself to Ottilia warmly and without condescension. I knew then he had something definite. He was treating her like someone bereaved, I thought, watching them talking out of earshot, up against the huge window of his office. Ottilia faced him, but it was he who looked away as he spoke.

'I want you to be here for this. I want you to see, make sure I'm not making a mistake' Ottilia fetched me and took my hand. I could see what Manea was thinking: that I had left his daughter for her.

'I'm here as Ottilia's friend,' I said to clarify things, 'to help her find out about her brother. That is my only connection with any of this.'

'Your *only* connection... how can you be so sure?' Manea sounded amused. Then, suddenly businesslike: 'There were two bodies found downriver from a border post downstream from the Iron Gate. They were taken to the morgue and cremated immediately. Fortunately – if that's the word I want – photographs were taken but there was no autopsy done. There was no need. I have had the photographs sent here at some trouble to myself. You will see that there are visible signs as to how the individuals died. I would like you to be ready for that.'

'Comrade, I have been a doctor in the people's health service for five years. I am ready for most things.'

Manea smiled. His assistant came back in with a brown envelope. It was ominously thin. Whatever story the pictures told, they told it quickly and unambiguously.

There were three photographs. In the first, two bloated grey corpses were arranged on a muddy riverbank. Scattered rubbish lay around: plastic bags, paint tins, a dark scud of foam. The bodies had been placed side by side and neither was recognisable in the sludge, their faces indistinguishable behind the dirt and the folds of slipped skin. One had a coat or jacket unzipped, his face hidden by a square of dark material. The next image was clearer: the uncovered face, short hair, eyes were open and filled with mud. That was neither Petre nor Vintul, though as I looked closer I recognised one of the high-fiving boys whose name I had never known. I had heard his shuddering intake of breath as the cold water enveloped him. It would have been one of his last.

In the next photograph the bodies had been cleaned up a little. It was more for identification than out of respect: beside their heads stood a bucket, and their hair was parted and still wet from having it emptied over their faces. Some of the mud had washed away, revealing on one of the bodies a large messy incision where I thought I had seen an unzipped coat. It was in fact parted flesh, a deep serrated cut from the collar down to the bottom of the rib cage. He looked half-climbed out of his skin, thick flaps of blood-drained flesh opened out into a crevasse filled with mud and sludge. Up close now, the skin was white as moonlight. The eyes were closed and part of the face eaten away by animals or by fish. It was the second boy. What had really become of Mel, who had set off with them, or to the two others? Petre and Vintul were not there to ask. This cleared up one mystery: these were not their bodies. But it brought us no closer to the answer.

In the third picture, the two faces were side by side on a morgue slab. It was the slab's texture that caught my eye: craggy concrete, pocked with holes and discoloured with seepage. A lit cigarette was balanced on the edge beside one of the faces, still smoking. Someone had cleaned the boys up and used a flash. Their skins were matt, absorbing the shock of magnesium light that rebounded against everything else: the surfaces, the scissors, a scalpel nearby, the kidney dish, the glass beakers.

I stupidly tried to shield Ottilia from all of this, but it was myself I was trying to protect. Ottilia saw this all the time, but I felt sick, stunned too by the violence of it all, violence that no amount of stillness and expressionless death could hide. Ottilia just looked at Manea and shook her head. Once she had ascertained that neither of the dead boys was Petre, and the convulsion of relief had passed, she became the clinician browsing through yet another library of death.

'Bloating, skin loosening... this is obviously a drowning. Can't see any other marks.' Then she pointed at the more damaged of the two bodies. 'This isn't straightforward though: looks like a messy slice through the sternum. A big, deep cut. He'd have had to be carried by a strong current over something serrated. Another half an inch and he'd have been disembowelled. He was alive when that happened. Not for long. Rapid blood loss. No sign of a bullet wound.' She pushed the photographs away. 'But I didn't come here to help you with cause of death.' She smiled the same ironic smile I had seen the day we first met in the hospital.

'That's what we thought, pretty much,' Manea said. 'I'm happy your brother is not among them. Any idea who they are?'

'None,' Ottilia replied without blinking. There was no reason she should have known; Petre kept that side of his life separate. I would find out later if she was lying.

'What about you?' Manea asked me.

'No. No idea.' It was Ottilia's turn to assess my truthfulness. I was learning: when lying keep it simple, brisk and decisive.

'I thought not,' said Manea wearily, 'so much for *quid pro quo*. No matter. If you had known, I would have merely asked you to tell their next of kin. No one else will. This story ends here – the papers and photographs will be destroyed or put somewhere unfindable. Officially, this did not happen, these do not exist, and we,' he swept the air with his hand, 'have not discussed them.'

Ottilia was not finished. 'That mutilation of the stomach...'

'I am afraid to say that some of the security emplacements are barbaric. "Deterrence" they call it, but since it is kept secret, it can hardly deter! Parts of the river have been filled with razor wire and metal spikes and industrial-sized factory saw blades. I am sorry. I will not justify that. Let us say that their use remains a matter of controversy even within the departments responsible.'

'There might be all sorts of words for it, but it looks to me like state murder,' Ottilia said simply. The typing behind us stopped.

'State murder is the fashionable term for it in some reactionary circles, though I would ask you to remember that those who attempt to cross the border illegally are breaking the law. That comes with its risks.' Manea recited the party line without conviction. Then he brightened and said something so startling I hardly believed what I heard: 'However it might be more of a deterrent if someone were to make these security emplacements public, do you not think?'

Ottilia knew at the same time as I did what he was suggesting – he was inviting us to do it.

Manea checked his watch. Nearly nine. The whole meeting had taken less than an hour. 'I have a breakfast meeting. You will please excuse me. Andrei will drive you back to wherever you want to go. Cinzia will be tagging along as she has some shopping to do.' Behind us, Cinzia, the secretary, was ready to leave. Even in the equalising uniform of the ministry typist corps, she looked beautiful. Outside Manea's office, a group of ill-clothed, overweight and greasy-looking functionaries waited in silence, sitting apart, avoiding each other's eyes. Regional secretaries, vice-ministers, provincial chiefs... they looked as if they both felt and provoked fear in equal measure. Another of the system's equalising mechanisms.

In the car home, Cinzia chatted with Ottilia. I caught some of the conversation, and discovered that they knew each other from before. Cinzia asked her about Petre, and Ottilia, normally so reserved, was happy to answer her questions. Gone was her prudence, her hesitation. When the car stopped, they swapped phone numbers, or, more exactly, Cinzia exchanged her phone number for Ottilia's address. In this country there was one private phone per three hundred head of population. The address Ottilia gave was mine.

'We were at school together,' Ottilia explained as we climbed out of the car. 'Friends, not close, but friends. Funny – you never imagine that when you'll meet again ten years later one of you will be a doctor in a state hospital and the other a minister's mistress. She was a clever girl. Could have done anything she wanted.'

'Explains why she's a minister's mistress, no?'

Ottilia smiled and put her arm around me. Though we were no further on in our quest to find Petre and Vintul, knowing those two bodies were not theirs had given rise to a strangely elated relief. The deaths of the two boys were violent and unnecessary, but they were at least not murder, except in the legal sense Ottilia had meant. For all that I was happy for Ottilia, Manea's information had also let me off the hook. For now.

'Sounds to me like Manea's clean, but what's interesting is

that he's prepared to help,' said Leo when we told him about our meeting.

'I got the feeling there was more to it than just helping us,' I offered. 'It's as if he were willing us to get hold of photos of the border traps and inviting us to get in touch with the families. I believed him.'

'Stoicu is in charge of border security, and he's also in charge of the shoot-to-kill policy right along the frontier,' Leo reminded us. 'Manea and Stoicu hate each other's guts. Stoicu's Manea's boss and he thinks Stoicu's a thick Stalinist peasant. Stoicu repays the compliment by reckoning Constantin to be a bourgeois/a Jew/a homosexual... delete as appropriate. I can't imagine Constantin is suddenly going to abandon his loyalty to the ideals of the Communist Party of Romania – after all, they've served him very nicely – but perhaps he's trying to stir things up.'

'And what's our role in all this?'

'We stir,' Leo said simply. 'With very long spoons...'

At four o'clock the next day I heard something slide under the front door. A brown envelope, A4 size, was half obscured by the mat. It was old and battered, and the original address label had been torn off. I opened the door and listened out. Nothing, just the echo of what might have been a step clearing the porch. I ran to the balcony, from which I could see a few dozen yards in each direction. Again nothing.

There were three poor-quality colour photographs and one black and white. All four were of the security 'emplacements' Manea had mentioned, and they certainly fulfilled a deterrent function when you saw them. In one picture a huge circular saw blade rose like a serrated moon from the water. Rusty and discoloured with moss, it protruded by a metre at its highest point and covered almost the breadth of this narrow bend of Danube. Two other shots showed different lengths of the river: what looked like a miasma of flies was in fact clouds of barbed wire clotted across whole stretches of the water. In the final shot three metal spikes reared out of the water. Typed on the back of each image was its location. The photographs were taken at three different points on the Romanian side of the Danube. They were separated by a distance, I calculated, of about two hundred kilometres. The date and time in small digital lettering at the bottom of each image showed all were taken within twenty-two hours of each other. Whoever had taken these had expensive equipment and had the petrol and permits to travel freely.

The phone rang: 'Fancy a *Kojak*?' Half an hour later Leo was examining the photographs. 'We've got your mate Manea to thank for this. I'll get these out to the German press in no time. I'll try the Brits too. I'll need to make copies as back-up.'

'I think I owe Wintersmith,' I said. Though the man made my flesh creep, he was the one who had given me the lead. After all, these 'emplacements', as Manea had called them, were secret. Only escapees or those charged with preventing escapes could get that close. Wintersmith might be able to do some good with them.

'OK,' Leo said doubtfully, 'you may be right, but he doesn't get the originals. Tell him you only got photocopies, and don't say anything else. In fact, you're such a bloody amateur, I'll come with you.'

'There's something I'm worried about,' I told him. 'I'm worried that we'd be doing Manca's bidding. I mean, Manea's no philanthropist. He's trying to find ways of getting Stoicu into trouble and taking his job. He might find factory-sized saw blades in the river disgusting...'

'Inelegant, even,' Leo offered, tying his shoelaces.

'Leo, I'm serious – what's to say he doesn't have better, cleaner, less obvious and ultimately more efficient methods up his sleeve?'

'What, fill the Danube with piranhas? Genetically engineered freshwater sharks?'

'I mean any number of sophisticated forms of intimidation, repression, brutality... physical violence... what's to say he won't be worse in his way?'

'Nothing. You know what they say: "You can't choose your friends".'

'No, Leo, they say that you *can* choose your friends; it's your *family* you're stuck with. That's the whole point of the saying.'

'Oh yeah? That explains where I've gone wrong over the years,' he grinned, punched me on the shoulder and headed out.

We walked to the department first. Micu raised himself up and saluted Leo, showing me the cautious sycophancy reserved for underlings with powerful patrons. Rodica stood up and congratulated him. He waved away the compliment with a generous sweep of the hand.

'We're all equal here, Rodica, I don't want you to treat me any differently. Well, perhaps just little,' he added, leaning his cheek into her face for kissing. 'The boss in?'

'Yes, yes, he is, er... Professor O'Heix...'

Professor?

'You've been so busy with your footling affairs that you've missed out on my recent and much overdue promotion,' Leo announced.

'A promotion? Leo, you're barely even here. You don't do your lectures. Haven't been to a meeting in months!' We locked the door and stood over the photocopier xeroxing the photographs.

'There's a dossier of records and attendance notes that says I'm a model lecturer. Who am I to argue?' The quality of the copies was surprisingly good. It was hard to tell how they would come out in the press, but their appalling gist would be clear enough.

'What is it you've got on Popea?' I asked Leo.

'Trade secrets, I'm afraid. Let's just say that for a man who believes in rigid hierarchies in the workplace, he has a very fluid sense of the gender divide when it comes to clothes...'

'You mean he's a transvestite and you're blackmailing him?'

Leo beamed at me: 'Actually I think there's an odd sense in which he likes it – blackmail I mean. In a kinky way, you know... it's another sort of *régime* to kow-tow to, and there's a kind of person who just can't do without fear, can't live without it.... Anyway, I won't tell you how I found out about him – let's just say it was a close shave for both of us. I was a little drunk, it was dark... and you've got to hand it to him, he scrubs up pretty well as a lady, which is more than I'd say for his wife.'

I shook my head. What shocked me more – Leo's grotty blackmail scam or the thought of Popea in drag? The poor man: being a transvestite in a surveillance society must have been almost impossible. Until Leo, Popea had somehow managed. It was probably Leo's hold on him that had ensured Ionescu was working in the university library and not unblocking drains in Turda.

The nameplate on my door still read *Dr F. Belanger*, but Leo's had already been changed: *Professor L. O'Heix*. On the Professor's desk, a thin fur of dust attested to his not having earned his title by conventional means. He sat and swept it with the palm of his hand and set about putting the copies and photographs into envelopes. With the fourth envelope, he wrote in fat childish letters GILES WINTERSMITH ESQ. He then dialled the embassy number and handed me the phone.

Wintersmith was waiting on the steps, wearing spy's sunglasses behind which his eyeballs slopped greyly like creatures in an aquarium. He was uncomfortable with Leo and wilted at his thick, exaggerated handshake. Leo had made our meeting as obvious as possible. I may have been repaying my debt to Wintersmith, but Leo was using him as a decoy.

'You must be mad,' the diplomat said to me as we arrived, 'calling me at the embassy from a bugged phone. Bloody stupid. Amateurs!'

'It's called the double bluff. Basic rule of espionage,' Leo countered.

We found a table in the Shit and Hassle where Wintersmith examined the photographs. 'Interesting, yes. Thank you. I imagine you won't say where these came from? Who gave them to you? So we can ... er... follow up their authenticity?'

'You've got a problem with their authenticity? Tell you what, Giles, you come with us, and we'll drop you in the water upcurrent from *this*,' he indicated the saw blade, 'and while you're sewing your ballbag back on you can *authenticate* it for us. How about that?' Leo jabbed his finger into the triangle of red skin in the open neck of Wintersmith's shirt.

'They were given to us anonymously,' I said, 'pushed through my letter box.'

'Photocopied?' Wintersmith was sceptical.

'Photocopied.' Leo got up for another pint. 'Take 'em or leave 'em. If you don't want them they'll go somewhere they will be wanted. And if you *do* want them, you bloody well use them.'

Wintersmith took them and slid them into his briefcase. 'I'll see what I can do. We don't like working with unauthenticated material. That's why we really need your source.'

'You need our "source" as you put it so you can chase them up for a load of useless info about oil or arms sales, and so you can help your chums in the trade missions to negotiate better deals.'

'Are these the only copies?' Wintersmith ignored Leo and addressed me.

'Human rights? That's for pantywaists...' Leo was levering himself up from the table, empty glass in hand, 'don't want to offend the comrades if they're about to buy some tanks from us...'

'So far as I know,' I answered. 'But since they're copies, I imagine the originals are somewhere. No idea where.'

'And you didn't make copies yourselves?' Leo was at the bar, so in this lie I was on my own.

I looked him in the eye and furrowed my brow in wounded disappointment, the way politicians do when someone attributes base motives to them. 'No. I told you I'd owe you for the info on the two bodies. Here it is.'

'Ah, the two bodies...' he said, suddenly reminded. 'What came of that?'

Leo had begun a darts match so I lied on solo. 'Trail went dead. We asked around, Leo made enquiries. Turned out they were a couple of gypsies smuggling a boatful of hi-fis in from Yugloslavia...'

Wintersmith finished his half and excused himself. He had taken the information grudgingly, but he would get any credit that was going. He would go to his boss and claim he'd received a tip-off from one of his local sources, someone from his network, build himself up as a 'Bucharest hand' with eyes and ears all over the city...

'He won't use them,' Leo decided. 'He might have a go, run it by the top brass. They'll dither, sweat a little, then decide to refer it higher, then higher, and on and on until it magically disappears into the clouds. Wintersmith will remind them of the need to keep things sweet for the next trade mission, and off it goes, into the file marked "No Action". Waste of time.'

At the embassy gates Leo pointed out the Securitate man across the street, brazenly staring us out. 'So we *were* tailed,' I said.

'Of course we were.' Leo raised a James Bond eyebrow. 'Triple bluff. Basic rule of the game. If there's one thing I've learned about bluffing, it's make sure you finish on an odd number.'

I heard a few days later that Wintersmith was off work for a week. He had been violently mugged the next night on his way home and his flat had been burgled and vandalised. Now he was unable to move without a Securitate tail and his diplomatic pass had been rescinded.

Two

At his Herastrau flat Trofim was sending out invitations to the Union of Writers' launch of his memoirs. *A Life of Service* was the safe, on-message title chosen for him. The preface outlined the nation's giant strides under Ceauşescu, from peasant sump to model 'scientific' society. Its ghostwriter, Hadrian 'The Wall' Vintile, was vetting the guest list. Trofim let it pass, as he let pass all the other humiliations that had been visited upon his manuscript.

He had finessed simultaneous launches. While we toasted *A Life of Service* at the Writers' Union on October 7, *Memoirs of a Betrayed Ideal* would be launched, in its author's absence, at the Club des Belles Lettres in Paris, chosen because it was three doors from the Romanian Embassy. Trofim's French publisher had sent out the invitations already, but had not specified what the book was, a tactic that had piqued French interest more than the book itself would have done. According to Trofim, the luminaries – or, as he had it, *obscureminaries* – of Romanian expatriate culture would be at the launch: Toninescu, the dramatist of the theatre of the absurd; Ciulan the pessimist philosopher; Elianu the historian of myth; even the nonagenarian surrealist Tristan Isoldou. It would be like one of Toninescu's own plays: a book launch in Paris for an absent author, while thousands of miles away in Bucharest the same author was launching a book he did not write.

Every now and then Hadrian would note the presence of a discredited author or politician on his guest list and ask Trofim to reconsider: 'Comrade, Mr *X* is a well-known reactionary, implicated in unsocialist activities... Ms *Y* is considered to have developed a close friendship with counter-progressive *cadres*, and as for Petrescu the icon-maker – a well-known cultist and trafficker in religious imagery...'

'You see, Hadrian is a model editor,' Trofim said in a mellow, indulgent voice. 'Now that he has finished editing the book, he has started to edit my friendships!'

Hadrian looked up from his work with his thin, mutinous smile and announced proudly: 'I have tried to help the comrade here and there, of course I have. There were a few lapses of memory and tone, and the occasional regrettable tendency to make subjective judgments when such things are better left to the objective perspective of history.' I had never heard the Party line rattled off with such conviction.

I leafed through the pages. It was like chewing cardboard. Trofim's eight years at the UN were dealt with in nine pages, three of which were devoted to the visit of Nicolae and Elena Ceauşescu. It was leaden stuff, censored for interest-value. Meetings with Nixon, Kissinger, de Gaulle were described in single sentences. The Cuban missile crisis, the Vietnam war, the Hungarian uprising, Paris '68: all events Trofim had been involved in or witness to were simply missing. Stalin featured once, though I knew from Trofim's genuine book that he had had a close and complicated relationship with him. Randomly injected throughout the book were non-sequitur paragraphs about Romania's productivity and extracts from homages to Ceauşescu by third-world leaders. The only photograph that did not feature Trofim in attendance upon Ceauşescu was a photograph of him as a baby, and even this had been doctored to remove his rabbi father from the cotside.

'This will be a very important book, eyewitness history,'

Hadrian raised himself up, emitted his phrase, then slumped back down like a mechanical bunny in an advert for long-life batteries.

We lived in a world of shadows and decoys, Leo's double and triple bluffs. This book, the product of endless censorships and siftings, was the decoy, the separated twin, of an altogether more explosive and dangerous publication.

Trofim saw them both side by side in his mind: the one marrow-stiffeningly tedious, the other risky and colourful and about to incur him the severest reprisals. 'Yes, I think it will make a splash. I hope so. I am very pleased with the way the publisher is handling publicity – it will be going to all the major papers, and I shall be invited to help promote it.'

Hadrian nodded in bemused assent, trying to remember what special events the state publishing house had planned. 'Well, the signing in *Luminea* bookshop next month will certainly bring out the grateful Party members, and I have seen the reviews for *Scînteia* and *Săptămîna*. Resounding.'

'I should hope so,' Trofim muttered, 'you wrote them.'

'Have you thought about what you will do when it comes out?' I asked when Hadrian had gone. 'You'll lose your privileges, you might be arrested, lose your flat, your Party pension.'

'All this I know. I am not beyond their reach, that is for sure, but there is a limit to what they can do without making a martyr of me. Besides, there is more to come. I do not think I will be alone in speaking out. I have seen what is happening in Romania now. Things are tightening up because really, underneath, they are coming loose. I have given my life to the Party, and to socialism. I do not envisage, and I will not support, any alternative vision. But it is the Party that must act.' It sounded like a prepared statement.

'You're a good communist and you want a palace *coup*, that's what it is...' I nodded towards the deserted chessboard tables, 'it's all about tactics, isn't it?'

'Nothing I see around me here, or out there beyond our borders – in Britain, America, Europe – has shaken my belief that the socialist state is the highest and most equitable form of human society. Nothing. I do not have American tycoons, the Pope or free-market politicians behind me, and I do not want to make my country safe for big business.'

'You think removing Ceauşescu will make that socialist state work again?'

'Again? It has not worked yet. But you are under the misprision that the liberal capitalist state works. For whom does it work? Not for your poor and your unemployed, your third-world workforce and their pillaged resources. For whom does cheap petrol work? Not for those who produce it. Cheap food? Cheap manufacturing? Nothing I have seen has changed my faith. Not Stalin, not Ceauşescu, not... not this...' He indicated the freshly painted EPIDEMIA on the wall of the Natural History Museum. 'Do you think that you who live in capitalist countries would believe in the right to a job, a decent wage, free health and education if socialism had not shown you the way? The welfare state? The National Health Service? Socialism showed you that what your employers and bosses sometimes gave you out of paternalism or pangs of social conscience was in fact life's necessities, the minimum. You only think of them as rights because of socialism. Until socialism they were merely privileges or random acts of charity or luck. And that is before I talk of social mobility! Without socialism, without Lenin, and Trotsky and Victor Serge such things would be unimaginable. Capitalism owes its better self to us.'

'And without Stalin?' I asked, wanting to put the brakes on his sudden outburst of idealism.

Trofim looked at me, at first with a look of hurt, and then with a wry, evasive, smile. 'What is it your friend Leo has been saying these past few months? Hold on tight or get out quick?'

'Something like that...'

We watched a stray dog, its speckled, moulted skin yellowish pink, absorbed in a streak of another's urine. It pushed its snout into the sodden gravel, inhaled, then slunk away into the bushes. 'Well, he may be right, but not in the way he thinks. No one will mistake me for a capitalist outrider. I have dirtied my hands for the Party, as you know and many others will soon find out. I have purged and discredited. I have enforced and repressed. I have even killed people, with my pen at least... with my signature. It is not a revolution I want.'

'I said it earlier, you want a palace *coup*...'

'I want a bloodless transition. There will be no revolution here. It is not the Romanian way.'

'If there is?'

'The Party will intervene and I will support that. Gorbachev is right – our survival depends on liberalisation and opening up, but also on keeping control. Ceauşescus come and go. They are expendable. The Party stays.'

He had become sullen again. An agile, subversive mind, a sense of humour, intellectual brilliance... Trofim had all this, yet there remained a sort of bedrock, a faith in the rightness of the cause which stayed unsubject to rational questioning. I had been wrong to think of him as a dissident. He was a fundamentalist – a pragmatic one perhaps, but a fundamentalist nonetheless, for whom all the failures of the ideal were due to the misapplication of the ideal, all the barbarity of the system was extraneous to that system and accidental to it.

'Sophistry,' said Leo later, 'or, to use the technical term, *Bollocks*. Trofim knows that if there is a revolution, they'll string him up. He won't be the first in line, but they'll get to him eventually.'

'I'm not so sure. I think he knows that if he lets go and reneges on his lifetime's beliefs he will have nothing left: he has no family, no life's work beyond the Party, nothing but the here and now. It's not his life he's worried about, it's what he's given his life to. The Project.'

'Mmmm.... the communists abolished God but they kept the theology. They knew it would come in handy when they cocked up. At least God has an excuse for screwing up – he doesn't exist. These bastards most certainly do...'

'I'm sure that's part of it, but I'm sure he's protecting himself too: the best way to defend yourself against charges of dissidence is by proclaiming your faith in the Party, not by attacking it.'

Leo sat and thought it over. 'Maybe he's got something else lined up...'

'Like what?'

'Like a comeback?'

It was the on the fifth of October that the German weekly, *Die Zeit*, carried the photographs Manea had sent us. They were the full-page feature in the international news section, beside a generalised account of Ceauşescu's 'two decades of misrule'. *The Last Stalinist* was the title. In powdery, news-ink monochrome, our photographs looked even more chilling, like the set of a Hammer House of Horror movie.

Leo read the article out twice, each time with a different emphasis, re-angling some new piece of information in the context of other things we knew. Had Manea seen it? This was his doing after all, and he would be watching the consequences. I imagined him in his office, *Die Zeit* splayed across his desk, waiting for the rumble from Stoicu's office after a bollocking from the Comrade and Elena. That was one scenario. This was another: Manea under arrest, his confession ready for signing. What had happened to his predecessor, General Anton, a few years ago? The defection of his son to the US had left the general in an impossible position. The general tried to distance himself from his son, and even made a show of disowning him. But it was not enough: after a visit from Stoicu, he took a pistol into the woods and shot himself. Murder was out; enforced suicide was in.

The Union of Writers' building, the Casa Monteoru-Catargi, stood on Calea Victoriei. Set back from the pavement, contemplating an impressively proportioned but now desiccated garden, the building's porch opened up with a descent of marble steps beneath a glass and iron canopy.

There were forty or fifty people in the Sala Arghezi, where tables were piled with copies of *A Life in Service*. I was impressed with the author photograph on the back: Trofim as a student in Moscow, Lenin-bearded and confident. It was what Leo liked to call the *I'm-On-The-Side-Of-History – Whose-Side-Are-You-On?* look, and these days we only ever encountered it in old photographs.

Despite its name, the Sala Arghezi was dominated by two huge portraits of the Ceauşescus. Beneath them was a poem by their court poet, Adrian Palinescu, praising Nicolae as a 'Danube of Thought', a metaphor I found chilling given my recent acquaintance with that deadly river. The poems were terrible: there was no hope for the art of parody in a world where this was the real. Leo had once joked about writing an allegorical sketch in which Parody packed its bags, shut up shop and put a sign on the door that read: 'Closed. Any enquiries please contact the Real.' Palinescu's poems would have been the last straw that pushed Parody into early retirement. Ottilia looked at them and laughed out loud, an incongruous, high-pitched giggle I had never heard before. People nearby squirmed and tutted, keeping their distance.

The walls were decorated with gold and scarlet silk tapestries, now dusty and full of bald patches, and a row of glass cabinets displayed Arghezi's manuscripts. Beneath the

243

portraits of the Ceauşescus was a handwritten page of
Arghezi's great poem, 'Blesteme', *Curses*:

> Let moles and worms crawl
> Over the corpses of the famous dead.
> Let mice squeak in their hundreds
> Among purple robes
> And insects and strange moths
> Nest in precious things
> Larded with pearls and gold.
> Over violins and guitar strings
> Let spiders stretch their silent threads...

Who had placed that particular poem there – subversive
not by intention or even content but simply by accident of
context – and got away with it?

Ottilia's giggle had announced our arrival. Manea waved
at me from across the room as Trofim, red-faced and tipsy,
headed towards us. As in a vast dressing room, there were
mirrors on every wall. Wherever you stood you saw the
people behind and to the side of you – the Union of Writers
building must have been one of the few places in the country
where you didn't need to look over your shoulder all the time.
The room was strewn with oddments of furniture: elegant,
thin-legged chairs and console tables which, up close, were
chipped and scraped, their stuffing flat and their joints loose.
Ashtrays fumed from mounds of smoking butts. Every now
and then, like a tune picked out from noise, came the scent of
a new western perfume, fresh from duty-free or Party shops.
It crested the banal wafts of old clothes, mothballs and garlic,
then faded away. I caught Cilea's scent, Chanel, and followed
the links in its chain of vapour across the room to a fat Party
wife pushing *vols-au-vent* into her mouth.

The diplomats mingled in a sort of levitating boredom. I

knew by now that boredom could be a sort of out-of-body experience, something like a state of transcendence. But the diplomats were professionals, and the doyen of diplomatic Zen was the Belgian bon-viveur, First Consul Ozeray, who had dedicated his working life to doing as little as possible. A few years ago he had been caught in a homosexual honey-trap with a Securitate agent. They had burst in on him *in flagrante* and taken pictures. The story was that Ozeray insisted first on finishing his coitus; then, when they demanded he turn double agent, pulled on his socks and trousers and went straight to his ambassador to explain. His foreign ministry left him in post as an example that some people were beyond blackmail. He noticed me watching him, smiled and raised his glass to me.

Wintersmith was mingling, or at least *mingling* was the verb he would have used for the shifty at-your-shoulder hovering he specialised in. This was the first time I had seen him since we had given him the pictures. The side of his face was still slightly bruised from the beating, and there were stitches on the bridge of his nose.

'It's all right to talk, is it?' Wintersmith sidled up to us and looked at Ottilia, 'I mean with her here?' Ottilia gave him a look of such withering transparency I was surprised he didn't pinch himself to make sure he still existed. She went to join Trofim and Ozeray. Ozeray kissed her hand and she jumped back, blushed, then let his old-world courtesies enfold her.

'You never *did* do anything with those pictures, did you?' I said to Wintersmith.

'Well, no, you see... I was all for it...' he squirmed, '*personally* speaking. But we had a meeting and, well, it wasn't seen as part of a viable strategy. There were no definable outcomes...'

'You mean it might have buggered up the next trade fair?'

'Well, let's face it, the Germans and the French are in bad odour here because of those pictures. They've had their ambassadors summoned and I've heard the Krauts have lost at least one big helicopter contract...' He smiled what he intended as a *conspiratorial* smile, 'and it's an ill wind that blows no good. We're well on the way to getting it for ourselves.'

'By we you mean UK Aerospace or British Defence Systems...'

'I mean legal and respectable British companies who employ hundreds, and on whom whole communities depend.'

'Since when was the British Embassy the diplomatic arm of private business? And if you want to see towns and communities dependent on industries that don't get government sweeteners or the Foreign Office rooting for them, try the miners and steelworkers...' It was a mistake to let Wintersmith rile me. I stood there flushed and angry as he watched me with satisfaction.

'Or possibly the printworkers?' He smiled: someone else who knew my story. 'Learn to change what you can. Pick your battles. My job isn't to approve or disapprove, and if I let my feelings get in the way I couldn't do it.' Then, to show his independence of mind, he added: 'There's a lot I don't agree with actually. But the fact is that economics are the powerhouse of politics now. Political decisions are economic ones. That's a fact. Nothing to be done about it.'

'Ah, Monsieur Midwinter? Gilbert, isn't it?' Ozeray loomed up between us and closed his fingers around Wintersmith's hand.

'Er... Wintersmith, Giles.' The Belgian had him in a diplomatic half-nelson.

'Ah yes, quite so. I could not help overhearing your wise analysis. I remember when I was just beginning my diplomatic career.' Ozeray paused and closed his eyes, inviting us to join him in a prehistory where diplomats and dinosaurs roamed the same mirrored banqueting halls, 'my mentor,

Baron Henri Nivarlais, – a great diplomat – oversaw fifty years of the most radical change the world has known without batting an eyelid – the Baron, he said to me: "Young man, in diplomacy there are two kinds of problem: small ones and large ones. The small ones will go away by themselves, and the large ones you will not be able to do anything about. The biggest challenges in your career will come from the temptation to act. The test of your mettle will be how nobly you surmount it." Very fine advice, Mr Midwinter, do you agree?'

'Well, that's not really what I meant, to be honest...' Wintersmith was struggling. 'I meant ... well... there's plenty for the diplomat to do...'

Ozeray's smile drained him of the will to go on. When the Belgian finally loosened his grip, Wintersmith backed off into the crowd, a beaten man.

'Thank you. I wasn't making much headway with him, and I was starting to lose my temper.'

'My pleasure. That man is dreadful. I fear that in your country at least he is also the future.'

'Did you mean that?' I asked. 'What you said about doing nothing?'

He was saved from answering by a loud knock on the table. At the end of the room a grey dignitary banged a gavel.

'It is with great pleasure that our Union of Writers plays host today to the launch of Sergiu Trofim's memoirs. They give unique insights into the great strides our nation has made on the world stage over the last forty years, and especially the last twenty – years, we may say, of fruition.' There was a loud clack in the background: edging through the French windows at the end of the room, a smartly dressed Leo was beckoning to someone I could not see. He stumbled in, knocking his foot against the bottom of the door. After him came Ioana, tipsy and resplendent with embarrassment. The speaker turned to look behind him. Leo waved at him to carry on. 'It gives me personally great pleasure to read out a message of warm good wishes from the President Academician, our *Conducător*, Nicolae Ceauşescu, known as much for his love of literature as for his expertise in other fields. A Renaissance man in the truest sense, a genuine Union of All The Talents...' He paused, drew a big breath. There was a general grunt of agreement; a few ultras clapped.

Then came a further twenty minutes of preamble. People swayed in boredom. Leo tiptoed back outside with a bottle of wine, while Ozeray went into a kind of trance, his metabolism shutting down, like a tortoise overwintering. Ottilia prodded me in the small of the back and stifled a giggle. I felt her body move closer to mine. I put my hand behind me and held her waist. She came closer, leaned into my back.

Now came Trofim's turn. He walked to the Party-crested lectern, lowered it a few inches, and began his address. For the next half-hour, without looking up, he delivered a speech encrusted with the most tedious communist euphemisms, buzzwords and aspicated jargon. No jokes, no witticisms, none of the expected urbane or learned comments. Petrescu and several of Trofim's friends from the park scratched their heads in bemusement. Leo scratched his head too and looked confused. He raised his eyebrows at me: *what's going on?* I raised mine back in bafflement. Ioana shook her head. Only Ottilia looked alert, pressing my hand, willing me to share a joke only she was in on. I sensed the broadening smile on her face without needing to see it. There was a long, full-body yawn from the back of the room, finished with a loud baritone grunt. Everyone looked at Leo.

Trofim was doing it deliberately, making a speech that was so boring it became subversive, not by standing outside the conventions and taking aim, but by dragging them down by the dead weight of their own leaden logic: subversion through over-compliance.

When the guests had gone he led me by torchlight down to a cellar where an old fridge hummed and trembled in a pool of rust-coloured leakage. Round about lay piles of books and papers, their pages eaten away, soaked through or greened with mould. 'The archive,' he chuckled tipsily and he opened the fridge door. Six bottles of French champagne glowed on its only shelf. I carried them upstairs in a flat box marked with the scratched-out name of some forgotten or disgraced writer.

'A gift from Les Belles Lettres, by way of First Consul Ozeray, to help us celebrate our Paris launch.'

So Ozeray, altruist of inaction, had been our third man, the one who oversaw the French end of things, negotiating with the publishers on Trofim's behalf? Before we reached the function room, Trofim gripped my arm: 'There's no going back now. It's out of my hands... Let us drink now, for there will not be much celebrating afterwards.'

Ottilia and I walked home. We had crossed unspokenly into couplehood. We went to bed together that night, made love silently, eyes closed, then turned and slept apart, saying nothing. With Cilea there was always something porno-graphic about our lovemaking: I watched myself fucking her, she watched me watching. I had to be conscious of it, of the unbearable pleasure, before I could feel it in my body. The carnality had to pass through the mind and through the eye first; it needed their validation. Ours were the disembodied bodies of watched sex, and even when we were together walking or eating or doing ordinary things it was always framed as if we were looking in at ourselves. It gave us a kick, it doubled the pleasure. Maybe that was because we lived under surveillance, but for me it was also a facet of my self-estrangement, my sense of being a lodger in my own consciousness.

With Ottilia there was just us and the darkness, followed by a sound of raw sobbing that woke me and which I found came from myself. It woke her too, and as she turned to cover me with her body and stop my mouth with hers, I felt something breaking inside me. It was a far-off feeling, ice on a long-frozen lake starting to crack at some tiny bankside seam.

Three

Ottilia's shift started at 7 am, but she allowed two hours to reach the hospital. As the mornings became darker only the pseudo-sunrise of the building site, its fake floodlit dawn across the rooftops, gave her a profile against the window: a thin, pale body dressing in the half-light. Across the flat, the kettle on the hob began its stifled whistle.

I flicked the light switch but nothing came on. Another power cut, or still the same one? When I joined her in the kitchen Ottilia was holding the sports bag that contained her possessions. She dropped it on the table. 'Maybe you can move my things into your bedroom? Won't take you long.' When she smiled and took my hand and kissed my mouth again, I sank into her arms. I was afraid that last night had been just an excess of emotion and closeness, a release of tension; that she would pull back from me, from my half-formedness. She felt me lose my balance and sat me down at the table.

On my way to work I stopped to call on Trofim. The old man would have one hell of a headache, but he would also be bracing himself for the fallout of yesterday's Paris publication of *An Ideal Betrayed*. I would take him to lunch, tell him about Ottilia; we would walk in the autumn sun and make plans for when his book made the headlines...

The street was blocked, checkpoints at both ends. I walked

on past. The militia men looked alert today. I crossed the road, better to see Trofim's door and the balcony that looked out over the street. The windows were shut and the curtains drawn. As I approached the building, the door opened and two militia stepped out, accompanied by three Securitate officers, and blocked my way. I asked them what they wanted, but there was no reply. I handed my papers over with an unconvincing air of weariness. This was no routine inspection.

'Officers, may I ask what this is about? I am visiting my friend, a senior comrade, the former minister Sergiu Trofim. I am helping him with his work...'

No one spoke. They looked over my papers and pocketed them. One of the plain-clothes men pushed me into a black Dacia. I kept talking. I was a British subject, an ordinary visitor, without involvement in anything illegal... I looked back at Trofim's window and saw the curtain stir. The men in the car were professional intimidators from the same assembly line that produced the likes of Stoicu. They called them *plain clothes*, but in fact theirs was a uniform, and they were never there to blend in. These existed to be seen and sensed, to inject every room, every street corner, every spontaneous gathering with the poison of overt surveillance. They had the same brown or beige suits with gun-bulging jackets and boot-cut trousers, the same heeled boots and regulation haircuts. Leo might have had a go at laughing at them, might have risked a beating with a witticism. Not me. For the first time since the visit to the Boulevard of Socialist Victory, I felt fear. Not fear in the face of spectacular danger or unimaginable evil, but the fear of the individual who has erred into the machine.

We did not go to Securitate headquarters but to a poky basement flat near the central police HQ. The walls were damp and covered in peeling wallpaper. I was shown to a small table with two chairs. After twenty minutes a calm, professorial-looking gentleman joined me. He smiled and opened up a dossier. My file was already two inches thick. If I saw out my two years' posting it would be eight inches and require two of those Monocom box files I used at work.

'There has been nothing confidential about your stay so far,' he began. 'This dossier is so well-stocked with information from your friends and colleagues that we might have saved ourselves the trouble of monitoring you...' He showed me photographs: me on the balcony, the first walk to work, the staff canteen, Leo and I coming out of Capşa that first night. Trofim and me on a bench. Cars leaving the museum after one of Leo's *soirées*, me and Ottilia on the way back from Trofim's. Ottilia outside my house. Leo picking his nose and changing currency with a pimp. Wintersmith talking to me at the embassy gates. There was no sign of Petre or of Vintul, the only genuinely dangerous associates I had, nor of Cilea or Manea. Surely that told me something?

'You'll have to remember to give me those for my auto-biography. My Romanian period will be a small but important part of the story. And certainly the best-documented. Now tell me why I'm here.'

'Ah, English wit,' he replied evenly, still smiling, 'we will see how well it serves you in this new situation... we have a large file on your activities, many of which can be considered against the interests of the state. Many of them also illegal in straightforward ways: changing money on the black market, attempted bribery of state officials, associating with criminals, using prostitutes...'

'Prostitutes? I've never *used*, as you put it, a prostitute in my life. As for *attempted bribery* I think strictly speaking 'attempted' is not the word, as I've yet to see these attempts rebuffed...'

'Do not waste our time. What this evidence points to is common criminality. If you are charged with that, there will

253

be no heroics. Your embassy will not intervene in cases of mere hooliganism and criminal behaviour. You will be on your own.'

'There is nothing I can do for you. Charge me or let me go.'

'*Charge me or let me go?* I think you have been watching too many police shows. My favourite is *The Sweeney*,' he laughed and took off his spectacles, while with his other hand he swung a punch that landed hard in the middle of my face. I felt my lip split across my front teeth and my nose buckle to a noise like bark being stripped off a tree. The metallic glut of blood filled my throat.

My interrogator went on reading my file as if nothing had happened. He ticked a box on his cover sheet and inserted the time – 10.38 – followed by his signature. I strained to make out his name but it was deliberately illegible. Later, when they opened up the police archives here and in other ex-communist states, most of the reports were signed in these plausible pseudo-signatures, a generic squiggle of a name belonging to no one in particular while symbolising everyone's complicity.

'We will talk again. You will help us eventually. There will be no choice,' he announced convivially, as if we had just laid the foundations for a happy friendship. He put out his punching hand for me to shake, then left the room. My head was swimming, my face a mess of blood and snot. My tooth hung on a hinge of torn gum. The two Securitate who had picked me up led me back up the stairs to the Dacia. Someone had put plastic sheeting across the seat to catch the effluvia of the recently interrogated.

Back at my flat the front door was open, and the lock broken – needlessly, since they had the keys. Every room was turned over, cupboards emptied and drawers tipped out. Paintings and posters had been pulled off the walls and vandalised. The phone had been ripped out, my books thrown off the shelves and the shelves torn from the walls. The kitchen was covered in broken glass. In my bedroom, the clothes were strewn across the floor and slashed. Ottilia's bag had been eviscerated with a single slice.

I cleaned my face up in the bathroom. My top lip was swollen and the split was scabbing over. One tug and my tooth was in my palm. I dressed in what I could find and went out. At the Museum of Natural History I called Leo. There was no reply at home or work. I tried Ottilia, but the hospital line was dead. I replaced the receiver and wiped the blood off the mouthpiece. My head was ringing with the boxed-up sound of a television after closedown.

No taxis stopped for me. I looked like a brawl-bruised drunk who had rolled out of a cell or the station toilets. My clothes were crumpled and mismatched: a red T-shirt bearing the logo 'The Champ', green jeans, Chinese basketball shoes and a tartan scarf to shield my mouth. By the time I reached Piața Victoriei I was waving dollar bills at passing cars, but no one dared to stop.

A car horn sounded behind me, and Leo's blue Skoda pulled up across the kerb. 'Jesus. I thought they meant business by what they did to your flat.'

'I don't know what happened. Or why. I was just walking to see Sergiu on the way to work. When I got there...'

Leo picked up the two newspapers from the back seat. 'It's all in there.'

The front page of the *International Herald Tribune* carried a photograph of Trofim at the head of article entitled: *The Letter of "The Five": Ceaușescu's Critics Break Cover*. The article published an open letter from five senior communists calling for Ceaușescu's resignation and sent to all the major papers in the West. Leo then showed me the French *Libération*, which carried an article on Trofim's book and coverage of its high-profile Paris launch. *Libération* was serialising it the following week, as was the *Washington Post.*

'Trofim's under house arrest. It's all over town. Ozeray called this morning.'

Trofim's letter accused Ceauşescu of mismanaging the economy and instituting a Stalinist personality cult, of emasculating the Party and imposing third-world living conditions on the country. It expressed support for strikes and protests and finished by calling on Ceauşescu to stand down. In a final rhetorical touch it concluded: *The megalomania of a single individual has reached terrifying proportions: we are now witnessing not just the disgrace of communism but the destruction of a nation's culture.* Trofim was the chief signatory, and there was little doubt that he had authored the letter, calling for Romania to join Gorbachev's train of reformed communism. Trofim's Writers' Union speech had been the joke, but this was the punchline. With the help of Ozeray and a few others, he had choreographed it all.

'Canny old sod,' said Leo, 'he's pressed all the right buttons: liberal, one-party socialism to keep the Russians on side, *Pere*-bloody-*stroika* and all that, and just the right amount of dissident derring-do for the Yanks and Europeans to stick him on a pedestal. Wouldn't be surprised if there's people in Washington and Moscow thinking "Sergiu Trofim, now there's a man we can do business with..." The old Stalinist fox turned reformist hero. Jesus.'

'He's finished isn't he?' I said , 'political suicide. He's already under house arrest. What else are they going to do to him?'

'Not much. Look: five big communist chiefs write a letter to the world press. It'll be on all the radio channels tonight: World Service, France Culture, Radio Free Europe, Voice of America, Radio Moscow. It's all round Bucharest already, probably the big cities too: Cluj, Braşov, Timişoara. The embassies, the consulates, the universities... They'll shake him up a bit, maybe move him to some factory town with shitty restaurants and no library, make him sweat, but that's about it. If they put him in prison they'll make him a martyr. He's seventy-three – that's young for communist leaders – and he's a well-known Party statesman. There's a few years left in him.'

'What about the others? Who are they?'

'Four top-ranking but marginal ex-ministers. Stanciu, Ralian, Slavnicu, Apostol... I only know Apostol to talk to. Good bloke in his way.' Leo tooted the horn and overtook a cement lorry. 'Designated successor of Gheorghiu-Dej back in the sixties. Suddenly found himself out on a limb, all his allies rooting for our Kojak-loving comrade, and condemned to a life of ambassadorial postings in places like Venezuela and Bangladesh. And I know Ralian's daughter, sort of. Apart from that, they're just names.'

The evening's radio news was full of the story. On the BBC World Service, a segment of the main news bulletin was devoted to Trofim's letter. Radio Free Europe gave it an hour-long 'Focus on Romania' programme, with potted biographies of the authors and rolling commentaries from seasoned communism-watchers. Voice of America joined in with an eight o'clock 'Special Report' on Ceauşescu's Romania. Radio Moscow had the *coup*: a recorded interview with Trofim in Russian, apparently given three days before the letter appeared, in which he reiterated both his opposition to Ceauşescu and his own credentials as a loyal but liberal communist. It was the most explicit sign yet that he had Moscow's backing.

'Bloody hell. I'll tell you what's going on...' Leo tuned the radio, chasing every sliver of the story across the airwaves, but he didn't get the chance. It was Ottilia who spoke next: 'That interview was conducted by the head of the Bucharest *Pravda* bureau, with the Russian ambassador in attendance, in Trofim's flat last week.' Leo and I looked at her, astonished.

'How d'you know this? You've only know him a few weeks.'

I blushed with jealousy, and then at the obviousness of my jealousy: blush overlaying blush.

She smiled and kissed my swollen mouth. 'Trofim is now untouchable. They may keep him under house arrest and watch him carefully, but Ceauşescu knows that if he harms him, the Russians will act. In the end he'll have to let him be.'

'Genius!' Leo clapped his hands in admiration. 'The crafty old bugger. I told you, he's trying to make a comeback!' Leo went to the fridge and returned with Ukrainian champagne. 'This calls for *Sovietskoi* fizz.' Then, to me, 'go and get some glasses and take that smacked-arse look off your face!'

That night we joined Ozeray at the Athénée Palace Hotel, where he was finishing a long meal with one of his diplomatic dining circles. He smoked a cigar, surveying the debris-strewn table and its inebriated diners like a commander taking stock of his exhausted army.

Ottilia and I stood at the bar while Leo and Ioana, going through a rare phase of harmony, danced to some 'groper's classics' next door. Ozeray levered himself up, excused himself from table and joined us.

'Trofim has been moved. We don't know where. I've just spoken to Maltchev and he says they took him and drove away at ten this evening.'

Maltchev, the Pravda bureau chief, sat at the other end of the bar. He gave us a brisk nod at the mention of his name, which he obviously lipread from years of espionage training.

'They will take him somewhere where he will be uncomfortable and hard to find. But not a prison. Apostol and the others were picked up at lunchtime.'

'All this is information – it's coming from the Russians?'

'New circumstances, new alliances,' replied Ozeray, raising his glass to Maltchev, who raised his back.

What had appeared to be selfless bravery on Trofim's part now looked like a flawless campaign to get back in the political game, the scheming of a professional strategist. Ottilia had worked it out much sooner than I had. Trofim had tried to tell me, in his way: those stories about Arghezi, the plots and the purges, the multiple betrayals. He had not lied to me; on the contrary he had given me as many clues as he safely could. I had simply preferred to think of him as a disappointed idealist, an old statesman put out to pasture. I had felt protective of him, even jealous of his confidences. In reality he had run rings around his friends as well as his enemies. A voice behind me called out goodnight to the hotel's *concierge*. It was Maltchev leaving with his minders.

The entrance to the Athénée Palace was a revolving door whose segments were only large enough for one person at a time. It was the favoured haunt of those who thought they were being followed, or who wanted to show off how many bodyguards they had: since people could only go through one by one, it was an ideal sieving system for a surveillance society. It worked like a prism: everything slowed down and separated out. Tailing Maltchev were two obvious Securitate stooges, clearly fresh from the provinces since they tried to squeeze into a single panel of the door, and behind them a single KGB minder in a coat and hat. Further back, a woman stepped discreetly in, followed by a man in a brown mackintosh and trilby. An entire eco-system of surveillance prospered on the back of one Russian journalist.

The figure in the mackintosh, whose profile I now saw through the glass, emerged from the other side of the doors and into the street. He had a beard and neatly trimmed hair, glasses and a hat pulled low down on his forehead. But there was something about him that refused the anonymity. Or is that just how, later, I would justify to myself the sense that I had seen Vintul, that I had recognised his profile, and that when I knocked on the glass and shouted his name he didn't flinch? Anybody else would have. Was it him? I banged on the window again, but though all around him people stopped and looked in at me, he continued to walk on.

There was a bottleneck at the door. An old woman with a poodle the colour of dishwater had her suitcase stuck in the door, which jammed and left her trapped inside with her yelping dog. By the time I had passed through the revolving doors and out into the street, everyone had gone.

I ran out to the corner of Strada Episcopiei but he had disappeared. I could run on ahead to the Boulevard Magheru, but by the time I reached it he would have melted away. I turned and walked back to hail a cab. I mentioned nothing to Ottilia. As I stared through the raindrop-beaded window of the taxi, I became less and less certain of what I had seen. An unremarkable man, hurrying through an underlit lobby, whose profile reminded me, for reasons I could not grasp, of someone I had been looking for. Already his image was clouding over: what colour was his coat? Had he worn a hat? A briefcase or a bag? What colour hair? Eyes? By the time we got home to my wrecked flat, there was nothing left of him but the aura of something missed.

They moved Trofim, Apostol and the others to the outskirts. Slavnicu caved in as soon as they came to take him away – he signed a retraction and claimed to have been put up to it by Trofim and Apostol. They let him keep his Herastrau townhouse. Stanciu was diabetic, and Ralian had trouble walking, so they were put in apartment blocks, without lifts, electricity or gas. According to Ozeray, Trofim was in a one-roomed flat at the top of an unready tower block, where the only running water was what came through the roof and air conditioning took the form of unfilled window cavities.

Trofim became big news: the US and Soviet ambassadors demanded to see him, while the Romanian ambassadors to both countries were summoned to the foreign ministries to receive official protests. The French foreign minister made a speech calling on Ceauşescu to release the remaining dissidents. Trofim's publisher came in on the act, declaring that his non-attendance at his own launch, held to full media fanfare, with human rights activists, ministers, political exiles, and a fractious array of absurdist philosophers, poets and playwrights, had created coverage that exhausted the first print run. *The Sunday Times* ran an extract about the rise of Ceauşescu, in which Trofim revealed that he had been in charge of doctoring the Comrade's war record to make him into an anti-fascist hero. He called Elena Ceauşescu a 'barely literate laboratory technician and professional plagiarist' and named the scientists whose work she had, over the years, put her name to. Another paper ran photographs of the Ceauşescus' state visit: the Comrade and his wife with the Queen, hunting with a Conservative minister of Obelixian girth, and Elena receiving an honorary doctorate from the West London Polytechnic. Trofim revealed that eight universities had turned her down, and that she had at first refused to shake the Vice-Chancellor's hand because he was Jewish.

The other dissidents were quickly forgotten. Trofim was the story, emerging as the country's leading statesman-dissident. Suddenly American secretaries of state and British ministers, French government officials and Russian spokesmen referred to his illustrious career. He was profiled in an article in the *Washingon Post* in which Kissinger called him 'an alert, humane realist and old school European gentleman'. In *Pravda* he was described quite simply as 'the Party's choice', which was far from the case but would quickly become so when 'the Party' read this morning's *Pravda*. It was a risky tactic on Trofim's part: if there was anyone the Romanians hated more than Ceauşescu, it was the Russians. But he calculated well – the Russians were now preferable: Gorbachev represented the only chance of democratic change; and to the Party apparatchiks he was the only chance of saving their skins if and when Ceauşescu fell.

It was ten days before we found out where Trofim was being held, and when the information came out it was Ozeray who passed it on. No one asked how, but it was accurate, right down to the routine of Trofim's guards. We had a half hour window between shifts, where the usual four-man watch was reduced to one. We also had the biggest bribe I had ever seen change hands: two bags of frozen steaks, six bottles of Johnnie Walker, a dozen cartons of Kent, three Walkmans and a hundred dollars. If the guard were discovered, he would probably be killed. In my mind thereafter that package of money, food and electrical goods came to represent the price of a life in Romania. I knew there were places in the world where life was cheaper, but this was the closest I would come to seeing it cashed in.

The terrified guard met us in the dark lobby of the apartment block, a looming, leaning edifice of wet concrete and rusty twists of metal. It was nowhere near ready, but the mixers and lorries and cranes had moved on to the next job. 'Fourteenth floor. Flat six. Here's the key. Please be quick. This is very dangerous for me.'

We climbed. Leo's torch threw tunnels of light up ahead at dog turds, broken glass, the flattened, dried-out carcase of a mauled cat. On the eighth floor, a dog shivered in the corner of the elevator cubicle, a bitch suckling tiny puppies. She looked up, summoned all she had left in her of fight, and growled into the torchbeam. Leo slammed the elevator grille across her. The corridors were full of puddle water and uncollected rubbish. On the fourteenth floor, a scratching sound revealed a feral cockerel who jerked his head critically, training first one eye and then the other on us before striding into the unfilled cavity that was his home. He was probably the second or third generation of urbanised farm animals picking away at a living in the new suburbs.

Leo unlocked the door. A curtain blew in at us from an unglassed window. The flat was a shell, unplastered concrete walls and unsurfaced concrete floor. The main room was a mess of loose wires and unplumbed pipes. The stink of a full toilet came at us from a room to the side and the floor was wet. Trofim himself was lying on a mattress in the corner. We had woken him. Leo shone the torch in his eyes and he rubbed them, sat up, called out.

'Who's there?'

Trofim was still in the suit they had taken him away in. They had let him bring nothing. No books, no paper, no radio. His hands shook as he embraced us. His head was cut from some fall in the darkness. He composed himself and pulled up the only chair in the room and lit the camping stove. Leo took out some provisions: candles, biscuits, whisky, tins of baked beans and Heinz soups and sticks of German salami. The *coup* was three bananas which he produced with a flourish. Trofim looked thin and ragged. He had a painful, hollow cough. I remembered he had spent two years in prison during the war and six months in solitary confinement after it. He was probably better able to cope with this than most septuagenarians, but it had taken its toll. He spoke slowly, breathing hard.

'The news?' he asked. 'I've heard nothing. I spend the days alone. No beating, no torture, just isolation. I am managing.'

Ottilia pushed past Leo and rolled up Trofim's sleeve. She checked his blood pressure, looked at his eyes and listened to his chest. She took two inhalers out of her coat pocket, a jar of protein pills, and sachets of rehydration powder. For the first time I noticed she too had a bag. From it she took three bottles of mineral water. She poured some into a glass and added the powder, and handed it to Trofim.

'Sleep, stay warm, boil the water here before drinking it. Try to exercise a little every day.' Trofim nodded and placed his hand on hers. 'Here are some antibiotics – you have a chest infection – three a day for a week.'

'The others?' Trofim asked.

'Slavnicu and Ralian have given in. They say you tricked them into it. Stanciu's holding out, but he's ill. We've heard nothing from Apostol except that he's in Baneasa somewhere,' I told him.

Trofim nodded. 'Apostol will hold out if he thinks he will win. Stanciu's different. A good man, pig-headed, awkward with everyone, friends or enemies. He'll hold out from sheer stubbornness. He didn't even want to sign the letter in the first place. Now he won't retract it!' His laughter segued into a coughing fit. 'And how has it been reported?'

'Ah, Comrade!' Leo replied. 'I wondered when you'd get to the point! I have prepared a folder of cuttings which you can peruse at your leisure, in your luxurious *garçonnière*, while your friendly cockerel patrols the perimeter.'

Leo handed over a scrapbook of cuttings. Trofim scanned them – *The Washington Post, The Times, Pravda, Libération...* – and looked pleased. He peeled a banana and munched it slowly, eyes closed, focusing on the taste, then gathered two tin cups, a chipped mug and a rinsed-out pilchard tin, and poured the whisky.

'To friends at home and abroad,' he raised his cup, 'I will be home soon. This is not a tenable situation for them. They cannot keep me here. Will you do one thing for me between now and then?'

'What is it?'

'Find out where they are holding Stanciu and his wife and visit them? With some supplies?'

There was a loud knock on the door, and the guard came in, breathless and terrified. 'OK, time's up. They're on their way now. Time to go.' He looked at Trofim's stash of goods. 'Hide that. Under the mattress, in the toilet, wherever, but don't let them see it. Please, *Domnul...*' *Domnul...* a sign that even here, even among his captors, Trofim was on top.

As I left I gave Trofim what I had brought: a small short-wave radio and some headphones. I had thought ahead and put in batteries. He thanked me with an embrace. There were tears in his eyes. It was the first time he had displayed such vulnerability. Usually there was only a witty rejoinder, a handshake or a nonchalant goodbye. As I stood there with my arms around his thin shoulders, smelling the smell, despite his attempts at keeping himself clean and in order, of stale clothes, sweat, dirt and urine, I felt protective and respectful. It was what I imagined I would have felt for a father, had my father lived long enough to get old and had he been... well, like a father. Trofim's frail body was so easy to kill off but his calculating mind remained ahead of the game: the puppet master running the show not just behind the scenes but here, in this damp and dirty cell.

For an extra half-bootful of goods, the guard told us where to find Stanciu.

'We're not going now, are we?' I asked Leo.

'Why not? We're close by. It's safe – he's not being guarded at night because he can't go anywhere.'

Otilia checked her medical bag and found some syringes and ampoules of insulin. 'He'll be glad to see these.'

'Stalingrad Boulevard, block nine, sixth floor: apartment thirteen,' Leo repeated the address. The lift worked and the building was clean. Stanciu was being spared the worst, though it would still compare badly with the Herastrau flat they had taken him from. The lobby lights were on, the regulation forty-watt bulb holding its own against the darkness.

We heard the lift grinding in its shaft, but did not risk it.

We knocked at the door and there was no reply. We knocked again. After a minute or two, Leo slipped a note under the door. There was the shuffling of slippered feet, a raised male voice followed by the placating voice of a woman. Then the timid opening of the door on its security chain. A jowly old lady with bedraggled hair peered out at us.

'Yes?' There was weary dread in her voice.

'Mr and Mrs Stanciu?' Leo pushed his face forward and she retreated and closed the door. Ottilia pulled Leo away and put her mouth up to the door.

'Mrs Stanciu, I am a doctor and I have some medicine for your husband.' There was a pause, then the unlocking of the chain. 'Sergiu Trofim has sent us.'

'Go away. That man has caused us enough trouble. My husband was not himself. He has nothing to do with this. He deeply regrets it all.'

A ferocious growl came from inside the flat. 'For God's sake, woman. Let the buggers in!' The door flew open. Mr and Mrs Stanciu stood before us: she a smooth-skinned and lard-coloured communist matron; he a barrel-shaped, gouty, triple-chinned old trooper with short legs and a walking stick. His skin was yellow and his eyes watery. He sweated and his skin was clammy. I sensed Ottilia adding up his ailments, dividing them by his living conditions and trying to calculate the amount of time he had left to live.

'Who are you?' he demanded. 'We've been through this shit. I don't care any more. I'm not recanting. I've recanted enough. All my life it's been *sign this, retract that, confess to this, deny that; purge him, rehabilitate her*. I've had enough. You can all fuck off.' He sat down heavily on the sofa and jutted out the first of his chins defiantly.

Leo was soothing: 'Comrade, I respect your fighting talk, but we have not come here to ask for anything. On

266

the contrary. Your friend Trofim...' Stanciu harrumphed contemptuously at the word *friend* but did not correct him. 'Your *comrade* Trofim asked us to visit you and see if there was anything you needed to make things more comfortable.'

The flat they were being held in was efficient but without luxuries. A packet of flour and some fruit lay on the kitchen table, and there was a television in the room. Mrs Stanciu may no longer be shopping in the duty-free shops, but she was getting the basics in somehow.

'My friend, the doctor here, has some insulin which I believe you need.' Stanciu looked at Ottilia and nodded, his face lightening. She handed him the medical purse with the bottles and some syringes. He seemed about to say thank you, but pulled back. 'I have some things which I shall leave here for you and your wife to do as you like with.' Leo took out some cigarettes, tinned ham and salami, a half bottle of whisky and a few bars of chocolate. Stanciu did not move, but Mrs Stanciu leapt up and hid them away in a cupboard. We rose to leave.

Stanciu stopped us. 'What's happened to Trofim?' We told him. He harrumphed again; then, rolling a glob of phlegm around his mouth for a few seconds, spat a gelatinous khaki mass onto a handkerchief. 'He always was a crafty old Jew. The only man who could go into a revolving door after you but still come out in front of you. That's Trofim.'

Leo laughed. Stanciu glared at him. 'And if you think I'm going to thank you for your capitalist pity and your little luxuries...' he called out as we left.

'Yes, I know, I know...' Leo raised his hands placatingly as we backed out towards the exit.

'...you can fuck off!' The door slammed behind us.

That was Stanciu. Rude, boorish, fat and ill, he was the unsung hero. He had thrown it all away with nothing to gain;

now he refused – whether from bravery or pig-headedness – to back down. It was as Trofim had said: friends or enemies, he wanted nothing more to do with any of them. When the journalists and historians wrote up their accounts of the end of communism, I wondered where Stanciu and his like would fit in. While some, like Trofim, set in motion their high political strategies, and others took to the streets and pushed from below, there were those, like Stanciu, who bogged the system down in its own absurdity with individual acts of courage or perversity. What history, obsessed with individual stories of great men or the myth of collective action, would find space for them?

They released Trofim a week later. He was back in his flat after two days in the Party clinic, and though still under watch he was able to receive visitors. Stanciu and Apostol too were allowed back into their homes, but it was Trofim people came to: a train of ambassadors, Russian, French, German, Belgian, American, all with messages from their foreign ministers. In theory the old man was under house arrest, but the guards charged with preventing people from reaching him quickly became his social secretaries. One day, when Ottilia and I were lunching with him, the police captain in charge of Trofim's surveillance detail came in.

'Sorry to interrupt, *Domnul*, but the Canadian *chargé* is here. I have told him he's early. Shall I ask him to wait in the lobby?'

Four

Trofim adjusted to his semi-clandestine celebrity like a man returning to work after a long vacation. From somewhere, visibly not the Bucharest tailors, he was kitted out with sharp new suits and jackets. The regime continued its intimidation – intentionally clumsy surveillance, break-ins, phone-tapping – while, out of deference to the Russians, allowing him plenty of leeway. He was free to travel, spending a week in Moscow at the beginning of November, and a week after his return he was invited to give a lecture in Paris. The Romanian authorities granted him a visa immediately. They sped him on his way but he disappointed them by coming back.

Two weeks after his return, Trofim heard that Stanciu had suffered a stroke, and took me to visit him in the Politburo health centre on Strada Mihalache. Stanciu sat in a wheelchair with an old peasant blanket over his knees. His face was the colour of ash, and his left hand shook. A party-crested ashtray overflowed with Havana cigar stubs. The shelves of the clinic's visiting room were stacked with improving literature: Marx, Engels, Ceauşescu his'n'hers volumes of speeches and scientific treatises. Two portable metal lecterns, symmetrically placed at each end of the bookcases, held one of Elena's ghostwritten tomes on polymers and a book by Ceauşescu entitled *Socialism and the New Society*. A half-read novel in Russian by Gorki lay upturned on Stanciu's lap. A nurse stood by, watching and listening.

'Bloody hell. Not you again! Haven't you caused me enough trouble?' Stanciu gave an effortful chuckle, coughed, tried to spit, and managed only a thick dribble down his chin which he wiped with his dressing-gown sleeve.

'Are they treating you well?' Trofim asked in the traditionally upbeat but tactful way one addresses the dying.

'No complaints. Fuck all to do except listen to your body packing up and the teacups rattling. Sometimes I feel my leg's wet and I check to see if I've pissed myself again or just spilled my drink.' He took a sip of water. 'And all that fucking Gorki: when they open the KGB archives I bet they'll find out the reason Stalin disappeared him was that he was so boring.'

'Is there anything I can do for you, Comrade?' asked Trofim, 'it was I who got you into this...'

'Saul,' Stanciu leaned forward confidingly and dropped his voice, 'I'm always sorry we never finished the job Marshal Antonescu started,' he laughed. 'But yes, please, come back next week. And bring me some more of these...' He waved an empty box of Havana cigars at us and called the nurse to wheel him away.

'Great sense of humour,' I said outside, 'that joke about Antonescu. Very funny. I don't suppose he cares much about the Iaşi pogrom does he?' I was referring to July 1941, when ten thousand Jews, among them Trofim's parents and sister, were murdered by Antonescu's fascist troops. Stanciu had used Trofim's real name: *Saul*, his Jewish name, the name he had changed to the more Latinate Sergiu. Trofim's own *Romanianisation* was complete, but to some he would remain *Saul Trofinsky*. The rabbi's son from Iaşi belonged to another world, another epoch.

'It's just his little joke. He knows about it all right... he was there, and not, I may add, on the side of the righteous... Stanciu was a corporal in Antonescu's army, fighting with the fascists. He's from my village. We knew each other. During the war I was chief organiser of the Iaşi Party, but stuck in prison, a communist and a Jew. A double death sentence – just a question of which would be carried out first. But I was lucky. When I came out I got a junior prosecutor's job at the Antonescu trial. I picked Stanciu for Antonescu's firing squad and shredded his war record. After that he escaped the reprisals and joined the Party. Being one of Antonescu's executioners got him a long way fast after the war, and he owed me.'

Trofim leaned on the railings of the old church on Strada Monetariei and caught his breath. The doors were open and the smell of incense hung in the still, sharp air. He sniffed and grimaced, then stood back and brushed the front of his coat clean of the taint of religion. 'It was Stanciu who put the last three bullets into Antonescu when the soldiers missed his heart. He dined out on that story for decades. Each time he pulled the trigger, the corpse jumped – "like he'd been plugged into the mains!", Stanciu used to say. When the next round of Jewish purges came in the late fifties it was good to have Stanciu on your side. He's no anti-Semite, not really... but then again, most of those who tried to kill us weren't either. That frightens me more than a few Jew-haters.'

Trofim and I walked in silence for some ten minutes before suddenly, out of nowhere and as if in conversation with himself, he said: 'All right, I'll take you...' Trofim needed me there so he could talk to himself.

We about-turned and rejoined Mihalache, passing the clinic again and going back towards Piaţa 1 Mai. It was a considerable walk for Trofim, still frail from his punitive weeks in that husk of a flat. He leaned on my arm, and I saw the skin hang from his neck, the ring of shadow between it and his tieless, buttoned shirt collar. We came to the corner of Strada Neculce and Mihalache, to a high wall covered in cracked plaster and cement inset with broken bottles. We faced a pair of heavy spiked gates with a chain across them but no padlock. I looked at Trofim, and he read the question in my eyes. His answer was to lift a handful of ivy from a dirty brass plaque on the left of the gate: *Cimitirul Israelit Filantropia*. The Jewish cemetery. He raised his cane and ran it along the bars – a deep bronze ring that somehow fitted the red-gold of the leaves, the timbre of a dying day. We were on the tip of the afternoon, the sun massing what was left of its light and falling in strips across the pavement.

A tiny man came limping from a caretaker's cottage, fastening the buttons of his jacket as he went.

'Shalom,' the old man greeted Trofim. Trofim gave him a brisk handshake through the bars: '*Tovarăşul*.' This was their ritual: the religious salutation and the communist greeting, neither giving way to the other.

The gates crackled with rust as they opened. Beyond them, a tangled necropolis: graves at odd angles, stooping into clumps of grass and bramble, crumbling, broken or defaced. There was the pale lettering of graffiti that had been washed and repainted and washed again, until it had taken the quality of bas-relief: nazi slogans, swastikas, the Iron Guard's fascist insignia. The anti-Semites still came here to hate and desecrate, while the state, which recognised only orthodox cemeteries, left it to volunteers to maintain. The paths were strangled by waist-high weeds, their directions deducible only from the flattened undergrowth that marked out, here and there, a solitary mourner's struggle to reach a headstone. There were no ornaments, no flowers, and no euphemistic words: just names and dates, in Hebrew or in Romanian. If you squinted, the tops of the gravestones looked like the crests of waves on a turbid sea.

Outside the caretaker's cottage, a wrinkled, photocopied

map marked out the avenues, the graves of famous Romanian Jews numbered and indexed at the bottom of the page. There was no better symbol of what had happened to the Jews over the last hundred or so years: these graves, overrun, overgrown, leaning over or sinking back into the earth, held men and women whose descendants lived in Israel, France, America. The lucky ones. This was a place of death, not because of the dead but because the living no longer came. I looked at the names: Jewish names like Avram, Gerschom, Binyamin, names from all across the diaspora broken up and standardised into pseudo-classical Romanian. *Trofinsky* to *Trofim*, *Saul* into *Sergiu*...

The caretaker looked fearfully beyond the gates, listening out. I imagined his ancestors, or, judging by his age and frailty, himself as a young boy, straining to hear the thunder of the hooves which brought the next pogrom or the turning engines of the next deportation. That was all finished now, they said, but from the inside of his cemetery he knew otherwise.

Trofim stayed on the periphery of the tombs. This was a place of religion, *his* religion, but he would be buried in one of the Party graveyards with their granite squares and their enamel hammer-and-sickle badges, overseen by some social-ist-realist sculpture that replicated, without ever admitting it, the shape of the cross. I knew – I had seen the party cemetery in Snagov, its regimented lawns, perpendicular avenues, and in the centre a vast bronze sculpture of an aeroplane. Beneath it, an airman stood with his legs apart and his arms at right-angles to his torso, disrobing from his parachute as if taking off a shroud. Christ as pilot – all that repudiated Christianity seeping back into the images designed to replace it.

'You go ahead, walk around.' Trofim waved his walking stick at the cemetery whose furthest recesses now disappeared into darkness as the first few rows of graves burned all the stronger in the last of the sunlight. I set off. The graveyard resembled an evacuated town, full of broken slabs and gaping family vaults, their gates pulled apart, the tops of the graves jimmied open. Cats loped around; skeletons of pigeons or small animals were splayed across the marble chippings. There was a shuffle behind me, the crunch of gravel and dry twigs. The caretaker joined me, out of breath after a laborious scramble.

'He comes every week but never goes beyond the peri-meter... just sits on the bench. I've been opening those gates for him for thirty years. Always the same thing: he shakes my hand, sits down for an hour, then leaves.'

'Where is his family buried?' I asked, turning back. I knew straight away it was a stupid question, but it was too late to pull it back.

'Buried?' The old man shook his head. 'No – everything else but not buried...' For a few minutes we said nothing, then he spoke again: 'His son came once. Maybe ten years ago, to say *Kaddish* for a schoolfriend. The rabbi. Lives in Israel. Domnul Trofinsky sat in his usual place on that bench. He said hearing it was enough, that he had a nice marble rect-angle waiting for him in Snagov, *all tidy and rational, no mumbo jumbo...*' The caretaker dropped his voice. 'But I know he is proud of his son.' Suddenly he said, in panic, 'Look!'

Trofim was slouched over the bench. As we got closer to him, walking faster, a fear took hold that needed no verbali-sation. The walking stick had fallen to the ground and his hand hung over the armrest.

'Sergiu,' I called out. No movement. 'Sergiu.' I ran down the gravel path, and with that sudden expansion of mental space that adrenaline liberates for irrelevant details, caught sight of the small, blue, ankle-high iron and enamel signpost dug into the path, 'Bulevard Gala Galaction.' A city of the dead with its own grid and its own white-on-blue street names. Another city of lost walks. 'Saul!'

Trofim jumped and emitted a strange, muffled cry. He looked around, disorientated, blinked and rubbed his eyes.

'I am sorry,' Trofim said, 'I was dozing...'

'I thought you'd...' I stopped. He looked so frail, so white, that in this place the word *dead* seemed more like invocation than speculation.

'No, not that. Just practising...' he laughed and coughed and leaned over to retrieve his breath.

I helped him up, and he leaned on me a little harder as we went home.

November brought the promise of a merciless winter. Leo would walk out in the mornings, distend his nostrils, sniff the air: 'Smell that... take a good long noseful... the smell of retreat.'

The trees seemed to lose their leaves in one overnight fall. As the building projects ate into the remaining parklands, people hurried from one wasteland to another, foraging for firewood, twigs, burnable scraps to keep them warm. One night I saw them, illuminated by the moon in a clinically clear, cold sky: twenty or thirty scavengers with axes hacking into the stumps and parcelling out the trunks of the felled trees. The silence was punctuated by the regular *thwup* of the blade parting the wood's flesh. It was a medieval vision, however outscaled by skyscrapers and cranes, like a scene from a Brueghel painting. It caught for me the desultory, sad mystery of the place far better than the brutal images in Leo's files.

Bucharest was braced for the Fourteenth Party Congress. The gas and electricity were intermittent in most parts of the city, and where a system existed it was this: power rotated, sector by sector, in two-hour segments, starting with the city centre and gradually rippling outwards, by late evening, to the outskirts. This led to surreal scenes in which brightly lit blocks of flats exuded the smells of cooking and the rush of showers and bathwater in the dead of night. These pockets of nocturnal society were scattered around the rims of the city. Later, when the uprising came, it meant that large sections of the population – mostly those on the receiving end of the regime's incompetence and brutality – were up and ready to mobilise. Many had even washed.

The stories leaked out: of men and women sleeping in their kitchens with their hobs on for warmth, then dying of carbon monoxide poisoning when the gas cut out and then resumed as they slept. All over town braziers blazed with burning rubber and plastic, ribbons of acrid smoke catching the eyes and throat.

The week before the Party Congress, I decided to tell Leo that I had seen Vintul at the Athénée Palace the night of Trofim's launch. I had meant to surprise Leo, but I should have known he would be a step ahead of me.

We had both seen him, and each of us had kept it from the other. But Leo had investigated. 'I went to see Manea. He told me he'd seen a dossier meant for Stoicu that strongly suggested Vintul is an Interior Ministry plant, a Securitate agent, always has been. That he's been in charge of monitoring student activities, especially the underground scene. That he's been running the defection and escape programme on behalf of Stoicu.'

'Stoicu? You mean we've been puppets for Stoicu? How long have you known?'

'A few weeks. After your visit to Manea with Ottilia. I called Manea myself. He didn't know exactly who was Stoicu's man on the inside, but he'd narrowed it down to a few people, all of whom had now disappeared. Two of them we know are dead – you saw the photographs – and around here being

276

dead usually means you're innocent. One of the other possible Securitate plants was Petre, but since you've seen Vintul and so have I, we know it's him and not Petre. There's still a chance Petre's got free, but I've got to say I don't believe it.'

'What's been going on?' I asked. Leo told me to take a seat.

'It's all been a con. I know it now for sure. The escapes, the defections, the middle-of-the-night adventures. Most of them fail, or get caught, or end up like those poor sods sliced up in the water. That's because it's all part of a semi-official plan. The only escapes that work are the ones where money's been paid. Mostly the girls get smuggled out to the west and put to work as prostitutes. They've got no passports, they don't know their rights once they get to wherever they're going. The men, if they aren't lucky enough to escape from the people supposed to be helping them, are dragged back and made to work in the mines or the prison details. The ones who do get out join the gangs, black-marketeering, people smuggling... Look at what's happening – people flooding into the West from everywhere. Next thing you hear is that the girl you thought had made it to a new life was giving hand jobs on the hard shoulder of some German U-Bahn.'

That lorry driver, I remembered, the one who boasted about the Romanian girls he'd had in his cabin, two at a time. What had kept Ottilia going was the thought that these people had made it, that at least *they* had escaped and started a new life. Now it all made sense, the lack of letters or phone calls, the smooth operations where the border guards were always absent and the electric fencing always cut out on time. They weren't escapes from the system; they were part of the system, ways for the system to export itself and replicate in new places. It was an appalling thought, like being trapped in a board game where the board never ended and the players never left the table. That was frightening enough, but what Leo said next had the effect of at once explaining things and making them worse than I had ever imagined.

'It took me a while to work it out. Vintul had me fooled. But there it is. I've known him for four years, and he never once dropped his guard. That night in the Boulevard of Socialist Victory, when the police came by with the dogs... that was when he nearly blew his cover, would have if they'd caught us. He got us out, but only for long enough to sort things himself, kill the dogs, divert the police. They'd have caught us if they'd wanted to. Even plodders like the militia nightshift can catch two lost drunks and a stoned girl. Mel...' Leo shook his head as he remembered her. 'The bastard probably pulled rank on them, told them to fuck off, that they were disturbing an operation... killed their dogs just to show he could.'

Those Alsatians with their throats torn out, the ground sticky with their blood. No knife. Just hands and teeth. Leo paused. 'It doesn't end here, on this side of the border. It goes on outside. For years they've been selling people. They started with the Jews, selling them to Israel – ethnic cleansing *and* a chance to make some money. Stoicu's speciality, the Ceauşescus loved him for it – especially Elena. Then they did it with the German minority. Since then some of the top brass have seen the chance to make a bit for themselves. Things are changing. They know it won't go on like this forever. They need to have something stashed away for when it all goes to shit. Vintul had a business on the side: get paid, get people out, have them caught again when they've gone over. But even he was working for someone else.'

'Who's on the other side,' I asked, 'I mean, things like this don't work without some kind of organisation. Money, networks...' But even as I spoke I knew. Belanger. Belanger was everywhere, had preceded me everywhere. Even gone he was more here than I was.

'Belanger started here, with me, a few years ago. We had a

278

good thing going. He took to the business immediately. A bit of black here, a bit of grey area there. Buying, selling, bartering. He was a natural. Had vision... well, I mean... he saw where the chances were – he was the first to start making pirate copies of CDs and videos, action films, porn, you name it.... Soon he was dealing in stuff I wouldn't touch. Drugs – cut with anything he could find, stuff much worse for you than the drugs themselves. One batch killed more than a dozen people that I know of, blinded God knows how many. Girls. Started to hang out with Ilie and the pimps... he had some kind of a hold over them. Bought a BMW. Made contacts on the outside – people who'd only ever dealt black-market petrol or fags now suddenly dealt in drugs and whores. Overnight it turned dirty...'

'Yes, sure, because of course all your stuff was strictly above board, wasn't it?' I said sarcastically. I was angry. I tried to persuade myself it was the righteous anger of outrage, but there was jealousy there too.

'Not sure when Stoicu decided to muscle in, but he and his cronies wanted a piece of his action. Maybe it was Belanger who went to him. Either way, Belanger became his man. The ministry and the Securitate have always been involved in the shadow economy. I've dealt with them for years, low-level stuff, you know, buying passes, changing dollars... Belanger knew that and played on it, but he took it a step further. Didn't just bribe them, he started to *employ* them. "Shareholder," that's what he called Stoicu. *Quid pro quo*, he began to do Stoicu's work too: information-gathering, entrapment, really dirty stuff. Eventually I confronted him with it. In there,' Leo nodded towards the living room, 'I told him I knew what he was up to and I wanted it stopped.' Leo looked at his beer and frowned, then took a long gulp. 'I gave him a bit of a slapping, nothing violent, just to get it across. He let me do it, didn't resist or fight back, just smiled as I blacked his eye. He could have beaten the shit out of me, but instead he just laughed me out of the house.' Leo shuddered at the memory, and nodded towards the inside of the flat. 'I hear it every time I come up those stairs, the laugh of someone who can't be hurt. But I tried...' Leo continued, 'I mean I tried to hurt him. I called in a favour.'

'Manea?' I asked.

'Yes. I asked to have him taught a lesson. You know, the old "we're watching you" stuff. Christ, it works in Northern Ireland, punishment-beatings for petty thieves and criminals, compliments of your local paramilitary.' He managed a weak laugh, then his face turned: 'Manea was only too happy to oblige – the bastard was seeing his daughter, this was a way of doing both of us a favour. A few days later someone took Belanger aside and smashed his legs; one of them's permanently damaged. Didn't work. He just upped sticks and left, but now he runs it all from abroad, and that's worse. He's got people in his pocket from here to Vienna. Thing is, I've seen it grow, his business, and it's different now: harder, deadlier, the drugs and the girls aren't a sideline any more, they're the business itself. What I do is chicken feed compared...'

Belanger had been the original apprentice, the high-flying graduate from Leo's school of contraband and racketeering. Now he had taken his master's work to another level.

'You're sure he's behind it?' I asked.

'Yes. Yes, I am. Belanger's been laying down networks, patiently building it all up as the structures of old East Europe come down. He's the one who started smuggling people out of the country, and to begin with I'm sure it was *bona fide*. At least, I think the money was not the main reason. But not for long. Vintul was his man on the inside, and the trail leads up to Stoicu and then across all the prostitution rings, the drugs routes, the pirated CDs and videos...

most of the people who work for me are doing jobs for him on the side... Christ, it turns out I've been doing his work without knowing it... we all have...'

'Where does that leave Petre?'

'What I think makes no difference, but what I think is that it leaves him dead. I don't know how, or when it happened, but he's dead.'

'What about his Social Fund, all those goods and money he put aside? What's going to happen to all that?'

'Whatever Petre built up, it's all gone, that's if it ever existed – remember Vintul was the banker, the man with the names and places. He probably siphoned the cash and the valuables back to Stoicu and Belanger, and let Petre think it was all getting distributed to those who needed it. It probably never existed. The only things that were real were the names on Petre's lists, and they're probably in Securitate hands now too. Oh, and the money, that was real enough. For a while.'

'And you let me go on thinking I'd had something to do with it, that I'd made the mistake of bringing Cilea in and that she'd blown their cover?'

'I'm sorry, but what else could we think? It made sense: Cilea was Belanger's girl, still is, you were the only one who didn't know, of course we thought she was involved.' Leo looked down and shook his head. 'Look, if anyone's to blame, it's me. I'm the one who brought Belanger in in the first place, set him up, started him off. You can see why I'd want to avoid facing up to that...'

I left the room and slammed the door, leaving Leo talking into the void.

It should have been us telling Ottilia that Petre was dead, but instead she found out in the most brutal way. I had left Leo in the living room, consoling himself with an epic measure of Johnnie Walker, when, at about 10 pm, the phone rang.

'It's me,' shouted Ottilia, her voice faint against the sound of engines and helicopters.

'Where are you?'

'I'm at the morgue. Petre's here. Come and get me please.' She rang off or the line cut out – it was hard to tell. Leo was up and pocketing his car keys. We had not spoken since I had walked out on him, but by now we didn't need to: Leo knew what was happening.

It took nearly an hour for what should have been a twenty-minute journey. Beyond Aviatorilor there was a sky of blood and rising smoke, and roadblocks every two hundred yards. The morgue was under police guard, its forecourt deserted. The phonebox from where I thought Ottilia had called was empty. If she had been unable to wait here, she would have headed home herself. We headed back a different way, hoping to pass her as we went.

Out to the east, the MetalRom factory was on fire, its chimneys stark against a blazing sky. At the mouth of the Boulevard of Socialist Victory stood eight armoured vehicles, their engines running and their doors open. Inside, like pods of alien eggs ready to hatch, were armoured paramilitaries in helmets, gas masks and night vision goggles, hunched forward over automatic rifles. They were absolutely still, waiting to be released, deadly and impersonal, into the streets. Nearby were two black vans with generators on their roofs: refrigerated morgue trucks.

Suddenly, from the burning factory, came the sound of bullets – not the full, round sound you hear in films but a thin, matt crack of steel splitting air.

Five

When we reached home Ottilia had not returned. By now Bucharest was crawling with Securitate. Something was happening in the industrial sector. Leo reached the radio just in time to hear Trofim's voice on the BBC World Service. Now billed as 'Romania's most respected dissident', Trofim was discussing the army's heavy-handed response to a sit-in at the MetalRom factory. It marked the first sustained show of resistance against Ceauşescu in the capital, he explained: the sit-in had become a riot, and now the neighbouring car plant had joined in.

On a crackling phone line Trofim condemned the violence of the government's response. There were dozens of dead, and the hospitals were full of Securitate tracking down the wounded: 'What we are seeing in Romania is a travesty of socialism. While our socialist neighbours take the necessary steps to liberalise, we are seeing a war against the people themselves – against the very workers our government exists to serve.' The line died. The newsreader apologised and moved on to the next item, the opening of the borders in Bulgaria.

Leo and I were so involved in the news that we failed to notice Ottilia until she was standing right in front of us. She had walked through town, through the checkpoints, past the guards, with the image of Petre imprinted on her mind. This time it had been him.

Campanu, the pathologist, had called her in the early evening after finding Petre's papers on one of the dozens of bodies that had been brought in. It was different from the others, he noticed: first of all it was cold to the marrow, *morgue-cold*, and he knew immediately it had been dead for weeks, stored and then suddenly released; second, it was an execution-style bullet to the head – the rest of the casualties were messy distance shots; finally, unlike the others who had been carefully stripped of ID, this one still had his papers. Someone *wanted* him identified. Ottilia's tone was appraising, a clinician's description, detailed right down to the O of burned skin at Petre's temple. It was the composure before collapse.

Ottilia's clothes were wet where she had tripped and fallen among the blocks of broken ice used to cool the bodies during the power cuts. Campanu, fastidious and sad, had tried to help, busy as he was with the MetalRom casualties. He had given her something hot to drink and somewhere to sit and gather herself. Then she had simply walked home, the soldiers and militia letting her pass unchallenged like a ghost walking through the tumult.

Campanu was unable to tell her exactly when Petre had been shot. All he knew was that the body had been cold-stored and brought in with five of tonight's victims by a squad of Interior Ministry troopers.

For the first time since she began speaking I noticed a polythene bag in Ottilia's hand. She held it tightly. It was thick and transparent and wet inside – beads of water were clustered around the neck where she held it clenched in her fist. She dropped it onto the table to the sound of loose change, muffled by damp paper. She stood and looked at us.

'Go on,' she challenged, 'open it.'

Leo looked at me and I shook my head. He sighed and sat down, carefully shaking out its contents onto the table. Petre's watch, an East German Glashütte model, the best you could buy in communist Europe. I reached for it. It was cold and heavy in my hand, working perfectly despite a smear of condensation inside the dial. I laid it out straight on the table-top. There were some coins and the notebook where Petre wrote his song lyrics with pencil stub attached by elastic band. A Havana Club keyring stripped of keys and an ID card which Leo fingered nervously, brushing the dirt off with his thumb. There was nothing else. He looked up at Ottilia.

'Open the ID card,' she told him.

Leo did as he was told. Tucked inside the soggy cardboard of the standard Romanian citizen's identity card was a laminated pass the size of a credit card. I didn't know what it was, but Leo and Ottilia did. They had seen many like it. Leo dropped it as if it had burned his fingers. Ottilia looked away. It stayed where it fell, face up, the photograph of Petre in uniform aimed at the ceiling: an Interior Ministry pass belonging to Major Petre Romanu.

Ottilia began to weep. I held her tightly as she sobbed, great convulsive tremors riding her body. Her clothes smelled of smoke and cadaver-ice; they had brought the mortuary into our home, that odour of formaldehyde that overrode the smell of death so powerfully that it projected it back in devastating negative, filling the room. None of us could speak: Petre, a major in the secret police.

Leo began some explanation or excuse: the ID was a plant, Petre had been forced into it, it was all a set-up. I don't think he believed it, but Leo's way was to get through each crisis as it came, bluff it out and move on to the next one, changing the terms of the problem in the hope of wearing down the problem itself.

'No more, Leo – no more speculation, rumours, wild guesses. No more double and triple bluffs!' Ottilia cut him off.

She went to our room and lay down, dosing herself on sleeping pills. When I was sure she was unconscious, I left Leo to his brooding and joined her. I was woken by a ring on the doorbell, and the low, unflappable voice of Manea. It was eight o'clock. We had been asleep for three hours. I rose and splashed water on my face. It was icy, so cold it was like rubbing broken glass over my skin. I looked at myself in the mirror: a scoured red face, heavy eyes, sallow, unshaven cheeks.

Manea had parked round the corner. Even he was wary of being seen as he entered the flat. 'I am sorry this happened,' he was saying to Leo, 'I knew nothing about it until tonight. You must believe me. These are not my tactics, and this is not my department.' Then, seeing me, he said: 'Sit down. I think we understand each other when I tell you that both Stoicu and I have people infiltrating the opposition groups. Both of us play dirty when we need to. That's normal. It's our job. Each of us wants to know what the other is doing. He spies on me, I spy on him. I had someone on Stoicu's personal staff. What I know is that one of his operatives was involved in the university's music and *samizdat* scene, in the people smuggling and defections. His cover was blown and he is now useless as an agent. But he did leave a body that night after a struggle, the night those two boys were killed, and this body was shot in the head at close range near the border. That accords with our own reports of a single shot fired. This was the boy you came to see me about, the boy I then did not know about. Petre. The body was carried back to Bucharest with the intention that it would stand in for Stoicu's operative, take the blame, and Stoicu's man could resume his activities. The rest you know, or at any rate suspect: that operative, whom you know as Vintul, was seen and recognised at the

Athénée Palace. By you and by Leo, though neither of you thought to mention it to the other...'

'Petre was killed for that?' Ottilia was standing at the door, 'to cover up some bastard's Securitate activities? To *stand in* for the Securitate officer who killed him so you could all get back to your Party power games?' She gripped her left arm with her right hand, her nails digging into the skin.

'No – Petre was killed because he had too much on Stoicu and Belanger and the others. Because he was working for them without knowing it, making them money, trafficking people when he thought he was helping them make new lives but the time was coming when he would find out... Unfortunately the only one of them he didn't suspect was Vintul, which is why he trusted him right up to the end.'

Manea moved towards Ottilia. She put out a hand, motioning him to come no closer. He raised his palms in surrender and stepped away from her. 'Petre worked for me. He was my man on the inside. His job was to track down the racketeers and block their money, their foreign links, smoke out the corrupt Securitate officers. His job was to find out who was running it all, and he did find out...' He looked at Leo. 'But of course, you know that, Leo, you know who's running it all, because you started it...' Leo began to say something in his defence, then looked away. Once again we had come to the edge of that name – *Belanger* – and pulled back from speaking it.

Manea turned to Ottilia: 'When you came to see me I had no idea. I didn't know the details of his involvement with Vintul, and maybe if you'd been a bit more forthcoming when I helped you we'd all have found out sooner. I waited for Petre to make contact. I thought he'd re-emerge, take back his double life. Nothing happened. Petre was a good man, a better man than most of us. He never informed on others, never took part in the repression of citizens. He helped many people, and he always used his position to make things better. You all know that. But he was also a socialist. He represented what the Party could have been if it had kept faith with its roots and its principles. We're not all like Stoicu and his cronies. Petre hated the corruption and the brutality, hated what Stoicu and Belanger and the others were doing. If there's any comfort in all this it's that we are now in a position to act against Stoicu. The evidence that Petre gathered is what will nail him.'

He opened the door, paused, then turned back to us. He took something from his coat pocket. It was Petre's red, bound folder of names – all the people he had recruited for his network of mutual help, all their addresses, jobs and details of their contributions in time and money.

'This...' he tapped the cover, 'this needs to be destroyed. The Securitate will be looking for it, Vintul knows it exists, and I'm duty-bound to copy it and take action against everyone whose name is written here. But I'm giving it to you. As far as I'm concerned it's lost somewhere at the bottom of the Danube. Burn it.'

Nobody moved. We were too stunned to speak, to follow him down the stairs, to ask any more questions. After a few minutes, I smelled smoke where Leo had kindled a fire in my metal dustbin and stood on the balcony ripping pages from the book and feeding it in. The pages caught, turned brown, then scattered in black flakes into the air. In the morning's fierce sunlight, the flames were invisible. Finally Leo threw in the hard binding of the book, Ottilia and I standing over the makeshift brazier.

Stoicu's fall was swift and bloodless and secret. If I had been Trofim I would have admired it aesthetically, especially now that Manea, with his new reputation as the scourge of Party corruption, was promoted to minister. From one day to the next Stoicu's power base was dismantled and his staff reassigned. The level of corruption he oversaw amazed even the *nomenklatura* who had most gained by it. But what had really done for him was the proof, meticulously gathered through Petre's work, that Stoicu had been running a network of people-smuggling gangs, prostitution rackets and money changing scams on behalf of 'foreign interests'.

'For *foreign interests* read Belanger,' Leo explained, 'Stoicu's gone, and Manea gets his job... tidy, eh?'

Was that what Cilea had discovered when she went to Belgrade to meet Belanger? Had he said something to her? Was that why she had seemed to know, but could not tell me without looking implicated?

As far as public disgrace was possible in a society based on secrecy, Stoicu encountered it: re-housed to the outskirts and given a job as a caretaker, his wife divorced him within days. Manea's was a better class of corruption. There were no gold bath taps in Manea's flat, no gilt-threaded kimonos; there were no pyramids of caviar jars stacked in his larder like Korean pilchards in Monocom. Manea never wiped his mouth with the back of his hand or belched after drinking Krug with a Tsuica chaser in the 'Madonna Disco'. He did not parade teenage trophy-fucks at party gatherings or wear three different French aftershaves at the same time. His fingernails were clean.

And now he owned not just the ministry but the dark and ramifying underworld of enforcers and informers that fed it. 'Cleaning up the ministry, eh?' snorted Leo, bitter that this was one plot he had not been involved in, 'a *Bulgarian bath*'s what they call it here: a couple of sprays of deodorant and then business as usual...'

Ottilia scattered Petre's ashes over Herastrau lake, speaking inaudibly to him or to herself or to their dead parents, while

Ioana and Leo and I hung back. Trofim sat with Campanu on a bench behind us. Even the plain-clothes man, one half of the surveillance double act who now watched Trofim all day, had his hat off. It was a blue expansive day, the sky wide open, the trees' black and leafless branches rooted in clear air.

Manea's mercy extended to ensuring Petre's work for him remained secret. Word got out that he had died helping others cross the border. It was true in its way, I supposed. I liked Manea, I was grateful to him, but I had no illusions: knowledge was good to hold on to. You stored it as you stored petrol or food or currency.

Petre had been the only person I had believed was untainted by the viciousness and deceit we all lived in. But Ottilia felt betrayed and held me complicit in the betrayal – complicit by ignorance, and more precisely *wilful* ignorance, the mind's averted gaze. We had believed in Petre and that belief had stopped us succumbing to the very cynicism and suspicion that would have protected us from his duplicity. To rise above the lies, you had to stop believing there was any truth.

And besides, I had known Petre was dead since the night I found Ottilia in their flat. The abandoned guitar in its case, the amplifier still plugged into the currentless socket: I knew the language of abandoned objects – I had learned it at home – and I knew it then. I just hadn't given room to the knowledge or shared it with her. She held that against me too.

For me, what Petre had or hadn't done was irrelevant. He really had believed in his project, just as Leo believed in his. The difference was that Petre's was not escapism or evasion of reality, but an attempt to change that reality, to use it as a basis for something better. According to Manea, Petre's relationship with socialism was more complicated than we thought. Like Trofim, he could never quite let it go. *The Project*, however unreal it was, however little of it was left, was evidence of that. Most people were closet dissidents. Petre had been a closet communist. The good he had done was real enough, though he himself might not have been. I tried to explain this to Ottilia. I told her that Petre's double life didn't cancel out what we knew and believed of him. She looked at me with pity and something like contempt. 'Go join a church,' she said. And then. 'Or the Party'.

Ottilia thought she was left behind to shoulder the shame. She punished Petre by punishing herself. Whenever people eulogised him or praised his music or his actions, she cut them off or left the room. Grief, they imagined. Now she barely spoke to me, and our life together was made of silence.

She came home irregularly, throwing herself into a frenzy of dirty, risky work. She did unnecessary, unpaid overtime, slept on the ward, volunteered a day a week at an orphanage or a cancer ward: penance for his guilt. The nights without her I spent fearful and apprehensive, but they were better than the nights she returned. I listened as she threw up in the bathroom or sobbed in the darkness, and when I tried to comfort her she shook off every touch, flinched at every tenderness. I lay sleepless in the Bucharest night, listening to the cold shower in the small hours as Ottilia washed herself clean of the day's horrors.

One morning as I woke before her in the blue metallic light of a winter's 5 am, I saw her white coat covered in mud or grease. I took it to the kitchen to wash in the sink, turned the taps on and scrubbed it with my fingernails, the dirt coming off on my hands. She came into the kitchen and switched on the light. I saw my hands wrist-deep in red water, my fingernails crusted with blood, the sink ringed with rust-coloured scud.

All around us were preparations for the Party Congress. There were flyovers and military rehearsals, soldiers parading to martial music. The sky was filled with the ripping of jets and streaked in squandered fuel, while down below buses remained in their depots for want of petrol and people froze in their homes. Even as shifts were disrupted and workers couldn't reach their unlit factories or offices, targets went up: more steel, more cars, more wheat, more corn. *Scînteia* carried news of broken production records, of a stupendous collective effort bringing us to the edge – *the very foothills* – of a new, *illuminated*, era. *Epoch of Light!* was the headline.

'Epoch of the forty-watt fucking lightbulb,' snorted Leo, hurling the paper across the room – lightbulbs too were rationed now. 'I'm off to see if I can meet my whisky targets. Anyone care to join me?' He unscrewed the top of a fresh bottle of Scotch and settled in for a glum solo expedition to its depths.

But the drink missed its mark, the dinners at Capşa failed to divert. Leo began to abandon his racketeering, losing customers here, forgetting deliveries there. All was spoiled for him by what had happened to Petre, and by Belanger. Only his work kept him going, his book of lost walks that grew fatter and fatter as there was less and less to describe.

The obliteration of the city now happened at such speed that vacant spaces appeared where just a few days before there had been people and buildings. It was not unusual now to pass a place you knew and to find it gone, as if the ground had swallowed it up in one mouthful. I remembered that silent Chaplin film where a man returns to his demolished house and fails to notice it has disappeared. He walks to the absent door, inserts his key into the memory of the lock, opens and steps inside, even wiping his feet on the missing welcome mat. It is not until he tries to sit on his favourite armchair – a composite of air and memory – that he falls on his arse and realises there is nothing left.

A British deputy foreign minister arrived for the promised official visit the week of the Congress. It had been due to be the Foreign Secretary himself, but the visit had been progressively downgraded as Romania became more and more isolated. Trofim and Leo refused to go to the reception, and Ottilia was not speaking to me, so I went alone. Wintersmith was in charge, and on unctuous form. He gave me a conspirator's wink as I passed him, and pointed to Cilea who, despite the cold, was alone on the terrace, smoking. I came up behind her, but she greeted me without turning.

'Will you take me into the Ship and Castle?' she asked, looking out across the embassy compound, 'I need to explain before it's too late.' She slid her arm through mine. We were strangers again, Cilea reverting to the careless, shallow intimacy of our first few meetings. As always I felt the power of her sexuality and the loneliness that had haunted me whenever I was with her. My fullest moments with her had been felt as lack.

'Too late? Isn't it too late already?' I asked.

'No,' she replied, 'there's more to come. There's always more to come...'

We sat at a corner table, she in her black cocktail skirt, I in my clumsy suit. People looked at her: her long black hair, her red mouth, the improbably tanned but unblemished skin. Her eyes were black and burning, and her cheeks red from the cold.

'You knew, didn't you? About what had happened to Petre...'

'Yes, but not all along, and only when Florian mentioned something about one of his men – one of Stoicu's men – dealing with my father's internal security agent on the border. It had been brewing for months, all part of the power struggle between my father and Stoicu. Belanger didn't order it, if that's what you're asking... actually it's been more trouble for him. When Manea's man brought down Stoicu he took down half of Florian's Bucharest network too... if it's any comfort, you had nothing to do with any of it.'

'Consider me comforted,' I said sarcastically, 'and that's the man you're going back to? The man you love?'

Cilea looked at me in surprise: 'Yes. I know what Florian is. I know what my father is and I love my father.'

'Tell me about him... Belanger I mean, tell me about *Florian...*'

Her fingers trembled, the cigarette ash shaking and crumbling onto the table. She blew it onto the floor, then took a long, sustaining drag. 'Where do I start?' she asked. 'Besides, you don't really want to hear...'

That was true.

They had met in 1984. He had just arrived, a young lecturer on his first posting from the UK, visiting the country of his ancestors. He knew Romanian from his grandparents, Frenchified Bucharestians – '*bonjouristes*' – who had emigrated after the war. He knew nothing of the place, but right from the start he seemed to be drawing on some buried familial experience of it. It was as if he had been there before. He called it *déjà vu*, she said, this feeling that he had from the moment he arrived at Otopeni airport and found the place opening before him. At first his own facility with the city took him by surprise. Then he mastered it. The map was already in his head; walking the streets merely unfolded it. He began with Leo. They took walks in the night; they were inseparable. He said that each step was like a switch reactivating the place beneath his feet. Leo had been here three years already. He had had time to put down roots, scout out the terrain. He had already started his contraband empire. But it was Belanger who really *knew* the place. He knew instinctively how far he could go, what would sell, how much for, how long to stockpile and when to release. Leo was an amateur, and besides, there were things Leo wouldn't touch which Belanger was happy to trade in. Within six months Florian Belanger was... Cilea searched for the phrase... *in the driving seat...*

'How did you meet?'

'My father. My father introduced us, though he regretted it pretty quickly. At a party at the French Embassy. Fourteenth of July. Belanger was there, he'd already started doing his own thing, cutting his own deals. Leo hated him because he had no respect for all those things Leo loved: art, buildings, books. Belanger didn't mind what they were doing to the city. It cleared space, he said. Made things sellable... moveable. Leo always said that fifty per cent of business was making things portable... *portable!* Belanger took him at his word, that's all...' Cilea smiled at the reminiscence. 'Everything was being dismantled, unscrewed, taken apart. Belanger packed it up and sold it. That first night he took me for a drive. He had a suite in the InterContinental, a penthouse, like something from an American movie. He stood at the window and showed me Bucharest in the semi-darkness and told me that one day it would be lit up like New York or London. There'd be all-night shops and nightclubs, twenty-four hour restaurants, theatres and cinemas, flashing neon signs. I laughed. I didn't believe such places existed. Not then.'

What Belanger had offered her was the Bucharest of the future. 'He took me to Paris, Madrid, Rome. My father disapproved, called him a criminal... tried to have him arrested and deported, but by then Belanger was working with Stoicu, and Stoicu overruled him. He was a protected man. Manea was humiliated. Then someone attacked Florian, smashed his legs. Threatened to kill him if he stayed. He never walked properly again. Then one day he left.'

I said nothing. Whatever kind of man Belanger was, Cilea had loved him then and still loved him now. She would never be talking about me like this.

'He wasn't a gangster or anything. He wasn't seedy or violent. I never saw anything of what they said he was involved in...'

I cut her off: 'The Belanger most of us know about was a drug dealer and people trafficker, who made money from the sex trade. He sold off pieces of a disintegrating city and colluded with the Securitate. He bought human misery at rock-bottom prices and sold it on at a profit.' I was surprised by my own vehemence. I hated Belanger, because of Leo, because of Cilea... I was living with his cast-offs, I had borrowed from his life to fund my own.

'Most of us? How dare you? You're not part of any us! You're not part of anything, not any of it. You watch, that's all! You float along. You just go with what there is, with whoever there is – Leo, Ottilia, that old Stalinist Trofim, that slimeball over there,' she jerked her head at Wintersmith, who was at the bar with the deputy foreign minister; he sensed he was a fleeting subject of conversation and waved at us. 'Florian made things happen, he changed the way things worked. He wasn't evil, he just wanted more than he had, like we all do. He didn't choose the system, but he made something from it. He didn't make the world. He's not Ceauşescu or Stoicu. He's not even Manea Constantin. He doesn't have to sit and be judged by thieves and murderers and collaborators.'

'That's shitty logic. Sick logic.' I had no image of Belanger, but in my mind I saw a photograph with a blanked-out face, and that blankness drew all my hate. 'Where is he now?' I asked.

A dampness behind me, like the musty draft that rides the backswing of a cellar door, told me Wintersmith was at my shoulder. Cilea pulled on her gloves. 'Pleased you could make it,' said Wintersmith, trying to kiss Cilea's hand, a greeting he must have felt behoved his promotion.

'I must go,' she said, giving me a dry hug and moving through the noisy bar room.

'I'll get you a drink,' said Wintersmith, raising his eyebrows, 'you can tell me all about it...'

While he was at the bar I left and walked home. There was a subzero undertow to the air. Winter was baring its teeth.

Six

That night I dreamed I was asleep on a train, that I woke and the train was still moving, the carriage swaying and the noise of screeching brakes and metal grinding against metal. The sound of sparks, the smell of sulphur. Clothes and suitcases tumbled from the luggage racks. Outside, a crescent moon swung from side to side like the rim of a hypnotist's watch.

Further down the carriage, my lost parents were unfazed. They moved calmly through the chaos, riding the air. As I struggled across the swaying compartment to reach them, they passed further and further back into the obscurity. Their expressions were neutral; then, as the shadow ate away at them, their faces contorted in horror and pain and melted to bone and darkness. They raised their hands to me as the blackness burned them like a reel of film catching flame, and when I reached for them they were gone. There was warm ash on my fingers.

When I woke a second time, the dream stopped, but its décor still moved. I looked around me. A great shuddering convulsion had taken hold of the whole building. The house shook from the foundations up, a long rippling wave followed by the delicate crashing of glass. Then came silence, that species of stillness we only hear as aftermath: the hanging air, time torn and gathering itself.

It was early morning. My bedroom curtain-rail had fallen

and plaster dust covered the bedsheets. The window frame was loose. The bookshelves hung lopsided. I got out of bed and was surprised to feel the floor still solid beneath my feet. It was cold, spiky drafts pushing their way into the room. The balcony, when I went outside, gave a little underneath me: the building settling into its foundations.

Outside the place had burst open: between road and pavement, pavement and housefronts, windows and window-frames. Every point where one part of the world was fastened to another had come asunder. The city's innards were coming out: water, burst drains with their cargoes of shit and slurry, compacted earth and rubble. Fire hydrants fountained up, peaked, then splashed the pavements. Sewage, a monster from the deeps, pressed up slowly from every crevasse, a shiny brown curdling that swelled up as it made contact with the air.

I pulled on my clothes and ran downstairs. The handrail was loose, the hall chandelier held up only by its wiring. The electricity had gone, which was just as well, given all the cables that now lay in water or drain sludge. There was a large crack shaped like lightning down the wall and you could feel the wind outside coming in, the darkness and the cold prising the bricks apart.

There were no voices, no sirens; there was no sound of people stirring or panicking. Just the wind singing of fresh cavities. There was another tremor. 5.15 am. Outside, the scene was not so much devastation as a protracted teetering: blocks perched ready to fall, walls leaning into mere air, balconies hanging from threads of steel. The place looked normal, just a little shabbified, as if subjected to a sudden accelerated dose of wear and tear.

I fetched my camera and set off to Leo's. Lipscani was a ten-minute walk away, and I would doubtless come across something he could use.

The quake had happened nearly twenty minutes ago. As I passed the lower end of Calea Victoriei I heard activity: sirens in the distance and militia cars without headlamps speeding towards the city centre. I passed Trofim's street, which was mostly undamaged and where fear had passed into a kind of self-interested curiosity. A man speculated that the quake would flatten the new monstrosity in the town centre and good riddance. Some cautious laughter ensued, followed by a *Shhhh...* as I passed by, a stranger with a camera.

Lipscani was full of noise and bustle. An informal action group had already taken control. Two gypsy men gave out bandages while a local Party man went around calling out names from what was, even in Romania, called the 'voting register'. Outside Leo's block three matriarchs fanned the flames beneath a vat of Tsuica-fortified tea. People huddled around its alcoholic fumes and queued with whatever they had – empty cans, plastic cups, broken china – for a ladleful. The power had gone, but ferocious braziers sent out waves of scorching heat. I asked one of the women if she had seen Leo. She handed me two paper cups of alcoholic tea and sent me to the next corner where Leo was eating aspirin from a jar as if they were peanuts at a cocktail party.

'They've been predicting another quake for years. We're lucky it's only this. The last one was in seventy-seven; killed two thousand people. Doesn't look to me like this one's done much damage, but the real test's going to be in the outskirts. The sort of gerrybuilt shit they've been putting up out there, you've got to wonder...' He sipped his tea, adding Tsuica from a bottle in his pocket.

'Lipscani's not done too badly. A couple of roofs fell in, chimneys came down... a big crack in Strada Lipscani itself, but nothing they can't sort out with a bit of resurfacing.' He noticed the camera strap over my shoulder. 'You seen anything interesting?'

I had snapped the convoy of militia cars as they headed into town, but wasn't sure the light was good enough. I hadn't wanted to draw attention by using a flash. From an open window a radio played folk songs, and down below Leo had his long-wave set tuned to the BBC World Service. There was no mention of this morning's earthquake. Unusually, there were no police here either – Lipscani had been left to its own devices.

'Probably all headed into town to check the damage to the Palace. Christ knows what it's like in the outskirts. You wouldn't want to be on the top floor of one of those apartment blocks this morning would you? Poor sods.'

Across Bucharest the old buildings were undamaged. The only one on Leo's street to suffer had been bisected by a falling crane rather than the quake. Only the back wall of the house remained, with its oddly undisturbed paintings and still-smouldering fireplace. Even the bibelots on the mantelpiece stood unharmed, draped in a layer of plaster dust but looking invincibly delicate.

'You see, it's always the small things – the luxuries, the decorations, that survive. The frivolous stuff. When they excavate ancient sites, it's a few jewels of beaten gold or bits of broken pot. An earring, a perfume bottle, we recreate the lost civilisation from. All that's built to last disappears... crashes down or ebbs away. No place ever tells the story of itself as it planned to do... look, a forty-tonne crane comes crashing down, but the little china dog on the shelf survives...'

There were flaws to Leo's argument, but he was not ready to hear them. Already he saw this earthquake as a punishment for the outrages that had been visited upon Bucharest by Ceauşescu. Everywhere we looked, old churches or houses stood intact, while their hulking new-built neighbours had cracked from foundation stone to roof tile. It was difficult, even without Leo's cranky urban animism, not to see it as an Old Testament-style retribution. I half-expected to see clouds of locusts bearing down on the city.

From the university's library dome where Ionescu had his attic office, we looked out at the damage while our former boss made Tsuica coffee. In the gathering light, Bucharest's skyline was piecing itself back together. In the city centre, things looked normal: the *Scînteia* building's needle-like spire still stood, as did the towers of the three cathedrals. Below them, like a range of minor hills clustered around resplendent peaks, the uneven roofs and domes of the old city. It was on the outskirts, in the places where Bucharest stopped and the Saturnal rings of urban blankness rippled off into the distance, that the real destruction appeared.

'Have you noticed what's missing?' Leo asked, pointing at an apartment block whose top two floors had collapsed into one.

'Noise?' I ventured. 'People and noise?' That was usually what was missing around here.

'Them too. No, look. Look at those flats. Look at the broken concrete. There's no steel framing – after a few floors they just build onto what's there. They don't bother with joists or girders. They just build floor upon floor, breeze block on breeze block. After a couple of floors there's nothing holding them up.'

The coming weeks saw a frenzy of demolition for which even hardened bulldozer-watchers were unprepared. The Buildings Directorate used the earthquake as an excuse to demolish swathes of old Bucharest. People were shifted from flats in places like Lipscani, Dudesti and Dorobanti and rehoused in buildings that were at once unfinished and dilapidated. After the earthquake many also came with a dose of the unromantic ruin, caught between the abolished past and a future that refused to arrive.

Leo and I continued to film or photograph the demolitions, but they were happening too fast. I filled a dozen films with images and could have filled a dozen more. Leo had them developed and sent them out, filing reports for Reuters, *Le Soir, Le Figaro*. Bucharest's diplomats, orchestrated by Ozeray, began protesting. What was happening here was only part of it: out in the provinces, in Sibiu, Timişoara, Moldova, areas where the minorities lived, all signs of different cultures were being eradicated. It was desolation: villages that had stood for centuries were bulldozed in a morning, to be replaced with high-rise blocks surrounded by scrubland or factory complexes that looked like abandoned galactic penal colonies. Romania was being turned into a huge, pastless no-place.

'You see that?' Leo asked, pointing at the world's largest structure, the Palace of the People, an entire horizon's worth of concrete, steel and marble cladding. 'That's the world's biggest mausoleum. When they've finished building it, the whole of communism will climb in there, shut the doors, and die. They think they're building the city of the future. What they've done is build their own tomb. The Megalo-Necropolis, the new city of the dead, waiting for its tenants.'

On the first of November we witnessed the worst of the demolitions, the one that would stand as a monument to all the vandalism, crudity and farce of the city's 'remodelling'.

The monastery of Saints Cyril and Methodias had stood for centuries on the south-west bank of the canal. Now it was in the way, its four-hundred-year-old tower an offence against the new skyline. It had withstood earthquakes, fires, woodworm, the Turks, rot and neglect, but now it would make way for the 'People's Leisure Park': a year-round communist pleasure dome with underlit arcades and static rides, grey candy floss and the all-day seepage of uplifting music. The

303

plans were on show in the Party HQ: neo-classical pillars and plinths holding up a huge glass bell, a crystal palace for totalitarianised leisure.

This was an unusual demolition. The tower would be dynamited – a new measure to make sure the very stones were smashed and not merely sundered from each other. It would be unrebuildable. When the demolitions started a few years ago, notable buildings were only dismantled and put in storage. They lay in their stone archives like the undead in their graves, ready to rise again and haunt Ceauşescu. Now it was more vindictive: buildings blown up and steamrollered, then heaved as ballast into great holes beneath where they had stood. It was like those death camps where prisoners were made to dig their graves before being shot as they knelt over them. *Megalo-Necropolis* Leo called it, and despite his apocalyptic talk we had all begun to feel that these were terminal times in a Bucharest that was becoming both its own ghost and its own grave.

We stood with a small crowd, braving the cold and the Securitate's cameras. I recognised Andrei Liviu the poet, deathly pale but walking steadily. He had made it from Constanţa for this protest, and his presence was drawing attention. His cancer was in remission but everyone knew it was only a matter of time. In his new poems he likened it to a group of plotters regrouping in the shadows, readying themselves for their coup against his body. The book had been banned because the Ministry of Culture censor had thought the cancer was a metaphor for the state. They were wrong: the state had become a metaphor for the disease.

Ion Marinaru was there with his wife. They made a handsome pair, the nearest Romania had to film stars. With them was the novelist Vasile Iorba, another good Party member now breaking cover. His last novel, a futuristic story about a penal colony on Mars, had only scraped past the censors because

Elena Ceauşescu herself had read it and adopted the idea as a policy goal. The Romanian Cosmic Research Centre, with her as its patron-director, owed its existence to the small, sarcastic man who now stood smoking and stamping his feet on the ground, unlikely father of the national space programme. These people were standing up to the authorities for the first time.

There was a whiff of experimentation in the air. Nobody knew how to stand or look defiant. They tried different postures and expressions and spoke loudly to keep up their confidence. The police were no better prepared. We knew some of the Securitate had been involved in the quelling of disturbances in factories and mines. We knew about all that, but this was different – these protestors were writers and artists, Party members, religious believers and technocrats, foreigners and diplomats. There was no blueprint for the authorities dealing with this.

At the back of the crowd stood Ozeray and the Russian *chargé d'affaires*. Behind them, moving along the edges, was Maltchev speaking into his Pravda dictaphone as his photographer took reams of pictures. The presence of the Russians emboldened the crowd. Shouts of 'Gorbachev! Gorbachev!' and '*Perestroika!*' could be heard towards the back. From elsewhere in the mêlée someone called out 'Trofim!' and a name I had never heard before: 'National Salvation Front!'

At sunset came the crack of dynamite. The tower flinched. A few tiles fell from the roof, then the little wooden belfry lost its rafters. There was another moment of hesitation, then the whole edifice convulsed, expired, fell down into its outline, sleeving its own descent. Up came a cloud of dust and rubble. The way was clear: the wrecking balls tore into the building like a pack of dogs, crashed through the barriers, flattened the gate, trampled the graveyard and burst through the monastery's walls. The wooden beams flew out like matchsticks.

Leo hurled himself at the police cordon. They pushed him back again and again until a Securitate officer pistol-whipped him and pulled him into a waiting car. The car started up, drove off then suddenly stopped a hundred yards away and threw him out into the waterless canal. By the time I reached the bank, Leo lay in a heap at the bottom, blood from his head spreading slowly outwards.

Two gypsies helped me drag Leo up to the roadside where I called Ioana from a functioning phone booth. Her first response was, 'What's he done now?' She came over immediately in a neighbour's Lada. We moved him onto the pavement; I was holding the back of his head, the sticky blood warm and slowly pumping from an open split in his scalp. Ioana sat with his head in her lap while I called Ottilia at her hospital, leaving a message in English, hoping it might ensure some response. Leo's lips were blue, his breath so faint it barely registered. If those who ministered to the living were unfindable, I had to try those who ministered to the dead.

'I'll do what I can,' said Campanu. I heard him suck on a cigarette, then the clink of something metallic on china. If I didn't know he was in the middle of a post mortem, laying a scalpel down in a metal dish, I would have thought he was putting down his knife and fork and lighting up after a meal. 'It's the other end of the process I specialise in, you know that... I'll do my best.'

He arrived within minutes in a morgue van with a stretcher and a pile of zip-up black bags, like bed-sized bin liners. Campanu felt Leo's hands. 'They're already cold,' he said, taking a pulse and listening for breath. 'We don't have much time...'

At the hospital I saw Ottilia immediately, standing in the lobby with a trolley ready. Beside her, one of the nurses smoked fiercely and stamped her feet in the cold. It was nearly dark now.

'I got your message,' Ottilia said, 'Diana was having a smoke in the office and heard you. Bring him here. Hold his head steady.' We transferred Leo to the trolley. As usual the hospital looked deserted.

Once inside, Ottilia took out her stethoscope and listened. I detected a tiny shake of the head, but refused to acknowledge it. No one else saw it – Ioana was stroking Leo's blood-matted hair as we moved, Campanu concentrating on guiding the trolley through the endless recession of corridors. She lifted his eyelids, Leo's pupils far up into the socket cavity, bloodshot white globes completely still.

'If he's got a cracked skull, a depressed fracture, the blood on the outside isn't the problem, it's what's happening inside. If he's having a haemorrhage I can't treat it and I can't do it here... there isn't the equipment. If any of the bone from the fracture has gone into the brain tissue, it may be too late anyway, and even if it isn't there's a chance of brain damage. I won't know until I've cleaned him up and given him a scan.'

We wheeled Leo into an operating theatre. 'I'll scan him and stabilise him. If we're lucky, it might just be a closed head injury, bruising of the brain tissue, some kind of contusion... there's still a risk of course, but it's something I can deal with. The other thing is that he's lost a lot of blood... he may need a transfusion...'

'No!' Campanu was shaking his head. 'No... you can't do that. It's too risky. The blood hasn't been tested properly. The morgues are full of people with hepatitis from infected blood. There's more people dying from that than from blood loss. You know about AIDS too. You can't do it. It's too much of gamble.'

'It's up to you,' Ottilia said, looking at Ioana and then at me. 'I'm giving you the options. We have blood. Campanu is right – it's unchecked, we haven't got the facilities to check it... we don't know whether it's infected or not. We don't know anything...'

'Do it if you have to,' I found myself saying. Ioana looked at me, but said nothing. Ottilia nodded.

The nurse assembled a drip and wheeled a ventilator towards where Leo lay. Ottilia taped in the mouthpiece, inserting a tube into his arm. She motioned us to leave. Campanu stayed behind. 'I'll come and tell you as soon as there's anything to tell,' she said, taking my hand and leading me out. It was her first act of tenderness since the day Manea had told her about Petre. The nurse came past with some bags of blood on a tray. They looked heavy, the blood dark and plethoric and dense.

'Why don't you go back to the flat?' I asked Ioana. 'Wait for him at home, rest, get the place ready for when he comes back. He's going to need someone with him. I'll call as soon as we know anything.'

'I was about to leave him, you know. I was going to tell him today. I've been meaning to for weeks but I just never plucked up the courage.' Ioana was crying, her hand covering her eyes. I had never seen her cry; I had always admired her ability to turn sorrow into anger, to turn the passivity of pain into an attacking energy. That ability failed her now. I said nothing. I was thinking about the logistics of a seriously ill Leo needing constant care. It was a difficult thing to envision, but it was better than the image over which I had superimposed it: Leo dead, his body wheeled through those double doors and out into Campanu's van. I was cold and afraid, ready for another bereavement. And not just afraid for myself. With Leo gone, the loneliness would be collective.

'He's impossible to be with. He's out all day or up all night writing. There's no life for us here – it's just his book and the city and the bloody black market. Cutting deals, taking pictures... we were never going to live normally. I wanted to get out. I'm going to – as soon as they open the borders. Maybe before. I told him. He didn't even look up from his scrapbook – "Mmmm..." he said. Just that. Wasn't even listening. Then I repeated it, hoping he hadn't heard, but he had: his answer was "You go if you want to." I tell you, he didn't even look up. Now he's in there, and he's going to die, and I was going to leave him.' She gripped my arm. 'He thought he was keeping the place together, he thought he was its rememberer, the one who'd put it back together again. He doesn't understand, he's just a higher parasite, picking through the debris. It's got so bad he's started to imagine places that were never there. They're more real to him than we are...'

Ioana lay on the bench and slept. I smoked and paced the corridor. After three hours Campanu emerged. Despite the cold, he glistened with sweat, his fingers trembled as he smoked. His hair was wet and spiky, his sleeves rolled up above his elbows.

'She's relieved the pressure on his brain, operated and stopped the haemorrhaging. His skull is cracked but it's going to heal. He's responding well. He's got a fractured ankle too, so he'll be in a wheelchair when he comes out, and he won't come out of that for a while.'

'Can I see him?' Ioana asked. Campanu nodded. 'Don't expect much – he's not going to be conscious for days, and he won't be up to much when he is. Go in.' He turned to me. 'He nearly died in there. I could have been wheeling him out to the morgue for his Y incision. Instead I'm here telling you you'll need to take care of him, nurse him back to... well... *normal*,' he gave an exhausted smile. 'I don't come across many reasons to believe in miracles in my line of work, but what Ottilia did in there, though completely explicable medically, was, in these conditions, a miracle...'

Ottilia came to get me, her white coat bloodied and her hair stuck to her forehead. I had dozed off – fear alone had kept

309

me awake, but when it went I fell into a chasm of soothing, imageless darkness. 'He'll be OK, but after a few days here he'll be best off somewhere else. Take him to yours, I'll come back and check on him when I can.' She led me inside, where Leo lay unconscious, connected up to a tangle of pipes and drips. In the background a machine bleeped evenly. I stood over Leo and touched his face. He was warmer, fighting his way back. 'Where's Ioana?' I asked, wanting to share this with her, to see the relief in her face. We looked around but she had gone.

They moved Leo to a room that was less a ward than a holding tank for sickness, a place where diseases recovered from their cures and came out fighting: better and stronger and more resistant to treatment. In the deserted corridors, infections patrolled invisibly, bugs and viruses sought out new flesh to fix on and dig into, their hunting grounds constantly replenished.

After three days Leo opened his eyes, his head creaked first to the left, raising a shaky salute to me, then to the right where Ottilia sat reading. Leaning on his elbows, he hauled himself up so he could see beyond the horizon of the bedsheet.

'Jesus...' he croaked, 'if I'm alive – and looking around I'm far from certain I am – then you've got to get me out of here before I die.'

Two days later we drove him to my flat, his ankle bandaged. Ozeray discovered an antique bamboo wheelchair, the sort used by white settlers in the Congo to tour their over-watered lawns. Attached to the rim was an adjustable parasol of grey silk, and the armrests held an ashtray and sockets for bottle and glass. It suited Leo, who spun around like a wheelchair Napoleon inspecting his troops. Our student Iulia turned up one day at my door and took him out for what she called a 'test drive'. She came the following day, and every day thereafter.

Leo knew Ioana had gone before we did, and knew she had gone for good. When I went to fetch his things from their flat, hers were missing. There was no note. Whatever farewell had passed between them had done so in the hospital: she had meant goodbye and he, by osmosis or mood-transfusion, had understood. He never mentioned her again.

Leo adapted well to life on wheels and, after a few days of zipping round the flat smoking and drinking Yugoslav sparkling wine, he returned to work. At first it was only in short bursts, since his head ached and concentration hurt, but as he regained his strength, he began asking for night-time excursions, me pushing and him taking notes in a Monocom exercise book. His first trip was to the site where the monastery had stood: a scraped-clean empty circle of dirt with a cordon of shredded ribbon flapping in the breeze.

Ottilia visited every day and stayed long beyond what solicitude for Leo required. Something had changed in her. After ten days, we bit the bullet and bathed Leo, who was half-drunk and as truculent and difficult to manoeuvre as a fourteen-stone baby. After we had washed him and changed his pyjamas, he fell asleep. We turned off the lights and tiptoed away, muffling our laughter.

As gradually as she had left, Ottilia came back. That night she asked to sleep on the sofa. I offered her my bed, which she refused. Later I went into the living room and heard her breathing and unsleeping. In the darkness, when someone has their eyes open, you can hear it. I touched her face, and she put my hand to her mouth.

'Why did you leave me?'

'I blamed you, I suppose, but not as much as I blamed myself. I looked up to Petre, I thought he was flawless, a perfect human being. I thought he was honest and principled. And because I couldn't blame him for not being all that, I

311

blamed us for believing that he was.'

'Everyone believed it. But he was all that. He was just something else too.'

A few weeks ago that comment would have drawn nothing but scorn. 'I know that now. I tried to stay pure, clear of it all, and always thought that, up against him, I was failing. I tried to stay uncompromised, to measure up, not to myself of course but to him. It would have been cleverer to realise we were all compromised and to work with what there was, with the reality given to us. Bend a little here, gain a little there...'

'You're sounding like Leo.'

'Am I? Maybe... maybe it's time I did, a little...'

'Everyone's compromised. We all are. Petre was, he would have been even without working for Constantin. It's a question of degree.'

'Are you compromised? I don't think you are.' She turned to me, frowning, as if considering the question for the first time.

'What d'you mean?' Was it a compliment? Maybe I *should* be compromised. Maybe that was my problem.

'Exactly that – to be compromised you need to have a stake in things, you need to have something to lose and something to gain. You have to be risking yourself, not all the time, but enough of the time to be weighing things up, principle over self-preservation, the gains, the losses....You don't have that. You don't have a stake in any of this.'

'That's a hurtful thing to say – I do... I've got a stake in all of it now, Leo, Trofim, my job... I don't have anything else outside what there is for me here. And there's you, isn't there...?' I trailed off. She kissed me and turned over, pressed her body into me and rested one hand on my thigh. 'Isn't there?'

Seven

On the night of the ninth of November I returned from walking Leo to find Ottilia hunched over the radio, straining to hear someone speaking against a huge noise, a noise distorted by the vibrating casing of my long-wave set.

It was the sound of a riot, but a riot of joy. A reporter was trying to make himself heard against a rolling turmoil of happiness. Several times he stopped to gather his own emotions – his words strewn across a debris of abandoned sentences – and started again. The pulsation of radio static, combined with the noise-barrage from the Romanian jamming satellites, meant we kept losing crucial pieces of the narrative.

We were listening to the fall of the Berlin Wall. 'They'll all be killed,' Ottilia said as the East Berliners hacked away at the concrete, some with pickaxes and hammers, others with forks and knives or just bare fingernails. The reporter described the police standing and watching, the border guards paralysed by the enormity of what they were seeing. An order had just come through telling them to stand aside. Many were beaming happily at the crowd, years of fear and the imposition of fear suddenly counting for nothing.

Leo and I cheered. Ottilia's reaction was different – she really believed they would be killed, that at any moment the tanks would roll in. It was just as well it was happening in reality, since she would not have been able to imagine it: the Fall of the Wall, even as she heard it unfolding, was not something real to her. It took Leo's expertise with a television and a cable signal box to give Ottilia what she most wanted: live images, direct from Berlin.

Erich Honecker, the GDR president, had resigned. He had visited Bucharest in May – I remembered his motorcade of shiny black cars seeping down the road like an oil slick unfurling over water. Only two weeks ago he was receiving Ceauşescu in East Berlin; it had been all *fraternal greetings* and *helmsmanlike discussions*. Now Honecker was gone, it was only a matter of time before the nautical metaphors turned to shipwreck and flotsam...

The news went on all night. At one point, a Hollywood actor with a German name, star of a prime-time show about California lifeguards, climbed on the Wall. A strutting, plasticated showbiz clown with a mullet, he was hoisted onto the rim of the Wall and sang so badly and so surreally that even the East Berliners pickaxing the concrete took a few seconds from their elation to gaze at him in weary affront. Leo nodded philosophically: 'That's the price you pay for freedom. There's always a price...' then tore the ring off a Becks Bier and raised it frothing into the air: 'To Freedom!'

But the morning of the tenth of November came with the same grey corrugations of cloud, the same steely wind, the same police in their usual positions. When the *Scînteia* vendor called out 'Read all about it... The world looks on in amazement... read all about it!' we stopped dead and waited for what came next, squinting at the front page. Had *Scînteia* reported the fall of the Wall? 'Read all about it!' he said with heavy sarcasm: 'Romania's new tractor successfully launched at the Albanian Agricultural Fair.'

Leo snorted and wheeled himself to the car.

'What's up, *Domnul*?' asked the *Scînteia* vendor, 'first the

Czechs, then the Krauts... won't be long now before they start printing some real news over there...' He jerked his head out towards the great concrete needle of *Casa Scînteia* where the paper was written, edited, censored and printed in one over-whelming Soviet-style building.

Leo disagreed. 'If I was the Comrade and I'd had my evening's *Kojak* ruined by the collapse of East German socialism, I know I wouldn't be thinking, *Well, perhaps I was wrong about this communist business, maybe I should reconsider the Era of Light, maybe what we need's a free election...* bollocks I would! I'd be speeding it up, I'd be coming at them harder, faster, more ruthlessly. And that's why the dying periods of these bastard regimes are also the bloodiest, dirtiest, most dangerous. What was it Ceauşescu said last week? "Stalin did all that a man in his position should have done."'

The Fourteenth Party Congress began on the first of December. The hotels filled with delegates from 'friendly' countries and organisations. The Greek communists camped out in the Athénée Palace with the French, the Serbs and various neo-Stalinist factions from the West. All the Africans were billeted in the InterContinental, which filled with Ethiopians, Tanzanians, Angolans and others, many still involved in conflicts they had forgotten the precise details of even as they slugged it out with fists in bars or spat at each other in the dim lobbies: about borders, airspace, trade embargoes.

For the regime's Pandar-in-chief, the arch-pimp Ilie, this was the busiest time of the year. He and his entourage prowled the edges of the social circuit ensuring the supply of sex and narcotics, and Bucharest's rail stations were full of young girls from the villages who had been brought in to swell the ranks of sex workers. Ilie made more from the Congresses and Party conferences than his whole year's income put

315

together, turning Bucharest into a vast incubator of venereal disease as the local strains met and crossed with foreign exotics. Leo said that VD brought out the good communist in everyone: it was the only thing that really got shared around.

But the city was dead at the core. Helicopters patrolled all day; at night the cylinders of white glare from their search-lights swung through the sky and scraped the empty streets. What they would have seen with their pilot's eye view was this: a cold, unpeopled city whose tightening rings of fencing resembled the circles of gunsights, and in whose crosshairs lay the party HQ.

The frosts had taken hold, a carpeting of white powder in the early morning and trees with their crystals of icicle-fruit. The first snow was a hesitant white glitter that had melted to grey kerbside sludge by midday. 'It's just a first sowing,' the *Scînteia* vendor told me on the morning of Congress' Grand Opening. Snow as seed – everyday language stayed close to the soil even as the people who spoke it were uprooted and herded into concrete shells. The next day it took hold: a dense crop of whiteness spread shin-deep over the city. In the Piaţa Republicii the gritters started harvesting it, leaving a stubble of salt and cobbles in their wake. The parks were desolate.

On the third of December, the Iraqi embassy hosted a reception for the Arabic translation of Ceauşescu's *Socialism and the Scientific Society.* 'The hottest ticket in town,' Leo boasted, waving his embossed invitation.

Ottilia and I dropped him off and went to the Palace of Light cinema to see Buñuel's *The Discreet Charms of the Bourgeoisie*, a surreal, political satire on capitalism that looked very much like a surreal, political satire on communism. It must have been the director's political leanings, rather than the film's content, that got it past the Romanian censor. In the film, people who looked and sounded much like Politburo members and their spouses gorged themselves on Capşa-esque food. Their shallow patter set off the only thing about them that was deep, or at any rate deep-rooted: porcine greed, fear, and a lethargy-blunted viciousness of spirit.

The auditorium was an ex-theatre with boxes and piebald velour seats with *art nouveau* ashtrays set into their armrests. You watched your films through a *Carpati* fug that barely covered the smell of chewed garlic bulbs and Tsuica-breath. The film was certainly getting a reaction, but I doubted the censor would pass this one again.

The audience of students and workers cheered when the bourgeois were shot and booed as the fine food passed their bourgeois lips in scene after scene of fine dining. From the back of the cinema, there were cries of 'Down with the Pigs' and 'Ceauşescu Bloodsucker'. When a particularly odious snob slurped her soup on screen, a man called out, 'Elena! Hurry up, the next course is coming!' The laughter was uproarious.

Suddenly the side doors of the cinema opened, and in the lit doorframes Securitate stood and blocked the exits. 'Get back into your holes!' shouted one voice in the crowd. Others laughed, 'Rats', 'Nazis', 'Thieves'. The doors shut and people cheered, but only the naive thought the Securitate had left. After the film, the Securitate combed the aisles demanding ID; now that the houselights were on only a few defiant protestors continued. One boy walked up to the Securitate pair at the exit and challenged them, waving his arms about and brandishing what looked a Party card.

It was my student Oleanu, the class informer, undergoing a cross between a Damascene conversion and a nervous breakdown. 'Why do you do this? Is this socialism?' He shook with fear and anger, waving his Party card in their faces, 'Is patrolling the cinemas socialism? Is state-sponsored fear socialism? Is this what Lenin wanted?'

This was the boy who toed the party line on every debate

from the social function of literature to the use of adjectives in a poem; the boy who censored what he read before he read it, edited his thoughts before he thought them. Now here he was, risking arrest, expulsion from the Party, the loss of his mapped-out career. I tapped him on the shoulder. For a moment he didn't recognise me, blinked and pushed his papers at me. I led him out to safety.

'Oleanu,' I said, realising I had never known his first name, that he was one of those people who didn't seem to have one, who would never get close enough to another human being to put it to use. 'Can we take you somewhere?'

He looked glassily at me. 'Looks like he's in shock,' said Ottilia. 'Who the hell is he? What's that stupid badge on his jacket?' She peered at his Party youth pin, then led him through the double doors of the Palace of Light. Police with dogs were moving people on. We sat Oleanu in the car and Ottilia produced her emergency Tsuica. She put it to his lips and he automatically glugged down a mouthful, coughed and whimpered. He looked out of the window, then at us for what seemed like the first time that evening.

'Oleanu – I'm sorry, I don't know your first name – it looks to me like you've just had a big and very public crisis of faith,' I told him.

'That's what happens when you have faith in the first place,' Ottilia offered with unwonted cynicism, 'it's a stage most of us skipped.' She swerved to avoid a herd of supermarket trolleys that had erred into the road like bemused cattle. Monocom's windows had been smashed, and people were looting it while the police looked on. A few doors away, at one of the state bookshops, a fire blazed.

At the Arab Centre Leo was fractious and tipsy. He jabbed his finger at the dial of his watch. 'What time d'you call this?' Then, swinging open the passenger door, 'And what the fuck's Young Lenin doing here?'

Leo softened up when we told him, but Oleanu found it hard to surmount his natural fear of Leo. For him, Leo *was* decadent capitalism. He had spent so many months informing on Leo's activities and reporting back on his lectures that now, when Leo breathed boozily in his face, put his arm around him and pushed a bottle of Chateau Musar to his lips ('Don't worry, it may be made by Arabs but they're Christian Arabs and it's fourteen per cent alcohol'), he didn't know which feeling to give in to first: terror or embarrassment.

'Where d'you live, Comrade? We're taking you home,' asked Leo.

'No, that won't be necessary. I can walk from here.'

'Bollocks, *Tovarăşul*. I know where you live, and it's a four-mile walk. As you see there's no buses or trams this time of night, and I'm buggered if anyone's going to accuse Leo of not helping out a Flower of the Party's Youth.' He rattled off Oleanu's address, a dismal block among blocks in a suburb of middle-ranking Party members. Life was better there, but not by not much, and no longer by enough.

'See, we all have our ways of keeping tabs, young man. Now go in and tell your parents you're safe.' Leo chuckled. 'For now...'

We watched Oleanu disappear into the forty-watt twilight of his block.

'Don't you think you were a bit hard on him, Leo?' I asked. Ottilia added: 'What he did was brave in its way, a bit mad perhaps, but it must have taken a lot...'

Leo rested his forehead against the car window. 'Maybe... maybe. Maybe Oleanu will be the hero of the revolution, who knows? What I do know is that for the last two years it's been him informing on all we say in class, selling his fellows down the river, setting them up... who's going to give them back the university places he took from them, who's going to erase the black marks he put on their files?'

'At least he was doing it because he believed in the system, or thought he did...' Ottilia came to Oleanu's defence but Leo didn't let her get far.

'And that makes it better, does it? Am I supposed to forgive him just because he actually believed in what he was doing? That makes him better than the ones who did it just for personal gain?'

'Yes,' Ottilia looked at him in the rear-view mirror, 'yes, I think it does.'

'Not this again...' Leo's voice was an irritated caricature of boredom, 'believing, not believing... how many times have I been through this, and with how many people: whether it's better to do wrong for the right reasons or do right for the wrong ones. I decided that long ago. I'm not changing my mind. I'm going for those who do bad things out of self-interest, because when their interests change, they'll change what they do. Simple as that. The others... well, look around you...'

'Sophistry, Leo, sophistry. Or as you prefer, *bollocks*. You say that because you run the biggest – sorry, the second biggest – racket in the city, and you've persuaded yourself it's a force for good because you're a good man and you do good things in your own small circle. But it's still racketeering, Leo. You make a virtue out of believing in nothing because that's what helps you live with the fact that you're living off a system you despise.'

'This... *system* as you call it was created by zealots like that little squirt with his Party badges and Communist Youth meetings...'

'Maybe it was, Leo, but when the zealots had finished designing it, they handed it over to the cynics to run, and that's why you've been given such an easy ride these last few years.'

Leo opened his mouth for a riposte, but there was nothing

there. He floundered grumpily for a few seconds, then raised both hands in surrender.

The special guest at this, the last Congress of the *Partidul Comunist Roman* was Yasser Arafat. He sat in the first row beside Elena and Nicolae Ceauşescu, a tiny, weatherbeaten man with busy, nervous eyes. The earpiece he wore to ensure he missed nothing of the speeches was obviously not working, or working too well: he rotated and cocked his head in quick, baffled jerks like a sparrow, or fiddled with the contraption and yanked it from his ear and stared at it.

I recognised several of the people in the rows behind the Ceauşescus: Palin the trade minister and Leo's best customer; the deputy foreign minister, the minister for cults, and a few others of middling to high rank. At the centre of the third row sat Manea Constantin, slick and well-dressed and with a suit that fitted him conspicuously.

They sat it out obediently, irradiated by boredom's invisible waves, vegetating through the hour-long speeches and rising for the palm-blistering applause. Tractors, five-year plans, miraculous crops, except that there were no miracles, just socialist-scientific planning yielding its socialist-scientific results. The second day's centrepiece was a speech entitled 'The Era of Light Taken in the Round' by the minister for culture, demonstrating how under Ceauşescu every individual aspect of policy had been brought to its highest and best form. The afternoon ended with a twenty-minute round of cultish applause which Ceauşescu brushed aside in unembarrassable mock-modesty.

'Pinch me,' said Leo, still in his pyjamas though it was past midday. This was to be his last day in my flat, now that he was able to walk and look after himself, but he showed no sign of being ready to leave. 'Pinch me so I know it's not a dream! I live in paradise! I live in bloody paradise!'

In the bedroom he had evicted us from, I heard him whistling, then straining to liberate a fart. He emerged businesslike and purposeful, flatulent and hungover but with a spring in his limp. 'I'm off to put in a good word for Young Lenin. I'll show the lovely Ottilia I don't bear grudges...' With that he was gone into the day.

Ceauşescu was re-elected unanimously on the fourth day of the conference. Unanimously? Not exactly. When I checked *Scînteia* for the list of Central Committee members, I saw a small paragraph with a dozen names of delegates who for various reasons had been unable to vote. One had died mid-Congress – he had felt a stabbing pain in his left arm during a marathon clapping session, and died in his Dacia on the way back to Snagov. Miron Banalescu thus became one of the first casualties of that Congress, a martyr not from the ranks of the brave but from the complicit and the cowed. Later, as the revolution mourned its heroes and persecuted its opponents, I wondered if there was a category for the Banalescus of this world, floating in the interstices of history like specks of dust: a great, grey purgatory of mediocrity that amounted to more than the sum of its parts because it was where most of us finished up.

The other names on the list of those who missed the vote meant nothing to me, but I knew the last one: Manea Constantin.

Eight

They released Oleanu after a week. Just like the people he had informed on, he arrived at the university to find that his place had been withdrawn. He knew the routine, having so often set it in motion: he handed over his university card and cleared out his locker. But there was a calmness about him, a singleness of purpose. Whatever had been done to him in prison, it had made rather than broken him. Popea, charged with expelling Oleanu from the university, tried not to look at the bandage on Oleanu's eye, the split lip, the way the boy held his ribs as every breath brought pain. But no one could ignore the new dignity he had; the way, even stooped over a bruised lung, he looked taller, stronger, surer of himself.

When Oleanu came out, Leo was waiting, his Skoda rattling in the morning snow. In the back seat sat an old man in a hat, with a French newspaper spread out in front of him, obscuring his face.

Leo was as good as his word. Better. He introduced Oleanu to Trofim, who made him his *de facto* assistant. Over the next two weeks we saw a complete transformation in Oleanu. Before, he had been a scheming, anal-retentive coward with a politician's time-buying stutter, square spectacles and flat, greased hair. His trousers were too short and his bony wrists stuck out from the sleeves of a barrel-jacket. Now his hair was tousled, he wore jeans and an open-necked shirt. Round spectacles and the beginnings of a sharp little beard made him look more like the young Trotsky than the young Lenin. He had filled out, muscled up.

Soon he was drafting Trofim's speeches, typing up his letters, accompanying him to events. He read dissident socialists – Trotsky, Victor Serge, Rosa Luxemburg, Gramsci – and reinvented himself as the intellectual guardian of a communism that might have been. Oleanu had not lost his faith, just transferred it.

The intimidation of Trofim increased. He received calls describing how his wife's corpse had been disinterred and given to the dogs to fuck, how the Yids were still good for gassing, how they'd come for him and skin him alive. It was a different voice each time, but always the same sneer, reading its obscene script at all hours of the night. Trofim coped. He even joked that there was more imagination in these phone calls than there had been in the last twenty years of official literature. But they wore him down physically, they broke his sleep; when he disconnected the phone they banged on his door or pushed pornographic images through his letterbox.

All this intrigue seemed abstract and faraway on the streets of Bucharest. Rumours came and went of workers striking, food riots, flashes of isolated dissent, but so too did news of their quelling: the midnight raids on people's homes, the bogus hospitalisations, the random relocations and imprisonments.

Communism was collapsing, but we didn't know it then, or not here. After the Wall came the opened borders, the promise of free elections, new parties, western aid and western goods. But not for us. Looking back it's easy to think that each brick knocked from the prison of communism brought another crack for the light to shine through. Perhaps that was how it felt in Prague or Warsaw or Berlin. In Bucharest it was a reminder of how much we remained bricked in, that sense that there would never be enough light to go round. Each relaxation outside brought a new squeeze. The Hungarians had opened their borders, but the Romanians tightened theirs. West Germany gave food and money to East Germany, but here new export targets were announced that left the people producing more and receiving less. Even the black market suffered, as the alternative avenues of supply closed down. There was nothing left to skim from the top of the quotas, the bottom of the inventories; nothing left to trim, no odds and ends to sell or barter. The luxuries were still there, rising like a glittering scum to the top of the day's deprivations, but the basics ran out everywhere.

As I trudged through grey snow to work on the morning of 17 December, I saw the Comrade's convoy, or one of its decoys, hurtling towards Otopeni airport to the crunch of snowchains on black ice. Here and there the thawing snow slid slowly down the roof tiles and fell in blocks, exploding on the ground.

Early mornings unnerved me: there was never anyone on the streets, but the criss-crossed footsteps testified to there having been some small-hours rush hour in the blue light, when hundreds of people had walked or run to work or stood and waited for their transport. You felt crowded out but alone – perfect police state weather. Leo told me after the first frosts: '*The Cold War*, ever wondered why they called it that? It's not just all that bollocks about icy relations between East and West. The cold is a weapon here, they use it just like they'd use a gun or water cannon... you remember what Napoleon said about being defeated by *General Midwinter*? Well, around here Winter's a colonel in the Securitate...'

At the university gates, Micu gave a stiff-jointed salute. He looked terrified, and I soon saw why. Two Securitate officers sat at his desk searching the students.

I knocked on Leo's door and went in. 'They're jacking up

security – shut down the politics department for the whole week. Something to do with Comrade Nic's official visit to Iran. They're tightening up.'

'He's going to Iran?'

'He must be bloody nuts, but that's not all. Guess who's in charge of the asylum while he's eating pistachios with the ayatollahs?'

I thought about it. The most obvious answer was also the most absurd. Still... surely not...

'You got it in one,' said Leo. I hadn't said anything, but my expression was enough.

'Comrade Academician Professor Elena Ceauşescu?'

'You forgot "Scientist of Broad International Renown", but I'll give you the point. The shit's hitting the fan in Timişoara, Brasov, Iaşi, and God knows where else, but what's the Big Man going to do? He's off to Iran. Iran for fuck's sake! Who told him to do that?'

Popea hovered at the door.

'Ah, good of you to come by...' Leo motioned him to stand by the window. There was no pretence any longer that Popea was the boss, but there was something about him today, something satisfied and authoritative. 'You're looking pleased with yourself, Boss. Well, fire away.'

'Very well,' Popea closed the door, looking ominously confident, and produced some papers. 'It's a letter from the Dean terminating your employment. One from the ministry rescinding your visa and work permit will reach you tomorrow. You then have fourteen days to leave the country. Sadly, owing to the traditional clerical error, the fourteen days began twelve days ago. It can't be helped. You have forty-eight hours.'

Leo had been beaten up, imprisoned, robbed and almost killed. But this was the first time I had seen him genuinely distressed. He leapt from the chair and took Popea by the lapels, but Popea pressed his advantage: 'Unless you are here, in this place and in this job, you are nothing... a nobody, an unemployable hack lecturer past his sell-by date. I've spent too long taking orders from you, I've watched you rub our noses in the shit, threatening and blackmailing people, corrupting the system... well, now that you're going I can tell you I have always held you in contempt. I had nothing to do with your expulsion, but go ahead if you want: expose me, humiliate me, lose me my job. Then it will be over. I'm calling your bluff.'

Leo sank back into his chair. 'What can you do to help?' he was the supplicant now, 'what'll it take this time?'

'Fuck you, Leo, I'm happy to say there's nothing I can do. Oh, I'm sure if there was I'd do it like I always have, just to save my skin. Actually, I already tried – no luck I'm afraid... I'm happy to say this one's out of my hands. There's something liberating about that, Leo, it's a relief. You should try it, just giving up and letting things take their course...'

Then, remembering a small detail, Popea turned to me. 'You too,' he said. 'You're out as well. Your Christmas break starts on the twentieth, but your visa won't be renewed. Best find another job, maybe one where they interview you...!' Popea smiled: I was just an additional bonus to his primary victory. 'Anyway, with Professor O'Heix gone you won't last long around here...'

'If those bastards think they're getting rid of me they've got another think coming. I've got contacts, I'm going to need to call in some favours. They'll have to tie me up and drug me and put me on the plane themselves while everyone watches and wishes they were in my place!'

Leo's letter was delivered by two ministry officials, revoking his working permit, his visa and his contract. I was not worth a visit: my termination papers were in my department pigeonhole and I was to leave by the twenty-third, two days after Leo.

Leo thought he could call in favours, reel in those dozens of powerful people who were in one way or another beholden to him. He was wrong. No one returned his calls and the few who agreed to meet him failed to show up. Only Manea replied, with a short note offering Leo a meeting for 28 December, his 'first window in the diary'. As Manea surely knew, Leo was due to be sent back on the twenty-first.

On 19 December, protesters in Timişoara stormed their Party HQ and set fire to its contents: Ceauşescu portraits, Party records, books and pictures, even the furniture went onto the pyre. The police stood by. In that protracted moment of hesitation perhaps, the end of the regime came and installed itself.

The first symbol of the revolution was hoisted from the balcony of the Timişoara Party HQ: the Romanian flag with a hole of blue sky where the communist insignia and PCR logo had been. People crowded to touch it, they carried it with them. The new national flag.

The Securitate presence from Calea Victoriei to the Central Committee building was stepped up. Young suited men with ostentatiously hidden guns stood every ten yards, smoking and watching, checking papers, pulling up cars, questioning anyone who stood and talked in the streets for more than a few seconds. 'Two's a crowd' became the motto. But sometimes it only took one: a construction worker with a megaphone at the top of the scaffolding on Piaţa Unirii bellowing out, 'Timişoara! Timişoara! Timişoara!' for half an hour before they managed to bring him down. On the Atheneum lawn 'Down with Ceauşescu' appeared in weed-killered grass. 'Death to the Vampire and his Bitch,' was daubed in red on the wall of the Party museum.

When the clampdown came it was easy to put an end to social life: all they had to do was stop the supply of food and drink to restaurants and cafés. Even the *ersatz* dried up. Only the dollar bars and international hotels stayed open, and even there the plain-clothes agents outnumbered you. And Capşa: Capşa had the diplomats and the Party *nomenklatura* to feed. It also had Leo's last week of decadence to host, a sort of Viking feast punctuated with flashes of mortal danger and the political surreal.

In the early hours of 20 December, Ottilia and I were awoken by a low rumbling noise close enough to the flat for us to feel the vibrations in the glass shelves in the bathroom. I looked at the clock: 4 am. Downstairs the police guard dozed upright. Two others stood and smoked a few yards away. If they saw me leave they gave no sign. The noise was louder now, an even, mechanised buzz that shook the ground. At first I thought it was the earthquake revisiting. I walked to the corner of Aleea Alexandru and Aviatorilor and then I saw them: dozens of armoured cars heading into town, their headlamps off. There were lorries carrying troops and tanks cruising at frightening speed. I'd always imagined tanks were slow and heavy. But it was their speed and their surprising, indestructible nimbleness that terrified me.

It was nearly daybreak when Leo returned. 'They're sending troops to Timişoara.' Leo was cold sober though he smelled of drink and smoke. 'Army leave's been cancelled. There's something big happening. Elena Ceauşescu's now taken charge personally of security.'

'They're bringing troops in here too, I saw them: tanks and personnel carriers.'

'No surprise there – always bring in troops from outside the area if you're going to start shooting your own people. I'll bet Timişoara's army units are heading over here and Bucharest's are on their way to Timişoara.'

'What d'you know for sure, Leo?' asked Ottilia. Speculation exasperated her. There were some who thrived on gossip, for whom rumours were more absorbing than the realities they brought wind of. Ottilia found rumours wearing: 'They distort your responses – by the time you've spent yourself reacting to the rumour, you're no longer able to react to the realities themselves...'

'Nothing. Not for sure. But I reckon there'll be competition for customers between you in the hospital and Campanu down at the morgue.' Leo's tone changed: 'I know I'm meant to be on that plane. But I'm not going. But if the two of you want to get out, now's a good time. I can help you.'

'I'm not leaving. This is my home.' Ottilia said it calmly and emphatically, the way Petre would have done.

Leo nodded. 'Tell you what, while you're mulling that one over, I've booked Capşa. I see my going-away party as a sort of rolling programme of events, culminating in my non-departure from Otopeni airport on Friday afternoon. We foregather at seven.'

Leo disappeared into the bathroom. We heard him shout as the freezing water from the hot tap crashed over his shoulders. Ottilia and I had not discussed what would happen when I left. Instead of making plans we continued to speak as if all would be well, as if we would all be here, together, the other side of Christmas. Unlike Leo, I could not pretend I would outface the police and find ways of staying behind. But if I wanted to be with Ottilia I needed to find a way of coming back. I could not imagine our life together anywhere but here; and in spite of its unreality, I had stopped being able to imagine my own life anywhere else either.

A tense, heavily policed peace reigned in Bucharest that day. Still in Iran, the *Conducător* released films of himself meeting the mullahs and outlining Romania's commitment to the socialist path. At moments of national or international unease, new homages were found for the Ceauşescus. Thus

Scînteia announced that the guild of artisan-basketweavers had bestowed on them their highest honour, the Order of the Golden Straw.

At three o'clock, as helicopters circled above us, they shut down the university and cleared it out. In the streets that afternoon random ID checks were everywhere, and police hurried people along whenever they stopped to chat. Food queues, obvious flashpoints of anger or spontaneous protest, presented more of a problem: move people on and you spark a riot, let them stay too long and you incubate one. Outside a butcher's shop on Boulevard Magheru, the queue was turning dangerous. Passing by, I noticed my sardonic *Scînteia* vendor waiting with his string bag. He called me over. People turned. He was taking a big risk speaking to a foreigner in front of a hundred witnesses and the police. There was a manic, past-caring mischief in his smile and wide-open eyes.

'*Epoca Luminoasa!* Era of Light, eh? Come over here, *Domnul*, come and queue with the happy people as they enjoy the fruits of their socialist lifestyle... come and watch as those goons, village idiots in uniforms, herd us like cattle from one queue to the next. You don't read about that in *Scînteia*, do you?'

People laughed bitterly, jeered and shouted at the police. Someone called out, 'Timişoara! Ceauşescu assassin!' Behind the *Scînteia* vendor two men who had been waiting in line moved towards him. In a few seconds they were at his back, yanking him by his shoulders away from the crowd: Securitate plants dressed as normal Romanians – tired ill-cut jackets and coats, cheap rabbit-fur hats and Monocom boots. He laughed madly, a lunatic grin on his face: 'Comrades why were you queuing? Don't they have special shops for Securitate? Don't tell me they're empty too...' I saw the furrows in the snow where his kicking heels dragged as they pulled him towards a black Dacia van. The police, out of their depth, moved to calm the crowd, telling people to get on with their wait, that there was nothing to see, but also eyeing the Securitate resentfully.

As I moved to intervene, one of the Securitate motioned me to stay away. I pressed on as their prisoner shouted: 'Fascists, murderers, scum!' People were emboldened, abusing the Securitate, who were now, even with the extra four who had appeared from the van, seriously outnumbered. A rock thrown from the crowd hit the windscreen and smashed it spectacularly across the pavement. In the confusion the *Scînteia* vendor disentangled himself, ran back into the crowd and out to a sidestreet where, as I watched him, three policemen let him pass. I saw his heel turn the corner and turned back, but now the police too had disappeared, leaving this to the Securitate and their plain-clothes agents.

This was a riot in the making. The pragmatists smashed the windows and looted the shop, running out with slabs of meat in bloody newspaper. The idealists faced down the Securitate who twitched for their guns and considered their options. The crowd pushed on; stones skimmed the van, smashing its remaining windows. There was only a matter of ten yards between the people and the Securitate when a second black Dacia van came spinning into the gap, all doors open, ready to gather in its agents. As they leapt into the back, one figure climbed slowly from the front passenger seat. He wore a fur hat and sunglasses, and as his colleagues called out to him to get in, he stood and looked slowly around, taking in every detail, pausing over every face. The crowd sensed the coldness, the authority. Faltering, the front row fell back and the advance stalled. They looked and found no fear in his face.

I knew it was Vintul even before he took off his sunglasses and hat. And something about him now made me know this was what he really looked like: fair, close-cropped hair, pale green eyes and light skin. No more disguises. He ran a gloved hand through his hair, a reflex from his days undercover. He folded his sunglasses, eyes sweeping over us without emotion, and slipped them into his pocket. He passed over my face three times. Maybe he hadn't recognised me. I breathed out. Maybe he had forgotten me. He said something into a walkie-talkie, and without waiting for a reply opened the van door. He was about to get in when he stopped short, turned again and looked straight at me, pulling the door across his body with his right hand and raising his left to make a pistol of his fingers. He closed an eye, took aim at me, jerked the barrel of his gun once into the air and smiled. One bullet. He wasn't the type to waste them, even imaginary ones.

He tapped the roof of the car and swung inside as it pulled away.

I doubted I would see my newspaper vendor tomorrow. Where did people go after confronting the Securitate? Where could they hide? How long could they run? The policemen had crept back and were inspecting the damage to the shopfront: smashed glass, splintered doorpanels, animal blood spattered along the snow. They began to clear up. Passers-by approached them and cheered them for not helping the Securitate. A rumour was being born. By evening I would hear it again, inflated by imagination, drink and wishful thinking: the police had stood up to the Securitate, they had helped the protestors escape...

Just before five o'clock I stopped at the TAROM offices. If I was going to buy a ticket home, this was the time. Perhaps it was already too late. Here too there were queues leading out of the doors. Most of the wealthy foreigners had arranged their exits: embassy people, defence contractors, the merchants of surveillance equipment and riot control gear they would soon have the chance to see being used. The only people left were student travellers, young families caught short in the middle of a cheap and spartan holiday, and East Europeans from soon to be ex-communist states trying to reach their bloodless revolutions before Christmas. No one knew very much about what was happening, but they knew enough to want to leave. I waited in the queue, feeling in my inside pocket for my passport, running my fingers along its edges and pointed corners.

Eight staff were at their desks, of whom six sat and read newspapers, smoked or fiddled with their cuticles. The usual fusion of panic and lethargy dominated. On the walls, maps of Romania were drawing-pinned to cork noticeboards, and posters of churches, beaches and folk choirs curled at the corners. How many of the churches still stood, how many of the singers had been relocated to the cities, how many of the beaches were choking on oil slicks, poisoned fish and bloated dog carcasses?

In front of me was a family of British tourists – two exhausted children and their mother – who had cut short their holiday in Timişoara. They had been put on a train to Bucharest this morning and were trying to swap their tickets. What had they seen, I asked. The woman looked around before she answered, already attuned to the dangers of speaking to strangers. 'We didn't actually see anything – the centre was cut off the day we got there, and for two days they wouldn't let us leave the hotel. Bloody awful. Then this morning they stuck us on a bus and drove us to the station...' She wiped her eyes. The children slept upright, leaning against her, while her husband waved ten-dollar bills at the staff. He was learning fast, but so was everyone else. It was more like a stock-market panic than a travel agency. 'The bus they took us in – the windows had been painted over so we couldn't see out. It stopped a few times, went back on itself, like it was changing route or something. Then when we got to Timişoara station the whole place was under armed guard.

They put us straight onto the train and that was it. Didn't see a thing except the inside of the hotel and the bloody bus.'

Her husband returned with some tickets: 'Who's this?' he asked aggressively.

'Dunno, I mean... just some Brit in the queue, I just started talking to him...'

'Yeah well, let's just get out of here, shall we? I've managed to get flights for tonight and we're going straight to the bloody airport. Sorry mate...' He placed himself between me and his wife and said, in the tone of someone imparting hard-won advice: 'It's each man for himself round here.' My smile puzzled him, then made him angry. He dragged a suitcase through the door and shouted back at his wife, 'You coming or what?' She smiled apologetically at me and hurried after him, a child in each arm and an Action Man with a tiny rifle sniping from her coat pocket.

I followed them out. The snow was four or five inches deep and the traffic crackled along the salted roads. Night was setting in. The weak streetlamps and the whiteness of the pavements gave the place the grey translucence of hospital skin.

At home I put my passport and papers back into the desk and flicked on the radio. The World Service said nothing about Timişoara or anywhere else, so I left the radio on and went for a shower. By the time I came out Leo was installed in my armchair watching *Columbo*.

'Single or return?' he asked without looking up from the television.

'What?'

'From the TAROM office... was it a single or a return?'

I opened the door. 'So, you've got Securitate on your pay-roll now too, have you? Spying on your friends...'

'I found out quite by chance actually. I popped in myself a few minutes later to pick up some tickets for clients, and it just sort of cropped up that you'd been. Maybe this is what

335

you were after?' Leo slapped a plane ticket onto the coffee table and walked out. It was made out in my name, and my passport number had been typed in: a single flight to London for the 23rd. I pushed it away. After a minute or two I came past again, took it and placed it with my passport and papers in my jacket pocket.

'Look. Think of it as insurance. I can't say exactly what's going to happen in the next couple of weeks, but just hang on to that ticket...' Leo was waving another ticket now. 'There's one for Ottilia too, but you know she hasn't got a passport... not a Romanian one anyway.'

'What other passport would she have?' I asked, but I should have known by now what Leo was capable of...

'I'm having her one made, a perfectly serviceable Russian one. One previous owner... it'll be ready in time.'

'You know she won't come. And as for me I went to TAROM wanting an excuse *not* to buy a ticket, not because I wanted to leave. And now you've bloody given me one...'

'Yes,' Leo guided me to the kitchen where he opened the window to reveal six bottles of Ukrainian champagne chilling in a snow-packed window box, 'yes, I have. Because I want you to choose, to decide for yourself. I want you to weigh things up, to stop floating in the slipstream of your own life.'

'You should write a self-help book.' I unhooked myself from his arm.

'I did, and I followed every step of my own regime. Can't you see?' Leo did a little fashion-model twirl in the kitchen. The jacket he had chosen for this evening was a metallic mauve colour I had only ever seen on toy cars.

He popped the cork. 'Timişoara's erupting. While we're at Capşa's eating our pork Jewish style and crêpes Suzette the police will be shooting to kill – it's either going to be a blood-soaked footnote in the history of communism or the start of the revolution. It's the right time to be making decisions, not just for you but for everyone.' He handed me a glass. 'For me, for Ottilia, and if they want to stay on top, for people like Cilea and Manea... for all of them, right down to those poor frozen pawns down there.' He pointed at the policemen stamping their feet in the snow as they sucked on Carpati, and raised a glass.

Leo stopped outside the Athénée Palace and picked up what looked like a big pot of jam from the parking attendant. Then he took me inside and told me to wait. I watched him disappear through the overlit lobby, his jacket pulsing with a new reptilian sheen as he passed under the spotlights. I waited for ten minutes. When he returned he was carrying a bag that moved. I peered in: lobsters wrestling slowly, elastic bands around their claws. 'Capşa,' he explained, 'it's bring your own starters night. The roads are blocked and nothing's coming through.'

Capşa was busier than ever. Most of the tables were taken, and the waiters skimmed along the deep blue carpets as if their shoes had invisible wheels.

Impassive at his post the Maître d'Hôte greeted us. He took Leo's bag and the jar, which I now saw was Iranian caviar. Obviously one of the Comrade's staff had done some shopping in Tehran. When Leo asked him what he recommended this evening he replied solemnly and with no hint of irony, 'The lobster, sir, it is very fresh,' and whisked his trawl to the kitchens.

We were shown to Leo's private function room, unofficially known as the 'Labis Room', after the young dissident poet Nicolae Labis, who, after a night of drinking and daring political talk in 1956, stumbled and was decapitated by a tram just outside Capşa. Leo had asked for it specifically.

In the main dining room apparatchiks and *nomenklatura* eyed both each other and each other's plates. A senior policeman in full uniform sat with three men in suits, an interpreter and some North Koreans in military dress, while a group of Arabs sipped Fanta from plastic bottles wedged into ice buckets. At a table near the string quartet the minister for work was softening up another scared adolescent for his under-table lunge. Nearby, behind calico screens, were tables of people so senior each had their own waiter. One of these, I learned later, was General Milea, the army chief of staff, in the process of making his greatest and last mistake.

In the Labis Room a long oval table was set in fin-de-siècle style. A fire burned, the red wine breathed and the cheeses sweated. Ozeray and Maltchev arrived first, followed a few minutes later by Professor and Mrs Ionescu and Rodica without her husband.

Ottilia joined us soon after. She kissed me on the cheek and whispered in my ear, 'It's bad – bodies are coming in from Timişoara. Dozens of them... so far. Campanu says they're dumping them at the morgue and cremating them, piling them into the incinerators...'

Leo tapped his glass three times.

'Friends! Let me thank you all for coming. As many of you are aware, these are my last few days. My last few days in this epoch of light, my last few days basking in the last few rays.... *ah*, I hear you ask, *whose last few rays, that's the question, Leo's or this luminous epoch's?*'

Nervous laughter. Ionescu scanned the room in panic, trying to calculate who might be tonight's Securitate plant. Satisfied that the likeliest candidate was himself, he relaxed. A few Party people had come, but I knew Leo had invited them as insurance for himself and for his friends – he had the lowdown on their corruption, since he had been its principal conduit. Leo's tactic was never to exclude people if they could be implicated instead.

Ottilia nudged me and nodded towards Maltchev who

338

stood at the edge of the crowd checking his pager and listening to something through a concealed earpiece. We knew there was something significant going on, but that was different from knowing what it signified. We sifted through portents, read the tea leaves, pored over the omens without ever knowing what they meant. Everything had a double meaning; you just never knew if what you had grasped was the meaning or its double.

Leo called me over. 'Where's Trofim? Give him a ring. See what's holding him up.'

'I'm not sure I've got the stomach for this "celebration" tonight.' Otilia joined me when Leo had gone. 'It's not right that we're stuffing ourselves and drinking and pretending it's all a joke when there's people getting killed around us.'

'I'm not sure anyone has the stomach,' I replied. 'Look...' Maltchev was reaching for his barely portable phone. 'I'll get hold of Sergiu for Leo and then we'll go home.' The phone near the kitchens was broken so I turned down into the corridor and past the storerooms. At the very back I came upon the door to the wine cellar. I smelled earth and cobwebs. The door was open and the Maître d' looked up at me silently, holding a paraffin lantern which swung its light across the bottles. Before I could ask about the phone he pointed to a door I had missed on my way down. He closed the cellar door behind him. I heard the sound of animated talking, smelled the familiar fug of Carpati in a cramped, unventilated room. I had passed this room without noticing it. The waiters' rest room. There must be a phone in there.

The talking stopped as soon as I entered. The smoke stung my eyes. My hand, which lingered on the handle, was seized and the door slammed shut. I had time to see people crowded around a table, some in military uniform, others in suits or jeans. A man I did not recognise sat at the head of the table, unshaven, with thin dark hair and a tanned face. He wore a check shirt and no jacket or tie and though the least well-dressed he was obviously the one in charge. Before I registered any more, someone had pulled my wrists together and was holding them fast with one hand, while pressing the base of my neck and grinding my face into the wall with the other. I did not need to see behind me to know the room was full, and not of waiters.

'What the fuck were you doing, Andrei? Dozing again?'

'Sorry boss,' came the voice behind me, 'I'd gone for cigarettes and when I came back he was just opening the door.' Andrei had his face up against mine. His breath smelled of raw garlic and Carpati.

'Great. What happens now?' A different voice, then silence. Finally a chair scraped against the floor and footsteps came towards me. There was a touch on my shoulder. My captor loosened his grip. 'Get him out of here, Sergiu.' I recognised Manea Constantin, alert and edgy. 'It's all right, we'll deal with this.' I should have been reassured but I wasn't. Then came Trofim's voice at my back, guiding me through the door, telling me not to turn around.

Back in the corridor I rubbed my neck. Trofim had my arm, ostensibly for support but it was myself I felt sagging as we walked. 'Do not ask,' said Trofim before I opened my mouth, ruthless beneath the kind smile, the bright, amused eyes. 'Now let us help Leo with his official send-off.'

Leo's party had run aground. Maltchev had returned, and stood with his back to the fireplace watching the door. He stopped talking when we came in and looked at Trofim, who nodded very gently. Maltchev had his cue. 'I have received reports tonight, minutes ago, that there is a full-scale uprising in Timişoara and that it is spreading. There are rumours, unconfirmed, of a great many deaths. The security forces are shooting to kill. Witnesses are talking about live ammunition, tanks and tear gas. It is a very bloody night.'

Leo stood to Maltchev's right, a glass in one hand and a bottle in the other. The food and drink lay untouched on the table. I felt the fear and apprehension in the room, but also rage and something like desperation – a sense that we were stepping into the beyond.

Ottilia rose from the table. 'I spoke to Campanu at the morgue earlier... he said he'd received bodies, dozens, with more to come... most had been shot, but he said there were signs of torture too... they're being cremated in the night...'

Maltchev again: 'It's gathering momentum: Arad, Sânni-colau Mare, Oradea... anti-Ceaușescu demonstrations. In Brasov a group calling itself the New Workers' Council has called a general strike. The ringleaders have been arrested but the strike is holding. Right across the country the unrest is spreading.'

Trofim spoke now, calmly pouring himself a drink and walking to Maltchev's side. 'The president is still in Iran, but will cut short his stay and return to Bucharest tomorrow. He does not believe these demonstrations are against him. He has been told that they are protests about wages and rations and he thinks he will be able to resolve them. We will see. At present, it is Elena who has taken over, and she has given specific orders for the security apparatus to respond to unrest. We have seen that response.'

'That'll be why General Milea is eating quails in the next room,' Leo chipped in. 'Has he been sacked or what? Does the fat sod even know what's going on?'

'I am not sure the General is master of his destiny right now,' said Trofim ambiguously. 'It is becoming clear that what Ceaușescu is doing to the country is not being done in the name of the Party, and I cannot imagine that the Party as a whole is behind the latest torrent of repression.' He turned to Maltchev for confirmation. Maltchev nodded.

I knew what Trofim meant. I had just walked in on a crisis meeting between dissident communists like Trofim and members of the Party high command like Manea Constantin: The National Salvation Front. The rest of those in the Labis Room, better attuned to doublespeak than me, grasped it immediately. Ozeray raised a glass to his mouth, the diplomat's way of hiding a reaction. Ionescu smiled, seeing the restoration of his old job ahead, which, coupled with the prestige of the injustice he had suffered, would make him an unstoppable force once back in place. Turda Technical College would be getting a brace of new janitors soon enough.

Though everyone knew what Trofim meant, Leo was the only one ready to question him. '*The Party...* what you mean, Comrade, is that the rats are deserting the sinking ship, isn't that right? But all they're going to do is regroup somewhere else, hose down the decks a little – Christ, I can't seem to shake off these bloody nautical metaphors – then back to business as usual...'

'I have no knowledge of any such plan, Leo.' Trofim glanced at me and I looked away, 'I am speaking in a personal capacity which, as you know, is an isolated and...'

'Sergiu, I don't for a moment believe that, but if it makes it easier for you, I'll say no more. What I do know is that all of you Party hacks have something invested in the system. What's the old Romanian saying? *New brothel, same old whores...*'

'What you are suggesting, Leo, is without foundation. I have no idea of any plans. I am as they say "out of the loop", but I was permitting myself to speculate...'

Leo cut him off. 'Some speculation. You think we don't know? For one thing, you're meant to be under house arrest, and yet you're here, getting more attention than you were as UN ambassador...! What does that tell us? Right across the country they're rising up and getting shot, the army's on alert, troops are coming in under cover of darkness... but Sergiu Trofim's suddenly got himself carte blanche to visit his chums in Capşa, and all day the black Dacias line up outside his flat... "out of the loop", eh?'

'Now come on, Leo!' Maltchev interjected.

'And as for Sergei Maltchev here, well, there's another story for the historians to unpick – I don't suppose Comrade Maltchev knows anything about the sudden influx of Russian "tourists" in Timişoara and Cluj and Brasov? In Bucharest you can't move for Russkis – what are they doing here? Christmas shopping?' Leo was right – the last two weeks had seen a suspicious rise in Russian visitors to Romanian towns and cities. Young, single men with cars, cameras and lots of dollars, none of them resembled ordinary tourists.

Ozeray stepped forward. 'I think we have all speculated enough. Tonight's occasion was to mark Leo's departure, the departure of a good friend who has kept us entertained, sometimes endangered, always well-supplied...' Leo raised his hands in surrender and beckoned Trofim and the others to table. Maltchev was still smarting from Leo's accusations, but let it go.

Ottilia took my arm and whispered, 'I can't take any more of this. I want to go home.'

I tried to catch Leo's eye but he was in the thick of things, shaking hands and raising glasses, ringing the bell for service. Ottilia and I left the room as the first course was arriving on trolleys: lobster thermidor. I had time to hear the gasp of amazement as the creatures were wheeled in, and Leo boasting that he had caught them himself.

The Maître d' raised his eyebrows as he held the door open for us, discreetly surprised to see us leave. He offered to call a black-market cab but we declined.

It was a mistake. The state-owned taxis had shut and there

were no buses. We began the long walk home in the snow. A few black Dacias were parked sufficiently far away from the restaurant to look as if they were not waiting.

'Leo...' said Ottilia as we crossed Piaţa Republicii round-about, 'won't he be angry? It's his farewell dinner. We shouldn't be missing it.'

'Leo's not going anywhere. He's got his ticket but that doesn't mean anything. They'll have to drag him through the airport... besides, he doesn't think it's going to happen... you know Leo, he'll find a way round, I wouldn't be surprised if there's a letter waiting for him at home, from Ceauşescu himself, telling him he can stay...'

'He really believes it, doesn't he? That between now and tomorrow afternoon it's all going to change?'

'I don't know, maybe it's just bluff, but I know he's not intending to be on that plane tomorrow.'

'What about you?'

'What about me?'

'What plane will you be on?'

'The same one as you, I hope. Leo's getting you a pass-port. It'll be ready in time.'

'We've discussed this...'

'No we haven't. You've said you weren't leaving, that's not the same as us actually *discussing* it...'

We were interrupted outside the Atheneum by a policeman asking for ID. Ottilia looked relieved to see him. He shone a torch into our faces and examined our papers, taking down our details, and keeping Ottilia's back. The snow was falling in flakes thick as blotting paper. 'Present yourself at the central police headquarters between 8 and 9 am tomorrow. Your papers will be returned then.' I saw from his face that he was calling out, but it came to us as little more than a whisper as wind and snow drowned him out.

At home the gas and electricity were cut off, the cold and

darkness so thick it was as if the flat had never been lived in. I struck a match, lit a candle and we groped our way towards the centre of the living room, where I fed a flame to the small butane heater. It gave off enough light to see ourselves by. The radio had batteries at least – we could hear the news – but as I put out my hand to switch it on Ottilia took my wrist.

'Please don't. I don't *want* to hear any more, any more rumours, any more speculation. I don't want to know what's happening...' I followed her into the bedroom, holding the gas heater carefully in front of me, and put it beside the bed. We stripped in the freezing darkness and made love in the dark, holding each other until the gas ran out and the sweat turned to ice on our bodies. Then we got up and dressed like people getting ready for work and climbed back into bed to sleep.

The National Salvation Front made its first official declaration that night. By the morning, Radio Moscow and Radio Free Europe had paper copies, in which they constituted themselves an official democratic political party, called on Ceauşescu to resign or on the Communist Party to depose him, and declared their support for the uprisings in Timişoara and elsewhere. In Timişoara meanwhile reports claimed hundreds of deaths. Workers at the Timis petrochemical plant had issued an ultimatum to the army: join us or leave the city; otherwise we blow up the factory and most of the town.

Ottilia and I spent the morning at the radio. We had forgotten about Leo, but I became aware of him standing, unshaven and in pyjamas, in the doorway. I began an apology for having left early last night but he smiled and waved it away.

'The Comrade's back,' he announced.

Bucharest had a strangely dislocated springtime feel to it on the twenty-first of December. It was sunny, the traffic flowed, shops were open, the cafés and restaurants that had been in hibernation were suddenly serving and full of people. We had morning coffee instead of *ersatz* at the Atheneum; butter and flour and meat had appeared in the shops overnight. Petrol was back at the pumps, and the smell of exhaust fumes returned as suddenly as it had disappeared.

The city was Rumour's forcing-house. The police in Timişoara had turned on the army; the army had turned on the police; both had turned on the Securitate. General Milea had been summoned to the palace and arrested. In Alba Iulia the party HQ had been stormed by protestors, and the police had simply let them get on with it. In Timişoara the death toll was increasing. Despite the international press reporting very few bodies, the rumours were calling them in their thousands. Then there were the rumours of lynchings: Securitate men strung up from lampposts in Maramures, Craiova, Targoviste. In Sibiu, Nicu Ceauşescu's fiefdom, a breakaway group of Party officials declared themselves supporters of the National Salvation Front. They were arrested, then let go. The Sibiu party HQ was burned down. The rumours about Nicu himself were that he was high on cocaine and personally shooting people, that he had surrendered to the demonstrators, and that he was in France whoring. None of these were unlikely, though it was ironic that only the most implausible of the rumours – that a brave judge in his home province had issued a warrant for Nicu's arrest on charges of rape – was true.

The atmosphere in the university was even more febrile. Students stood in groups, plotting, the police only half-heartedly moving them on. Someone had stencilled images of Gorbachev dressed as Santa Claus along the corridor walls. Beside him was a large ribboned present the shape of the map of Romania. 'TIMIŞOARA' was painted in white letters on the front facade, and again across the cobbles of the courtyard. I passed the photocopying room, which was always locked. Today it was open and guarded by Rodica while inside our student Iulia was making hundreds of copies of the front page of today's *Herald Tribune*. 'Massacre in Timişoara', ran the headline, and beneath it, 'Fears grow of new Tiananmen Square: thousands dead'. 'Is this true?' I asked, pointing at the word *thousands*. Her answer: 'True, false, it's irrelevant, what matters is that people find out.' Clearly her dialectical education had not been wasted.

I was the only one in work, and I busied myself with inconsequential tasks. It was a way of avoiding the terminality of my position, of persuading myself I would still be here on the fifth of January. I cast small hooks into the future – a date here, an appointment there, filled in my desk diary with January's events. I looked out at university square for what might be the last time. These were Belanger's views, his chair, his office. His handwriting too: as I picked off and flattened out the curled-up Post-it note with Cilea's number, I wondered if Belanger was reading the *Herald Tribune* and listening to the BBC, if Belanger was watching events as they unfolded on TV, if Belanger was choosing, from fifty different rumours, the one that would best serve him. My phone rang.

'There won't be any *Kojaks* tonight,' Leo shouted into the receiver. He was calling from a phone booth, and I could hear a plane overhead. 'The Comrade's giving a speech on telly, live, an address to the nation. Six pm.'

'What's he going to say?'

'What's he going to say? How the hell should I know? Am I his speechwriter now? Anyway, it's not what he's going to say that's important, it's that he's saying it at all, that he needs to say it.'

'Where are you?'

'At the airport.'

'What – you're going?'

''Course not, I just thought, since I've got the ticket and the passport, I might as well pick up some duty free, get my visa stamped, then get back out in time for the Comrade's state of the nation address. I've got Ottilia's passport ready too: you'll be travelling with a Miss Tatiana Pullova, engineering student. A Leningrad girl.'

I forbore to ask how Leo would make his way back out of the airport or how he might persuade Ottilia to take the passport and run. Anything was possible now, the country was tightening up and falling apart at the same time. Leo would be filling his suitcases with booze and fags and bribing his way back out of the terminal building, his name safely on the list of passengers. It would buy him a day or two at most, but maybe that was all he needed.

We met at the Carpathian Boar, where Leo had gone to ground by buying everyone drinks. At six o'clock, the bar so full we were standing on each other's toes, we watched as Ceauşescu addressed the country, bent over and reading from a shaking sheet of paper. Behind him Elena loomed with a handbag, disconcertingly Thatcher-like in her demeanour, with three nameless barrel-suits at her side.

The Comrade looked tired and old. Against the rumoured thousands of deaths, he claimed no more than ten, every one of them a 'foreign agent'. He rambled on in lumpy communist clichés, praising the police, the army, grinding out phrases like 'imperialist saboteurs', 'enemies of Romanian sovereignty', 'capitalist provocateurs...' It was the language of Stalinist show trials. People laughed, spat on the floor, called him an old fool, 'Stalin', 'Dracula'. Ceauşescu finished his fifty-minute discourse by announcing pay rises, along with an increase in the student grant. 'And what the fuck do we spend it on?' called out one of the drinkers from the back, to general applause. If this was any gauge of the public mood, the Comrade could no longer count on his most effective weapon: fear.

Ceauşescu had miscalculated. He looked weak and shifty and slight. Usually alert, he seemed jetlagged and confused. His voice was high-pitched and breathless and his skin pasty, a diabetic mix of gaunt and puffy. His performance tonight would affect how all of his subsequent actions were interpreted. He had shown his weakness, and they would take revenge for his weakness now as much as for his strength before this. 'Stalin did everything a man in his position should have done'; yes, but Stalin had fear on his side until the end. Ceauşescu was like his palace: a facade laid over a ramifying hollowness.

Ottilia returned at eleven without her papers. At the police station they had made her wait two hours then told her to leave. The militia who had taken her ID card had suddenly been transferred to another sector, and no one seemed interested any more. 'They spend all their time watching you, then suddenly no one gives a shit.' Leo was right: the system was breaking down into its constituent parts, paranoia and apathy, and as the centre started to give way the two were left to engage in their great, blurred, inconclusive Manichean struggle. Apathy and paranoia: two drunks fighting slowly around a park bench.

Leo handed her her new Russian passport. Ottilia looked it over and laughed. 'Tatiana Pullova? Since this is the only ID I've got, I might as well hang on to it... see where it takes me.' Leo looked at me and raised his eyebrows. We both knew better than to press her, but perhaps she might be using that TAROM ticket after all.

At five the next morning, 22 December, a kilometre-long convoy of armoured vehicles clattered down Boulevard Aviatorilor. More troops were being imported. Hundreds more had arrived at Basarab station to be met by lorries taking them down Calea Griviţei into the city centre, where they disappeared into dozens of closed-off security compounds camouflaged as ordinary houses.

If the radio was our source for large-scale news, then the street gave us the details: the city crematoria had been busy all night burning the Timişoaran dead, bussed in and unloaded namelessly into the ovens. In Timişoara the army had retreated and given in to the workers. The strike was solid and spreading. By now the whole of the west was in revolt, and in the border areas with Yugoslavia, Russia or Bulgaria, the structures of repression were faltering. Something else was emerging from the disorder: a radical, systemic inefficiency, where parts of the security apparatus just faded away, while others reacted with unimaginable ferocity. In Iaşi, the army and police stood back and let people storm buildings and ransack the shops. In Maramures they joined in. In Cluj they tortured them, killed them and burned their bodies in rubbish incinerators.

Radio Bucharest made its first allusions to the state of emergency. The announcer read out a roster of the usual suspects – imperialist-capitalist insurgents, reactionary forces and foreign terrorists – before reassuring us that the situation was well in hand. Another speech by the *Conducător* was announced for later today: a deliberate echo of his great triumph of twenty-one years earlier, after the Prague Spring, it would be televised live from the balcony of the Central Committee HQ in Piaţa Republicii. The man who had condemned the Russians for intervening in Czechoslovakia was condemning them for not intervening now.

The National Salvation Front made its second announcement within minutes. It called on Ceauşescu to resign, on the army and police not to obey him, and on the workers to observe the general strike. That the NSF was now issuing declarations to the western media within minutes of drafting them, suggested an extraordinary degree of access. I thought of Manea, Trofim, and the others in that room. Were they now in permanent session? Who was protecting them? How were they getting their statements out?

After so many weeks of stiff upper lip, it was a relief to see some genuine panic at the British embassy. It came in the form of that peculiar blank-facaded institutional turmoil I recalled from public-service information films from school: in the event of nuclear explosion, hide under the table with six months' supply of baked beans. A similar spirit prevailed now. It was the hardwired British response, to hoard tinned foods and set up vats of tea. Those who hadn't left last week were now bunkering down. Embassy wives were opening cartons of long-life milk and packets of Rich Tea biscuits. Fistfuls of teabags dropped into metal teapots so huge they had a handle on the front as well as the back. A good crisis allows both heady involvement and a kind of modest self-spectatorship, and this was a good crisis by any standards. The Shit and Hassle was showcasing the Best of British.

Wintersmith was riding high. No matter that he had assured us all along that things were OK, and that it was 'business as usual, with the emphasis firmly on the *business*, if you get my drift...' Ozeray was right: the nature of diplomacy is that mistakes are never remembered because they are never one's own mistakes; events themselves are at fault for not making clear their intentions.

Right or wrong, there was an OBE at the end of this tunnel for Wintersmith. It was in the bag. He wore camouflage trousers and a panama hat, with a Swiss Army knife hanging from his belt. He had been taking lessons from Franklin Shrapnel and looked like a survivalist boy scout.

'We have had communication from the National Salvation Front, and we are interested in talking to them. There's no evidence that things will turn dangerous here in Bucharest. If the government remains in power nothing will change. If it doesn't there is every reason to suppose an orderly and bloodless transition. On the model of the rest of communist Europe.'

'When are we going to actually know anything for sure?'

'Well, President Ceauşescu is making an announcement this afternoon, in which I expect things will become much clearer. There will doubtless be some policy announcements followed either by a smooth transition or by a general liberalisation of the current system. Change isn't a Romanian *forte*.'

Diplomacy: the ability to stare the future in the face without meeting its eye.

The Comrade's big speech was to be televised live that afternoon at two. It was 11 am now. Dirty snow was banked up and thawing on the roadsides and against walls. The police and the army were now under the supervision of the Securitate in a *mise-en-abîme* of surveillance. In the glass-fronted news boards the front pages of the day's papers flashed morale-raising declarations and implausible figures from the cooked books of economic growth. The propaganda had been intensified. New roadside placards suddenly appeared, and the heroic murals were freshened up: 'Unity, Strength, Leadership', 'Long Live the Romanian Communist Party', 'Ceauşescu, Heroism; Romania, Communism'. On *Scînteia*'s front page, I skim-read Palinescu's new ode, which used the image of the national electricity grid to describe ordinary Romanians' love for their leader, each citizen contributing his individual voltage to the great power station that was the country.

Calea Victoriei had been checkpointed to a standstill. Crowds of men climbed out of rattling, clapped-out buses with tired old banners. Infantile music rattled the loudspeakers while police with loudhailers and batons shouted instructions and streamed the crowds into lines. Above all this rose the mutual hostility of the three security forces watching each other rather than the workers – if they noticed the mutinous resentment building up among the marchers, they did not show it.

This was the vast popular demonstration we had been promised, the workers 'electrified with loyalty'. I looked across the street to the corner of Aviatorilor and Modrogan and saw the familiar, slightly hunched figure of Trofim. He was alone, Astrakhan hat and scarf carefully placed to hide all but his eyes. A bus passed and when I looked again he was gone.

In half an hour I counted twenty-eight buses, each carrying over fifty people. Unsurprisable though I had become in my short time here, I was still puzzled at how contemptuously the Securitate treated them. Surely this would be a time to show a semblance of camaraderie? Besides, how wise was it to fill the city centre with thousands of angry, ill-fed, working-age men at a time of national crisis, then prod them like cattle through the self-abasement of this 'popular demonstration'? Workers dragged their banners along the ground, soaking up mud, grey snow and dirty water, spitting as they were handed their Ceauşescu portraits. A few argued with their superiors, union goons or shop-steward yes-men who were barely in control.

Even if it started on time, there were more than two hours to go until the big speech. Whose idea had this been? It was stupid beyond belief. Only a leader absolutely sure of popular support and loyalty from the institutions could afford to take this sort of a gamble. But Ceauşescu could have no such certainties. He had looked old and confused on television. He or his wife had just ordered massacres in Timişoara and Brasov. There were strikes and demonstrations all over the country. A new opposition group was calling for his removal. Despite all this, he had decided – or had he been persuaded? – to bus a hundred thousand people to the city centre to exhibit their devotion to him. 'The people love us...' Elena later said at the trial, 'the people love us and will not permit this outrage...'

My mouth was dry, my chest tight, my skin prickled with excitement. I could not say I knew what was going to happen – *knowing* is what comes after – but I felt it then, that pregnancy of unhappening that precedes major events. It was a sense of imminence that others had – Leo, Ottilia, Trofim, Ozeray, Maltchev and the rest – but that had until now failed me. It was as if I had entered the weave of things, not that I could control or even predict them, but that I felt them massing, blurred and indistinct but ready to happen.

I passed Trofim's on the way home and found his house unguarded. In fact there seemed to be a sudden drop in police presence everywhere except the city centre. I knocked. No one answered. I heard people talking, and then the silence of hushed voices. The spyhole went dark for a moment, then Oleanu answered. He wore a suit and tie and was clean-shaven. Gone was the young Bolshevik look, the round glasses and dissident-chic stubble. What he looked like now was a politician.

'Sorry, we have the radio on in here and it's hard to hear the door.' He looked at me with a liar's overcompensatingly steady eyes. He wanted me gone.

'Tell Sergiu I'm leaving tomorrow. Midday flight. It would be nice to see him before I go. Not sure when I'll be back, or even whether it'll be possible after...' But I was speaking to a closed door. I felt light-headed, cut loose again. Even here, even at the centre of things, I was drifting away to the margins, dragged by some invisible current further and further out.

It was nearly one o'clock when I reached the flat. I switched on the TV to find a medley of nationalist songs, footage from Party conferences and state visits, all of it cut with flashes of standing ovations and celebratory statistics about outputs and production levels. I couldn't tell what was being outputted, but whatever it was, it was going up and up, year on year. Tractors, oil, Dacias, flour, steel, iron... all of it so plentiful and so efficiently produced that it stretched the vertical axis of every graph that plotted it. What it never stretched was the credulity of the people watching. They had never believed any of it in the first place.

I turned the sound down and had just settled on the sofa when Leo hurtled into the room. 'It's madness out there. Crazy. They've got all these people in the main square, just waiting. There's already been scuffles. At the front you've got Party goons leading the cheering. They're about three rows deep. At the sides, Securitate. In the middle you've got these "loyal" workers and they're getting more and more pissed off. And believe me – I've seen them – they're on the verge of ripping the eyes out of the Comrade's portrait. They've started arresting people already. Every now and then the Securitate jump into the crowd, drag someone out, and they're gone. Where do they take them? Christ knows.'

'I've seen the buses unloading the poor sods. They weren't looking too happy when they got here.'

'No doubt about it. Things aren't under control. I was passing Kiseleff and I saw hundreds of women being turned back at a roadblock. It wasn't loyalty *they* were displaying. They were shouting and pushing, and the police had no bloody idea what to do. Some of the women had their kids with them. Babies in slings, kids running around everywhere, heroic mums and grannies waving their beefy arms. There's sit-ins in every factory, miners in the streets... the police aren't doing anything about it. Right across town: fights and lootings and attacks on Party offices, and the army's too busy keeping hold of the parade to get on top of it. As for Timişoara, who knows how many people they've killed, but whatever's going on there it's beyond their control. I've heard of army commanders refusing to obey the shoot-to-kill directives...'

'So why d'you think that with half the country in revolt, Ceauşescu's decided to bring hundreds of thousands of people to the capital city to demonstrate their loyalty, just when they're likely to be at their most rebellious, and at a time when he obviously can't rely on his security services?'

Leo looked at me and lit a cigarette. 'Well, there's two possibilties. One, he's really got no idea what's going on and he's decided to act tough, give a big speech and get the flags and banners out. It's always worked before... or someone's advised him to do this, and they've advised him badly. That may be Elena, or any of the pet sycophants who ply him with stories of how much he's loved. Or it could be someone who wants him to go too far, to engineer a no-return situation... There'll be people out there, not so far away from where we're standing –' He jerked his head in the direction of Herastrau, 'waiting and watching and hoping for a spark.'

When Ottilia came home the big speech was already fifteen minutes late. Leo had brought beer and wine to the table but no one was drinking. We wanted our wits about us for this.

What we were about to see for the first time I have now seen so often that it has become impossible to isolate it from the subsequent viewings, when it already had its place in the narrative of the Ceauşescu's fall. It has been played over and over, on international television, on Romanian television, on radio, and on the new technology of the internet. It is the totemic moment, both the symbol and the thing it symbolises: the Revolution. Though it is a scene full of finality, it remains for me embalmed in a perpetual present tense: 'Fresh as Lenin in his mausoleum,' Leo would say.

Ceauşescu stands on the Central Committee balcony, a pair of microphones at his mouth. He is alone, but behind the silver-grey lace curtain at the French windows, we can make out Elena's face, defiant and watchful. Ceauşescu wears a dark coat and an Astrakhan hat and looks fragile – more fragile than yesterday. He starts to speak before his voice is ready – a croak, a thin rattle – then clears his throat. The noise that rises as he steps up to the podium is unnatural, a cold snarl topped with a thin layer of cheering. At the front, the loyal plodders wave their banners and chew through their scripted eulogies. Behind them, something elemental is happening, something that comes from the stomach, that gathers and swells up. On the balcony, they can only hear what is directly below. We can hear that second sound, and we can hear it live: low, menacing but above all authentic. It is the cry from the throat, the stripped-hoarse larynx; the sound of fury and hate.

Ceauşescu starts to speak again. In his mind he is recreating his moment of greatness, twenty-one years ago, when he opposed the crushing of the Prague Spring, but his voice is drowned out. It is indistinct, but you can see a movement in the crowd, a fraying at the policed edges, people leaving and others pouring in from cracks in the cordon. Then the camera cuts back to the *Conducător* condemning provocateurs and enemies of socialism.

Ottilia and Leo are open-mouthed, their drinks untouched. Leo has been lighting cigarettes and forgetting about them, and there are five in the ashtray heaping their fug into the room like the smoke of the factory chimneys of Pitesti. Ottilia grips my hand; I think she is whispering something but it's only her breath through clenched teeth.

There is shouting. Very distinctly now we hear it: 'Timişoara! Timişoara! Timişoara!' Ceauşescu can hear it too. We can hear it on the television, and now outside our own balcony – we are experiencing both the event and its simultaneous mediatisation. We are there and not there. Ceauşescu puckers his face impatiently and sweeps the air with his hand. It is an authoritarian reflex only, because now there is no authority; he falters and falls to angry pleading. It is all beyond his grasp now. He promises more food, more money, an extra national holiday, but it's no good. The loyalists are scattering and people are barging past them to the front. Ceauşescu looks helpless and terrified as the fantasy melts like a wall of wax before his eyes. It occurs to me that he has the same look on his face as the Princess the day she came back from Paris.

There is a shot and the camera cuts to the crowd for a moment before pulling back to the president. People are bursting through the ranks of agents and stooges, and out to the sides the police cordon has given way. People are running past the militia, others joining them from the streets to the side of the square. More shots. Our first thought is that the Securitate have started to fire. Hence the thin rattle of single shots: snipers or close-range handguns.

A fat bodyguard in a suit and hat who looks like a butcher in Sunday best hurries out and says something into Ceauşescu's ear. He says it briskly, aggressively. Ceauşescu, who has never been spoken to like this, keeps going, but it is now just a pathetic ramble. The bodyguard comes out again, takes the Comrade's arm and pulls him indoors. A few faces peer out from behind him to assess the heightening chaos, the curtain parts for Ceauşescu then ripples closed again behind him. It is like water recomposing itself over a drowning man, but to say that is already to read the end into the beginning.

The screen goes blank, then dark. For a few seconds, nothing. No announcements, no explanations. Then patriotic music. Outside there is a roar. From where we are it is muffled like an underground explosion; then suddenly the streets are full.

People are running in all directions, and still not a police-man, not a soldier, in sight. The streets I have known these last eight months, streets I imagined only half-populated, are full of people. They pour out of houses, doors swing open, men and women head out towards the city centre.

The shooting is still far away, but denser. Machine-gun fire; black smoke rising from somewhere just off the main square, close to the university. It *is* the university says Leo, sure he can pinpoint the exact spot: the library.

In Aleea Alexandru two of the militia men had changed into jeans and shirts. Whether they were joining the people, trying to save their skins or going undercover it was impos-sible to tell. Whatever the case, they were uninterested in stopping us as Ottilia and I left the flat to see what was hap-pening on Aviatorilor.

A cold breeze brought the tang of tear gas, still powerful enough to sting the eyes, and the smell of burning. People were singing and shouting, exchanging rumours and news, debriefing anyone who had come from the city centre. Des-pite the savagery of what was happening the mood was elated, carnivalesque. A hundred yards away the tanks rolled by. The army could move in any time, kill us all. But here, now, people were free; intensively, dangerously, and perhaps not for long, but they were free.

This was what Petre meant, I told Ottilia. 'It's what he meant, yes. I wish he could have seen this.' She added ambiguously: 'Then we would have known for sure what side he was on.' She smiled and went upstairs ahead of me. When I reached the hallway, she had placed her half-empty bag beside mine at the door, her new passport on top of mine.

'What's made you change your mind?' I asked.

'I'm going with you because it's the only way to make sure you'll come back.'

By midnight the army had regained Piaţa Republicii.

Ceaușescu remained holed up in the Central Committee HQ, but made no announcements, no broadcasts; there were no declarations from either the government or the National Salvation Front. Radio Bucharest announced the suicide of General Milea at 1 am, just as Leo returned smelling of burned rubber, Tsuica and petrol. The sleeves of his reptilian jacket were charred and he had a nasty-looking burn on his arm. 'That?' he said proudly as he saw me eyeing his wound, 'Molotov elbow I think it's called... seems to be a lot of it about at the moment...' He had news: a British Airways flight had landed three hours ago to take home the remaining non-essential UK staff and citizens. 'Good of them to tell me,' I remarked. 'I went to the embassy too,' said Leo, 'I saw Wintersmith – he said they tried three times to call here, but the phone was dead. Anyway, he's gone too now. Last on the plane, first up for the OBE.'

I checked the line. It worked perfectly well. Not only that but it was incongruously clear. No clicking, no static, no bugs. No one was listening in any more. So much for Wintersmith trying to call me, I thought.

'Another thing,' said Leo, 'Manea wants to see you. Meet him at Cilea's in the morning. Ten o'clock. Don't ask why – I didn't. Be back here by eleven – I'm getting you to the airport by twelve and there's no telling what things will be like by then. And we need to allow time for Ms Pullova here to get through customs.' Ottilia took a bow and said something in Russian.

By 8 am it was clear that the army and police had won only a temporary victory. Piața Republicii was filling up again. There were thousands more people today and peaceful demonstrations right across town. The general strike had brought the whole country to a stop. There had been no word from the president now for over twelve hours. There was no shooting, no tear gas, no fighting, just a swell of peaceful sit-ins, demonstrations and rallies. Yesterday it had mainly been men. Now it was women and children and old people, quiet and disciplined and dignified.

In Herastrau guards stood at their posts waiting for orders that never came. The deeper in I went, the more I felt the muffled panic of the *nomenklatura*, torn between staying on and protecting their possessions and getting safely out of town. The Party food shop near Cilea's had been looted by its own customers: the padlock had been jimmied off and a pair of women who looked like opera singers were making off with stuffed suitcases. They were chewing fast – anything they couldn't carry, they tried to eat.

Outside Cilea's flat the guard waved me through. He was no longer in uniform either – he too had taken the precaution of going civilian. I had first seen him that May Day afternoon when Cilea and I had repaired here for sex and chocolate. It felt like a decade ago. It was certainly a regime ago. In front of me was a courtyard of shivering, denuded trees, shovelled snow, empty window boxes and verges of dormant grass. I must have been standing there, taking it all in one last time, because he knocked on the glass of his sentry box and shooed me in.

Cilea's living room had been turned into a centre of operations. Manea Constantin was reclining across a deep sofa, his head resting on Turkish cushions, his leg in plaster from heel to thigh. Two televisions were on simultaneously: one showing German satellite TV footage of the events just a few hundred yards away, the other showing the TVRom testcard and playing patriotic songs. One of Manea's men was feeding papers into a row of shredders, while another stuffed the chewed paper into black bags. There was no sign of Cilea.

Constantin had telephones at his side, lights flashing like the rotating beacons of police cars. Next door I heard the low calm voice of Cinzia taking messages. Manea nimbly swerved his plastered leg off the sofa and made room for me to sit down.

'Your leg?'

'Yes, that has been something of a... a bugger, you might say. Tripped down the ministry steps on my way to an emergency meeting with the Comrade, I've had to cancel all engagements for the foreseeable future.' He gave a wince of pain so false it might as well have been in inverted commas. 'Can I get you a drink? A whisky perhaps?'

One of the phones flashed its green light. Cinzia answered. Manea levered himself up and opened an elaborate peasant cupboard which had been gutted and customised into a drinks cabinet with mirrors and cocktail shakers. The sunlight, angled through the half-tilted blinds, caught the glint of his library of malts.

'Shouldn't you be out there giving the Comrade a hand?' I asked sarcastically. He feigned not to hear and poured a pair of daytime measures. 'Where's Cilea? You moved her out so you could set up your headquarters? Well, at least you can tell me what's going on out there.'

'It's difficult to say what's going on, I will be honest with you, very difficult... this is all unforeseen and I know little more than you...' He looked at me to make sure I knew he was lying, which was his way of telling me a sort of truth. '...but I think the Comrade is facing some trouble. I'm afraid,' motioning to his leg again, 'I will have to – what do you say – sit this one out. Literally...' His dry laugh was not without some real pleasure. He knocked back his drink, refilled the glass. He became serious again. 'Cilea has gone. She left for Paris last week. She wanted to see you.'

'Not enough to come to find me... last week? Sounds to me like she'd had plenty of advanced warning of this, er... *unforeseen* uprising...'

'Yes, well... she read the signs and chose to leave. It's what you should have done. I will always regret that you and she did not stay together. You might have been happy back in Britain, away from all this.' The red light on the phone flashed. 'I'm sorry,' he said, 'this call I have to take.' He picked up the receiver and listened. 'Da,' he said simply. *Yes.* Then in reply to someone querying him, he repeated it brusquely and rang off. 'Look, I had a reason for wanting to see you and it has nothing to do with saying farewell. It is a warning. When the Comrade falls there is no guarantee that what comes after will be substantially better, not to begin with at least. What concerns me, and it should concern you too, is that when that happens all sorts of people will return to Bucharest. The regime had its problems, but it kept some control over the criminal class...'

'Mainly by taking its place...'

'Maybe, maybe... there'll be time to address that in due course, but the moment the borders open and the government collapses, they'll be back...'

'Who's *they*?'

'The gangsters, dealers, traffickers, the pimps and fascists, the Jew-haters and ethnic cleansers... you've seen it starting already in Yugoslavia, or whatever it's called now, and it'll happen here.'

'What's that got to do with me or Leo?' I knew where Manea was going with this, but I wanted to hear him say it.

'Florian Belanger is coming back. That's what they're saying, and I believe it. I always knew he would. That's why I sent Cilea away. When he does he'll be richer, more powerful and more ambitious than ever. He'll have his scores to settle: with me, with Leo, but also with you. Cilea was besotted with him from the start – I hoped you'd take her away from him, and maybe you did for a while, I don't know – but he'll be coming back for her. He won't be happy to know she's been with you, and when he finds out you're Leo's friend he'll have plans for both of you. Maybe he knows already.'

'I can look after myself.' Manea let it pass as the hollow bravado it was. I put my hand out to shake his but he hauled himself up out of the sofa and embraced me. On my way out the guard was gone.

Nine

Leo and Ottilia were waiting in the car, luggage and passports ready and engine running. I didn't even have time for a last look at the flat, to shut the door marked 'Belanger, Dr F' behind me as I went.

At Otopeni airport there were roadblocks and perimeter checks. Leo predicted that the chaos would make travel easier, but he was wrong. We got past the first militia checkpoint, and our papers were examined and approved by the army guard outside the departures gate. Crowds were being held back, but we managed to pass the next checkpoint without obstacle. Inside the terminal we thought we were through – Ottilia was already kissing Leo goodbye – when I saw the notice at the TAROM check-in desk: all flights had been grounded. The desks had been vacated; the staff had disappeared. Our tickets were worthless. The only operators running were Air China and JAT, the Yugoslav airlines. 'Beijing or Belgrade... that's the choice...' I turned to Ottilia, but she was gone. Three Securitate men had pulled her from the queue and were examining her passport.

'Shit,' said Leo into my ear, 'I've buggered it up. I thought being Russian would be OK, but it's not. It's the Russians they're stopping – I should have bloody seen that coming! The Russians are the regime's enemies! Fuck! What have I done?'

I heard Ottilia pleading with them in Russian, then in convincingly broken Romanian. She looked over to me and waved me off. 'Go!' she mouthed as they took her passport into an office for checking.

'Go on!' said Ottilia as we approached her, 'that passport's not going to survive a proper check, and I need to be gone when they get back.'

'She's right,' said Leo, 'I did my best – couldn't very well get her a Chinese passport could I? We've got to get her out of here. Take this,' he handed me a JAT ticket, one-way to Belgrade. How he had got past the chaotic queues at the JAT desk I didn't know.

'I'm not going,' I said, 'I'm not leaving without you.' I took Ottilia's arm.

'Yes you are.' She kissed me then pulled free. 'You're leaving now, take that ticket and when it's safe you can come back. Either that or Leo can make me a better passport and I'll come to you. Go...' She pushed me hard in the chest and was gone in the crowd, Leo lurching after her, keeping hold of her hand.

I was alone at the airport again, just as I had been eight months ago. At the JAT desk they said I had missed check-in, so I left my suitcase on the marble floor and headed through customs to find the same pair of uniformed thieves who had fleeced me when I arrived. If they remembered me they gave no sign of it, just checked my expiring visa against a list on their wall, stole fifty dollars and waved me through. The system was falling apart, but here, in the microcosmos of their customs booth, it was business as usual.

Belgrade was cold and wet and as heavily policed as Bucharest. I chose my hotel because of its name, its price and its proximity to Belgrade station. There was nothing Romanian about the Hotel Bucarest unless you counted the lack of hot water, refreshments and heating. From my window I could smell the wafts of pavement buffets and hear noises of transit around Central Station. I hoped there would be a television, but in that too the hotel aspired to Romanianity. I had been without news for several hours, and now, in the early Belgrade evening, I went in search of somewhere to eat where I could watch the latest images. In the station buffet a large-screen television showed rolling satellite news from across the border. The western TV crews had arrived.

Ceauşescu had escaped by helicopter that afternoon after his failed attempt to rally the troops. Army factions loyal to the president retained control of the TV station and telephone exchange, but Radio Bucharest was now in rebel hands, transmitting news and declarations by the minute. In Timişoara, Brasov, Cluj and elsewhere, the army and police had switched sides; the Securitate and some army units were resisting. Already the dead were being laid out on the pavements to be identified and mourned. Only in the streets of Bucharest was the fighting as vicious as ever. The university library was burning, its great dome smashed and the rafters poking out into the smoke. Tanks had turned their fire against the Central Committee HQ and blown holes in the facade. Ceauşescu portraits were being burned in the streets. Snipers fired from windows and bodies of civilians lay in the rubble. The Securitate were fighting in small deadly groups, but those who were caught were strung up from lampposts and left to seize up with cold or rigor mortis, whichever came first, as they swung in the breeze.

It was on the night of the twenty-third too that the camera crews discovered the underground torture rooms, with their tangles of piano wire and implements that looked like straightened coathangers, their exposed electrics, hose pipes and clotted blood. Strewn across the floors were the papers and box files of victims and their torturers no one had had time to burn. All over Romania documents were being fed to flames and shredders, but the really foresighted people would not be destroying papers. They would be making copies.

It was past midnight when I returned to the Hotel Bucarest. My bag had been stolen, along with all my hard currency. I appeared to have been the only victim of the burglars, but the hotel staff lost no time in blaming the influx of Romanians – *Here just a few hours and already they've started stealing*. The manager pointed to a notice which declined all responsibility for theft or damage. When I threatened to call the police he slapped me on the back and laughed so hard the hem of his moustache lifted like curtains in a draft. I had lost two hundred dollars – all my fare home – and my clothes. All I had left was twenty dollars, the passport in my pocket, and the copy of Arghezi's poems Trofim had given me with the photo of myself and Cilea as bookmark.

Christmas eve in Belgrade brought rain that froze as soon as it hit the ground. The borders were open, and the westward flow of refugees was unrelenting. The Yugoslavs didn't mind. They were just a staging post. Thousands of Romanians were arriving in Berlin, Paris, Brussels. They were filmed begging in western streets and sleeping on blankets in gyms, cresting the waves of pity. They were right to make the most of it. Within a few weeks these 'gypsies' were being blamed for crimewaves, muggings and disease.

I had to reach the UK consulate before midday. With luck I might be able to arrange a bank guarantee and borrow enough money to get home. The Vice-Consul was a sad-faced, gentle man who wore a summer suit and sweated tropically despite the cold. He smoked a medley of cigarettes, lighting one off the other as if trying to economise on matches. I filled in some forms and he advanced me enough to pay for a hotel and some meals. The rest usually took forty-eight hours, but given that it was Christmas it would have to be the twenty-ninth at the earliest. Did I have somewhere to stay? He recommended a two-star hotel on the next corner, popular with visitors because it was cheap and clean and had remote control TV. The Lasta Hotel – 'I wouldn't read too much into the name,' he smiled tiredly. He gave me his card: *Francis Phillimore, Deputy Head of Mission*. I had heard the name before but couldn't place when or from whom.

Outside the Lasta Hotel I was approached for money by a man claiming to be a refugee from Timişoara. I spoke a few words of Romanian to him but he was unable to reply. He spat at me and walked away: already the situation was providing new openings for fraudulent begging. At the Lasta Hotel the vaunted remote control turned out to be attached to the television with a six-inch chain, making it impossible to use without getting up and crossing the room. It was the object-equivalent of those absurd communist jokes I had laughed at and learned from over the last hundred days. I settled down on the bed with a bottle of Slivovitz and a meat pie, drinking from a tooth mug as I watched the first footage of the National Salvation Front in session. This too is stored in the perpetual present.

Behind them stands a Romanian flag with a hole in the middle. They are in a room in the Party HQ, large but already befogged with smoke. Everyone is talking at once. Papers are being shuffled, most of them blank, and one man, sitting at the centre of the rectangular table, receives faxes and telegrams, scans them and dictates responses to Oleanu who stands at his back with a dictaphone and pen and paper. The man wears the same clothes as when I saw him in Capşa: Ilinescu, head of the NSF, former Party chief and lately high-profile dissident, now the NSF's undisputed leader. Manea Constantin is there, near the middle of the table: interior minister and now also information minister. He is underdressed, and to one who knows his usual snappiness of attire, the dishevelment is deliberate. He has even taken care not to shave. He has the air of someone who has been on the barricades all night, though in his case the barricades were a Turkish sofabed, a drinks cabinet and satellite television, and the weapons were phones, fax machines and a choking shredder. Manea is at the inaugural cabinet meeting of the first post-Ceaușescu government, the only minister with two portfolios. There is no sign of his leg plaster.

The other men in the room look like the sort of people they have replaced. In most cases they are the same people. Then I see him. The camera picks out the end of his cane, sweeps across the room, then pulls back to where he sits on a chair a little to the left of the new Prime Minister. Trofim feels no need to underdress; he even wears his Party lapel badge. When he talks everyone listens. The expression on his face is one I have never before seen: concentrated, penetrating and completely impersonal. Trofim seems transfigured. A commanding presence, he is not in charge, but from the way they all consult him and ask his opinion, show him the new decrees as they pass them – eighteen in the first hour of government – he does not need to be anything so crude as *in charge*. Trofim has been transfigured into himself.

The NSF spokesman declares that Ceaușescu has been captured after escaping by helicopter and will be brought to trial. The people's representatives have taken control of the radio and television stations, and of the *Scînteia* building. They blame the Securitate loyal to Ceaușescu for continuing fighting and claim the army has been on the side of the people from the start. It may not be their first lie, but it is certainly the first I can recognise.

I am surprised by a fresh belly laugh, a great, enveloping cackle of cynicism and bitter hilarity. It is coming from myself, and it soon veers into something that's full of anger and ridicule and self-mockery. And then tears. I can feel them stinging, mixing with the cigarette smoke and the fumes of

370

Slivovitz coming up from my guts. *New brothel, same old whores,* wasn't that what Leo had said?

I slept in my clothes and woke late, parched and sweating alcohol. At the hotel desk was a phone message from Phillimore inviting me for Christmas lunch. *Drinks from 11 am,* the note said, and gave an address. The hotel receptionist told me it was only two blocks away and outlined the route on my JAT tourist map.

Phillimore opened the door holding two cups of mulled wine, a crepe cracker crown angled rakishly on his head. 'Merry Christmas.' His living room was decorated with portraits of distinguished ancestors, admirals and commodores with names like Fortescue and Phillimore-Mannering, who watched over the latest and, judging from the disconsolate bachelorhood of his flat, the last of their bloodline. Phillimore's only festive concession appeared to be a single bauble hanging from a rubber plant.

A smell of roasting wafted from his tiny kitchen. A small woman in a headscarf was basting goose and uncorking wine. In Phillimore's living room, Euro News played the familiar images, except now the Ceauşescus were under arrest and stared, wrinkled, wild-haired and terrified, into the camera.

'Sorry. You've probably had enough of that,' said Phillimore, turning off the television and refilling my cup. 'If I'd known you were a friend of Leo's – no reason you should have said, of course not – but if I'd known I'd have sorted you out for cash immediately and put you on a flight yesterday. You'd at least have had Christmas at home.' Phillimore was pointing a cracker at me.

'You know Leo?' The cracker came apart and its tiny explosion made me jump.

'Known him for years, though it's been a while now since we met. I used to keep an eye on things over here for him –

you know, paperwork, visas, export permits... low-level stuff but still basically corrupt.' He gave a glum smile and raised his cup. 'I'm afraid you're my only Christmas guest, but there's plenty to eat and drink. I've got no plans for today, except the Queen's Christmas message at four and embassy staff drinks tonight if you're interested...'

Phillimore was easy to be with. He had the undemanding sadness of the lonely-by-choice. Just being with him was an unburdening, a clearing-out. 'So Leo called you?' I asked.

'Last night, late. On some sort of portable telephone. Terrible reception. Said to look out for you, and I told him you'd actually already been. He said to tell you everything was fine, that they were safe. Then he told me to help you out with cash. Actually he made me promise to tell you to come back to Bucharest, but I'd be going against Foreign Office advice if I did that. Look, here's three hundred dollars, more than enough to get back – *back where* is up to you. Take them and I'll settle up with Leo later.'

We listened to the Queen's speech over roast goose stuffed with buckwheat and some Croatian wine.

Christmas day for the Ceauşescus ended early, because that morning they were executed against a wall and their not-yet-dead bodies were finished off by handgun.

By five o'clock, Phillimore and I were watching film of the trial on television.

It is only the Ceauşescus we see, sitting at a small table in a Targoviste bunker. They were defiant to the end, and strangely tender in their small proprieties. It is always the small proprieties that stick in the mind. Perhaps it's because they seem to take death's measure and, for a brief moment, to square up to it: the way she buttons up her coat and juts out her chin decisively; the way he strokes her hand, smoothes his hair, puffs out his chest. Is it my memory playing tricks or does she, minutes before the end, wrap a scarf around his neck? She is disorientated and in terror, but musters a mad defiance. Asked how old she is, she replies, 'You shouldn't ask a lady her age,' this, no more than half an hour before they are shot.

Every dictator's trial has one of these moments of unexpected dignity or fastidiousness when the bloodlust that has been stirred up in us begins to waver. What is he saying? There are subtitles, but it's just a desolate life-and-death patter: 'I am the president', 'I do not recognise this bandit court...', 'I will answer to the people, and to the people only'... She: 'We made you. We looked after you. Is this how you repay us?', 'This is nonsense: the Romanian people love us and will not stand for this *coup*.' Bravery? Or just fantasy outlasting its relationship with reality, like the last note of a symphony hanging in the silence that will swallow it up?

They are found guilty of a range of crimes, from starving their people to owning too many pairs of shoes. At one point, their defence lawyer has to be reined in by the prosecutor because he is shouting abuse at them. Their accusers are kept out of sight, and their names, when either Nicolae or Elena mentions them, are blanked out of the subtitles. One of the voices is Manea's, I recognise it, but though the names of those at the trial were eventually released, Manea's does not figure among them.

It's all finished now. The camera pans across the corpses. Their faces are intact, the entry wounds tidy; on the other side the exiting bullets have ripped through their skulls, and the backs of their heads flap open like hoods blown off in a gale. She lies across the pavement while he has died on his knees with his torso and head thrown back. Someone opens their eyes and checks their pulse.

There's a sudden jolt and we see an irrelevant snatch of blue sky as the cameraman loses his balance: a perfect azure expanse, empty, weightless. Then he steadies himself, stepping across first the one body then the other: the close-up of their hands, parted where the bullets' force tore them from each other's clasp. The clothes of the dead are what stay in the mind, not their faces: she has a shoe missing, his Astrakhan hat is by his side; her bag, which she kept until the end, still lodged in the crook of her elbow.

Afterwards, before the Christmas pudding, Phillimore brought me a consulate compliment slip with a long phone number. 'It's Leo's, his portable phone... he said to give it to you. Ring him from here if you like.' He set a bottle of Slivovitz on the table, poured a few shots over the pudding and lit it with a match.

Leo was breathless, excited, radio and television loud in the background.

'Where are you?' I asked.

'I'm in the flat. Well – your flat. We're all here, Ottilia, Iulia, Ozeray's come over, we might even get a visit from the new government's senior policy adviser, Comrade Trofim. Ottilia's sleeping right now, she's been in the hospital all night. She wants you back, but I think she knows she wasn't meant to leave. This is where she belongs.'

'I know that. What's it like?'

'It's carnage, but we're winning.' I noted the *we*. 'Where are *you*?'

'Where you knew I would be. At Phillimore's. We're on the Christmas pudding.'

'Did he give you an advance? Good. Now that you've had a couple of days to think about things, it's about time you came back... anyway, it's safe now.'

'*Safe?* What d'you mean *safe?* I can hear the bullets! I can see it on the bloody TV! Doesn't look safe to me... what about Vintul, Stoicu, the rest of those bastards?'

'Bullets? No, just the odd ricochet... dunno about Stoicu. I expect he's keeping his head down. He might resurface – but he's harmless enough so long as Manea's in charge.' Then Leo's tone changed. I could feel him looking around to see who was listening, then I heard him change rooms, his voice drop. 'Vintul won't though. That's been dealt with.'

'What d'you mean *dealt with*?'

'Let's just say we got a tip-off from someone in the know – the Lieutenant and a couple of his people took care of him. He was rounded up with a bunch of Securitate goons and, as the phrase goes, *The People exercised summary justice.*'

In other words Manea had told Leo where to find Vintul, and Leo had put the word out. There was always room in a revolution for the settling of old accounts – Manea's, Ottilia's, Leo's. Mine too now, it seemed.

'Hello? You still there?' Leo shouted. 'So – what's your plan? Let me tell you what you're missing...'

'Save your breath, Leo.'

There was an overnight train to Bucharest and if it was running I would be on it. One of the advantages of communism was that Christmas was just another working day.

I checked out of the Lasta Hotel and walked with Phillimore to the station.

At the *guichet* I asked for a single to Bucharest and counted out my money. The woman at the till looked up in astonishment and asked me to repeat first my destination and then my ticket type. Phillimore accompanied me to the platform and gave me a bag containing the remains of lunch and a bottle of mineral water.

'Regards to Leo,' he said plaintively, 'perhaps now he'll be able to visit more often.'

Two platforms away stood the Brussels train: BEOGRAD/BRUSSELS. People were piling onto it already, standing in the corridors, dragging in their luggage. The Bucharest train was a ghost train, twelve carriages empty but for a few news crews. With the borders open, the street-fighting, the Ceauşescus dead and the storming of the luxurious palaces and villas, Romania was now journalistic gold.

I took a compartment to myself. Belgrade's rain had turned to snow, mounting up on the rubber seals of the windows. I leaned my forehead against the freezing glass and watched the Brussels-bound intercity pull out. After twenty minutes, our crew arrived, unshaven and in unbuttoned grey tunics. After forty, the engines started up.

A few compartments down my nearest and only neighbours were paramilitary-looking men with black berets. Some were obviously armed. All were Yugoslavs. They smoked and drank and listened to pogrom-rock. In the next cabin, sitting alone surrounded by newspapers in French and German and English, their boss, a muscular, blond-haired man looked me over, raised his eyebrows, and pulled the blinds across his window.

Eight hours later, after unexplained stops, passport checks and a two-hour wait at the border, we pulled into Bucharest Central station. It was a chaos of departures and aborted departures. Trains pulled out with men and women hanging off the doorhandles, bags and cases strapped to the carriage roofs, people in the sleepers sitting four to a bunk.

I was prevented from leaving my cabin when one of the Yugoslav black berets blocked the door, giving his employer and the rest of the bodyguards time to make their exits. When I was allowed to disembark I saw up ahead of me the tall blond man flanked by his guards and luggage carriers. Though he moved fast and powerfully, he limped hard. He carried a walking stick but didn't use it – it was there to remind him and those around of his infirmity and how completely he had overridden it. If he saw Leo standing under the old clock on the empty arrivals board he gave no sign. Leo meanwhile was talking into a mobile phone, his back half-turned, a rolled-up copy of *The Times* under his arm. There were no police to be seen, and though I heard gunshots in the distance, normality was pushing through like weeds in cracked paving: the smell of bread, the sound of trams and buses, kiosks open for business. There was even a new newspaper, *Adevarul*, with its headline 'Trial of a Tyrant'. A new poem by Palinescu was announced.

'What's up?' said Leo as we embraced, 'you look like you've seen a ghost...'

Over his shoulder, leaning against a black Mercedes, I saw Cilea in her sunglasses and grey fur coat. I felt my stomach seize up. Back from Paris? More likely she had never left. I followed Belanger with my eyes, still holding Leo against me, stopping him from turning towards them. Cilea faced me, but I do not know if she saw me. In any case, her smile was for Belanger. As he lifted her up she laughed and threw her head back, then covered his face with kisses. He carried her into the back of the car, then they were gone.

'No, nothing. I thought I saw someone I knew,' I said, letting Leo free himself. He set off, pulling me through the crowds, a counterflow to the human traffic. His ambassadorial Skoda had a new laminated card on the dashboard – 'On Provisional Government Business' – and a detachable siren lay on the passenger seat. A few shots rang out nearby. Some people ducked. Leo didn't even hear.

'Ottilia's waiting, and I've booked Capşa for you both – you'll be glad to hear there's been no regime change *there...*'

'That's good to know,' I looked out as we passed the Boulevard of Socialist Victory, its gravestone facade eerily undamaged. 'As for the rest of the country, let me guess: *New brothel, same old whores* – isn't that what you told us?'

Leo waved it off. 'Well, you know how it is... after all, experience is what you want in a whore...'

About the Author

Patrick McGuinness was born in Tunisia in 1968 of Belgian and Newcastle Irish parents. Brought up in various countries, including Iran, Venezuela, France and Belgium, he studied at Cambridge, York and Oxford. He is the author of two collections of poems, *The Canals of Mars* and *Jilted City*, which have been translated into several languages, and of various books on French and British literature. He has won an Eric Gregory Award for poetry, the Levinson Prize from the American Poetry Foundation, and in 2009 was made Chevalier dans l'Ordre des Palmes académiques for services to French culture. He has also written and presented programmes for radio, including the Radio Three features 'A Short History of Stupidity' and 'The Art of Idleness'.

He is Professor of French and Comparative Literature at Oxford University, and lives in Caernarfon, Wales. This is his first novel.